I0822904

OLDEARTH

GEORGIOS

ENCOUNTER

A. K. Frailey

Hardcover Edition

Cover Design: A. K. Frailey and James Hrkach

ISBN of hardcover: 979-8-9861803-9-7

The Writings of A. K. Frailey
Books for the Mind and Spirit
https://akfrailey.com/

Contact
akfrailey@yahoo.com

Historical Science Fiction Novels
OldEarth ARAM Encounter
OldEarth Ishtar Encounter
OldEarth Neb Encounter
OldEarth Georgios Encounter
OldEarth Melchior Encounter

Science Fiction Novels
Homestead
Last of Her Kind
Newearth Justine Awakens
Newearth A Hero's Crime

Short Stories
It Might Have Been—
And Other Short Stories 2nd Edition
One Day at a Time and Other Stories
Encounter Science Fiction
Short Stories & Novella 2nd Edition

Inspirational Non-Fiction

My Road Goes Ever On—
Spiritual Being, Human Journey 2nd Edition
My Road Goes Ever On—A Timeless Journey
The Road Goes Ever On—A Christian Journey Through The Lord of the Rings

Children's Book

The Adventures of Tally-Ho

Poetry

Hope's Embrace & Other Poems 2nd Edition

Audible Versions Now Available. Check book details on Amazon for current listings.

A Covenant formed between God and Man.
He chose a people for His own.
Becoming a Man among men.
A King among kings.
Many would know Him.
Some would choose Him.
From Aram's seed rose Alexios.
And his wife brought forth Georgios.
Who knew Him well.

Prologue

I Was Bitten Once

-Jerusalem-

Noman surveyed the white walls, considered the silence of the empty tomb, and knew that hell existed. He wiggled his sand-encrusted toes and straightened his back, his loose tunic rippling with the movement. Sweat dripped down his back as blazing sunlight glared from an unrepentant blue sky.

Where is Abbas?

With a smothered curse, he shifted his gaze away from the gaping hole. There was no point in torturing himself with what might have been. If only Abbas had listened. If only someone had cared enough to believe him. But it was too late. He was on Earth, the challenge had been made, and he could not unmake it. He could only prove them wrong.

Abbas' face appeared before his eyes—a man he could have loved heart and soul. Instead, he had another mission. Love had its limits.

A squeal turned his attention. A woman stood frozen on the rocky path, her eyes wide, terror-stricken.

A scorpion poised in her path, ready for attack.

Bumbling woman! Humans had an ever-ready supply of idiocy. He stepped forward, then stopped. Why should he? What was this archaic inclination to assist lesser beings? *The very image of Abbas*. Noman stayed in the shadows.

A hillside covered in small shrubs with a cave at the far end made for a mute wilderness. Few birds twittered here.

A young man jogged along the worn, rocky path and

halted. He glanced from the scorpion to the woman.

Her voice shaking, the woman lifted her trembling hand. "I was bitten once, nearly killed me."

The youth leapt aside, grabbed a stone, and whisked it at the pest.

The venomous creature scuttled away.

Clutching her chest, the woman closed her eyes and swayed.

The young man's hand shot out, and he gripped her elbow, holding her upright. "You're safe. It's gone."

She opened her eyes, gratitude softening every feature. "Thank you. My name is Anna. I was too scared to think."

"I'm Georgios. No worries. Will you be able to—?"

She clasped her hands with a formal bow—humility matched with gratitude.

After a parting smile, Georgios jogged off, heading toward the harbor.

A glance ascending like a prayer, the young woman paced forward and a serene expression replaced her former anxiety.

Noman stepped onto the path and shook his head.

The scorpion was still nearby. Its mission to paralyze and eat its prey had not changed. *Mutant kindness means nothing. One day, she'll not be so lucky.*

He peered along the path the young man had taken, a grin hovering over his lips. The perfect object lesson. Georgios would prove his point. Fools made the best argument for humanity's eventual defeat.

-Planet Lux-

Teal held Sienna close. Her head rested comfortably on his chest as she slept in perfect security. They didn't need to maintain human form, but he realized, with a luxurious sigh, that the human body offered something the Luxonian experience lacked: a wide range of physical pleasures.

Despite humanity's limited knowledge and absence of technology, they did know a thing or two about adding spice to life, literally as well as metaphorically speaking.

Before leaving Earth, Sienna had rubbed coconut butter into her skin, and the exotic scent still pulsed erotic sensations through his body. Her hair, rain-washed and lightened by the sun, rippled through his fingers as he ran his hand along her back. After they returned to Lux, they had made love late into the night, but arousal returned with a vengeance as the first streaks of morning light filtered through the window.

Sienna stirred, stretched, and opened her eyes.

Their gazes met.

Will I ever stop falling in love?

"You're awake?" Sienna stretched. "I thought you'd be worn out—ready to sleep through the day."

With a grin, he ran his fingers along her side and—

Sienna sat up, clutching the bedsheet. "I don't feel so—" Leaping from the bed, she ran to the lavabo, the Luxonian refreshment room. As a light being, she didn't need the same care as humans, but she did need refreshment at times.

Teal frowned.

Trying to realign his plans for the morning, he climbed out of bed and grabbed his clothes. Disgruntled, he glanced at the doorway Sienna had sped through and considered following her. No, if she needed help, she'd ask. He pulled on his tunic and slipped on his sandals.

A muffled call. "Dad?"

Teal stepped to the door, opened it, and met the gaze of his young son in his human form and dressed in a simple brown tunic. "Cerulean, what's wrong?"

"Nothing. I just wanted to know when we're going. I read a report about an unusual—"

Heaviness pressed Teal's chest. He had promised, but a visit to Earth wasn't high on his agenda right now. He glanced back to the bed. "We haven't decided yet. There's a lot to think about."

Sienna, now arrayed in a long, dark blue tunic with a matching belt, swayed forward. She lifted Teal's arm, snuggled in close, and pressed his hand onto her hip. She grinned at her son. "You'll go soon, darling. But your father and I have some decisions to make. Let's figure out the best time, and we'll get you all set." She arched her eyebrows. "You'll be a guardian your whole life; don't rush your childhood away, all right?"

Shifting his gaze from his mother to his father, Cerulean bit his lip, his words stifled.

Teal knew that look. His heart ached in response. When he was a child, he'd wanted to go on his first mission so much he could hardly contain his enthusiasm, but it had taken several tries to find the right placement. Once he'd discovered humanity, he never wanted to leave. He ran his fingers over Sienna's belly. Until lately.

Practicing every human mannerism that he had learned from his off-world studies, Cerulean offered a curt nod and a slight bow. He respectfully turned away.

Teal closed the door behind him.

Sienna sighed as she turned to her husband. "He really wants to go. His heart is set on it."

"We just got home. He must learn patience. The most important lesson in guardianship is knowing how to bide your time." He leaned over and kissed Sienna, first on the cheek and then on the lips.

She groaned in pleasure, but then she slid her hand between their chests and halted his momentum toward the bed. "I can't." She wrinkled her nose. "I'm not feeling well."

Glancing away, Teal tried to regain his composure. Anxiety crawled over his spine. He frowned. "Are you ill?"

After a playful pinch on his arm, Sienna strode to the window. She leaned against the low railing and rested her head on the flower-entwined post. Light twinkled over the blue-green ocean spread before them. Rays of sunshine cascaded across her face. Her whole being shimmered. "I can feel sick without being sick."

A lightning bolt could not have shocked Teal more. He leaped across the room and grabbed her arm, tugging her out of her reverie. "Are you—"

A languid smile spread across Sienna's face. "I think so." A shadow darkened her features as she met his gaze. "It's so rare these days—to be twice blessed. I must be one of the lucky ones."

Cold fear shivered over Teal's body. "But is it safe?"

Sienna stared at the sun and shimmered, her whole body wavering into colorful beams. "Life isn't safe, my love." She stood there, a brilliant chorus of light rays, her voice clear as crystal. "Take Cerulean to Earth and let me rest. The future will unfold as it must." She blinked away.

Joy and terror ran riot through's Teal's mind. He peered at his trembling hands. Humanity may have an edge on physical pleasure, but the two races endured fear much the same.

~~~

Ark stared at the vial clasped in his mate's tentacles. She was grinning. He could not respond in kind. Still, it
~~~

was an honor, though an unwelcome one. "Are you absolutely sure?"

Meta shook the clear tube. "As sure as a triple-check can be."

She should've had the sense to wait until they were in the pool to share this news instead of shocking him with it while he'd been immersed in his studies in the laboratory. *But what can one expect from a female? They're always so blasted unpredictable.* "Watch where you put your tentacles" and "Don't turn your eyes from a female in the lab" were two oft-repeated truisms bandied about the private male laboratories. The females had built their own scientific centers, ones Ark avoided with diligence.

He adjusted his nostril tube and smoothed down the cilia on the top of his head. *What I wouldn't give to speak with Teal at this moment.*

"You will own it, won't you?" Meta was clearly in no mood for obfuscations.

"I'll run my own tests if you don't mind. But in the end, if the pod is mine—as I suspect it is—then, of course, I will own it."

Meta exhaled, bubbles forming around her breathing tube, and her smile widening. "Good. Once I give birth next cycle, it's all yours!"

A crash splintered the silence.

Ark peered at the floor where his latest experiment had spilled in a gelatinous goo across the floor. One brief, well, three brief, pleasant encounters, and he'd be paying for uncountable cycles. *Perhaps for the rest of my natural life!*

Meta shrugged her shoulders and waved all six tentacles. "Make sure you clean that up carefully. You don't want to get sick. New father and all." With a giggle, she waddled through the open doorway.

A throb building behind his eyes, Ark lusted for a tall

glass of green and a trip to Lux. Yes, he'd stop by and see Teal. Compare fatherhood stories. After all, it was Teal who made interacting with the opposite sex so appealing. *Had it all been a lie?*

Before he officially met his offspring, he must find out.

~~~

Zuri paced before the closed ornate oaken doors, his hands clasped behind his back. Still wearing much of his Ingot armor, he wrenched his helmet off his head and flung it in the corner. Never should've taken the job. *By the Divide! She could die, and I'll—*

The door creaked open.

A petite Bauchi woman slid through and nodded at Zuri. "You can come in now. She's stabilized. But you'll have to be careful. She's very weak."

His heart pounding and every synapse on overload, Zuri stuttered the most fighting words he had ever formed. "And t-the b-baby?"

Despite the perfection of her features, the woman's face crumpled, grief disfiguring all that was good and holy.

Her words barely rose above the roar in Zuri's ears.

"I'm sorry."

Pain crushed Zuri's chest. He couldn't breathe. He could hardly stand. He staggered and reached out.

Surprisingly strong, the Bauchi woman grabbed him. Wrapping her arm around his, she led him to the bedroom.

Familiar decorations met his eyes: seven miniature trees arranged decoratively on the windowsill, twelve dolls from various planets in holiday apparel on the shelves to the right, three seaside paintings adorning the back wall, and a woven blanket from Earth lay across the
~~~

foot of the bed, a gift from Teal and Sienna upon their return trip.

Kelesta lay on the bed, her eyes closed, her brow contracted in pain.

A venerable figure rose from the bedside. A Bauchi woman well past youth but with timeless beauty marking ancient wisdom. Her frame, elongated by the dark cloak around her shoulders, made her appear tall for a Bhuac. Her hood lay on her shoulders, while a blue tunic rippled to her toes.

"Song?"

"I came as soon as we realized the danger. She had been doing so well."

Zuri stared at his wife, aching throbs building like a raging sea against his eyes. "What happened?"

"She's never been robust. And with all her travels, she undoubtedly picked up a strange virus. It lay dormant until recently. She never came for help, insisting to friends and family that all was fine."

Zuri shook his head. "She never breathed a word. I never would've left—"

"No one could've known. Each person handles anxiety differently. In the past, she would've played it up. But she's learned hard lessons. This time she pivoted in the opposite direction. She told no one."

Swallowing a lump stuck in his throat, Zuri bit off his words in small chunks and stared out the window. "Will…she…live?"

"I believe so. But—"

Zuri swiveled his blurry-eyed gaze to the woman.

"Her life came at a cost. They couldn't both survive. Kelesta had the better chance. Your daughter wouldn't have survived another day, no matter what we did."

The wail that shrieked from his lips sent shudders down

his spine, but he could not stop his words. “You should’ve done something!”

“If we could have, we would have.” She sighed in plaintive despair.

Zuri followed her gaze.

The bassinet he had fashioned with nascent skills hung from the ceiling like a floating bed, his love poured out in beautiful invention and attention to detail.

Soul-bruised and spirit-beaten, Zuri tromped forward and slid the lacy curtain aside.

There lay a perfect baby girl, beautifully locked in time.

He caressed the blue-tinged fingers, toes, and the pale face. A perfect combination of Ingot and Bhuaci features.

“Did she ever have a chance?”

“I don’t know.”

Zuri paced to his wife’s side.

Pale but tinged with pink, Kelesta breathed shallow, pained breaths.

“How will we live now?”

“You have to discover what it means to live.”

Zuri sat on the edge of the bed and clasped his wife’s hand.

CHAPTER ONE

WHAT MADNESS DROVE HIM

—PATMOS—

CIRCA ANNO DOMINI 100

Georgios stood on the cliff outside his home and stared across the Aegean Sea, his stomach clenched and his heart constricted, bound to a world he both loved and despised. Home drew him like a bee to honey, while his name sent shivers down his spine.

A white, stone house surrounded by walls with thick tufts of green moss perched on top of a mighty cliff on the island of Patmos.

Eyes peered at him through the large open windows.

His grandfather had inherited the land from his father, and they ruled over their portion with autocratic supremacy, though far from the glory of the Roman Empire.

His mother's parents, Myron and Roxanna, treasured him beyond words. His life at fourteen was both comfortable and pleasing, except when his father, Alexios, returned from his travels as a legionnaire for the Roman army. Then old yearnings haunted the boy's days and filled his dreams.

"Georgios! Come here, son!"

Georgios trotted to his father and dutifully knelt on the sunbaked earth and bowed his head. He did not speak first; that was not an option.

"Walk with me a while, Georgios." Alexios stood waiting, the sun beating mercilessly down on his short black hair.

Georgios' heart leapt to his throat. He took a large step to fall into alignment with his father, keeping his shoulders aloof to the effort.

"I am called away, and it's my duty to respond quickly and obediently," —he dropped his large hand on Georgios' head— "as I hope you would do in my situation."

Georgios stared at the hard-baked earth as depression settled over him. His father's hand moved from his head to his shoulder and squeezed, begging reassurance that his confidence was not in vain. Georgios nodded, fearing that his voice might betray him.

"Your mother has been gone for over a year now, but you are from strong stock, made for greatness." Alexios peered into the bright sky, a faraway expression crossing his features. "You're almost a man." He shook Georgios' shoulder playfully. "And you have your grandmother and grandfather. You're hardly alone."

Georgios clenched his fists, but he dared not show any further displeasure.

Alexios knelt on the hard path and pulled his son toward him, emotion straining his voice. "I wish that I could take you with me, but I belong to the empire. I can't risk—The safest place for you is here." Alexios pushed Georgios back. "You understand?"

Georgios swallowed hard and nodded.

"Don't nod like a dumb animal. Speak! Say what you think. I can accept discord as long as it is explained and defended. I cannot accept limp acquiescence."

Georgios sucked in a breath and, in a swift motion, flung himself against his father, hugging him around the waist. An impulsive move. He didn't know what madness drove him. Afraid to look up and see his father's reproachful expression, relief enveloped him when his father's firm hand smoothed the linen tunic on his back. Georgios lifted his head. "I'll miss you."

Alexios' dark, penetrating eyes grew thoughtful, even sorrowful. "I am grateful. Since your mother died, I have not been a favorite son."

Georgios rubbed away unshed tears with the back of his hand. "Surely everyone reveres you!"

Alexios laughed mirthlessly and turned home again. "Reverence is not love."

Georgios felt his spirits climb in the warmth of his father's trust. "You are a great man; everyone thinks—"

"Georgi? Where are you?" The high-strained voice of his grandfather wavered as the old man shielded his eyes from the glare of the sun.

Georgios glanced at his father.

Instantly, Alexios' Roman face appeared. He straightened and returned to the road.

The boy quickened his pace.

His father slackened his own.

"Yes, Grandfather! I'm just saying goodbye to Father."

The old man nodded and turned inside the sunbaked villa.

Alexios stopped on the dusty road, staring into the distance.

Georgios bit his lip then gathered every ounce of his courage. "Can I go with you—some day?"

Slowly Alexios' eyes focused as he rubbed his jaw. "Possibly. Soon you will be a man, and it's the duty of every father to see to the training of his son."

Georgios' heart rose.

Birds danced in the bright sky.

He held his breath in anticipation.

"Yes. In one year, when I finish my tour, I will pick you up and take you with me back to Rome. We'll be warriors together and conquer the world!"

Georgios' heart hammered in his chest as he clasped Alexios' hand and knelt in the dust. No longer the subjugation of a dutiful Roman boy but the loyalty of an honored son. "I will wait for you, Father."

Alexios smiled and he placed his hand upon his son's head.

Georgios' grandfather, Myron, poked his head out the doorway, a scowl bearing heavily upon his brow.

His life changed in this instant; Georgios would be a great son to his noble, distant father.

CHAPTER TWO

I'LL BE NO OTHER

—PATMOS—

Georgios leaned against the stone wall, watching the ships on the sparkling sea, marveling at their beauty and silent charm.

His father's ship stood ready in the harbor. He gazed intently until the magnificent Fides broke free and slipped over the blue stillness, growing smaller until no more than a memory in his mind.

He turned his steps toward home.

Soon his one-story home came into view. At the doorway, Myron, a slight man, stood stooped, while Roxanna, round and buxom, emitted solid strength with perfumed persuasion in her every look and gesture.

Irritation filled the air as the two lined the way awaiting his return.

"Georgi! What took so long? Dinner has been waiting, and we've been worried." Myron scowled while Roxanna ushered Georgios into the dining room.

The servants dutifully shuffled aside.

Roxanna waved to the table set with a grand assortment: quail, fish, bread, eggs, olives, figs, carrots, asparagus, and a large carafe of wine.

Myron peered at his grandson, the two sitting across from each other. "Did your father upset you, Georgi? You've not said a word. Normally, you are such a magpie."

Georgi grinned, though his gut twisted. His father's plan wasn't a secret, yet he wanted to keep it to himself. "Sorry. I didn't mean to be so late." He stared at the decorative plate. “I’m very hungry.” With the ambition of a child who wants to grow big and strong instantly, Georgios piled food on his plate and shoveled food into his mouth.

Roxanna’s smile disappeared.

Myron’s scowl darkened.

He set his gravy-soaked bread aside. “Has something happened?”

Roxana’s eyelashes fluttered in accompaniment with her hands. “We wondered the same thing. Your father was so reserved when he arrived, and then you two had such a long, earnest conversation. Is there news?”

A blush crept up Georgios’ face; his heart pounded. The truth would out. “He’ll be on tour for a year, but after that, he’ll return, and I’ll begin my training.”

Fury, like a living force, reared up in Myron’s eyes.

Roxanna leaned in, silently demanding more.

“He’s my father, after all, and it’s perfectly right that he should want to train his son. I’m going to be of age; it’s about time I learned the ways of real men.”

Myron thrust down a crushed olive, his voice rising to a squeak. “Real men? What possessed him to say such a thing. Is he mad?”

Roxanna trembled and tears filled her eyes.

Dumbfounded, Georgios wiped his fingers on his napkin, the food in his stomach churning.

“He’ll do nothing but bring you among savages who drink strong wine, eat rich food, and brutalize their enemies. Warriors are little better than beasts, hired to kill when the need arises.” Myron waved his hand in command. “I’ll not have it! No grandson of mine will accept such a fate! You are destined for greater things.” He rounded on his wife and shook a long finger accusingly. “I told you what would happen when you allowed Helena to marry that man! But you bustled about and flung your arms around her and said that she loved him, as if that solved the problem. And when we knew the full truth, still, you did nothing to stop it!"

Roxanna's hands flailed like birds caught in a snare. "Don't blame me! I suspected he was not one of us. I told you to speak to Helena and order her to give up the match, but you said it was too late. You said he was too powerful. And now, look, he killed our daughter, and he'll take—" Tears flowed. She scurried to the door.

Confused, Georgios rose unsteadily. "What do you mean, he killed—? Mother died of an illness. Father loved her—he called for the best physicians. No one could've saved her." His jaw clenched as he bit off his words. "You never liked father...why? Because he's Roman—"

Roxanna stared at her grandson, then, in a mad rush of maternal protectiveness, she grabbed Georgios, hugging his head to her chest and covering his ears. "No! It doesn't matter."

Georgios jerked free of the smothering embrace.

Myron wrenched Georgios aside. "His father will have the right to take him! Unless we tell him, we'll relive the agony of seeing our child bound to an unworthy—"

Fury and horror giving him strength, Georgi broke free and ran to the doorway.

Well-dressed servants clustered, murmuring, astonishment widening their eyes.

A pulsating need to understand forced words into Georgios' mouth. "What do you mean by unworthy? How could so—"

"A Jew!" Myron's shriek startled everyone. Even the servants jumped.

Georgios stepped forward, his world slipping away like a ship at sea. "Jew? My father? Then I..." Words failed.

Roxanna dug a small white cloth from her sleeve, dabbed her eyes, and then waved her feminine banner in truce. "Of course not! You carry our daughter's blood. Our blood. You look nothing like them! You're not like them at all."

As he stood transfixed, Alexios' face appeared before him. The truth stared him in the eye. "But I am." Tears burned. "I am my father's son. I'll be no other."

Myron lifted a fist. "You are our grandson. That means something. He's nothing."

Georgios clenched his hands, his body trembling. "That's not true! My father wants me. My mother loved me. I'll not deny that they're mine." Scorn filled him as he glared at his grandparents. "If I were to deny anyone, it would be you!"

With those words echoing off the blazing walls, Georgios shoved past the murmuring crowd of servants and left his grandparents far behind.

CHAPTER THREE

I'M NOT YOUR ENEMY

—VOYAGE TO AN ISLAND—

Georgios had to talk fast to convince the captain he was worth taking on board, for his slight frame and youth suggested that he was too weak and too inexperienced to manage the hard labor assigned to a crew member.

To his humiliation, Georgios was not destined to do much labor, for almost immediately upon sailing into deep waters, the captain's misgivings proved prophetic. Georgios took ill, and there was little anyone could do but hope he did not die. Being a kind man, the captain let Georgios sleep in the aft of the ship and did not ask anything more than to keep his moaning to himself.

Georgios could never, in later years, recall the details of that terrible voyage other than the boat heaving and an awful stink.

He became vaguely aware when they approached land. He was rowed to shore and roughly carried into a sparse wooden hut out of the sun. A few others debarked, but they were soon on their way to unnamed destinations and never spoke to him.

His grandparents' anguished yells when he had rushed out of their home—the only home he had ever known—replayed in his mind. They had called for hours, even as the sun sank behind the purpling mountains and dark night descended. There were not many places he could go on that first night, so he paced along the shore, cold and miserable, but his determination returned full strength with the morning light. After countless inquiries, he found a merchant ship that would accept him as an inexperienced crew member.

Now, shivering, he pressed his hand to his burning forehead and wondered about his sanity. By daybreak, he was ravenously hungry. In the strange hut on the shore of he knew not where, as he alternately clutched his stomach and throbbing head, he remembered his resolution to follow his father.

Images of crawling back into his grandmother's welcoming arms and being stroked by her firm, loving hands haunted him. What kind of a man would his father think him if he saw him now?

As he rocked back and forth in misery, he wondered if there wasn't a better way to learn the truth about his heritage.

Georgios imagined his father's strong chiseled face. As a Roman-Jew, his father must have known trials, indeed.

Maybe I should return home and wait for Father.

As the waves rolled onto shore, he closed his eyes and vowed, *I'll never be so stupid again.*

With his resolve set, new strength enlivened Georgios' weary body. He tried to stand, but the earth seemed to sway. He grasped a firm beam and took one slow step and then another until he reached the doorway. Squinting against the strong light, he peered over the sand to the sea, which ran upon the shore in meditative intervals.

He whispered a small comfort to his lonely heart.

"We can't have gone far. I'll beg for passage…Myron will pay."

A low snort.

Georgios glanced over his shoulder, but after staring at the bright day, only blackness met his eyes.

A young man shuffled toward him from the dim interior.

Georgios stepped back. "Who are you?"

The stranger poked him in the shoulder. "I could ask you the same thing."

Georgios stepped backward into the full glare of day. Being too well brought up to get into physical contact with the sons of lesser men, he shivered at the thought of touching this ragged young man. He cleared his throat. "I'm a Roman citizen, the son of Alexios—"

The stranger leapt on him and pummeled him with both fists.

Too surprised to put up a proper defense, Georgios took the first blows straight on, but then a searing jab to his cheek and a slug to his middle forced the realization that unless he did something, he might be beaten to death.

Backing up, he slapped and clawed his enemy. *I won't lie down and die!* As exhaustion overwhelmed him, a wooden staff leaning against the interior wall caught his eye.

Georgios scampered under the larger boy's arm, darted toward the staff, and in one swift motion, swung with all his might.

The impact of the heavy cedar against the skull resounded with a loud crack.

In slow motion, the stranger crumpled to the ground.

Sweating and panting, Georgios collapsed; his head throbbed, his stomach churned, and his body ached.

The sunrays slanting into the rough dwelling revealed the stranger's face contorted in agony. He rubbed away tears of outrage.

The sun lowered at a snail's pace. White birds circled the frothing sea, and rolling waves crashed against the shore.

Recovering some of his strength, Georgios climbed to his feet and, stepping warily, he stumbled outside.

The distant walls of a small village shone in the evening light.

Eyeing the distance, Georgios nodded and lurched forward. *I can make it—*

A low moan rose from inside the hut.

Georgios froze. He closed his eyes and sucked in a deep breath, relieved. At least he's not dead. He took another step.

Another moan.

Georgios wavered. He swallowed back burning thirst and remembered his desolation at finding himself alone in the dark with no one to aid him. He could feel his father's grip pressed on his shoulder. *It is my duty to respond quickly and obediently...as I hope you would do, my son.*

Silently, Georgios waited. This young man was a relation to someone. He would eventually be found, dead or alive, and Georgios might be blamed. He turned on his heel and strode to his tormentor.

The young man sat up, holding his head. Blood trickled down the side of his head where a spreading purple bruise marked Georgios' accurate aim.

"You all right?"

The youth attempted to lift his head, but a yowl of pain escaped. He thrashed at Georgios. "Do I look all right? You nearly killed me."

Georgios shuffled his feet. "There's a town not far off. Does your family live nearby?"

The youth spat and struggled to his feet. "My family? I would like to see them again! Can you bring the dead back to life—you murdering Roman?"

Astonished, Georgios straightened, his back arched. "You attacked me!"

The boy groaned, reaching for the wall to steady himself.

His stomach flip-flopping, Georgios reached out. “Where do you want to go?”

“To the devil and take you with me!” With a stifled sob, the stranger winced in pain.

Georgios stepped closer. “I am not your enemy—at least, I don’t mean to be.”

Red-rimmed eyes peered at Georgios. “You want to help me? How very un-Roman! You’d help a Jew, the son of a crucified man?”

Stifling shock, Georgios sucked in a breath. He offered his arm. “I’d like to—very much.”

CHAPTER FOUR

IT'S WORTH YOUR LIFE

—ROMAN VILLAGE—

Georgios steadied his companion, and they shuffled away from the shore in silence. Georgios had never cared for anyone, though he had played with a stray dog now and again. He felt the same compassion for this stranger, despite the beatings they had exchanged. After stumbling halfway to the village along a dusty road, his side ached, and his parched throat burned. Dizzy with hunger, he slid to earth and let the young man fall in a heap at his side.

A man strode their way.

Georgios lifted his aching arm and waved, calling. "Help us!"

The man looked their way and then stepped off the path so as to go around.

Georgios blinked in the evening light, dumbfounded. He glanced at the setting sun and the distant village.

On Patmos, people had gone out of their way to help him. When his grandparents went to market, the servants moved through the crowds clearing the way. Merchants stepped forward and smiled, displaying their finest wares.

A tug on his sleeve forced his mind back to the present. Georgios pulled the young man to a sitting position. Too weak to stay upright, they scooted back-to-back and leaned against each other for support. "What's your name?"

A throat clearing, like rocks rubbed together and a wracking cough shivered over Georgios' sensibilities.

"Rueben, son of Benjamin, of the tribe of...oh, what does that matter?" He snorted. "They're dead. Murdered.

My father and every uncle there ever were of our accursed race."

Nausea boiled into Georgios' throat. "I'm from Patmos, a Greek." He stared over the rocky shore to the far-reaching sea. "My grandparents raised me. My father is a Roman soldier, and my mother died of fever." He hesitated. Only labored breathing broke the silence. "I heard about the massacre in Jerusalem. A great temple once stood there. Though brave, they could not withstand the Roman army. When I asked my father about it, he said that the destruction of Jerusalem brought dishonor to Rome. He ordered me never to speak of it again."

Rueben straightened, his voice stronger. "That was thirty years ago, long before you were born."

Georgios sighed. "My father was the son of a Roman officer and a Jewish mother. My grandparents on my mother's side despise the Jews. When I learned the truth, I ran away."

Rueben turned and squinted at Georgios. "You're a Roman-Greek-Jew?"

Georgios stiffened. Tears threatened. "Of three worlds, I am your enemy and your brother. The son of a Roman warrior, the grandson of a Greek merchant"—his voice dropped to a whisper— "and I carry the blood of a people I hardly even know."

Rueben struggled to his feet, pressing his hand to his head. Grimacing, he steadied himself by sheer force of will.

Sitting in his shadow, Georgios flushed with alarm. *He's so big.*

Rueben peered over the Aegean Sea. Then he turned and stared at the village, as if studying it. He tapped Georgios on the shoulder.

Wiping sweat from his brow, Georgios climbed to his feet.

"We must move on. Raiders roam the seas, and they have a preference for young men. I should know...." Blinking in the bright light and squaring his shoulders, Rucben's face broke into a sheepish grin. "You are the first person I've ever met who's worse off than myself." He shook his head, his smile dissolving. "To be of mixed blood is the worst curse of all."

Anger boiled inside, flushing his already over-heated face. "My father is a noble man, and my grandparents are wealthy Greek merchants. Perhaps I've inherited the best blood of all."

With a snort, Rueben laughed. "God help you if you have the worst blood of all!" He plucked Georgios' sleeve. "I can walk again, but I'm so hungry I could eat—"

"A lion?"

Rueben grinned. "That would do."

"I could eat a lion and a bear and have room for more."

The two shuffled along shoulder to shoulder. "You're surprising, Georgios of Patmos. When I heard you were a Roman, I had no other thought than to kill you."

"I noticed." He glanced aside. "But now?"

"I understand you better."

The sun fell behind the hills, and the two marched faster.

"How could your father have died in the massacre thirty years ago and yet bring a son into the world?" Georgios asked.

"My father was not in that battle. That massacre was just one of many battles our people fought. My father vowed revenge and spent his life trying to organize his brethren to oppose the Roman oppressors, but eventually, he was caught and killed. I was very young when he died, but I will never forget the sight of him hanging—" Rueben's voice broke. He clutched his aching head.

Reaching out, Georgios steadied his companion. "Don't. I'd want to kill all the Romans if that had happened to my father." His heart pounding, Georgios remembered his father's face. *How did he choose a side?*

Rueben halted. "What are we going to say when we get to town?"

"I'll just ask about the quickest way to get home."

Wide-eyed, Rueben stared in disbelief. "Why would anyone care who you are or what you need? Do you have anything valuable on you?"

"Of course not, the servants handle—"

Rueben sniffed. "I thought so. When you ran off, you had only your honor to keep you warm and fed? How did you get passage?"

"I planned to work."

Rueben pinched Georgios' thin arm.

Georgios scowled, his temper rising.

Rueben rubbed his temple. "What have I gotten myself into?" He strode the last paces to the gateway and glared at the thickset, muscular guard. "Sir, my relatives are within, and I must give them urgent news. May we pass?"

The guard grimaced, vexed. "It's late, but…" He glanced at the setting sun and shrugged. "Urgent news? A shipwreck?"

Rueben nodded emphatically. "And more besides. I don't know the details." Rueben shoved Georgios through the gateway and into the bustling village.

The guard mumbled discontentedly to himself.

After a bewildering ramble through town, Georgios halted on an empty, narrow street and leaned against a wall, exhausted and out of breath. "So—where—to?"

"What would you have done without me? You

wouldn't have gotten past the gate."

"I'll do you a good turn when we get back home."

Rueben draped his arm around Georgios' shoulder and dropped his voice to a conspiratorial whisper. "You still don't understand? As far as the Romans are concerned, we're runaway slaves or worse."

Clammy terror shivered over Georgios.

Rueben glanced down the quiet road. "There's time enough to teach you what you need to know. But tonight, we need food and rest." A light entered his eyes. "Being a Jew is worth more than gold or jewels."

"How's that?"

"I have friends who understand and are willing to help. Come along, and you shall meet some members of your heritage." He frowned at Georgios in the twilight. "This tunic is too fine. Take that off and trade with me. I can explain a fine tunic better than you can."

They exchanged tunics in silence.

Uncomfortable in the threadbare tunic and irritated at Ruben's authoritative attitude, Georgios bit his lip. He glanced toward the sea.

Three ships lay anchored in the harbor.

Rueben grabbed Georgios' tunic and the thin fabric ripped. "I'm taking you to my people, to the Jews who have survived. It's worth your life not to be Roman tonight. Don't talk about your Roman father or your rich Greek grandparents. You must understand, these people have had their husbands, fathers, brothers, and sons murdered. They can't see beyond their suffering."

Georgios swallowed a lump in his throat and motioned for Rueben to lead the way. He rubbed his face with the back of his hand, mixing mud with tears, but no amount of washing would erase the pain that crushed his heart.

CHAPTER FIVE

FORCE OR DECEPTION

—PATMOS—

My Dear Cecilia,

My heart aches. Every day I wander, staring at the endless sky as it melts into the endless sea. Though their beauty has not changed, the world seems cold and dead.

When my beloved daughter Helena died, I thought I would lose my mind. For a long time, I couldn't even speak, but I realized that Georgios needed joy, so I acted happy, even when my heart ached. Pretending to be cheerful lightened my heart, and Georgios grew less despondent.

Myron continues in his dour manner. He is never a cheerful man, even when things go well. What a heavy rock I chained myself to when I married him!

I cannot pretend to be happy anymore—for whom would I pretend for? The only antidote to old grief is the source of fresh sorrow—my dearest Georgios. I have few friends—you are my oldest and therefore my best. I wish you did not live so far away. Visitors who express their condolences look about the place to see how far I have let things go. Gossips and talebearers everyone! They don't care about Georgios or my loss. They only want to see my agony so as to tell others how thin I've become or how I no longer care for myself.

When that wretch, Melitta (She's finally been recognized as a priestess – to her infinite delight.) stopped by, she was hardly civil. "Oh, what grief you bear. Two heavy losses in two years! I wonder what you did to earn such ill-fortune. Surely the fates have oppressed you for a fault. Perhaps if we could discover it, perhaps we could make a proper sacrifice. It's the only way, my dear."

Conniving witch! She thinks I'll offer a beast to the fire and bear my soul so that she can appear to lament with me. And then she gets to take the best leavings of the offerings. She'd profit from my misery!

My soul cries out. Why did Georgios leave me? Wasn't I a loving grandmother?

It's all Alexios' fault! Poor Helena was deceived. He may have accepted his Jewish mother, but he never acted like a real Jew. He was so sure that as a Roman citizen, he would conquer all. Look at us now!

What could Georgios possibly find in the world that he could not find at home?

I have no respite from this awful grief. Yesterday, Clorinna told me about an oracle that lives in a cave on the other side of the island and how he might help me find Georgios. I've never had much faith in such things. It would be a long trip, and I hear that oracles can be temperamental.

But I can't live with this pain. Myron doesn't understand my sorrow.

Perhaps I will go to this oracle. His name is John. He's supposed to be both wise and powerful. The trip will take planning, but I will do it.

What else is there for me but despair and death? I am not ready to die, and despair bores me.

Remember me, my friend,

~Roxanna

—Dispatch from Myron to Lysander—

Lysander,

As noted in my previous dispatch, your exoneration from debt depends on my good report to the authorities.

You must do everything possible to bring my grandson, Georgios, home. I understand that he left the island on a merchant ship bound for Corinth, so you may have to travel some distance to find him, but I give you my oath that your recompense will be in just measure with your effort.

You were sent to this island as a punishment for a crime against the empire, but I have spoken with the proconsul, and he has agreed to my request. Therefore, I assure you, you have permission to leave the island in search of my grandson. If you bring my grandson safely home, I have his word that you will never know exile again. An attractive opportunity, indeed!

I suggest that you take the first ship heading toward Corinth and follow every lead. Make certain that all dispatches are marked for me alone and sealed. It would not do to publicize our loss. Keep this between ourselves. I await your report.

With confidence,

~Myron

P.S. When you do find Georgios, if by some chance he does not wish to return, use force or deception, whichever is most effective.

CHAPTER SIX

NOT YET A MAN

—A TOWN NEAR CORINTH —

Georgios opened his eyes, stretched, and smiled, feeling little pain, except his split lip stung when he ran his tongue over it. *I didn't know a night's rest could make me feel so much better.* He surveyed his surroundings and frowned. *Where am I?* He sat up on a pallet situated against a rough stone wall and glanced around.

Voices murmured around the corner.

Vacant pallets lay against the wall, and a doorway led to a room where voices rose and fell in comfortable conversation.

Light streamed in from the window slit, illuminating particles of dust that floated in the light rays, a surprisingly beautiful sight.

His stomach rumbled, so he climbed to his feet.

A young woman stepped into the doorway, her hands on her hips and her eyes glowing with amusement. "So, you're among the living again. I was wondering if you'd be forever in the world of dreamers."

Her cadence was unfamiliar, but the lilting quality of her voice appealed to Georgios.

She studied him in brazenly. "Well, you're not much to look at, but with proper food, you might fill out. If we put some decent clothes on you, we might make you look like a man, though small you are to be sure!"

His face flushed hot. "Who are you?"

His anger seemed to kindle the woman's mirth. "Oh, a man you are! I should've known. Men come in all sizes and shapes, and I can see by your face that you've had troubles enough."

In defiance, he clenched his jaw.

Her eyes softened. "It'll do you no good standing there as the sun flies across the sky awakening the world. Might as well get something hot into you before we begin the journey. Rueben has plans and Seanan will not wait for the slow of foot." She chuckled, wrapped her arm around Georgios, and led him into the next room.

"I could tell you *long* stories about the marches we took into the hills." She chuckled, wrapped her arm around Georgios, and led him into the next room.

Forlorn in his isolation, Georgios sighed as exotic smells teased his nose. Confusion swarmed. *A journey—where?*

In the middle of the cream-colored room lay a table covered with wooden bowls. A large jug stood prominently in the center. Men sat on benches, eating and drinking.

Georgios stared. He looked for Rueben, but his friend was nowhere to be seen. "I think there's been a mistake. Am I in the right house?"

The men glanced up, grinned, and then laughed uproariously.

Georgios' face burned with embarrassment.

A tall man pulled Georgios to the table and pressed him onto the bench. "Come, lad, eat. We know all about you. Your plans have changed. Rueben didn't expect to see us here, but he was glad all the same. He's searching for news. In the meantime, eat and get what rest you can. We have a long journey ahead."

A plate of meat and bread was shoved in Georgios' direction.

With a shrug and tired of fighting hunger pangs, Georgios dug in with undisguised relish. The men chatted about matters he could not understand. Thirsty but unwilling to interrupt, Georgios pulled the wine jug in his direction, his gaze searching for a cup.

A burly man snatched the jug away, swung the mouth to his lips, and took a long swig. He wiped a drip from his chin. "That's how a man gets a drink around here, and if you want to quench your thirst, you'd better learn to do as well."

Georgios grasped the heavy jug and attempted to swing it, but the handle pinched his fingers, and it slipped from his grip.

The woman marched over and held it so Georgios could drink better "Like feeding a babe. Such weakness and ignorance, I wonder how he survived weaning!"

More laughter.

Georgios spluttered, thrusting the jug aside. He leapt from the table, blinded by fury. "I'm no babe, and I have long since been weaned by a mother finer than anyone you've ever known." He nodded stiffly to the man at his side. "I thank you for your hospitality, but I'll be on my way. Tell Rueben I'm grateful, but I don't need him anymore." Georgios stomped to the door.

Two men stood languidly and blocked the way.

The woman waved her hand, her tone soothing. "I was only teasing. I meant no harm."

The burly man raised his hand. "Stop, Brighid. The boy has a right to go, but first, he must understand what he'll face when he walks out this door." Shifting his gaze to Georgios, the man pointed to the bench.

With little alternative, Georgios plunked down with a snort.

"My name is Seanan, and I'm from a faraway land. My home is the most beautiful place in the world, though I dare say you'd say the same about yours. But things can happen that make a place a living hell." He pointed to the woman. "This is my sister, Brighid, and it's for her sake that we sailed, for in our lands some gods demand the flesh of the living to appease the spirits of the dead. Some keep the custom of offering a victim to keep 'em happy, but I was not willing to pay that price when it meant my sister's life.

"After we sailed, we made a living as traders. Until we were attacked. After a short battle, we were rewarded with a small merchant vessel, and onboard we met a dying slave—your friend—Rueben. However, during a storm, he proved most resourceful, so we accepted him as one of our own.

"We both have missions. I make a living by trading merchandise, while he is on a quest to find his God. I've found Rome not to my taste, so I'm returning home. But this time, I'll fight to keep what is mine, including my sister."

Brigid smiled.

"When Rueben showed up last night looking for friends, I told him that they'd moved on, but he's welcome to come with us. On hearing your story, we've decided to take pity on you. You'll serve us on our journey, and when you're strong enough, you may choose who you wish to be and claim your heritage."

He looked down at Georgios. "I'll treat you like my own son. I have several at home who wait for me to gather strength and take my proper place. I'm the clan leader, or I soon will be. Once I rid the world of Gutun." Seanan raised his hand in oath. "There will be no more human offerings! In the meantime, you come with us."

Georgios blinked as if he'd been staring at the sun. "But I'm a free man. My family will pay a handsome reward."

A grin spread over Seanan's face. "Aye, you may be a

free man to those who know you, but who knows you here? Besides, you're not yet a man, and far as I know, children have no rights, Roman or otherwise.

"But they'd pay well!" Georgios blurted, irritated that the man didn't seem to understand him. "I'm certain—"

"All the riches we need are at home on our own land. What could your grandparents give us that would make it worth our while? They could pay us the worth of a good slave, but we already have that in you." Seanan shook his head ruefully. "No, you're coming with us. Make no mistake about that."

Leaning on the table, Seanan stared into Georgios' eyes. "If you think you can run free in Rome, think again. There are worse masters than me."

Seanan stepped away and rummaged through a wide-mouthed bag. "I know how to make use of an honest man." He drew out a knife; its blade glinted in the light. "My son made this when he was a wee thing. Take it and see if it doesn't make you feel better. It's not much as weapons go, but it's the spirit of the thing. Someday you'll be ready for a more impressive weapon." He pressed Georgios' shoulder in a fatherly manner. "You'll see your grandparents again—but after a few adventures."

Stunned, Georgios rubbed the smooth handle of the knife. It was beautiful with a keen edge and fine craftsmanship. True, he wasn't a man yet, but that would change soon enough.

CHAPTER SEVEN

NOT FORSAKEN

—A TOWN NEAR CORINTH—

Rueben hustled into the entry, clasped Georgios by the arm, and whisked him to a side room. "Sorry I wasn't here when you woke up, but I had to get some information."

His hands on his hips, Georgios spluttered, "You said you were going to help me, but you left! They're preparing to sail, and I'm supposed to go with them. Seanan has as good as captured me. Uh, a-adopted me. I am not sure which."

Snorting, Rueben laughed and headed to the table, where he wrenched a piece of bread into bite-sized pieces. "Adopt? That's better than I got. Your wide-eyed innocence must've beguiled him." He chewed with vigor.

Georgios raised his hand, but a man's cough turned his attention. One of Seanan's men sauntered past the doorway.

Rueben wagged his finger teasingly at Georgios. "Stop worrying. You're among friends now."

Georgios threw up his hands. "Friends? You're not being dragged away from home. I don't even know what island I'm on!"

Rueben drank deeply from the wine jug, then wiped his mouth with the back of his hand. "You idiot! You're not on an island. The whole world is not made of islands!" Rueben fended off Georgios' raised hand, grasped Georgios' arm, and squeezed it. "Listen, fool, or you'll face a fate worse than homesickness! Believe me, I know. My father was killed and many of my family have been destroyed by the long years of battles—"

Georgios yanked hard to free his arm.

"Listen! I was like you, filled with anger, and I wanted to find my place in the world, a place where I could win honor from those who would keep me in poverty and subjugation. Instead, I met more trouble than I could handle. I've been hurt in more ways than I care to remember, but when I met Seanan, he found my wits useful. Some men understand that the measure of a man is not in his body but in something deeper—something noble, unseen. Something from above." Rueben flung Georgios' arm away. "God is bigger than we can imagine."

Georgios scowled, his words dropping to a low whisper. "I thought God abandoned you." He lifted his hands. "I just want to go home. Is that wrong? I care for no man's god. Can't you help me find a merchant vessel heading toward Patmos and let me go in the right direction?"

"You're a long way from home."

Slamming his foot down, Georgios grunted in frustration.

"Listen, Seanan plans to sail near Olympia, then on to Syracuse, and finally to Rome. He'll trade, take on supplies, and make bargains. He's no fool! You'll find each stop interesting, though you may not see much, for he doesn't let his men stray far, but still, he might let you see a bit of Rome."

Rome?" A glimmer of hope flickered inside Georgios. "My father is there. Maybe I can find him." He frowned, a headache building between his eyes. "Though I'm not sure..."

Rueben scoffed. "You don't even know where you are now! You don't know where Rome is, how far, or in what direction."

His face burning, Georgios clenched his hands. "I know Rome is west, the direction in which the sun sets. I could find it if—"

"If you knew where you were!" Rueben laughed. "I'll tell you. We're not far from Corinth. We'll sail to all the ports I mentioned, then to Rome, and next, we'll cross over land on foot. Then we'll take to a new sea, visit an island, and finally land on the other side of the world. Then the fun will really begin!"

Georgios choked, his breath coming in short gasps. "How will I ever get back home?" He stopped mid-stagger and peered at Rueben. "Did you say we?"

Rueben clapped Georgios on the back. "Sure. I'm not about to let you go by yourself!" He sucked in a deep breath. "One land is as good as another to me. At least with Seanan, I have already proven my worth, and he's shown me that he's fair, though—" Rueben leaned in closer. "He is a wild man."

Georgios blinked. "*He's* a wild man? What are you?"

"I can read and write."

"You—?"

Rueben put his finger to his lips. "It's best not to say too much." He nudged Georgios to the doorway. "Things are never as simple as they seem."

"But will I find my father? How will I find my way home?"

Rueben flung his arm around Georgios' shoulder as they strolled into the main room. He adopted a slow, patient tone. "You'll come with me, and we'll have great adventures. Have you ever heard of a prophecy?"

Nausea stirred inside Georgios' stomach. "The fortune-telling of old men and hags?"

Seanan and his men filed into the room.

Seanan smiled knowingly as he approached the table.

"No, boy, he doesn't dabble in the arts of the accursed. He's a Jew. He believes in the One God." Seanan sighed, wistful. "Wish we had such a god. All our gods are fickle and act no better than men."

Rueben snatched up a handful of figs and chewed. "Being the children of the One has its price. Not all love the relationship." Rueben considered Georgios. "But don't be afraid. God is strong and righteous." He took a last swig of wine, wiped his mouth, and faced Seanan. "I have one more thing to do. I'll be back soon."

Completely befuddled, Georgios shook his head. "But I thought your God had abandoned you?"

Rueben glanced at Georgios as he headed for the doorway. "For those who died in agony, it must have seemed so, but I've learned something that gives me hope."

Both Seanan and Georgios spoke at once. "What?"

Rueben's eyes twinkled. "First, we'll take this voyage. Then, we'll see..."

Seanan smiled, fatherly benevolence in his eyes. "That's the spirit, my boy! I'll walk with you—we have things to discuss. I need you to translate…"

~~~

Georgios felt his stomach drop to his feet. None of his questions had been answered. *Why is fate sending me to the ends of the earth with a host of wild men?*

A gentle voice responded in his mind. *"Your son's sons shall know Me."*

A skin-tingling sensation raced over Georgios. He stood frozen, terrified.

Brighid stepped into the room and set fresh bread, a new jug, and a pot of hot porridge on the table.
~~~

Seanan's men found seats and ladled porridge into their bowls.

Brighid strolled to Georgios. "Eat while you can. We'll be leaving soon, and food may not agree with you the next few days."

Confused, Georgios blinked at the men. The warm, inviting scent of spiced porridge dispelled his nausea.

Brighid led him to the board. "My brothers have taken a liking to you. You'll be well cared for, though you'll work harder than you've ever worked in your life." She ladled the porridge into a clean bowl, shoved it before him, and gestured to the wine. "It's not as good as red meat and mead, but Romans thrive on it, and it'll give you strength and courage enough." With a smile, she strolled around the table, seeing to the men's needs.

Feeling like a grasshopper as he sat next to Seanan's men, Georgios squeezed his eyes shut.

The voice returned. *Your son's sons shall know me.*

Peace settled over Georgios. He fingered the knife tucked in his belt, then pulled a bowl of porridge closer. Straightening his shoulders, he tore off a piece of bread and popped it into his mouth.

CHAPTER EIGHT

DO NOT LOSE HEART

—PATMOS—

My Dear Cecilia,

My plans are complete. I feel like a girl again. I'm going on an adventure! Phoebe is going with me. We have everything we need and two men to help us, plus a good guide. I've told Myron that I am going to the other side of the island to take the baths to relieve my aches. Stupid fool doesn't even know that there are no baths there. He didn't even hear me. He just stared like a hawk with his piercing eyes, understanding nothing. When I pressed him for his approval, he merely nodded and said that he was busy.

He has decided to try trading again. We have enough money for ourselves, and since Georgios left, we have no one to pass it along to. Myron will probably fail, and we'll end up as poor as the sparrows.

But before then, I have everything packed. All need only sleep the night away and set out before Myron stirs and thinks up a stupid question. He's like that. He'll seem unconcerned and then, just when I have everything in order, he'll ask searching questions. It'll be a pleasure to get away.

I can hardly wait to explore a mysterious cave and meet new people. If only morning would come quickly.

Remember me,

~Roxanna

—Dispatch from Lysander to Myron—

Sir,

I regret to inform you that Georgios boarded a ship, became gravely ill, and was left on shore near Corinth. It's difficult to ascertain the full truth, for if he perished, his body would likely have been thrown out to sea or buried in an unmarked grave.

But as your faithful servant, I feel it is incumbent upon me to investigate further. I have searched every ship on this coast and will now search the nearby towns. If there is any news to be had about your grandson, I will know of it.

In the meantime, do not lose heart; I will search diligently for your sake.

Your servant,

~Lysander

CHAPTER NINE

A WORLD APART

—COASTAL VILLAGE—

Georgios would never say that he enjoyed sea voyages, though he could say that during his second seafaring adventure, he discovered that travel meant more than raging seasickness alternating with deadly boredom.

Seanan kept his word. It seemed that they traveled the length and breadth of the entire world before they landed. Georgios had had no idea that the world was so large, varied, or wonderful.

He had never experienced unrestrained Greek life before. In his first coastal village, he enjoyed the outdoor shops, colorful crowds, enticing scents, and the cacophony of human and animal sounds.

Once disembarked, he dragged Rueben toward the center of town.

Letting himself be tugged along, Rueben only laughed.

After a whirlwind tour, they rested and watched the villagers stroll through the market. Fine ladies with heavy-laden slaves and burly men tromping beside companions ambled through the narrow byways, talking, browsing, and stopping to argue prices.

By noon, hunger pinched Georgios' stomach, and he set out again, but Rueben pulled him back.

A group of young men jostled each other, making their way to the seaside.

Rueben slunk aside, melting into the crowd.

Georgios stood his ground and watched openly, fascinated by the boys' fine clothes and rough speech. Romans born and bred.

A tall boy with a scar above his right eye flicked a glance in Georgios' direction. Then he marched forward, speaking in a rapid, commanding voice. "Get me fruit from the market."

Georgios hid a smile. *He thinks I'm a servant.*

The youth pointed to a fruit seller. "I'll pay later."

Baffled, Georgios decided to comply, but when he told the fruit seller, the man cuffed him. "Get yourself gone, vagabond!"

His face blazing, Georgios returned to the smirking youth.

The boy shouted, "Get my fruit, fool. Hurry up!"

Flushing with fury and confusion, Georgios turned away.

The group followed.

"Coward! Useless slave!"

"You should be flogged for stupidity."

Stark fear combatted with anger as Georgios measured the distance to the ship. He kept his head down and focused on the shore.

"Whore's son! You don't even know how to obey!"

Georgios whirled around, his fists high, fury toppling his fear.

The mob of boys rushed forward. One grabbed him by the hair and flung him to the ground.

Georgios tried to rise but a swift kick in the stomach curled him into a ball of agony. Sweat dripped in his eyes, and mind-numbing fear gripped him.

Suddenly, Rueben leaped at the throng, wild-eyed and clawing each boy who came near.

The group backed up. The tall boy smirked. "Jew!"

Like a pack of wolves, the assembly jumped on Rueben, beating and kicking without mercy.

Georgios staggered to his feet. With a twisted knee, bile

rising from his stomach, and dizziness throwing him off balance, he flung himself into the middle of the fray. Blocking blows with his body, he protected his friend. "Rueben!"

Angry men's voices crashed together as burly arms pulled the youths apart.

Georgios crumpled in a heap next to Rueben.

Jostled and dragged off, a few youths yelped as they were smacked on the head and shoved forward.

A wet rag was thrust onto Georgios' bleeding mouth. Strong arms lifted him to his feet.

Rueben lay on the ground, two men standing over him.

Georgios tried to shake his benefactors away and jerked toward Rueben, but strong arms held him secure.

"Hold on and let them help your friend."

Braced by helping hands, Georgios staggered to a bench, plopped down, and wiped his bleeding mouth. He heaved a painful, deep breath. "Thank you. I was just standing by that tree, thinking about getting something to eat, when they—"

The men nodded. One rubbed his ear, and another stroked his beard.

"Rueben tried to help me, but they attacked as if they wanted to kill him too."

A gray-bearded man steadied Georgios, patting his shoulder. "You needn't explain."

The first man pointed at Rueben. "Your friend can stand. He'll live to tell of this adventure." He glanced around. "Where do you belong so that we may see you safely home? Sadly, the circus alone does not fill Romans' appetite for sport."

Rueben approached, one eye swelling shut and bright red marks and bloody scratches marking is body.

Georgios clasped Rueben's shoulder, and they started for the ship.

With several of his men following and enormous scowl etched across his forehead, Seanan jogged toward them. "What happened?"

Graybeard pointed to the market. "They were attacked. They fought bravely to defend each other. Are they brothers?"

Seanan gestured for his men to assist. "Brothers? Hardly. The way I hear it, they tried to kill each other the first time they met. One is a runaway Greek; the other is a Jew who's lost most of his family to Roman justice. If they now defend each other like brothers, well—it's another one of life's mysteries."

Graybeard smiled at his companion, waving his hand between them. "We, too, are like brothers, for we believe in the same God."

With a helpless shrug, Seanan bobbed his head. "It was good of you to help the boys before they were beaten to death."

Graybeard's companion grimaced. "We help each other because it is God's will."

Seanan sighed. He turned to go but stopped and faced the two loquacious benefactors. "If you're ever in need, I'm in your debt. My name is Seanan."

The men bowed.

Seanan waved his men who assisted the two boys forward. "Let's get them on board. Brighid will see to their wounds."

As he was led onto the ship, Georgios watched his saviors stroll back into the village, bent close in conversation. His whole body ached and his mind whirled. If it was God's will to help them, by whose will were they beaten?"

~~~

Seanan watched over the boys anxiously, but as Brighid's ministrations took effect, he felt more confident of their recovery.

Yet when Rueben finally did rise and look about, he was not the same. All the spark had disappeared from his eyes, and every motion was labored.

Georgios appeared exhausted; his shoulders slumped in permanent defeat.

When the two stood before Seanan, reporting for duty, his other men went about their business, avoiding eye contact with him and the boys.

Dissatisfied, Seanan rubbed his lips and considered his options. "When I took you boys on board, it was with the understanding that you'd make yourselves useful. But now, after four days, you look as weak as the day you were beaten. You needed time to heal, but this is a hard world, and we must endure much."

Georgios swallowed. "But we—"

Seanan shrugged off excuses. "Cruel men are always ready to attack. Still, one must carry on. A man must choose—to die in despair or to rise again."

He touched Georgios' bruised face and then stared into Rueben's unfocused eyes. "You'll be trained to avoid becoming mats for other men to scrape their feet upon. Reports say that you fought with spirit but lacked skill." He glanced aside. "Rueben, you should've won for the spirit you showed."

After a nod from Seanan, three men stepped forward.

"Here are your teachers, the best fighting men in the known world: my elder brother, Tainair, a leader like myself, and my younger brother, Ronan, a quiet man who
~~~

will teach you how to oppose an enemy successfully. And this"—he pointed to the third man—"is an old friend who saved my life on three separate occasions. Olcan can devise an escape from any trap. He rescued my sister from the bloody hands of a Druid priest."

Seanan raised his hands and his voice in the style of a man making a solemn vow. "I, Seanan, put Georgios and Rueben into the hands of Tainair, Ronan, and Olcan that they be trained to become worthy fighters who will bring honor to their names and ensure mutual success."

He dropped his hands and studied Georgios. "The difference between the great and the small lies in the heart." He patted Georgios on the shoulder and then shoved him toward Ronan.

Seanan peered hard at Rueben, who stared vacantly across the sea. "My boy, how could you have survived so much and let a seaside brawl bring you so low?" He gripped Rueben's shoulders. "If you give in now, where will we be tomorrow? You're not the only one to endure loss and grief."

Deadpan, Rueben's voice barely rose above a whisper. "No one has suffered as much as me."

Seanan stomped away, his stomach churning with irritation. "Many of my men have lost family and friends to the evils that men do to each other. But they don't give up. They stand and fight. They still care."

Rueben's eyes flickered. "I lost..."

"What?"

Rueben's face crumpled. "God."

Frantic, hysterical laughter bubbled from a dark pit in Seanan's middle. "How does one lose God? I thought Jews didn't worship graven images. You can't lose the real God."

Rueben shouted. "My *faith* in God, the creator, the

father of Adam and Abraham, the covenant maker—"

"I know of the Jewish God. I admire Him, but—"

Rueben lowered his gaze. "I heard He came and lived among us as a man named Jesus. He brought a message."

Sadness enveloped Seanan. "Gods are fickle and care little for men."

Gulls flapped against a strong wind and called out.

Tears welling, Rueben glanced aside. "The Savior suffered the same fate as all men who care too much."

Seanan flung his hands up in the air and perched on an overturned wooden barrel as sunshine glinted off the water. "So, what happened?"

"He commanded us to love as He loves."

"He loves all men or just His own?"

Rueben's eyes flickered toward his friend in scorn.

Seanan shook his head. "How did you manage to lose faith in such a good God?"

"He was crucified...like my father."

Rising, Seanan sighed and flapped his arms against his side. Time to get back to work. "I'm sorry, Rueben. It was a good story. I wish it'd been true."

Rueben regarded Seanan. "It is true. God did die, and He rose again. He is alive."

"If you really believe that, then why do you doubt? Your spirit has been as cold as a winter moon."

Rueben sniffed and rubbed his sunburned nose. "When I felt their vicious claws rake my face, I wanted to kill those beasts."

Seanan shrugged. "I would've felt the same way, but I would have seen it through. That was the point of my talk—"

"But don't you see?" Rueben's voice cracked. "I'm no better than the rest of raging humanity. I'm a savage beast."

Seanan tapped Rueben's shoulder. "No. Your problem is that you want to be God. Would anyone be fit for the Land Beyond if we stood by while cruelty charged across the land? Your God must understand that." He nudged Rueben toward Georgios, who sparred with the men. "If I return home and defeat the evil ruling there, then perhaps I'll go with you to learn about your God. Where did He live?"

Like an awed child, Rueben whispered, "He lived in Nazareth and died in Jerusalem, but he traveled all over."

Seanan stroked his chin. "Far away, almost a myth..."

"But one of His followers lived on Patmos, where Georgios is from. I'd go there."

Foreboding filled Seanan. "One mission at a time." He pointed ahead. "First, learn how to be useful, and then we'll see."

Rueben strode to his teachers, his shoulders back and his chin up.

A smile played on Seanan's lips. *A God-man, killed by Romans, yet still lives—what next?*

Chapter Ten

Define Real

-OldEarth, Rome-

Noman smoothed down his tunic as he paced before a wooden table spread with the evening meal: wine, boiled fish, nuts, olives, bread, honey, cheese, dates, and pomegranates.

Abbas was coming to see him.

He played with words in his mind. Abbas was coming… to see him…to see him…

Boys' laughter crashed against his ears. He stopped before the window of the Hospitia and considered the bucolic scene.

Three children chased each other across hard-packed earth, their clothes tattered, their feet bare, and their eyes bright.

A shout split the air, and the children scattered.

A gesturing heavyset man, flushed and furious, jerked forward. "Didn't ya hear me! Get back to work, you fools, or I'll cut your useless legs from under your bodies."

An elder dressed in a long white tunic with a fine robe draped over it stepped close upon the angry man's heels. He raised his hand as he passed.

All bombastic bravado fled. The heavy man bowed low, scraping the ground in a servile fashion.

Unimpressed, the older man stopped and eyed the window.

Noman caught his breath.

Abbas had come. To see him.

~~~
~~~

Noman poured wine into an ornate cup and passed it across the table. The food sat untouched. Neither needed to eat but that fact had never stopped them before. He spread his hands wide, a genial host. “Please, enjoy.”

Abbas, ever the master of kindness, broke off a piece of fish, slipped it between his lips, and chewed with a hum of pleasure. “Very nice.”

Pride fought gratitude in the playground of Noman’s mind. He smirked. “I picked it out myself. Best fish this side of the Divide, they say.”

Abbas choked and grabbed the goblet for a quick swallow. He wiped his lips daintily with the edge of his sleeve and leaned against the hard-baked wall, his penetrating gaze searching. “You know about The Event?”

Noman wasn’t going to play. “Event?” He smirked. “God’s attempt to make humans appear worthier than they are. A trick, really, to see how we’ll react.”

Abbas stroked his bearded chin. “Is that all, you think?”

“I know so!” Frustration needled Noman like a thousand biting insects. “I told you. They are a mere plaything. A toy. God just pretended to become one of them. He wouldn’t really send His Son to be sacrificed. Ridiculous! Just His way to see how we’ll respond. If we throw ourselves at his mercy and beg for forgiveness—”

“We need forgiveness?”

“Of course not. But if we’re fools, we might think so. Lesser beings are always ready to beg. It’s what they do. Humiliate themselves before greatness.”

Abbas sighed. “You’d certainly never do that.” He rose from the bench and strode to the window.

A little boy sat on the ground, playing with round stones. A gray sparrow landed and hopped nearby. The boy watched, then raised his hand, a stone poised. The bird pecked at the ground, unconcerned.

Noman stepped over and propped his arm against the wall, his gaze fixed on the opposite side of the room. "We know our true place in the universe."

The boy's gaze softened as he watched the bird, his brows knitting together. Slowly, he lowered his arm and dropped the stone. With his other hand, he dug into a pocket.

Abbas sighed. "Do we?" He glanced aside. "Really?"

"Our power informs us." Noman threw his arms wide. "I could remake this entire village into a treasure of pleasure—if I wanted to."

Abbas returned his gaze to the scene outside.

The boy held out his hand, palm up, offering breadcrumbs.

The wary sparrow hopped close and stopped. With a cock of the head, it eyed him.

Smiling, the boy tipped his hand and scattered the crumbs within easy reach. Eagerly, the bird snapped up the morsels.

"Steward."

Noman cocked his head and stared at Abbas. "Excuse me?"

"I keep hearing the word in my mind—like a verse, a song."

"Ah! Song—the Bhuaci witch. She's always playing mind games."

Brooding irritation flooded Abbas' eyes. "No, not that Song. A song. Music. Harmony and melody. Beauty in sound."

Noman shrugged. "Never understood the concept." He peered out the window.

The boy grinned as the bird pecked the crumbs.

Annoyance flushing through his body, Noman shouted, "Go on, boy! You've no business here."

Abbas sighed and started for the door.

Jolted, Noman gripped the man's arm. "Where're you going?"

"You may be right. Song may be exactly who I'm thinking of."

"But what about me—about my mission?"

Abbas peered at Noman's fingers gripping his tunic. "I think you've underestimated The Event. There's more to humanity than meets the eye. At least, God thinks so." He jerked free. "I'll take my leave now. But I suggest that you don't do anything you'll regret."

Cold seeped through Noman. *Regret?* Not possible. Chilling that Abbas could even suggest the word. He bowed and peered at the door.

Abbas had come. Now, it was time for him to go.

–Lux–

Teal reviewed Arc's holographic message twice and sighed. He passed his hand over the holopad; the wavering image disappeared.

With a soft touch, Sienna placed her hand on his arm, slipping around from behind. "What's wrong?"

The thrill of her unexpected touch dissipated too quickly for Teal's liking. He glanced from the low couch to the shelf packed with OldEarth crafts—a decorated pot from Aram's clan, a woven blanket from Ishtar's clan, even one of Neb's forgotten obsidian knives. He shrugged and turned away. "Arc's worried. So, he's got Zuri worried. And before you know it, I'll be worried."

Sliding around her husband's waist, Sienna snuggled under his arm. A smile played on her lips. "Cerulean has been begging to go. Maybe…"

"I should have followed up before this. It's just—"

Sienna nodded. "It was a big event. Everyone talked about it, but then things died down. We'll probably never know what God meant by it."

Teal padded to the window and contemplated the Luxonian skyline, the suns setting and moons rising. "Things are happening, changing. I don't think humanity will ever be the same."

"Can they handle the responsibility?"

Giving a snort that sounded rude to his own ears, Teal shrugged. "Of course, they can't. No one can. It's impossible. The very notion. God-man? Eternal life with Him—as family? We don't even dare define—"

"Children can imagine what adults don't dare dream of—the limitlessness of youth, perhaps?"

Teal rubbed his forehead. "I can't even begin to go there. It must be a misunderstanding. Wishful thinking."

"And if it's not? If it is real…" She joined him at the window, sharing the view.

Heat working through his body, Teal swallowed. "Define real." A soft sound caught his ear. He glanced over his shoulder.

Cerulean, youthful, eager, and ready for anything, stood in the open doorway. "Ark sent a message. He has something for me."

Teal closed his eyes. *Oh, God.* He opened his eyes and met his son's innocent gaze. "I'm sure he has." He glanced at his wife. They both knew. No one would be the same.

–Crestar–

Ark zipped up his bio-suit, dragged on his boots, and glared at the pod swimming energetically in the murky pool against the back wall.

The door swished open, and Zuri tromped in, his head and hands bare but wearing a modified version of Ingoti armor. "You ready?"

Ark huffed through his breathing helm; bubbles rose. "Now or never."

The pool swished spasmodically, a riot of bubbles rising. The pod stopped and hung weightless, its large eyes staring imploringly at Ark.

Zuri halted and glanced back. "What's—I mean—who's that?"

Ark cleared his throat and tugged at the collar of his bio-suit. "Uh, my son, Tarragon."

Zuri's eyes couldn't have opened any wider if he'd had implants. "What? You never told me you had a son!" He slapped Ark on the back. Hard. "Congratulations!"

Stomping to the doorway, his boots smacking the ground with emphasis, Ark aimed for his escape. "It just sort of happened."

Zuri swiveled his head as if testing the limits of his joints. "What does that mean? You have a son and you're—what—irritated?"

Stopping on the threshold, Ark waved all six tentacles and forced a smile at the pod. "Just out of sorts, really. I wasn't expecting it." He scowled at Zuri. "I have important work to do. We both do." He turned his back on the pod. "There's a new player on Earth, a mysterious being, who has a bet to win…a challenge. He's trouble, make no mistake."

"In proper diplomatic response, we're going to…?"

"Meet Song and discuss possibilities. Then we return to Earth."

"I thought we couldn't."

“Couldn’t is a strong word. Shouldn’t perhaps…” Ark clumped out the door.

Zuri looked back.

The pod waved, its eyes over-wide and grievous.

“But your son—”

Charging forward, Ark already knew. He simply refused to see.

CHAPTER ELEVEN

IS ANYONE FREE?

—ROME—

Georgios nursed his bruises but knew, with some small measure of pride, that he had given a few bruises to his instructors as well. He had learned to parry and thrust with a sword as well as with a short knife, using both hands, and how to wrestle to keep his opponent off-balance, using his weight to his best advantage. He liked to spar with Ronan, a man who fought with both strength and wit. Olcan gave good advice, but he was too much of a thinking man for Georgios' taste.

As they traveled south along the coast toward Olympia and across the sea to Syracuse, Georgios enjoyed developing his muscles, though he despaired whenever he compared himself to the other men. Still, he sensed a pleasant change as his legs adapted to the sweep of the ship's movement, and he hefted loads upon his slim shoulders that he would never have dared attempt back home. He could fold a heavy canvas better than he could have managed a bedcover.

He worried that perhaps his father would return sooner than intended and, not finding his son, would go off in search of him, and they'd spend years looking for each other.

But then he would survey this wondrous new world, and his worries would vanish like a mist in the heat of the sun's glorious rays. *When I get home, we'll find each other soon enough. Now, at least, I'll be fit for a proper adventure.*

On a sultry morning, Seanan informed him that

summer was almost over, and their stay in Rome would be as short as possible.

Georgios' spirits immediately dropped into gloomy darkness. His work turned into drudgery, every motion taking exorbitant effort.

Ronan crossed the deck in a hurry but then glimpsed Georgios and stopped abruptly. "What ails you, boy? I could cure you of world-weariness with a drink or two, but I doubt it would take that tragic expression off your face. We're nearing Rome and have to arrange the ship's repairs and exchange supplies in quick time. If we don't keep our wits about us, we'll lose more than we gain. Above all, we must keep the Roman authorities from looking too deeply into our private affairs."

"Why would the Romans investigate this ship? Do we have something they want?"

"If we have anything of value and stand about too long, someone will surely notice. If we're not broken into during the black hours of the night, we could be waylaid by Roman justice and see our things carried off by a rich merchant or powerful senator who thinks that what is in a Roman harbor naturally belongs to him. Being the most powerful people on Earth, they tend to claim much!"

In disbelief, Georgios shook his head. "But Roman laws apply to everyone. The Senators must defend the rights of the people."

"Are we Roman citizens? Do the laws apply to us? And even if they did, could we argue the law in front of those who wrote it?" Ronan snarled in derision. "Don't fool yourself. Being the son of a Roman soldier won't protect you from the villains who take advantage of those ignorant of written law and their courts."

Georgios stared across the sea as a wave lifted them high. "It's beautiful though—green hills and magnificent buildings. What men can create when they have a mind to!"

Ronan tapped Georgios' shoulder and pointed to the Roman shoreline. "Don't forget the brutes that nearly beat you to death. This is where cutthroats learn their trade!"

As Ronan bustled to his next duty, Georgios leaned on the railing. If he could introduce Seanan and his crew to his father, they would finally meet an honorable Roman. He sighed wistfully and returned to his work.

The next evening, they drew nearer shore, and Seanan made arrangements for fresh supplies to be brought on board and to trade the goods that he had bought earlier.

Georgios looked for Rueben so they could search for his father, but Rueben was nowhere to be found. When Georgios asked Seanan, he appeared distinctly uncomfortable and beckoned to Olcan. "Take Georgios in the city and ask after his father, but be discreet."

Olcan nodded, his eyes glinting in amusement.

Georgios sighed as the two strode into the bustling Roman world. If bullies attempted to have fun with him now, he would be better prepared. He glanced at Olcan's muscular build and watchful gaze and grinned. He had nothing to fear.

All day they tromped through cobbled streets asking merchants and innkeepers if they knew of Alexios, a soldier in the Imperial Army. Many offered irritated scoffs and bewildered stares. One irritated old man shook his fist and shouted, "There are thousands of Roman soldiers and half of them are named Alexios!"

Georgios grew too dispirited to go on and found a hedge bordered by a stone fence. He leaned against it and sighed. "It's no use. There are too many people, and the city is too big. I'll never find my father."

With his arms crossed over his chest, Olcan watched

men shuffling through the narrow streets and women with colorful long tunics carrying bundles and tugging children by the hand. Stately Roman men wearing leather sandals, long robes, and sporting oiled and scented hair strolled languidly before weary slaves.

He smirked as one such man crossed his path.

Then a group of four slaves with ropes tied around their necks and hands traipsed by, like trapped animals, their heads bowed and their expressions frozen. One beautiful woman gripped the hand of a handsome little boy.

A lump rose in Georgios' throat. He recognized their suffering and identified with their despair.

Olcan clenched and unclenched his fists in a particular rhythm he used before a mock battle.

A twinge of anxiety passed over Georgios, his skin tingling.

Olcan pelted after the slaves, dust flying from under his feet. He caught the man holding the lead rope and grinned innocently. "My master is in need of more slaves to take aboard. I was sent to find a few and, by luck, you walk by."

The man, a tall Persian, considered Olcan with shrewd appraisal. He wiggled his fingers in a cajoling manner. "How much money do you have?"

Olcan's eyes widened in mock horror. "My master must see them for himself and decide."

The slave-dealer sighed, disgruntled. "So be it. I hope your master is not the kind who thinks things over for a ponderous time. I've had enough thinking men this day!"

Olcan nodded with a sympathetic expression. "My master is very efficient. I'm sure he'll take immediate action."

The slave master wrinkled his brow in indecision.

Without thought, Georgios leapt forward, his voice

loud and beseeching. "Our master wants to get home before winter sets in."

The merchant's face cleared, and he picked up his pace. "Right. Winter is coming on, and you'd better make the most of your opportunities. I won't bicker over prices. I'll sell them for what they cost me and go my way so I can see my family before the evening gets too far spent."

Like a wolf, Olcan grinned. "You're too kind."

The slave woman slipped, her son falling from her tight grip.

Georgios rushed ahead and lent a stabilizing hand.

The woman glanced up; their eyes met.

A torrent of emotions washed over Georgios.

She looked like Alexios—both Roman and Jew, bound by histories as palpable as the rope that tied her hands. He glanced at the child. What if this had been my father—or me?

After stumbling on the rough cobbled road, he caught himself.

They approached the ship where Seanan's men bustled about fulfilling assorted duties.

Georgios glanced all around. Seanan was nowhere in sight.

Olcan put his finger to his lips and motioned to the merchant. "Stay here and don't say anything. I want this to be a surprise. I'll leave my brother with you, so you needn't be alarmed." Olcan shot Georgios a stern look.

Weariness overwhelmed Georgios. As they waited, cold and hunger swept over him. He promptly forgot Olcan's warning and tried to cheer the shivering slaves. "Don't worry. Seanan is kind. You'll get good food and a decent place to sleep tonight."

Irritated, the merchant waved his hand. "Not if he doesn't pay a fair price. Mind you, I'm reasonable, but I'll not be cheated. Besides, what need have they with good food and soft pallets?" His eyes narrowed.

Olcan jogged forward with Tainair and Ronan and stood guard.

The two others took positions behind the slaves and began to untie their ropes with alacrity.

"What do you think you are doing? These are my slaves, and no one has paid me! We have not even struck a deal. I'm a kind man, but I want to see the money first! Are you barbarians?"

Breaking from a gathering crowd, Seanan stepped forward. Sniffing, he pressed the merchant's shoulder. "Yes. And I'm taking your slaves, for I need them more than you do, and they need me more than you need them."

The merchant's face flushed with fury. "An outrage! I'm an honest merchant—"

Seanan laughed. "You are a merchant of stolen goods. This woman was free, living with her lawful husband—a good man by all accounts. How you managed to get hold of her, I don't want to know."

"Her husband plotted against the emperor and was killed for his crime. She was taken, as was her whole household. I've done nothing wrong. Don't bear false witness against me! I paid a fair price for her and her son, and these two others are of little enough value, one being stupid and the other weak. They'll be no use to you. I'll take them to the market square and get what little I can for them. Now, be reasonable—"

Olcan, Ronan, and Tainair led the four bewildered slaves onto the ship.

"You'll pay for this! Roman law cares nothing for foreigners who think they can rob an honest man. Soldiers, help!"

Seanan shoved the merchant backward. "Get your

Roman soldiers. I'll explain how you stole your goods and how you cheat as a matter of course."

The merchant backed away. "You don't have what it takes to earn Roman justice, but I—"

A rock whizzed by the merchant's glowering face. He turned and fled, screaming for assistance.

Seanan signaled for his men to set sail.

Georgios stood by confused. Seanan had intended to stay in port for several more days, and now all that was cut short. And for what? There were so many slaves. They could not free them all. Worst of all, he had not found his father, and he would have no other chances.

Barking his order, Seanan glowered at Georgios. "Get on board and hurry!"

Georgios stumbled forward.

As the shoreline bustled with interested gossips and talebearers, Georgios stowed wooden boxes and heavy ropes and repacked things that had been unpacked so recently, working like a man in a dream.

Rueben carried food and bedding at Brighid's direction.

Seanan took the helm and beckoned to Georgios.

Georgios shuffled closer.

"Quite an adventure, eh, Georgios?"

Desperately wanting to close his eyes and forget his disappointment, Georgios nodded.

Seanan tousled Georgios' hair. "It's not what you were hoping for?"

As if he were standing in front of his father again, Georgios merely nodded.

Seanan sighed. "You are a young man in a big world. Many have lost more than you and yet lived to great purpose. Think of what you did for those four people today."

Georgios tried to break free from his stupor. "Free? Just because the merchant lost them, does that mean they are free?"

Seanan slapped his hands against the rudder. "By the stars above, you and Rueben ask the most befuddling questions!" He pursed his lips, a prim father taking his son to task. "I stole those slaves for a reason. Trust me."

A shiver passed over Georgios. "I'm not any freer than they are. I have no choice about where I go or what I do. We're all slaves, even you, for you have to run from Roman justice and are forever trying to make a bargain. Is anyone really free?"

Seanan gestured for another man to take the helm. Gripping Georgios' arm, he led him to a sheltered spot out of the wind. "You're a true philosopher, Georgios. Perhaps there is more Greek in you than I realized. No more questions. Rest now."

Georgios slid to the deck, his eyes closing even as he slumped against a wooden post.

He could hear Seanan muttering as he strode away. "Good questions, though."

CHAPTER TWELVE

A CONSOLATION

—PATMOS—

My Dear Cecilia,

I have never been so frightened in all my life! The very air seems to hold the power of the man who once lived here. I believe every story I've heard about him. Oh, how I wish he were still alive! I would have followed him anywhere, for surely this Iohannes had the power of prophecy and could have told me where Georgios has gone.

But as fortune would have it, he was sent back to the mainland and there he died only a short time ago. I hear he was quite old, and his death was peaceful. Oh, I am bereft! To have missed him by so short a time is horrible indeed.

I find some consolation in discovering that the people here have some of his writings, and they remember his stories. He claimed he knew God Himself. Of course, I find that to be quite extraordinary, but something about this place that puts all doubt aside. The walls seem to proclaim wonders—if only I understood.

Tomorrow I'm going back, and I will speak to one of the men, a cheerful old man who smiles constantly. I enjoy his humor and light heart, despite his toothless grin.

My nerves tingle with awe, fear, and joy. I know nothing more about Georgios, yet I feel strangely content.

I am eager to learn more about this John. I feel so strange. I hardly know myself.

Remember me,

~Roxanna

—Dispatch from Myron to Lysander—

Lysander,

Do what you must, but do not give up your search until you find Georgios or learn indisputable proof of his death.

My wife has discovered some new prophet, and she now believes that Georgios is still alive, though far from here. She was told by some friend of this prophet to look west.

I'm going to check on her for I fear she is being led into some weird, foreign cult. Her letters to me have been most unusual. If I did not know better, I'd say she was happy in this very unhappy time.

In any case, your mission remains the same. Search diligently for my grandson.

~Myron

CHAPTER THIRTEEN

AUTHENTIC JOY

—SEA & LAND—

Georgios shaded his eyes with one hand and watched a bird dance carefree in the bright blue sky. *Will I ever be free?*

Apparently, Seanan could not take a deep breath until they had moved further from the center of Roman territory. After their hurried departure from Rome, they sailed west and stopped on the island of Corsica long enough to complete their repairs and make the trades that had been interrupted in Rome. As soon as possible, they sailed again and made for a place near Massilia. There they took a long rest and traded once again.

The new town was pleasant enough. When a group of young men headed his way, he stood his ground, his head held high.

They looked his way but did not stop.

Vitality pulsated through Georgios' whole body.

Each day melted into another. He never felt as lonely as when wandering through a market town. Occasionally he saw something he wanted, but he never had any money. Finally, an intricately carved fish with strange markings caught his interest enough to force him to ask Seanan if he could buy it.

Like an indulgent father, Seanan handed him the sum needed, though Georgios winced at the need to ask, for at home, he had been the master of his fortune. With new humility, he suppressed his indignation and bought the carving.

As he turned to leave, the merchant told him that he

was a lucky man, for it was a sign from the one true God and could make a man's fortune if he knew how to use it.

Georgios merely smiled at the merchant's drollery and moved on.

That evening as they settled on board, Seanan informed him that he had sold the ship. "We're going to leave the ship behind and travel on foot. Then we'll take one more sea voyage, and finally we'll reach home."

Georgios listened halfheartedly. It seemed that Seanan had lost interest in him and found only Rueben's literacy skills useful. He had tried not to be jealous, but a flush of irritation rose as he tried to imagine his part to play.

Seanan clasped his shoulder. "I have a problem, and I need your help."

Georgios waited, perplexed but interested.

"You must agree of your own free will or nothing will work. In fact, you have to really want to do this thing."

Perplexity turned into confusion. *This ought to be interesting.*

"Do you remember the slaves that Olcan recovered?"

Georgios lifted his eyebrows.

"Well, this is rather a delicate matter and—"

Georgios had never seen Seanan blush before.

"I need to give you a little history of my people. That'll help to ease the point across." Seanan leaned nonchalantly against the rail, crossing his arms over his chest. "I'm descended from a noble clan that has lived in the valley for generations uncounted. We've always been a brave, daring people, well versed in the laws of our religion. I was brought up an honorable son of a valiant father. I married young and brought into the world my first son when I was only a few years older than you are now. I had two more sons and, later, a baby daughter, but she died soon after."

His gaze shifted away. "After my father died, I became the leader of our clan, and I took my responsibility seriously. But there was a man, a certain Druid priest named Gutun, who did not like my father. When it came to matters of authority, my father always claimed the right to make the final decision. Inevitably, they clashed over some inheritance laws. Furious at being challenged, Gutun left the discussion, taking his servants with him and calling on Dagdg, the king of the Otherworld, to judge my father for his insolence, thus foretelling our doom.

"Well, not long after, my father died—of purely natural causes, mind you. But some saw it as the judgment of Dagdg for offending the Druid priest."

Seanan propped his hands on his hips and his voice hardened. "I defended my father's name and went about my business in defiance of Gutun's dread warnings. Strangely, things went from bad to worse. Livestock sickened, my baby daughter died, and one argument resulted in a man losing his right arm. The clan looked at me as if I were to blame."

Seanan snorted. "One fool, an idiot named Bronach, implored Gutun to come back, offering the sun, moon, and every star in heaven if only he would. Of course, I thrashed the fool for his betrayal, but the damage was done, and Gutun returned with the importance of a god.

"Then the worst thing happened. Everything got better. The fighting ceased. The cattle got well, and there were no more mysterious deaths. It was a trick of some sort, though I never figured out how it was done. In any case, I could not force Gutun away without an uprising, even in my own family, for my wife believed in him. She blamed our daughter's death on my stubbornness."

Seanan dropped his gaze and all hint of humor died. "I tried to ignore him, though I wanted to kill him. He wanted me to bow down, as he had wanted my father to do, but I would not. So, he told the people that unless we made a proper sacrifice, we'd be cursed. The summer grew terribly hot, the creeks dried up, and some were willing to see me sacrificed. But Brighid spoke her mind. She challenged Gutun." Seanan unfolded his arms. "You can imagine the rest."

His imagination on fire, Georgios leaned in with bated breath. "No, tell me! What happened?"

Seanan turned around, stared across the rising waves, and squeezed the rail. "I awoke late one morning, after a long night with a very good jug of mead, and I heard wailing. My brothers armed themselves for battle. Gutun had sent men to take Brighid as the sacrifice. I knew that open warfare, with too many of my own clan fighting on the wrong side, was inopportune, to say the least. I did the next best thing. I grabbed my sister and brothers and a few loyal friends, and we fled."

Entranced yet alarmed, Georgios slapped his thigh in frustration. "But what about your wife and sons?"

Seanan winced and rubbed his jaw. "My wife was not as loyal as she should've been, and Gutun believed that she supported him. My sons stayed to protect their mother, while pretending to accept Gutun's decisions until I return. And when I do, we'll give him the surprise of his life!"

Combing his fingers through his hair, irritation ran riot over Georgios. "But what do you have now that you didn't have then? What good can you do against a whole clan and a man who has ruled in your stead for all the time that you've been away?"

Seanan smirked. "Leadership is easy when you have an enemy to hate and promise the stars in the sky, but it's a different matter to rule when the enemy is gone, and you have to keep those promises. By now, the clan and Gutun have taken each other's measure and, surely, all is not well. Also, I have something now that I did not have then."

"Profit? You are a good trader, I'll admit."

Seanan's eyes sparkled. "You and Rueben."

Georgios pursed his lips, his irritation cooling to mild annoyance.

"You'll act like a Roman lord and claim my sister and the slaves as your property."

Georgios swallowed a lump in his throat, trying hard not to choke.

"By all the stars above, must I explain everything? I need someone with authority to claim my sister so she will not be taken by Gutun again."

"But I'm your slave, remember?"

Seanan wiggled his fingers in the air, a jest between friends. "I invited you to come along. You'd have been killed wandering about. Remember, we're the barbarians, and Romans love to lord over us. If you can act the part, you'd convince even the Druids that you are the rich son of an important Roman officer who has claimed the land. They won't be surprised. If you say that you have been sent in advance to see the lay of the land and to make arrangements, they'll stall for time before making a move."

Georgios crossed his arms, an unmovable tree planted in the earth. "What would their move be?"

Seanan shrugged, all innocence. "To kill you, of course."

Basking in the absurdity of it all, Georgios laughed. "You want me to set myself up as a sacrificial distraction so you can prepare an attack?"

A smile stretched across Seanan's face. He slapped Georgios on the back. "Exactly!"

Reason asserted itself. "I'm not good at such things.

Have one of your men do this! Or Rueben."

"Great bovines! My men are known, and none are Roman." Seanan frowned. "Rueben is too slight a figure, while you have grown into a strapping young man. Besides, he's a God-fearing Jew. He'd never attempt such a thing. Only an impetuous, rich Roman youth with plans to conquer my poor, barbaric home would ever think of something so outrageous."

Georgios waved his hands from head to toe to demonstrate his point of reason. "But I am too young."

Seanan gripped Georgios' shoulder. "You're not the boy you used to be. Besides, you can always lie."

Georgios could hear the squeak in his voice. "It'd have to be one mighty lie! Who am I working for, anyway?"

Seanan stroked his chin thoughtfully. "Say you have your father's interests in mind and suggest that he has legions at his command. That ought to earn us plenty of time."

Georgios squinted at Seanan. "You're trying to get me killed?"

Seanan stared Georgios straight in the eye. "I will not abandon my home. If you won't help me, fine, but remember this—men do not use evil as evil uses men. If I don't stop Gutun, he will destroy my people. I've grown fond of you, boy. I'm looking forward to introducing you to my sons."

The desperation in Seanan's voice touched Georgios where logic did not. "Well, if there is any sport in me—I'll learn of it now."

Seanan's head bobbed approvingly. "First, we must make you look and act like a Roman brat."

~~~
~~~

Rueben sat at the table, enjoying their evening repast of wine, hard cheese, and bread, and listening as Seanan explained his plan and his expectation that Rueben would support Georgios by acting as his slave.

Rueben retreated into silence.

Seanan and Georgios waited, their eyes anxious and alert.

Even the shorebirds quieted in somber expectation.

Rueben lifted his hand. "Since I am risking my life—again—I think I have the right to make one simple request."

Seanan nodded agreeably.

"Georgios must do whatever I tell him, no matter what."

"So, I'm supposed to be your slave while attempting to be the master? How very convincing when the slave rules the master."

Rueben stared Georgios in the eye. "If we don't succeed, then Seanan will never take us to Patmos."

Georgios looked from one man to the other. "You will take me home after this?"

Seanan sighed wearily. "If we succeed."

Georgios squinted at Rueben. "You'll come with me?"

Rueben nodded. "But in the meantime, you must do what I tell you, even if you don't like it."

Lifting his arms, Georgios surrendered. "Trusting you has become a way of life."

Seanan rubbed his hands together, exultation gleaming in his eyes.

Rueben considered Georgios with a critical eye. "We have a lot of work to do. I'll teach you how to act like an imperious Roman scoundrel. In other words, act like a selfish brat, and we may survive."

Standing, Seanan beckoned to his men impatiently.

"I'll send word ahead that a representative of the Roman Army is on his way. How Gutun will squirm!"

Georgios rose, started forward, then halted. "Why would a Druid priest, friend of the underworld, be afraid of a Roman soldier?"

Seanan spat his words. "Even the underworld fears Rome's approach!"

~~~

Georgios waved to the ship as if parting from a good friend.

The sun rose over the hills, and Seanan's men threw heavy packs over their shoulders and followed their leader as he marched along an unmarked path away from the foaming coastline and toward the verdant, hilly interior.

Seanan followed, muttering to himself as he prepared a dreadful speech for his first encounter with Gutun.

Strolling near the end of the line, Rueben peered meditatively inward.

Birds whirled in the sky and a fresh breeze swept across the land. Small animals scampered aside as they passed by.

Enjoying his newfound strength and health, Georgios smiled. Roman, Greek, and Jew—a pretend master ruled by a pretend slave.

For the first time in months, he hummed in joy.
~~~

CHAPTER FOURTEEN

YOU HAVE A JOB TO DO

— HISPANIA—

Georgios fell in love with the earthy scent of rolling hills and arching trees, so vastly different from the high cliffs and rolling sea of Patmos.

The horizon marked a dividing line between undulating green land and the spacious orange-pink sky. The invitation to go deeper into the mystery pulled Georgios along through days of wandering.

By evening of the fifth day, weariness enveloped the assembly, and Seanan and his men gathered in one group. The women huddled in another.

Georgios perched on a half-buried boulder and watched both.

As usual whenever in deep discourse, Seanan's hands flailed like birds unable to find rest. His brothers listened, while Rueben stared into the distance. The other men sat hunched, munching meditatively on thick brown bread, chewing figs, dates, and slabs of venison, and washing it all down with strong wine brought from Rome.

Finally, Seanan stopped talking.

Tainair launched into an impassioned speech—unusual for him.

Georgios frowned. Why had Seanan been chosen as clan leader when he was the second son?

It was true: Tainair expressed himself best with the aid of strong wine. Georgios suppressed a smile as Tainair vented his feelings and little else. Their faces set, it was clear that the others listened out of respect, not interest.

When Tainair ran out of words and returned to the

wine, Olcan asked Seanan to explain their next steps.

They had been traveling through woods for days, and had now entered lush, open land. Just when their supplies had run low, a deer bounded across their path. Now they had enough meat for a few more days, but it was time to make more detailed plans.

A shriek turned their heads.

The older slave woman pointed a wavering hand at a large snake slithering before her son.

Georgios and the men jumped to their feet.

The younger woman pulled the children back.

Rueben grabbed a staff.

"Wait!" Seanan gestured for everyone to stand back. Taking Rueben's staff, he stepped near the snake's hissing head and with one downward stroke, smashed it.

The air fell silent.

The mother embraced her children, while the younger woman hovered, wringing her hands.

A stab of guilt needled Georgios. He sidled closer.

Brighid clasped the older woman's shoulder. "You all right, Isadora?"

The woman trembled, a picture of nervous exhaustion.

Stepping forward, Georgios helped Brighid settle Isadora on a flat rock. Before he moved away, he leaned toward Brighid and whispered, "What ails the woman?"

Brighid shrugged. "Ask her. She thinks that because her husband was a great man, she should be counted as great now. The proudest fall the farthest, I always say."

Georgios wrinkled his brow in concentration. "The merchant said that her husband was accused of a crime. What did he do?"

Isadora's head snapped up, her eyes flashing. "Leander was a lion! A great man among great men, but when he tried to speak the truth to those who were false, no one would listen. My husband was a senator but also a man of the people. He understood that Rome's strength lies in her sons, sons who come from all lands, bringing true vision. He followed the One rather than men who pretend to be gods."

Brighid lifted her hand. "Hush, woman. We're in a land of many gods—kind and brutal both. Don't tempt the forces which prevail upon these lands."

As if pulled by an invisible cord, Olcan strode to Brighid and bowed respectfully.

Brighid dismissed Isadora's tantrum with a wave. "A fool. If she is not careful, she'll get us all killed!" She met Olcan's gaze straight on. "What do you want, man?"

Olcan raised one eyebrow. "In the morning, Seanan, I, and the others will move ahead and make arrangements for ships across the channel. You follow behind, and we'll meet up at home."

Confused, Georgios interrupted. "Why the hurry? I thought we had to make more preparations."

"We can't arrive together. That would spoil everything. We're leaving the women under your protection, so prepare well."

Aghast, Georgios choked, "Under my charge?"

"You are the Roman. There are legions who'd say that a Roman has more rights than a barbarian. Remember, everything depends on your loyalty and quick wits."

Stroking her cheek, Brighid considered Georgios. "Ay, my babe has grown these past months." She pretended a formal bow. "In our abject fear, we'll convince everyone that you lead Rome's might into the wilderness. No one will challenge you. At least not right away."

With a snort, Isadora turned away. "I made no bargains. I will act as I truly am—a slave of dishonest fate, not of birth."

Facing the woman, Olcan winced, even though his eyes searched her fair face. "Isadora, your husband is dead. You're no longer a Roman matron. This venture is our only hope of reclaiming what is ours. Perhaps, in time, you'll build a life as noble as the one you lost, but that won't happen if you don't help us now."

Brighid pursed her lips in a look of distaste. "She's bent on self-destruction. My only fear is that she will take us—"

"I will not die a slave!" Isadora stood though her legs trembled. Her little boy tugged at her filthy gown, watching her every move with fearful interest.

She bent down and embraced the child. "Oh, Timo, my little man. I can't risk losing you."

Seanan strode up with a bag slung over his shoulder, a sneer of pity and aversion marring his face. "You're not losing anyone. Just do your part." Seanan glanced around, apparently surveying the heart of the assembly. Finally, he turned to Georgios. "Come with me. We have matters to discuss." He glanced from the women to his sister. "Brighid."

Seanan pounded off with Georgios jogging at his side. After rounding a large tree, he stopped and pulled clothing, ornaments, and a bottle of scent out of the bag.

Without a word, Georgios stripped off his old clothes and dressed in the new garments and accessories.

Smiling, Seanan observed the transformation. When it was complete, he marched with Georgios back to the group. "Show proper obeisance to your new master!"

The entire assembly bowed, though some of the men did so while grinning.

Georgios stood before them wearing a fine, red tunic. Over this, a leather lorica segmentate and a bright red cape flowed from his shoulders. He carried a shiny helmet in his right arm and wore leather sandals with shields strapped on his feet. Leather bands encircled his arms, and an exotic spice filled the air.

Seanan clapped his hands and bowed. "Say what you will. It shall be done accordingly."

Georgios swallowed.

Isadora considered them through narrow, haughty eyes, her chin high.

The men sauntered near, smothering their laughter.

A flame sped over Georgios' face. Squaring his shoulders, he spoke with the deepest voice he could muster. "I am Georgios, son of Alexios. Go and prepare a ship for me. I wish to see new lands!" He gestured impatiently.

The men smirked as they threw traveling bags over their shoulders, grasped their staffs, and clutched near-empty wine sacks. Laughing, they strode into the dwindling evening.

As he followed his men, Seanan shouted over his shoulder, "I leave them in your capable hands, Georgios!" With a half-salute, he then turned and led the way across the green lands.

One of the men began singing and the rest joined in.

Georgios watched their figures diminish into the evening light, and his stomach plummeted. Darkness took them from his sight. "Strange time to leave, just as night is falling."

"They'll travel unseen, unhindered by questions or challenges."

Georgios glanced aside at Rueben. "But what if we need them?"

Rueben made a wry face. "We best not need them." He shrugged. "I'll keep first watch."

Georgios glanced at the women and children preparing

their beds for the night. He nodded sharply and practiced his new authority. “Wake me when the moon is high.”

Rueben beheld the stars shimmering overhead. “We’re not alone, even out here.”

Comfort flooded Georgios. He threw his fur cloak on the ground, lay down, and after wrapping the folds about his body, he fell into a deep, dreamless sleep.

CHAPTER FIFTEEN

YOU HAD BEST PRAY

—PATMOS—

My Dear Cecilia,

I never liked Myron, even when we were first married. Our parents arranged the whole thing. We were so young; we didn't dare ask questions. But after a time, questions were my constant companions. I was disgusted by his personal habits; he was so flighty and disorganized—a spoiled, petulant child. He could never admit when he was wrong even about simple matters. Oh, his arrogance!

But I found comfort in our little ones. When the first two died, I thought I'd never recover, but finally, we were blessed with Helena, and we were so happy. Myron gave up his business, and we were both content.

When Helena grew up and met Alexios, I thought it was just an infatuation that would die away. But Alexios was very handsome and had a good future, and Helena loved him.

I saw no reason to protest too much. But when she told us of their plans to move to Rome, I became concerned. Then she revealed his Jewish heritage, and I knew they weren't a fit match. Still, nothing I said changed her mind. She was like her father, stubborn.

Eventually, I accepted the inevitable. When Georgios was born, she gave up the idea of moving to Rome, and we forgave everything. But our peace couldn't last.

Alexios' ambition took him further away from home for longer periods of time. Helena grew anxious, sick with worry, and before I knew what was happening, illness took her.

After her death, Georgios took it into his head to worship his father. Telling Georgios about Alexios' ancestry shouldn't have caused this tragedy, but now Georgios is lost to us too.

The guide here, Eusebius, has become my friend. He is a wizened old thing, not much taller than me, but I've discovered that he has wit and wisdom. When I first looked for Iohannes, Eusebius told me that he was no longer alive in this world, but he still lived in spirit.

I didn't understand a thing he said. As if to comfort me, he told me that Georgios was alive but far west, on another land. I supposed that meant I would never see him again, but Eusebius assured me that was not the case. He spoke so cheerfully that soon I grew confident too.

He invited me to meet his wife and family. They were the most marvelous people I've ever met. So peaceful. Imagine it. A poor family with no luxuries—happy! At first, we talked about common things—the Empire, families, farmers, merchants. Then they told me about the Christ named Jesus. I'd never heard anything like it in my life.

What God would die for His creatures?

Eusebius told me. I listened and learned. When they celebrated, I saw their joy, and I was completely won over. Now I believe.

I wrote to Myron, telling him that I have found a pearl of great price, and though I know he won't understand now, I hope that someday he will.

Eusebius told me to pray to the spirit of Iohannes for Myron and Georgios so that we may be joined as a family once again.

It is my dearest wish.

Your friend,

Roxanna

—Dispatch Lysander to Myron—

Sir,

Georgios is sailing with companions to a distant land. I am in pursuit but have little hope of finding him, for they are entering into barbarian territory.

You had best pray.

Only a god can save him now.

Your servant,

Lysander

CHAPTER SIXTEEN

GUTUN AND THE SONS OF SEANAN

—GAELIC LANDS—

Gutun loved finery. Ornamented weapons held a particular fascination for him. People who narrowed their eyes in suspicion when he praised light as it struck a sharpened blade baffled him. For him, beauty was like a woman—youthful, alive, and vivacious. He would go out of his way to watch an artist work. Genius enabled mere mortals to imitate the gods, thus men of vision ruled the world, as well as the underworld.

Seanan's eldest son, Ian, gave glorious shape to ordinary tools. It galled Gutun no small amount that so despised an enemy should have so worthy a son, but without a doubt, Ian was gifted. His ability to craft fine metal and forge strong, graceful weapons knew no bounds.

Gutun watched him work on several occasions, and though Ian's reaction was as carefully crafted as his work, his words conveyed annoyance. "I'm not an animal to be observed in my habitat. Besides, I can't teach my skills, so you're wasting your time."

Sitting on a bench outside his hut a few yards from Ian's workplace, Gutun moodily chewed a wedge of bread. He reached for a vessel of mead. He studied Ian at his forge inside his three-sided thatched hut, helping his younger brother Earan repair a hunting spear. Gutun scowled.

The youngest brother, Liam, dutifully tended the furnace with a faraway look in his eyes, while his brothers worked, and three craftsmen attended their own stations, etching, painting handles, and oiling each piece in concentration.

Gutun had tried relentlessly to find fault in their work, but in their devotion to family and craft, they did everything as perfectly as any leader or priest could ask.

Seanan's wife, Fiona, strode by, obliterating every other beautiful object in view. With her long black hair and passionate, flashing eyes, she was artless in her dress and nature, but she loved deeply and was turned from fury to grief in a short time. Lines of sadness etched her somber face, drawing her mouth down and her gaze inward.

When her baby girl had come into the world, Fiona's heart swelled in joyful gratitude. But when the child weakened, Seanan had treated her with casual disinterest, a father who couldn't face suffering. He scoffed at Fiona's worries and told her that she was imagining things.

Gutun knew that Seanan's weakness lay in his excessive devotion to his family, something even a husband and father feared to express too openly. When Fiona grew angry at her husband's obstinate nature, Gutun fed her bitter heart with accusing perceptions. "The man cares more for hunting than the lives of his children."

In Seanan's refusal to grieve, he infuriated his wife and satisfied his priest.

When Seanan escaped with Brighid, Fiona's sons stayed by her side, but sorrow and confusion etched irregular lines in her brow, marring her once-perfect face.

Gutun continued to feed her loneliness and grief, but she returned only sadness, while her sons offered distrustful glares.

Perturbed, he stuffed the last bit of brown bread into his mouth.

Ian had fashioned a glorious sword, a representation of the aspirations of man and god, and Gutun's heart pounded every time he saw it. But Ian insisted that it was not ready for inspection.

Gutun rubbed his chin. *Why won't they allow me near their shop? What are they planning?*

He harrumphed and stood up, brushing crumbs from his robe. *Ian is as obstinate as his father.* He glanced around.

Ready for the end of the workday and satisfied with the spear, Earan offered a skin of mead to the men. They drank, chatted playfully, and gathered their weapons for an evening hunt.

Gutun shivered. He hated marching long distances, especially in the cold, getting dirty, and the slippery feel of blood on his hands. He dug a speck of dirt from his nail.

Abruptly, Earan laughed, slapping one craftsman on the back. "Watch out! your hem is touching the mud."

Another burst of laughter.

Gutun's eyes narrowed.

Earan turned, met Gutun's glare, and his smile vanished. "Let's get ready. No more delays." He tossed the empty skin bag to a companion.

Liam, small and thin, stopped pumping the bellows as he watched the men gather their weapons and throw empty sacks and drinking horns over their shoulders.

Gutun stood and passed his hand over his long-oiled hair. He marched forward. "Wait a moment, Earan. I must speak with you."

Earan glanced from his companions to the Druid priest, smirking, "You want us to kill a fat stag for your table?"

Gutun forced a smile. "I have not planned a feast, though a bit of venison would please the gods. They like the loin best."

Earan's lips twisted. Straightening with a posture for

quick departure, all amusement disappeared from the assembly.

Gripping Earan's shoulder, Gutun leaned in and whispered into Earan's ear. "The gods see all." With a knowing look, Gutun nodded and turned away. "The meat can be delivered to my door—before dark would be best."

~~~

Earan stared after Gutun, drumming his fingers against his thigh. Turning, he met the wary stares of his men. They admired Earan but wanted no trouble with the priest.

Earan stroked his short beard as he faced his men, laughing off the exchange. "The Druid is always in need of meat and wants us, not the gods, to supply his table."

Liam stood with his hands on his hips, a frown digging its way across his forehead.

A dangerous idea crossed Earan's mind. He wanted no suspicions confusing his thoughts on the hunt, so he indicated for his men to wait, and he strode into the forge. He clasped his brother Liam's shoulder, and they strolled to the edge of the village.

"Listen, Liam, that Druid hints of secret knowledge. Do you know what he means?"

Shaking off his brother's arm, Liam peered at Earan unblinking. "I don't know Gutun's concerns. I don't even know matters within my own family. How could I? No one ever tells me anything."

Guilt stabbed Earan as he studied his brother's innocent face. "That's what I thought. Here, come with me, and you shall be a wiser though no more honest man. Never trust that snake in the grass. He worked mother into his confidence."
~~~

Liam gritted his teeth. “She was grieving, and Gutun tricked her.”

Earan nodded. “You’re a good son. Though mother has her part to play in events.”

The men waited while Earan directed his brother to the back of the shop. “Look well without saying a word.”

He led the boy to a chamber off the main room and then into a smaller room. Irregular pieces of lumber leaned against the back wall. Earan removed the wood, opened a small door, and gestured toward the interior.

A stash of weapons lay upon a table.

Liam gasped and spluttered, “W-What—?”

A husky whisper interrupted. “Don’t talk! You’ll give us away.”

His heart leaping to his throat, Earan jerked around.

Ian strode forward.

His shoulder’s relaxing, Liam grinned.

Slapping his hand to his wildly beating heart, Earan struggled to regain his composure. “It’s time for him to know. He’s old enough, and besides, Gutun tests us with hints and sly looks.”

Without ceremony, Ian directed them out of the weapon room and shut the door. He restacked the lumber against the wall.

Earan and Liam assisted, tension in the air, for when Ian was most angry, he was most silent.

Once satisfied, Ian led Liam and Earan to the main room. He glanced around the empty forge and leaned closer. “Father is coming. He’s sending someone ahead, a Roman youth with Brighid, two women, and children. We must be ready.”

Liam’s voice rose to a squeak. “Father, coming? How long have you known?”

Waving his hand to lower Liam's excitement, Ian whispered, "Not long, though I'd hoped and prayed every day, and I'd started preparing months ago. He'll need more than just our loyalty; he needs good weapons and men willing to use them."

Ian pressed Liam's shoulder. "No one questions your loyalty. But the fewer people who know, the better. Clearly, Gutun suspects something, though I've tried to divert his attention with my metalwork."

Liam clasped an enormous sword carved with intricate designs and a fine, sharp blade. He grinned.

Amusement shone in Ian's eyes. "He has lusted after that piece. I keep telling him that I will show it to him when I'm done. He longs to smite my head off with it, I imagine. He thinks himself an expert, but he is deluded. Still, he's dangerous as a serpent."

Earan grinned. "You are every bit as wily."

"Gutun is a leech that sucks the blood of our family." Ian met Liam's wide-eyed gaze. "We need every able man, and I know your strength of arm as well as your spirit. We make ready for our father's return. Soon, it will be Gutun's turn to learn the meaning of exile."

Earan nodded and strode to the door. "My men are ready for the hunt, but I will share the news. They will be pleased."

Ian lifted his hand in warning. "Be sure of your men before you say anything. Gutun has many followers, and even among those who do not like him, many fear him."

Earan bowed in acceptance. "I'll be gone several days. If Gutun grows too hungry, tell him that he can kill a cow." He met Ian's steady gaze. "I'll be back before you need me."

Ian nodded.

Liam grinned.

As Earan marched toward the woods with his men, he glanced aside.

His ornate robes dragging in the dirt, Gutun stepped into their mother's house.

Fear like a lash of fire tightened Earan's gut. His father could not return soon enough.

CHAPTER SEVENTEEN

THE BEST MEANS OF CONQUERING

—GAELIC LANDS—

Seanan dreamed of revenge. Gutun must cower before him—with his hands clenched in a beseeching attitude, begging for forgiveness and the right to slink into obscurity. And if his wife regretted her injustice to him, so much the better.

He marched swiftly over the short grass, his leather sandals straining against weary muscles. With his bags slung over his shoulder, his arms moved rhythmically at his side. Small huffs of breath bloomed white in the morning chill. He flexed his arms and stretched his neck in the habit of a man who knows that he must be prepared for sudden action.

His long black hair ran down his neck, blowing in the breeze. He scratched his short beard. An irritating insect plunged its hapless body against his neck, and he swatted it with more force than necessary.

Tainair glanced over, eyebrows up.

Seanan frowned and tried to think of an appropriate curse for an insect.

A distant figure approached. A large, lanky man marched forward.

Seanan halted.

The stranger increased his speed. Connan, a clansman and friend, ran forward, gesturing toward a grove of trees.

Seanan relaxed.

Once hidden in the thick grove, everyone gathered around.

Connan knelt before Seanan. "We have waited long for

your return, hoping that the gods would see fit to preserve your life and set us free from our oppressor."

Seanan wrinkled his brow and tugged the man's sleeve none too gently. "Get up, man! I am no god to worship."

Connan rose to his feet, his gaze on the ground.

Exasperated, Seanan cajoled his friend in his best I-will-be-calm voice. "You got the message that I was returning. So, what has Gutun been up to? Is everyone sick of his tricks yet?"

Still frowning, Connan sighed and lifted his gaze, sparing Seanan a glance. "Worse than Gutun. Romans are coming! One of their greatest fighting men and several legions has been sent to conquer our island. Rome is never satisfied. She wants the whole world!"

Delighted, Seanan's smile widened. "A Roman warrior, eh? With legions?" Seanan looked around at his men and lifted his hands in wonder. "This is better than I had hoped. I mention to a few people that a Roman is coming with plans to take a piece of our territory, and now a great Roman warrior is coming with legions. I feel as proud as a papa to see my humble little story grow to such mighty proportions!"

Connan considered Seanan through narrowed eyes. "They landed on our shore only yesterday. How could you have heard about it when you've been far from home? Have you been traveling with Romans?"

Undaunted, Seanan shook his head. "Oh, Connan, you never did get anything straight. I know about it because I invented the whole thing. I've been traveling with a Roman boy for months. We split up a short time ago. He won't arrive for another day or so, and by then, I'll have arranged passage aboard a ship. You'll meet him and make sure that he gets on the right ship." Seanan's eyebrows rose in speculation. "So tell me, how far to shore? We're tired and in need of rest."

Connan jerked his thumb back. "The shore is about a half of a day's march, and a ship is ready. Your message got through all right. Still, I don't understand. How can a Roman youth leading a legion be both in front of me and behind you?"

Seanan swung his bags over his shoulder. "You're just confused. Georgios—that's the boy's name—is behind us. I left him not long ago." A new thought intervened. "Are there other ships arriving soon?"

"The port is always busy. Ships arrive every few days."

"But will one sail to our island soon after the one we take?"

Connan shrugged. "I think so."

"Good, that's all I need to know. Normally, I wouldn't split up, but this plan was too good to fail. Wait here and meet Georgios and the others and lead them home. We'll go ahead and get everything ready." A painful memory flashed through Seanan's mind. "How are my sons?"

Connan's face brightened. "Very well indeed. They've become mighty in the sight of the gods, and Gutun does not pursue them openly, though he'd like to. You'll find a welcome surprise awaiting when you return." His gaze turned inward, a worried frown building between his eyes. "If you get home. I hear the Roman warrior and his men are heading into the valley."

Seanan shook his head. How can such a well-meaning a fellow could be so obtuse? With hearty encouragement, he clapped his arm around Connan's formidable shoulders. "I have a plan. Don't I always have a plan? By the green grass of our ancestors' graves, did you think I'd walk into a trap?"

Connan sighed, bewildered. "I don't see how you can have men before and behind you at the same time." He shrugged. "I'll wait for Georgios and pray that he is as good a warrior as the ones landing on our shores."

With a snort, Seanan gestured to the men behind him. "Didn't I tell you that everything would work out? We'll give Gutun the surprise of his life—and then I'll say hello to my wife!" He patted his bulging pack and sighed, well satisfied. He might allow her a glimpse of the treasures he had acquired before leaving her for his new home—a green knoll set off by four great oak trees, a spot he had always loved. He would build a luxurious home, and Fiona could see him from a distance and know what she had rejected. He smiled dreamily as he continued his homeward march.

~~~

Connan sat down to wait for the Roman boy. *How can a Roman warrior be both in front of and behind me?* He lay down, resting his head on his arm, and watched the grass as it swayed in undulating waves. He let his mind wander, for it was not his place to question the clan leader. And, anyway, things usually worked themselves out in the end. *At least, that's what I've always been told.*

~~~

Alexios wondered if he should disobey an order. He had been ordered to take a small training unit, do a little terrorizing, and make a foothold on this northern island. He planned to strike at one of their established holdings and raze it to the ground. Then, in suitable fear, these barbarians would listen to his council.

Later, Rome could send legions to occupy her newest outpost. Alexios peered across the verdant hills toward the valley occupied by a thriving clan. Strong and heavily armed, the natives would not be conquered easily.

He knew full well that if he failed, he would never see his home or his son again. He could voice his concerns to no one, for no one would understand. Rome was more than a mother country; Rome was a god upon the Earth, and she had the divine right to rule everyone she could hold within her grasp.

Alexios turned to his right-hand man, Marcus, and pointed to the valley. “How would you attack these people?”

Marcus cleared his throat and gestured in an arc, indicating the area north of the valley, where ancient trees topped a border of low hills. “Word has undoubtedly reached them about us. We must circle around and attack from the north, remaining well-hidden until the last possible moment, coming from a direction they don’t expect. Like tying a noose, we choke them from all sides by setting fire to their fields and homes. If we start before the sun rises, when they are still sleepy or bemused by drink, the task should be accomplished by noon.”

Alexios rubbed his temple, where a headache throbbed. He took a deep breath. Rome neared her breaking point, and the futility of this exercise exhausted his spirit. Still, he must try. “Yes, every clan on the island undoubtedly knows we are here. They’ll prepare for our attack from every direction. So, we must do what they don’t expect. We will form a treaty with them.”

Marcus’ eyes rounded in horror. “A treaty with barbarians? Are you out of your mind? Forgive me, sir, but we were ordered to conquer, not make an alliance.”

“You have much to learn, Marcus, for alliances are often the best means of conquering.” Alexios gathered his gear and motioned for Marcus to do the same. “Come along; they won’t attack unarmed men. They are as curious about us as we are about them.”

Scowling, Marcus muttered, “I’m hardly curious.”

Alexios frowned. “Look proud! No muttering curses or glaring, do you understand?”

Marcus hesitated.

Alexios gripped the younger man’s shoulder. “I asked you a simple question.”

Marcus stiffened. “Your will is my command.”

According to Rome’s will, Alexios led his men toward the largest dwelling in the center of the small village.

CHAPTER EIGHTEEN

WORTH DYING FOR

—GALLIC LANDS—

Georgios met Connan dutifully waiting for him, and relief washed over him like a gentle rain. He had secretly wondered if they'd be devoured by wild animals or murdered by unfriendly barbarians.

Rueben only laughed. "Seanan knows what he is doing." He grinned. "I can hardly wait to see Gutun fall!"

Georgios leaned against the ship's railing as Connan trotted forward with a wooden platter piled high with brown bread, honey, wedges of cheese, a flask of barley ale, and an assortment of small fish. He set the tray down and bowed low. "Brighid is seeing to the needs of the others, so this is all ours." He smiled sheepishly. "Does this meet with your satisfaction? The captain sends it with his compliments."

Accustomed to his imperious role, Georgios nodded.

Rueben reached out and stopped, remembering himself. He smiled at Connan in an ingratiating manner. "My master is pleased with your humble offerings." He pointed to the horizon. "When will we arrive?"

Connan broke off a piece of bread and stuffed it in his mouth. He talked around chews. "We have to go around. It'll take us a few more days. But don't worry, the weather and the crew are good. We'll have to make a stop or two, but that won't take long. It pays to keep moving."

Georgios sliced off a large chunk of cheese with his ornate knife. He chewed meditatively. "Why is that?"

His eyebrows rising, Connan snorted. "You should

know! If you keep trading and getting fresh goods, your wealth and reputation grow. There's always some enterprising fellow willing to relieve a merchant of his heavy burdens."

Georgios scowled.

Drumming his fingers, Rueben waited for his turn to eat.

Georgios took pity on his friend and threw a hunk of bread and a wedge of cheese in Rueben's direction. "I need you in good form when we arrive. Don't fall down in a faint."

Rueben bowed and shuffled to the far side of the ship.

Connan's gaze trailed after Rueben, his brows puckered. "He any good?"

Georgios swallowed a hard chunk and stared at the man.

Connan lifted his chin, indicating Rueben. "Never owned a slave, though I've often wished for one. To have a man at your beck and call is better than having a wife; wives talk too much while slaves don't dare."

Squeezing a piece of cheese, Georgios stared ahead. "I've never been fond of slave-owning. It seems a waste of a man. But I bow to reality and accept what I must."

Connan shrugged. "You're the master. I'm not a thinking man, not like you and Seanan. Seanan can think in ways I hardly understand. He has Roman lads coming behind him bringing a few measly slaves, yet insists that they are the same Romans landing on our shores. If I didn't trust him so—"

His heart slamming hard against his ribs, Georgios gripped Connan's arm. "What Romans?"

Wide-eyed with surprise, Connan shook himself free. "I told Seanan, but he was sure I was mistaken. Still, I know what I saw. A mighty Roman leader and his soldiers came ashore the other day. Only the gods know what they're doing now."

Georgios jumped to his feet, glancing wildly about. The edge of Rueben's tunic billowed in the wind as he leaned against a post. Georgios glared at Connan. "When will we reach your island?"

"You mean the stop near home?"

"Yes, when?"

"It'll take another couple of days to travel north. My people are situated in a valley between two of the most delightful hills you could ever hope—"

"Can we get there faster?"

Chewing his lip, Connan rubbed his temple. "I don't know why you'd want to do that. Seanan only has a two-day lead, and he needs to get organized. He doesn't want you arriving on his heels."

Georgios trembled in rage. "Idiot, don't you see? Seanan is walking into a trap."

Connan's slack face broke into an artless grin as he rose to his feet, muscles relaxed, like a common man taking his sweet time. "No, he is *setting* a trap for Gutun."

"Are there or are there not Roman warriors on your land?"

"I believe so, but Seanan knows how to handle himself. He'll find a way to make things work out. See if he doesn't."

His breath catching in his throat, Georgios spluttered, "How many Roman warriors have you met personally?"

Connan's bottom lip protruded. He ran his fingers through his hair, tugging a bit. "None, but that doesn't mean I don't know Seanan. Gutun will get the surprise of his life and so will that Roman leader, whoever he is. He'll learn a thing or two about the men of the green isle, a lesson he'll never forget, trust me. Now sit and finish eating. You make me nervous jumping up like that. We can't push the ship any faster, and the stops can't be skipped, for if you asked the owner such a thing, he'd throw you overboard. It's as much as your life is worth to get along until we get home. Then you can race ahead and see what is going on. Only the gods can arrange things differently, and we're no gods, to be sure!" Connan stuffed the last chunk of cheese into his mouth.

Georgios nodded and started for Rueben. If rage wouldn't save them, perhaps prayers would.

~~~

Seanan stood stock still, amazement spreading like wildfire through his body. His eyes worked as well as any man's, but he kept blinking to make sure that they were not playing tricks on him. "What is this? Gutun's magic? How is it possible that I see Roman warriors on the hill over our valley?" He whistled under his breath. "The idiot was right. There were Romans before and behind me!"

Tainair chewed on a long blade of grass and seemed to find the situation less of a marvel than his brother. "I thought perhaps something like this might happen."

Seanan swung around. "Did you envision legions invading our shores?"

"Rome has an insatiable appetite."

"She won't eat me or mine!" Seanan sucked in a deep breath as he drew back. "Time to make new plans!"

~~~

Gutun wondered why he had been chosen to suffer the pains of hell while still a poor mortal. "Why me?" Standing in the front room of Fiona's home, he cringed in agony. "They're coming to kill me, I'm sure of it. What am I going to do?"

Fiona bit her lip, straightened her shoulders, and exhaled. "You'll go right out there and meet them! Tell them that my husband is away, but he'll be home soon and he's bringing many warriors with him."

Gutun shivered. "But they're Romans! I can negotiate with men from our island or even across the water but not Romans. They have the protection of mighty gods!"

Fiona's lips hardened into a taut line. "Romans may be known for conquering, but we are an unconquered race, and we shall not fall now. Men have died so that we might live. Are you going to stand there cowering and give in without a fight? If you don't do something, you'll die—you and everyone else who lives here, coward!"

Gutun stared at the ceiling, his pounding heart making him dizzy. Finally, he spoke in whispered resolve, "If that's how it must be, I will sacrifice myself for the good of the clan." He gazed at Fiona for a beseeching moment. "Know that I did it for you alone."

Fiona brushed past Gutun and hustled outside.

Hesitant, Gutun tapped his hand against his thigh. Shuddering a deep breath, he gathered his courage, and trailed behind.

~~~

Alexios strode purposefully through the village looking for any sign of the clan leader. Surprised that no one had come out to meet him, he quickened his steps. *Is there a place left on the earth where men do not fear Rome's approach?*

A tall man with muscular arms and shoulders protruding from a sleeveless tunic marched toward him.
~~~

He stopped and folded his arms across his chest, defiantly blocking Alexios' path.

Alexios took another step forward and smiled, pleased. Here, at last, was a man he could deal with. He motioned for his aide to stand back. "I am Alexios, a representative of the Roman Empire, come to speak with the people of the green isle. You're their leader?"

"I am Ian. My father is not here."

Alexios' brows knit in surprise. "Then why bar my way? I could speak to another—"

"You may speak with me."

Alexios' frustration level rose as the situation grew more complicated.

With long robes dragging on the ground, a hunched old man rounded a hut and stopped dead, his eyes wide.

Then a woman, beautiful and shapely, came up from behind the old man and nudged him forward. She lifted her voice and called over the distance, "This is the priest of the village. Gutun. Speak with him."

Gutun paced nearer, lifting his hands dramatically in prayer and murmured inaudible words.

The woman sniffed, apparently satisfied.

The old man halted before Alexios, who towered over him. He glanced back, shifted his gaze from Ian to the woman's glare, and squared his slumped shoulders. He lifted his thin, querulous voice. "You dare come to this isle dressed as conquerors! You must offer homage to our gods, or you'll find your way home again."

Alexios stared at the little rooster crowing before him. He pointed to the sky and dropped his voice to bedrock seriousness. "Rome has her own gods; she hardly needs yours. It is the strength of Rome that meets you now. Consider yourself blessed, for I come offering peace."

Gutun's eyes widened. "Peace?"

Finally, the fool understands. Alexios smiled patronizingly. "The peace of your allegiance, of course. Rome claimed this land the moment we landed on shore. We have already conquered it. Accept us, or we prove our ownership with your blood. The choice is yours."

Ian stepped beside Gutun, hatred burning in his eyes. "We become *your slaves*?"

The woman rushed closer and grabbed Ian's arm. "Ian, let's hear—"

The young man reared back and glared at the woman. "Mother, we cannot accept Roman authority! It means nothing less than—"

Lifting his hands high, Gutun swayed. "Help us, oh gods, see your people's need and save us." He glanced aside. "Fiona, go home and wait—"

Weariness enveloped Alexios. "Stop chanting, fool!"

Stomping forward, Ian glared into Alexios' eyes. "Rome thinks that it can touch a thing and claim it for its own! But you're mistaken. Here, Rome will meet her defeat. This is a land she can never conquer. Go home, or the proof will be in your blood!"

Any desire for mercy and goodwill vanished. Were their positions reversed, Alexios would do as this man, courageously defy the strongest empire in the world like a hero of old. His stomach tightened. Once he'd had such an opportunity, but he had sided with Rome. A bitter taste made him want to spit. Alexios glanced at his men and then returned his gaze to Ian. "We will meet in battle then. May I know your name first?"

"I am Ian, son of Seanan."

"My men and I have a worthy opponent, Ian. If you change your mind, we will offer generous terms, and you and your family may live."

Gutun darted forward and groveled at Alexios' feet.

"We'll listen."

Ian thrust Gutun aside. "There is no bargaining with Rome."

Sadness filled Alexios. "I would have bargained gladly." He shook his head. Fate was never kind. "Battle it must be. Death will decide." He turned abruptly and swept his men with him toward the crest of the hill. Though this would be an easy triumph, slaughter was never simple.

~~~

Ian watched Alexios and his men stride away in grand formation. He squinted in the evening light as he pondered the strength of well-trained Roman warriors. He sighed and looked first to his mother, then down at Gutun bowed in the dust. "What're you doing, man, if man you can be called?"

Gutun slowly lifted his body off the ground, seemingly caught between humiliation and rage. He chose rage. "You idiot! They have already burned one port and wreaked havoc as they traveled here. Don't think you can overpower them with your simple blades and inexperienced kin. You will die a tortured death, as will every member of this clan—every man, woman, and child will be put to the sword because you would not be reasonable!"

Ian sneered. "You expect *Rome* to be *reasonable*?"

"No, but I can pretend! You could've pretended to grovel so as to gain time to make weapons and warn other clans that Rome is upon us. We shouldn't have to fight alone—to die alone, I should say. Now they will rush upon us, and we'll all die."

Ian glanced at his mother. "We are not unprepared.
~~~

Some of us are ready." He turned and strode away.

~~~

Gutun stood up, rubbed his neck, and winced. "That son of yours is worse than your husband. You thought that losing a daughter was bad, wait until every child you ever bore is slaughtered before your—"

In the next instant, Gutun felt the sting of Fiona's anger on the side of his face. He spluttered, stunned and confused.

Fiona wagged her finger in his face, her eyes mere slits. "If you're not careful, you won't live another day. My son is right. You speak for no one. I was a fool to believe in you. Once the Romans bowed to us! We will see victory again or die trying!"

Gutun spat. "What good is it to die in battle when we could live—"

"In submission? Treachery? Gutun, you're blind. There are things worth dying for. You might try learning that before the day of battle." Fiona stalked off in the direction her son had gone.

Gutun rubbed his cheek, which still stung from Fiona's slap. He had no intention of dying. But he wouldn't mind if the Roman's took a few lives before they left
~~~

CHAPTER NINETEEN

I WILL NOT LOSE

—GAELIC LANDS—

Seanan planned on sneaking into his village unnoticed during the night while the moon was hidden behind wispy clouds, but he had not considered all the roots, rocks, trees, branches, dangling vines, and forgotten storage buildings between him and his dwelling.

Destined to bump into everything in his path, he stumbled and fell, cursing under his breath, while his brothers kept a discreet silence and slithered like shadows.

Finally, he reached home and gestured for his brothers to move on to their own dwellings, which they did with little difficulty.

Seanan took a deep breath and mentally prepared himself. He pushed back the heavy flap covering the doorway, hoping to remain silent, but, as luck would have it, a mouse scurried across his path and squeaked in earnest when he stepped on some unknown part of its anatomy.

The sharp squeak shot Fiona to her feet. She darted to the darkest corner and crouched low, grabbing a stout cudgel.

In an attempt to soothe her fears, Seanan crossed in front of her, waving his hands.

Fiona screamed.

Seanan's heart stopped.

The clouds parted and a thin shaft of moonlight came through the window and illuminated Seanan's face, nearly blinding him.

After slapping one hand to her chest, Fiona grinned and

dropped the cudgel. She flung her arms around Seanan, nearly strangling him in her joy. "I'm so glad to see you! You have no idea what it has been like since you went away."

After the initial hair-raising, skin-prickling surprise of soft arms thrown around his neck, Seanan dared to breathe again. He peeled her arms away, no more used to this exuberant affection than her rejection at their parting. He frowned. *Have I ever understood this woman?* "Don't choke me to death. We have Roman company, and I might want to talk to them."

As if in drunken hilarity, Fiona giggled.

Shivers. Seanan had never seen his wife like this, though he could not honestly say he could see her now, for it was so blasted dark that he only caught glimpses of her between shadows.

Taking her hand, he attempted to step outside to better light. He took a few swaggering steps and hit the wall.

Fiona chortled.

What's gotten into the woman?

She tugged Seanan's arm. After maneuvering around pots, piles of skins, and a blasted lot of hanging herbs, they finally stepped into the open air.

Fiona clasped Seanan's hands. As the clouds broke, the moon shone full on her face. Her gleaming eyes stared intently at her husband.

Seanan looked down at her, and his proud heart sank, for she was more beautiful than ever.

With affection and gladness, she bowed her head and kissed his hand. "Seanan, can you ever forgive me? I was wrong to blame you for the baby's death and stupid to think that Gutun was an honest man. I did everything badly, and I'm sorry." Tears slipped down her soft cheeks.

Man enough to battle a deadly enemy, but against

repentant tears, Seanan had no defense. With a sigh, he enveloped his wife in a warm embrace.

Fiona snuggled in, resting her head on his chest.

After his confused apprehension, now mixed with joyful relief, Seanan regained his bearings. “How are my sons?”

Fiona pulled away and clasped his hand. “Come and see.”

Seanan wanted to ask her not to lead him into a tree, a building, or over the smoldering embers of last night’s fire, for she stepped quickly across the village grounds, but he smothered his fears.

When they arrived at the next dwelling, she rapped on the door frame.

A figure stopped in the open doorway. Apprehension scrawled across his face and a knife in his hand, Ian peered at his mother. “What’s happened?”

Standing behind Fiona in the shadows, Seanan cleared his throat, ready to surprise his son.

Quicker than Seanan had thought possible, Ian rushed forward and thrust a blade against Seanan’s throat.

Too well-trained to scream, Seanan allowed hot irritation to flood his body without physically reacting. “I was expecting this from your mother, not my loyal son.”

Ian released Seanan, yanked him inside his dwelling, and exploded. “Father! I was expecting you, but not in the middle of the night.” A smile broke over his face.

Seanan rubbed his neck. “It seemed like a good idea at the time. Your uncles came with me. They should be settled by now.” He looked at his son, curiosity getting the better of him. “You didn’t move the buildings while I was away?”

Ian frowned.

Seanan shook off his confusion and paced to the open

window. He pointed to the hills. "I saw Roman soldiers up there. Wait a couple of days, and my friends will arrive. Then my plan will be ready." He sighed. "If only we had a supply of weapons at hand."

Fiona hugged his arm, and Ian clasped his shoulder, grinning.

The clouds parted and starlight shone brilliantly.

For the first time in much too long, happiness found Seanan's heart.

~~~

Seanan slept most of the first day, taking ample refreshments to replenish his exhausted body. The second morning dawned clear though cold. Seanan's breath clouded before him as he strolled around the village. After happy reunions, he and his brothers met with his sons, and together, they planned their strategy.

Seanan stopped in the middle of their compact village and appraised their situation. Even with an army encamped against him, it was good to be home. He savored the sight of the forested hills and sloping valley. He scratched his head, trying to reconcile the overwhelming beauty before his eyes with the approaching danger before his people.

With reluctance, he turned to view the proudest dwelling in the village, a structure at the foot of a hill built onto the largest cave on the island.

How the cave came into existence was a mystery of nature, but how Gutun had acquired it for his personal residence was an epic tale. Seanan had heard many variations of the tale that morning. *Why did the clan stand by and let Gutun have his way?* A solid structure with boulders on either side and wooden posts carved with
~~~

imposing figures, forming a silent guard, it was the most magnificent dwelling on the island.

Seanan squared his shoulders. Time to confront Gutun.

Liam jogged forward. "Father, I need to speak with you!"

Seanan smiled. Here was his ruddy child with thick red hair, sparkling blue eyes, and skin white as milk. A memory of Rueben and Georgios stabbed him.

Liam stopped and waited, his face twitching in impatience.

Seanan clasped his youngest son's shoulder. "Yes, Liam, I haven't had a chance to speak with you yet. How are you and our many fat cows?"

"I saw something—"

Gutun appeared at the entrance of his dwelling, glaring through narrowed eyes, his jaw working. He shook his finger at Seanan. "Death and curses, you're not wanted here. I forbid you to stay in our village. Go and never return!"

Suppressing explosive fury with all his strength, Seanan swerved from his son, pounded forward, and gripped one of the wooden figures. "Eager to die, are you? You'd send your salvation away! Listen, Gutun, I should send you to the Romans as a first course. You deserve it, but being a kind man, I plan to send the Romans off our shore in such manner that they'll lose all appetite for our green isle. I can do this alone, or we can work together. But I will deal with your misdeeds later. Promise."

Gutun spluttered.

Loping forward, Tainair shouted, "Seanan! There's action on the hill. They are moving in formation. I wager we'll fight today."

His heart pumping with fresh incentive, Seanan grimaced. "I thought all Roman commanders liked to plan out long, involved strategies! What kind of Romans are they?"

"The kind that like to do battle. Come, Seanan, we must prepare!"

As he strode away, Seanan tossed one last glare over his shoulder. "Pray to your gods, Gutun. The fate of us all depends upon me. If I lose, this isle will never be free again."

Running alongside his father, Liam tugged Seanan's sleeve. "But, Father, I saw—"

Tainair called, "Not now. We have to go!"

Seanan glanced aside. "Later, son."

Liam's eyes darkened as he stopped, letting them move on without him.

Seanan forced a grin. "Don't worry. I won't lose." Stripping off his outer garments, he and his men joined forces.

Chapter Twenty

What on Earth?

-OldEarth-

Noman didn't think much of sea voyages. Nor for long tramps through woodlands, down slippery hillsides, or across verdant valleys. Plagued by biting insects, sharp stones, blinding sunlight, chilling breezes, and questionable water sources, his frustration levels soared. *Oh, God, the humiliation of it all!*

One day of outdoor travel among earthly elements would have been enough to convince anyone that humanity lay on the lowest rung of development. Mere beasts, really. How else could they stand it?

Still, the upcoming battle should be diverting.

The irony of Alexios and Georgios, father and son, facing off on a strange island, as enemies no less, sent a thrill down his spine. Naturally, their evil inclinations would rise, showing their true—

Noman stopped short; his fur-lined boots squelched in the mud.

Georgios stood on board a ship just offshore, his hair fluttering in the breeze, his cheeks ruddy, and his eyes bright.

But that's not what caught Noman's attention. Along the shore, a small group hid under the shelter of a rocky embankment. He squinted. Unless his eyes deceived him, two were Luxonians, one was clearly Crestonian, and—Noman slapped his hand to his cheek—an Ingot! *What on Earth?*

~~~
~~~

Teal, staying close to Cerulean, nodded formally to Ark and Zuri.

Clasping his hands in prayer-style, Zuri bowed low and whispered well-practiced words.

Teal squinted. *A prayer?*

Then, as if pulled by invisible strings, Zuri tromped to Teal and threw his arms around him in a tight embrace. "God, it's good to see you again!"

After awkward arm flapping, Teal gave in, pounded Zuri on the back, and grunted in reply.

Ark waved all six tentacles, then bounded toward Cerulean and stated the obvious. "You've grown!"

Stiff in trained formality, Cerulean attempted a proper bow.

"None of that among old friends." Zuri embraced Cerulean.

Ark's bulbous eyes glistened.

Teal cleared his throat and pressed Ark's shoulder, half in greeting and half in hopes of restraining the impending tears. He clapped his hands and pointed further inland. "There's a spectacular view of the ocean just around that bend." He patted Cerulean's shoulder. "We came early and did a little scouting." He glanced aside. "Where's your ship?"

Zuri grinned. "You can't see it."

Cerulean's gaze fixed on the Ingot. "It's invisible?"

Chuckling, Zuri pointed to the waves. "Not if you're a fish." He glanced at Teal. "Song arranged it. We're using a Bhuaci ship—good for space and underwater travel."

Teal's heart ached. An old sensation, almost forgotten. "Song? How is she?" His eyes widened as his memory and embarrassment kicked in. "I'm sorry. I meant to ask first, how is Kelesta?"

Ark twisted his neck so hard his breathing helm popped

from one nostril. Huffing, he adjusted it and glared at Zuri. "Something wrong with your wife that I don't know about?"

Silence landed hard.

Otherwise still, Cerulean's gaze bounced between the adults.

Zuri blinked rapidly, his shoulders dropping. "We lost—"

Befuddled, Ark thrust his tentacles on his hips. "Lost what?"

Teal sighed. "Their baby."

A fresh flush worked over Ark's face and new tears threatened.

Zuri waved his friend's gloom away. "You don't even like children. Besides, I'm learning to accept what I can't change. I've found faith in something bigger than myself."

Ark rounded on Zuri. "Who said I don't like children? I love pods of all kinds. I—"

"Not your own. You left yours swimming about with those big sad eyes following your every—"

Sucking in deep draughts from his breathing helm, Ark swelled beyond his usual stature.

"Enough, you two." Teal pounded up the green sward and headed for the rocky cliff. "If you can't behave yourselves, you can leave. We've got enough trouble without you two acting like stupid children." He glanced at Cerulean. "Not that all children are stupid—just—"

Cerulean scowled as he zipped up the incline.

Ark shoved past Zuri, waddling over damp grass. He slipped.

Zuri reached out a steadying hand.

Huffing, Ark glared at the offer.

Jogging back down the hillside, Cerulean stopped short

before Ark. “Your message said you had something for me.”

Snorting, Ark straightened and slapped his tentacles over his bio-suit to search for it. “Yes. I do.” He pulled a vial from a deep pocket, making a show of his effort as he held it out for inspection. “I perfected a solution that detects poison in your food. Just a drop, and you’ll know if your meal is safe to eat.”

Cerulean squinted in the strong light. “You think someone will try to poison me?”

An eye roll answered the question eloquently. Ark dropped the vial into Cerulean’s waiting palm and glanced at Zuri. He slapped his tentacles against his rotund middle. “Sorry I snapped. Just a bit put out that you didn’t tell me—I know how deeply Kelesta longed for a baby.”

Zuri swallowed. “She wasn’t the only one.”

Ark wagged his head, repentance in his dejected gaze. “I know.” He shrugged. “I’m not like you. Never was.” He pursed his lips. “For one, I can’t leap around like a goat on uneven ground.”

“All right. We’ll help.” Circling around to Ark’s back, Zuri shoved, waving directions at Cerulean. “You pull, and I’ll push. We’ll get him up there. Hey, Teal, you can help, anytime.”

Ignoring the antics below, Teal’s body tingled as he stood on the crest of the rocky cliff. He was being watched and not by a human. Someone he’d never encountered before stood on the shore, staring at him.

He shuddered.

CHAPTER TWENTY-ONE

I SEE IT IN THEIR EYES

—PATMOS—

My Dear Cecilia,

Myron is here now, and I wish I could have explained things better. He looks so tired and harassed. I'd never noticed how hunch-shouldered and beaten he looks. When he first got here, we just stared at each other like strangers.

We spoke only of servants, household matters, or the weather. We certainly never discussed anything inside ourselves. We may have told each other how furious we were, but we never explained why. We've never revealed our pain. Not to each other, anyway.

I think that Eusebius is wonderful but dangerous. I'm thinking thoughts I never had before, noticing things I never noticed before. He told me a story about a rich man who wished to serve in a great army but failed because he wouldn't leave his possessions. Eusebius asked me what I would've done. Would I give up my comfortable life to follow a great leader?

I told him I was no man and following great lords was not for me, but he only smiled and asked if I would offer my life to save a loved one. Of course, I said yes, thinking it was the noblest answer, but he just smiled in that peculiar way of his.

Irritated, I left him and took a stroll.

By evening, I found myself at Iohannes' home. Then the strangest thing happened. I was alone and very tired. Everything was quiet, so I lay down on a pallet and had the strangest dream of my life.

I dreamt that a wild beast, something between a lion and a boar, chased me home, but when I called for my servants, none came. When the beast was nearly upon me, I called for Myron, and he appeared, brandishing a cudgel. He beat the beast to death.

Then I woke up.

Even though I knew it was a dream, I was so relieved that I wanted to hug Myron when I saw him next, but as I said, we are strangers. When we next met, I asked him about his business, but he said nothing. I told him about the wondrous old man who lived here. Myron listened, but his eyes narrowed. I told him about my new friends. He said he would meet them later. He wanted to see the places that I had described in my letters. So, we went to the cave, but with Myron standing there, it had shrunk into a dank, dark space.

I wanted to cry.

Myron thought I had lied, but why would I deceive him about an old cave? Truly, I was as bewildered as he.

Three days have passed. Myron has decided that there's nothing left to see. He has met my friends, but I'm afraid they did not make a good impression on him. He certainly did not make a good impression on them.

We will return home tomorrow, though why I came and what happened while I was here remains a mystery. I learned nothing about Georgios, and what pleasure I had is quite gone.

Myron says they are just tricksters who play with ignorant minds.

It would be easier if I could agree with him, but my memories are too vivid, and I know deep inside that he's mistaken. These people know something that is hidden from him, but I can't explain.

Still, I remember my dream and wonder if perhaps I should trust his judgment. Myron might be saving me from a terrible fate. I don't know. I feel divided against myself.

Eusebius is wise. His words were like balm on my troubled spirit. His family was kind. How could my joy be completely mistaken? Who do I trust if not myself?

Myron is calling. He says the sun is setting, and we should take a walk before night settles in. Strange. He's never asked me to take a walk with him before.

I will go. After all, what harm can it do?

Remember me,

~Roxanna

—Dispatch from Myron to Lysander—

Lysander,

Do not talk to me about gods. I am sick to death of gods. I have spent three days being immersed in the superstitions of a little-known sect that has rooted itself on the far side of the island. If you ever meet a follower of Christ, walk away as fast as decorum will allow. Run if you can. They are deceivers, though they believe their own words. I see it in their eyes.

In any case, continue to the unknown lands. You are a man of many resources. Use them. Do not lose Georgios' trail if you value your life. I would hate to tell the procurator that you have disappointed me.

If you do not find my grandson, you'll have no home to return to, so don't rush on any account.

I await your next dispatch.

~Myron

CHAPTER TWENTY-TWO

CLAIMING TO BE YOUR SON

—GAELIC LANDS—

Georgios insisted that they disembark on the first open shore at daybreak. After packing a few meager provisions, he told Rueben that he was going ahead, pulled forward by an anxiety that would not be denied.

Standing before verdant hills with his arms crossed and a petulant scow digging a furrow into his brow, Rueben insisted that they travel together at a reasonable pace.

Bullheaded and angry, Georgios retorted, "If the Romans have come ashore, they'll attack soon. I must warn Seanan!"

Without listening to further arguments, he left Rueben red-faced in blustering fury.

Following Connan's directions as he ran across the wide-open fields and after taxing his strength to the breaking point, Georgios collapsed at noon, forced to give his exhausted body a rest. In a matter of moments, he fell asleep.

A few hours later, he awoke famished, but his food bag lay flat at his side. Even his water skin lay empty. He stood and surveyed his surroundings, noticing signs of the Romans' passage—smoke rising over ruined huts in a distant village. Urgency drove him forward. Forcing his feet to obey, he labored onward.

By evening, he saw Connan's landmarks and knew that Seanan's village was just ahead. Relief filled him at the sight of the peaceful, undisturbed village. Gazing upon the ridge of the next hill, he spied the outline of a Roman encampment. Though Georgios was Roman, and as a

Roman he had a right to speak to another Roman, even on foreign soil, terror filled him at the thought of approaching such a formidable enemy.

After taking a brief rest, Georgios scampered into the valley, skirting the village, and climbed the far hill. With exhausted but determined steps, he proceeded toward the Roman encampment.

The sentries, apparently not concerned about the prospect of surprise attack, ate and drank in relaxation, only two stood watching a hundred yards away.

Keeping his profile low and bleary with exhaustion, Georgios plopped onto the grassy hillside, out of sight, and considered his options.

The sun set in a beautiful array of gold and red hues, turning into pinks and purples and finally melding to black. The quiet scene calmed his troubled spirits. He stretched out and once again fell into a dreamless sleep.

Bird song overhead awoke Georgios.

A tiny brown bird perched on a long weedy stem not far from him. He reached out to touch the slender figure. It flew out of reach.

Georgios sat up, rubbing his eyes. His urgent mission flooded his mind. Scrambling to his feet, he hurried toward the Roman camp.

At first, the sentries, chatting in the pleasant morning air, didn't notice his approach.

Swallowing back fear, Georgios thrust out his chest in bravado and shouted, "Romans, I've come to speak with you! I have news." Georgios raised his hands high, proving he was harmless.

Wide-eyed and clearly suspicious, the taller of the sentries directed him to halt with a gesture. His powerful voice easily crossed the distance. "Give us your name."

Georgios replied in the customary manner, "I am

Georgios, son of Alexios, of the Roman Imperial Army. Will you let me approach?"

A murmured consultation followed.

Anxiety, hunger, and thirst grew into barely contained irritation as Georgios shifted from foot to foot.

The tall soldier cupped his hands to his mouth and yelled, "Your name again!"

Georgios enunciated each word, "Georgios, son of Alexios, of the Roman Imperial Army. May I approach?"

More consultation. The two sentries beckoned other soldiers, and one man ran back to camp. A hefty man stepped forward; an irate scowl etched across his forehead. He marched up close to Georgios and patted him down, checking for hidden weapons. Then ordered him to follow. "If this is your idea of a joke, you'd better be prepared to die. I doubt our commander will find it amusing."

Georgios blinked, confusion toppling his anxiety. He followed in silence.

At the main camp, a large tent dominated the field. Guards flanked the entrance. The insignia on the flagpole appeared strangely familiar.

Georgios took a deep breath, bewildered by the appraising looks the men gave him.

A man stepped outside and surveyed Georgios from head to toe, his arms akimbo. "My name is Marcus. I am second in command, and you claim to be Georgios, son of Alexios. Is this right?"

Nearly fainting from hunger and thirst, Georgios merely nodded. "Yes. I'm here to—"

A commotion rose as men snapped to attention; their eyes riveted ahead.

Instinctually, Georgios straightened and readied himself as the commander approached.

Marcus' features became rigid as his eyes fixed over

Georgios' shoulder on the man approaching. "Sir, a boy has come here claiming to be your son!"

Georgios' jaw dropped and shock, like a cold rain, drenched his body. His mouth going dry, he turned and stared into his father's eyes.

CHAPTER TWENTY-THREE

NO WELCOME TODAY

—GAELIC LANDS—

Rueben tromped across the blowing grass with only a brief glance behind to assure himself that the women and children were still following. Though the sun showered bright rays from the noon sky, anxiety wearied him to the bones.

Connan trudged at his side, silent and morose. In one of his exasperatingly overzealous attempts at helpfulness, Connan had explained to Fiona—and every listening ear—the details of Gutun's attempt to sacrifice Brighid, as if it were nothing more than an amusing contest of wills between the Druid priest and the clan leader.

Her eyes wide with horror, Isadora gagged as she tripped over tufts of grass.

Brighid, normally cheerful, shut herself into an impenetrable shell.

Zoe, her four-year-old legs unable to maintain the long march over uneven ground, fell down, sobbing, exhausted by the endless walk.

With slumped shoulders, disheveled hair, and face smeared with dirt and sweat, Isadora's eyes filled with tears as she panted, too exhausted to carry anyone.

Connan offered the useless comment that once they got to the village, they would never travel again.

Saying nothing for fear that he would explode in fury, Rueben strode to the frail child, picked her up, and carried her in his arms.

Comforted, Zoe rested her head on Rueben's shoulder and closed her eyes, her whole body swaying to the rhythm of his steps.

They marched until nightfall. Despite their exhaustion, they snatched a few bites from their provision bags, sipped water from a fresh stream, and lay down on the grass without a thought for wild animals or marauding Romans.

In the morning, after a long undisturbed slumber, Connan shared the last of his ale, and they prepared for another long day of hiking across the land.

Isadora mumbled incoherently as Timo ran about, fascinated by birds, butterflies, and every insect he chased in innocent abandon.

How long before she unravels like the frayed end of a rope?

Agnes cradled Zoe in her arms, tripped repeatedly, and barely kept pace.

Rueben called for a short rest for her sake, knowing that if she fell, they would either have to carry her or leave her. Neither alternative appealed to him. As they chewed dried fruit and sipped the last of their water, Rueben threw small stones to the boy. He caught each one handily, delighted with the game. *How is it that some children resist the evils around them, overcoming every hardship?*

As the sun reached its climax, Rueben's exasperation heated to the boiling point. Where was Georgios? He looked askance at Connan, reluctant to get the man chatting again. Without any alternative, he braced himself. "So, how long before we reach your village?"

Connan grinned. "Guess."

Rueben detested guessing games. He offered a ridiculous answer. "Three days?"

Big thigh slap. "Oh, no, you are wrong again, slave boy. No—you're not quite as smart as you think! We're almost there. See those hills in the distance? Those are our hills. Once we climb this bare ridge, we'll see the whole valley clearly. My home is right there. You'll sleep in a proper house tonight!" He wrinkled his nose at Rueben. "Or a stable. My people don't especially take to strangers. We're a proud clan. Our ancestors pushed the Roman invaders—"

Isadora stepped forward, her brow furrowed, and pointed to the hills. "Your hills have been invaded by ants!"

Brighid pushed past Connan, staring intently. Without explanation, she sprinted forward.

Anxiety filling him, Rueben scooped Timo into his arms and jogged ahead to see what Isadora meant.

Agnes hefted Zoe and trudge along behind.

Connan jogged along, mumbling, "No hurry. The village isn't going anywhere."

They struggled up the ridge. There, before their amazed eyes, the valley spread out like a blanket.

And on the western hill camped a Roman army.

The village looked nearly deserted, but Rueben's searching eyes quickly spotted women and children scampering to the crest of a distant hill. His heart sank. Undoubtedly, somewhere in that melee, Seanan stood with his brothers and his sons and with Georgios by his side.

Sobbing, Brighid fell to her knees.

Isadora hummed a wretched tune while Agnes clutched Timo's hand and squeezed Zoe in an embrace, tears meandering down her dirty face.

Rueben sighed. *No welcome home today.*

CHAPTER TWENTY-FOUR

WHY ARE YOU ROMAN?

—GAELIC LANDS—

Georgios stared at his father and tried to speak, but words utterly failed. Though his mind acknowledged the man staring at him, reflecting his shock, every muscle in his body froze.

Alexios, gaunt and weary, seemed to have shrunk. Or perhaps, Georgios realized, he had grown larger than his father.

"Georgios, how can you be *here*? I left you with your grandparents, safely at home on Patmos."

Despite his father's authority, a wall of impenetrable anger stood between them. Georgios squared his shoulders and thrust his confusion to the side. "I learned of my Jewish heritage and ran away to follow you."

"You what?" his father whispered, his scowl deepening.

"But then I . . . I got sick and was abandoned somewhere, had to be rescued." Georgios hesitated, his thoughts crashing together in a storm of uncertainty. "I sailed here to help a friend regain his rightful place and then . . . we learned of the Roman threat, an even bigger enemy." He swallowed. "I-I didn't know the enemy would be you."

Alexios worked his jaw, his eyes narrowing in consternation. He gestured sharply and beckoned his son to follow him.

Georgios hesitated as his thoughts crashed together in a storm of uncertainty. He took a deep breath and followed his father into the interior of the sand-colored tent.

His father pointed to a wooden stool, lifted a cup from a wooden box, then poured a healthy measure of wine. He was about to put the wine to his lips when he recollected himself and gave the cup to his son. He took a second cup from the wooden box, poured another measure, and raised the cup in salute. "Drink up, son! You're practically a man now, I see. If you've spent any time with these barbarians, you must know how to drink deeply and eat heartily. I hear they love roasted meat and can kill a large animal, skin it, and prepare a feast in less time than it takes us to prepare a decent porridge."

Georgios nodded, in no mood to be amused. Anger surged through him, though he could not account for it. His father had done him no harm, had not lied to him. He had always presented himself for what he truly was: a Roman warrior who served his emperor and his country with unswerving devotion. But what had once been a simple fact was now laid out before Georgios' eyes as a much crueler reality.

To assert their authority, Rome had crucified thousands of Jews, destroyed the Jewish temple, and strewn an entire people across the land so that they would never know security as a single nation again. Rome had killed Isadora's husband for speaking his mind, taken his lands and his family, and tried to crush their identity by selling them into slavery. Rome had conquered the mighty and proud clans of Gaul and took a heavy yearly tribute for the honor of their iron rule.

Now Rome stretched her hand further, claiming a beautiful island and demanding the villagers' allegiance to an imperious, powerful emperor who they would never know and could never love. Resistance would be crushed with merciless force. Seanan would be killed, as would his sons and brothers. Those who survived would never know the enchanting breath of free air again.

Georgios smoldered but did not speak. He was still too much his father's son to show open disrespect, and he was not Roman enough to demand his right to be heard.

Alexios took another sip and stared at his son. "Speak! You are a man now. Say what you think!"

Georgios did not blink, though tears ached behind his eyes. "Why are you Roman?"

A snort. "Why did I choose to identify with the most powerful nation on earth rather than a beaten race, crucified and scattered throughout the land? Think, boy! Would you choose to be a Jew?" He frowned, a startled expression flitting across his face. He shook his finger, admonishing Georgios. "You'll have to make the same choice. Are you a Roman conqueror or a Jewish slave?"

Georgios stepped to the open doorway, the flap held back by leather ties. He looked upon the lush, green valley and the silent village. His gaze traveled to the frightened women and children winding their way up a distant hill. He spoke with his back to his father. "I will be free without enslaving myself to conquerors. I am Jew, Roman, and Greek. I'm—"

"A blind fool who thinks that a mixed identity will draw admiration, but you will *have* to pick a side. You cannot be all things to all men." A chuckle. "Don't choose Greek. They're slaves, too, but just won't admit it."

Turning, his fury rising, Georgios glared at his father. "My grandparents did not think so. Their Greek heritage endowed them with greatness, renowned for their intelligence and ferocity, too."

His lips puckering with a sour expression, Alexios waved the thought away. "Long ago, perhaps, but today Greeks are idle scholars and thieving merchants, too weak to conquer outright. Their method is to poison slowly.

Their words do the most harm."

A memory of Isadora falling on the road flickered through Georgios' mind as he stared at his father. "What happened to your family?"

Irritated, Alexios glanced at the distant hills. "I have no time for this. There is a battle to be fought." He stepped closer and clasped Georgios' shoulder. "How you've grown! You must have more strength and endurance than I realized to have survived such a long, dangerous journey with barbarians. The fates have decided; you shall take your place at my side now. This battle will not take long, and then we can sail home. I'll have you trained properly in Rome." His eyes swept over the distant village. "I almost want to thank the man who brought you here. I'm sure he would do differently if he had known how useful you were going to be to me."

Georgios shook his head. "I am not your Roman. In this conquest, there is no honor, only shame."

Alexios shrugged and tossed the dregs of his cup out the doorway. "I tried to talk with them, but they wouldn't listen. We are only a small force, as you can see. I was ordered to take a Centuria and tame a portion of this barbaric land as a foretaste of what Rome has to offer. If they resist, they'll be slaughtered. They could have paid the yearly tribute and been left in peace. But the son of the clan leader—a big fellow named Ian—is a stubborn man. He wouldn't listen. Their Druid priest is a worm, but the women are beautiful." His gaze wandered to the line escaping up the hill.

Fear flooded Georgios. "I can't fight against these people! The clan leader, Seanan, is my friend and another man, Rueben, is like my brother now." His heart pounded. "Let me talk with them. I can reason with Seanan. I'll tell him that you will leave peacefully if he offers a token of friendship to Rome. That way you both keep your honor, and no battle has to be fought."

Alexios frowned. "Rome does not accept tokens of friendship. We are a conquering race, and we take what belongs to us by right of strength. If we return without a complete surrender, it'll look as if I were defeated." He stroked his chin. "No, a token will not do, but perhaps you can help." He delved into Georgios' eyes. "Convince them that there is no valor in death. Tell them that I will leave in peace if they admit that Rome rules here as she does throughout the world."

Georgios stiffened. A strange smoky scent tickled his nose. He ignored it. "They should admit defeat without battle? Where is the honor in that?"

"Honor is best left to the living. The dead do not reap much benefit." Alexios sniffed, his scowl deepening. He stepped outside and glanced around.

A soldier approached. "The barbarians set fire to the grass, but we have put it out and everything is secure."

Confused, Georgios stepped closer. "Why burn the grass? What would that serve? They must feed their cattle."

The soldier sneered. "Who knows the minds of barbarians? They probably thought they would frighten us away."

Alexios shook his head in wonder. "Why do they wish to urge the moment of their death forward?"

Georgios stared at the quiet village and stepped forward. "They do not look to be defeated."

"Then they are wrong." Alexios' eyes followed his son's movements anxiously.

"We will see." Georgios nodded respectfully to his father and started down the hill.

"Wait!" Alexios shouted, "Where are you going?"

"To fight with the Jews and the barbarians."

Marcus called after him. "But there are no Jews here."

"Only a few, true. But then, I'm not much of a Roman."

His tone guttural and demanding, Alexios ordered his son, "Come back here!"

Hesitating only once, Georgios refused to look back. He leapt down the hill and into the quiet village.

Shaky with hunger, he glanced around. *Where is everyone?*

He stopped at an empty hut and slipped inside. A bed with a blanket folded neatly at the foot invited his weary limbs to rest a moment. A bucket of water stood by the wall. He plucked a cup off the wall, dipped it into the warm water, and drank his fill.

Midday sunlight filtered through the cracks in the walls and a smoky scent lingered in the air. It had been a long while since he had eaten, and the wine from his father made his head swim. He sat on the pallet, squeezing his eyes shut to erase his father's face from his mind. *Who am I?* Georgios groaned and flopped back onto the bed.

Suddenly, a deep chuckle vibrated above him. "Dreaming, Roman boy? I have you at last!"

Stunned, Georgios' eyes snapped open. Just as quickly, relief flooded over him.

CHAPTER TWENTY-FIVE

YOU KNOW THIS MAN?

—GAELIC LANDS—

Rueben removed his foot from Georgios' chest, smiling. "Nice to see you. I saw movement on the hill and thought"—he looked away, embarrassed—"maybe you'd been captured."

Georgios blinked and glanced around.

Filtered sunlight angled through the slats of the quiet hut.

"I must've fallen into a stupor." He met Rueben's gaze. "I'm glad to see you. You'll never believe what happened!"

Rueben's relief somersaulted into amusement. "You were attacked by Roman sentries, fought them off single-handedly, and then fell into a dazed sleep from sheer exhaustion?"

Grimacing, Georgios rubbed the back of his neck. "No, but that's a good story. I'll keep it in mind. What really happened was even more amazing."

Rueben draped his arm around his friend's shoulder and led him into the sunshine. "Tell me about it as we walk. Connan nearly talked my ears off coming here, so I don't see why you shouldn't finish the job. They're resting by the stream. I told them to wait while I looked around." He glanced in the direction of the Roman encampment. "We'd better get going. Those Roman friends of yours won't wait much longer."

"My Roman friends? Oh, you mean—" Georgios shook his head, marched across the village, and laughed. "You won't believe it. Let's get the others. But keep in mind,

I'm still the master."

Rueben shoved Georgios' shoulder. "I've played slave long enough. Tell your insolent friend Connan, and everyone else we meet along the way, that I'm every bit as free a man as you, or I'll beat you within an inch of your life."

Without breaking his stride, Georgios stretched to his full height, aware that he now towered a good two inches over his friend. "I will tell them you are a free man because it happens to be true. Now quit dawdling!"

The two climbed the hill and gathered the women and children from a hilltop lush with grass. Cows grazed in contentment on the west side as rays of sunlight slanted across the ground, over boulders, and set the treetops glowing.

Connan ambled to their side.

Georgios took the lead. "Trouble is brewing on the hill." He squinted into the slanting rays of light. "We've got to find Seanan. But I need to tell you something first."

Rueben shoved Georgios forward. "Talk as we march back to the village."

With an anxious frown, Connan's temper sparked. "What're you doing? Don't touch your master, or I'll—"

Too irritated to play the fool any longer, Rueben shoved Connan to the ground. "Get out of my way!"

Connan jumped to his feet and dove into Rueben's middle.

Rueben took the onslaught and pummeled the large man's back. He then rolled away and stood up in one fluid motion, huffing to catch his breath.

Georgios called a halt, shaking his fists for emphasis.

With a smirk, Connan taunted Rueben. "Think you're better than a sniveling slave, eh?"

Grateful for all the fighting lessons, Rueben backed up

a step then charged forward, leading with his right shoulder. He knocked Connan to the ground.

Isadora screamed, Zoe sobbed, and Timo yelled to no one in particular.

Surprised, Rueben fell backward as Georgios landed on him and pinned his arms to the ground.

Connan lay on his back, stunned.

Brighid ran to Connan and dabbed a rag to his bleeding mouth.

Furious at himself as well as at the whole world, Rueben thrashed until he shoved Georgios aside. “Get off me, you Roman oaf! I won’t take another word from that overgrown—”

Georgios shook his head grimly. “Stop talking and stand up.” He stood and stretched out his hand.

Cursing under his breath, Rueben clasped the offered hand and climbed to his feet, wiping dirty sweat off his face.

Connan rose, spluttering revenge. “I’ll teach you—”

Georgios held his arms between them, stalling any further action. “Stop it! We’ll have plenty of fighting soon enough. The Romans won’t stop until they take this whole island. Unless we want to be Roman slaves or worse, we’d better find out where we can be the most use.”

Rueben brushed dirt and grass from his clothes, glanced at the women and children huddled together, took a steadying breath, and faced the hills. “Brighid, where should the women go?”

“There are caves in the woods.”

With a nod, Rueben gestured for them to hurry along. “Take Isadora, Agnes, and the children and go. There’s no welcome awaiting you down there.”

Connan spat dirt out of his mouth, wiped his lips, and marched to Rueben, his voice low and threatening. “Who are you to give orders? I'm a member of this clan, you're just—"

Georgios shouted, "Don't start again! Connan, Rueben isn't a slave. He never was. He's a friend who only pretended to be one so that we could outwit your Druid priest, but we have bigger troubles now. A very determined man leads those Romans. His job is to take this island at any cost. He will conquer you—or die trying. Believe me, I know."

Connan stared open-mouthed at Georgios.

The certainty in Georgios' tone snared Rueben's attention. He raised an eyebrow. "How do you *know*?"

"He's Alexios, my father." Without looking back, Georgios jogged down the slope, heading toward the quiet village.

Stunned into silence, his disagreement with Connan thrust aside, Rueben sprinted after Georgios.

Connan called after them, "Wait up. I know where to find Seanan!"

Rueben grabbed Georgios' arm, stopping him. "What do you mean, he's your father? You mean symbolically, or—"

"I went to the top of the hill, met the commander, and he is none other than Alexios, my father." Georgios' face froze as if he had not an ounce of emotion left in his body.

Clasping his head in his hands, Rueben tried to make sense of this insane possibility. "But your father is in Rome! I can't be—"

Georgios stomped forward. "I don't care what you believe. Go up the hill and ask him if you want, but it's the truth. He offered me a position at his side."

Running up from behind, Connan gripped Georgios' shoulder. "What did you tell him?"

Rueben shook his fist at Connan. "He said he'd be

honored to butcher his friends and their families! What do you think? He's here, isn't he?"

His face flushed and his shouldered hunched forward, ready for another fight, Connan stared at Georgios. "What did you say?"

Georgios yanked his arm free. "I said that I was a free man and not as Roman as I once thought."

Rueben scowled.

Connan pointed at the hills. "They are coming! Hurry, Seanan will need every able spear."

Rueben watched the figures marching in perfect formation down the hillside.

Georgios stood frozen.

Clasping Georgios' shoulder, Rueben led him the last steps into the village, a sick foreboding seeping through his body. "Let's go. You've made your choice, and I've made mine."

~~~

Seanan stood outside a storage hut before the large pile of weapons and studied his son with renewed respect.

With calm authority, Ian parceled out the weapons to a line of waiting men.

Seanan lifted a sword and examined it. "You've accomplished a great deal. These are well made. Even the handles inspire strength and—"

From the outskirts of the village, Olcan sped forward, huffing. "Seanan! Liam saw a Roman youth on the crest of the hill talking with the Romans. Could Georgios have been captured?"

Liam, his gaze down, tread the last paces behind his uncle and stopped respectfully before his father.

Alarm clenched Seanan's stomach, nauseating him. He
~~~

faced his youngest son. "What's this? Liam, why didn't you tell me?"

The boy met his father's gaze. "I tried to tell you this morning, but you were too busy. I told Olcan, and he thought it sounded like someone you brought home with you. But why would he be conversing with the Romans? He didn't look like a prisoner. He asked to speak with their leader."

His insides twisting, Seanan swallowed back bile. "Georgios wouldn't betray us!" He glanced at the advancing army. "Where are Rueben, Brighid, and the others? He'd never betray them into Roman hands. He wouldn't!" Fear clutched his heart. *Would he?*

Olcan gripped his spear, his fingertips white. "There must be some mistake. Surely, they'll be here soon." Olcan searched the horizon. He chuckled, relief rippling over his face. "I'm sure of it."

Seanan stared at Olcan. "Having a vision, are you?"

Olcan pointed over Seanan's shoulder. "You could say that. Look."

Surprise warred with relief until joy unclenched Seanan's heart. He clasped Liam's shoulder, remembered his son's words, and confusion wormed into his mind. He counted three figures, Georgios, Connan, and Rueben. *Where are the women?*

Seanan rubbed his face, took a swift, appraising look at the approaching enemy, faced the newcomers as they stepped close, and shouted in exasperation, "It's about time! Were you waiting for better weather? You were supposed to be here yesterday!"

Panting, Georgios halted and bowed respectfully.

His stomach sour, Seanan couldn't care less for formalities. "Where in blazing fires is my sister?"

Rueben and Connan joined Georgios before Seanan,

each bowing in respect.

Rueben pointed to the western hilltop covered in thick woods. "Your sister is well-protected in the caves behind us with Isadora and the others."

Georgios lifted his hand. "I ran ahead and spoke with the Roman commander. We just met up again and have joined you as quickly as possible."

Relief spread through Seanan. The protective covering of caves in the woods offered a time-trusted shelter for women and children. He blinked as Georgios' words sank in. He pursed his lips. "You spoke with the *Roman commander*? Had a few words of advice for him, perhaps?"

Georgios observed the advancing enemy, his frown deepening. "I've a lot to tell you, but now is not the time. Have you weapons for us? We've come to help save your people or die trying."

His good humor instantly restored, Seanan pounded Georgios on the back. "That's what I like to hear. You're a good lad." He glanced at Ian, who stood exchanging news with Connan.

"Stop talking to that big oaf and get these two warriors the best weapons we have. We've a battle to fight. Tell the men to gather at the mound. We'll take our stand alongside our beloved dead who risked life and limb preserving these lands."

~~~

Georgios stood alongside Seanan's brothers at the crest of a high grassy mound, while Ian and Earan took up their positions next to their father. The men ranged in ragged lines, shaking their spears and swords, impatient for the battle to begin.
~~~

Olcan led a group on the left, and Liam was ordered to the back of the line to keep weapons ready for any man in need.

The men chanted a guttural rhythm, setting hearts throbbing, stirring even Georgios' blood.

Ever since leaving his father, cold had settled inside. His eyes climbed over the hills where his father led his men, descending into the valley. He must defeat the Roman army, but he could not kill his father. He had to keep as far from Alexios as possible.

Rueben swung his sword over his head with expert strength, hate and fury glowing from his narrowed eyes.

Connan's mouth gaped open. He breathed loud and cursed often, stomping his feet, his eyes unnaturally bright.

The men, their limbs bare, scorned the security of armor, proclaiming their nature as true warriors. Swords, knives, cudgels, bows, and arrows were poised for action. Everyone stood in readiness.

Seanan raised his arms. "My people! I have returned preserved by the gods for such a day as this! We will throw the Romans into the sea! They shall not conquer here! Free men—we will ever remain so!"

Georgios closed his eyes. *My God, I hope he's right.*

~~~

Alexios knew that his fate would be decided today. There would be no second chances. His son had made his choice. It was cruel fate to fight his own son, but he could not reverse the fortunes of war. Rome offered the best hope. Perhaps if Georgios lived through the day, he would be freed from delusion and able to follow a more hopeful path.
~~~

Once at the bottom of the hill, his men reconfigured themselves into the phalanx formation, prepared to attack but protected at the same time.

Clearly unwilling to wait for the Romans to approach, Seanan's clan charged, screaming and howling, their nearly naked bodies plummeting forward with all the fury of men protecting their homes and families.

Alexios watched the barbarian forces spurt forward in ragged lines. Somewhere in the throng, his son bore arms against him. His heart quaked, but trained to stand against all forms of agony, he ignored his heartache and thrust his sword into the air, shouting, "For Rome! Valor for the victorious!"

His men roared, "Valor for the victorious!"

The shout briefly stirred Alexios' blood, but his heart did not rise to the challenge.

The fighting quickly turned fierce and bloody, for even though the armor and shield offered excellent protection, the barbarians knew their weaknesses.

Celts leapt on their shields and thrust spears between their helmets, armor, and shields, devastating the value of the phalanx formation.

Shocked by this unprecedented breach in their protection, Alexios swallowed the bile rising in his throat. These barbarians were men and intelligent at that.

~~~

Seanan took a breather and wiped sweat from his brow. His warriors pummeled the Romans, scrambling like wild men over shields and bodies, stabbing and slicing at every opportunity. The Romans broke formation and fell back. Sucking in deep breaths, Seanan glanced around.

Rueben ran from one quick thrust to another. He
~~~

weaved in and out, dropping his enemies to the ground by slicing them behind the knees. Stouter opponents then finished them off. Thus, he did the work of ten warriors by setting up his victims for quick slaughter.

Connan had the good luck to be following Rueben, so the men who came his way were not hard to defeat.

Ian and Earan worked in tandem, fighting back-to-back, while Olcan took up the perimeter, directing his men to catch any enemy trying to escape.

Ronan and Tainair fought, strong and fierce. Their combined efforts slew Romans left and right.

A glint caught Seanan's eye.

The Roman commander had taken off his helmet to wipe his bleeding face.

Grinning, Seanan knew that his enemy lay in his grasp. He circled around and stabbed the commander in the back, though his blood-soaked hand slipped, and the thrust did not achieve its full impact.

The Roman leader fell to his knees.

Seanan viewed the field of victory; the battle had turned his way, and his confidence soared. He pulled his knife free, raised it, and cried out, "Victory is ours!"

Alexios doubled over in agony.

Confidently Seanan stepped in front of the man's face that had brought death and destruction to his people. "I will look you in the eye before you die, Roman!" He grabbed Alexios by the hair and lifted his head, staring at the man face to face. He gasped. The familiar look, so like Georgios, just older and rougher, took away his breath.

Ian ran to his father's side.

Seanan stood transfixed, his body trembling.

Ian glanced around and called, "Georgios! Seanan needs you."

In the thick of the fight on the bloody field, Georgios turned.

Ian beckoned to Georgios over.

Leaping over bodies, Georgios ran to Ian, and when he came close, he stopped, frozen.

Seanan released his hold on the Roman's hair, and the bleeding Roman collapsed to the ground. Seanan stared at Georgios, his throat tight, his words choking as they tumbled forth. "Do you know this man?"

CHAPTER TWENTY-SIX

CHILDREN OF THE SAME GOD

—PATMOS—

My Dear Cecilia,

My world had changed! It all happened so simply and naturally. I am bewildered. Are the stars still in the sky? Myron and I took a walk on the last evening before we were to leave, and I felt so miserable. I asked him how he felt. I wanted to know how he managed to keep his mind occupied when he must suffer too.

Myron stared at me as if he had never seen me before. I glimpsed his fear. Grieved, I clutched his arm, clinging like a child seeking refuge from a storm. I could do nothing but weep.

To my utter amazement, my stoic, distant husband sobbed. Tears streamed down his cheeks.

For the first time, I saw him as he really is. Eusebius said, "We are all children of the same God and need understanding. When we feel for each other, we serve God. Then we love Him best."

After we dried our tears, we talked about our thoughts and feelings, our fears and hopes. Myron is a new man, and I am a new wife. Myron spoke again with Eusebius. This time, he listened.

Yesterday, Myron rose before the dawn and walked to the cave by himself. When he returned, he said he spoke to a man who was no man and yet had the bearing of a lord. He said the figure told him many things, revealing that he was a servant of the Most High.

Myron is quieter now, not sullen but peaceful. We smile

and laugh like people gone mad. We are happy. We plan to travel to the lands where Jesus lived. We've put Georgios into His hands. Someday we will see our grandson again.

I am happy! Myron is calling. I don't know when I will write again. May you come to know Him as I do.

I will never forget you.

~Roxanna

—Dispatch from Myron to Lysander—

Lysander,

I am leaving this island to go to the mainland. I have discovered something of great value, and I must learn more.

I regret my previous threats. I ask that you find Georgios and bring him home of your own free will. I will do all I can to assist you when you return, regardless of your success or failure. My dispatches may not reach you after this point. If you find my grandson, care for him until I return.

Your faithfulness will be rewarded.

~Myron

CHAPTER TWENTY-SEVEN

GOD KNOWS

—GAELIC LANDS—

Marcus had never entertained the possibility that barbarians could defeat Roman soldiers. As he stood in the corner of the hut, a mere hovel, where Alexios recovered on a primitive pallet spread across the floor, reality insisted that he reform his opinion.

The battle had been decisively won shortly after Alexios' fall, and the escaping soldiers were chased to the sea. They left as quickly as their sails could carry them. Those who had fallen were buried in a mass grave. Only two Romans remained behind, Alexios, soon to die, everyone assumed, and Marcus, who would not leave his commander's side. Only Georgios' plea for mercy spared them immediate execution.

Grateful, but furious at his need for gratitude, Marcus endured the humiliation of accepting food and a place to sleep from his enemy. When Brighid offered to see to his wounds, he brushed her away with a scowl. He could do little more than watch Alexios waver between life and death. Only Fiona's gentle ministrations and Brighid's medicinal sense saved him.

After years, serving loyally in hopes of rising in rank so as to lead his own force one day, Marcus now sat helplessly by Alexios' bedside, trying to decide if he could ever return home. What would he find in Rome but disgrace?

With wary speculation, he observed Georgios' devotion. Georgios would even thrust him aside whenever Alexios called for help. Marcus sneered as he watched

Georgios' dedicated care—a man who had betrayed both nation and family. His disgust doubled with every encounter.

Even if his own future lay desolate, at least he could be faithful to his commander. In this, he could cobble together some measure of self-respect.

Staying in the shadows, he waited for Georgios to leave them alone. Then he would do as he always did, act like the son Georgios had never been.

~~~

Georgios ignored Marcus standing against the wall and focused his attention on his father. Guilt twisted his gut as he sat on the edge of the pallet, watching his father's labored breathing. Had he stayed with Alexios, the battle would have turned the other way, and his father would have returned to Rome in triumph.

In weary anxiety, Georgios stepped away from his father's silent suffering and left the hut, finding fresh air and sunshine outside. He considered the verdant hills as mist hid the mountaintops. Smoke rose from village huts, families worked in gardens beside their homes, and he realized once again that he had made the right choice. He could never have forsaken this glorious land and these humble people to Roman cruelty.

Seanan had allowed Alexios—his bitter enemy—to be nursed by his wife and sister for no other reason than he was dear to Georgios. And for this kindness, Georgios would always love him.

Everyone ignored Marcus, though the man's presence irritated Georgios. *Why didn't he flee with the rest?*

Between heartfelt gratitude to Seanan and his clan and a growing hatred for all things Roman, Georgios struggled
~~~

to keep his emotions in check. He could not deny his heritage. He was just as much a Roman as he was a Jew or a Greek. As a dutiful son, he must return Alexios to Rome so their physicians could heal him. But at present, Alexios was too ill to be moved, Rome was a long journey away, and he had no wish to travel again so soon.

He shuffled back inside, passed Marcus' silent shadow, clasped Alexios' hand, and wished through gritted teeth that Marcus would go away.

~~~

Rueben helped the women and children resettle in the village and, with Seanan, Olcan, and Georgios' help, built a dwelling for Isadora, Agnes, and the children.

Though Agnes watched his every move with intense interest, smiling shyly whenever he came near, he merely nodded but never let his eyes linger on her face or form.

He enjoyed the comfortable rhythm of village life. Mornings were invariably spent working the land, gathering food, taking care of the herds of cows, goats, and sheep, or mending broken tools.

Rocks were plentiful, but it took a prodigious amount of work to move and shape them into something useful. Still, as backbreaking as that was, it did not take a genius to accomplish this job. Stone would last, so once a foundation or a border was built, it would stay put. Rueben found consolation in that. The afternoons were spent much the same, except when it rained. Then villagers would gather around peat fires and chat in soft voices well into the evenings. When the sun sank below the horizon and coolness descended, they trundled off to bed wrapped in furs and woolen blankets.

With thoughts nagging him in the back of his mind,
~~~

Rueben pondered his purpose in the Celtic village. A private mission haunted his nights and distracted his daytime thoughts.

On a clear day after the village had recovered their daily rhythm, Rueben strode to Seanan's garden, where the men broke up of clods of earth. He beckoned to Georgios.

After passing his hoe to another, Georgios clumped across the broken soil and paced up to his friend.

Without ceremony, Rueben launched into his newest plan. "I want to get away to pray and consider my life. Seanan is so busy building fences, enlarging his garden, and giving everyone orders, it's an ideal time for me to decide my future."

Georgios smiled. "But we know your future. You're coming home with me as soon as my father is well enough. Then we'll head to Patmos so you can meet my grandparents."

Vividly recalling Georgios' stories about his grandparents' aversion to Jews, Rueben wondered at his friend's naiveté. Just being Georgios' friend would hardly make him a welcome guest in Myron's home. He glanced around and scratched his head, uncertain what to say.

Georgios grinned. "Don't become too enchanted with this land. It's not ours."

Rueben contemplated the sky, trying to shake his pensive mood. See what I have to put up with. He met Georgios' inquisitive gaze. "I admire the beauty here, and Seanan and his family have grown on me like barnacles on a boat; still, I have a dream that enchants me more. I must see it through or die in the attempt."

"To see the Christ who died in Rome?"

"He died, but his words live on. By all accounts, he is not really dead. I must understand what that means."

Georgios shrugged. "A fool's quest, perhaps."

Rueben pointed to the largest hill. "On that hill, like Moses on the mountaintop, I'll spend time alone with God. Maybe I'll understand my purpose better."

Georgios stared at the rounded hill, amused acceptance rippling over his face. "Enjoy yourself but be ready to travel soon."

Rueben gripped Georgios' shoulder. "I'll pray for you as well."

"Be careful or lightning might strike! Rest, pray as you please, and come back soon."

Rueben collected supplies: bedding, food, and a wine sack left by the fleeing Romans. Then he set out toward the hillside. He climbed throughout the afternoon, sweat beading on his forehead at the exertion, and rejoiced when he reached the top.

After finding a sheltered spot under a large oak, Rueben settled in, resting and praying until glorious stars dotted the evening sky.

After enjoying strips of roasted meat and chunks of barley bread, he took long draughts from his wine sack. Satisfied, he leaned against the tree trunk and watched the black limbs sway in the night breeze.

In the distance, a disheveled branch pile loomed like broken fingers from the horizon. *Barbarians! They can't even store their fuel properly.* He sipped more wine and soon slid into a comforting repose. To the tune of cooing doves and the low mooing of a lonely cow, he slipped into a deep, peaceful sleep.

~~~

Gutun saw the happy villagers bustle about in productive duties and realized, beyond all doubt, that
~~~

Seanan had won back his leadership. Though the Roman defeat was glorious, it was not as dramatic as Gutun had hoped. He had prayed for a great wave to sweep the enemy into the sea, though he realized later that perhaps it was just as well his prayer hadn't been answered, since the entire village might have been swept along with them. Still, he held his chin high; though only a few faithful knew of his great deeds, he had done what no one else had thought to do—he had appeased the gods.

On the day of battle, he had climbed to the top of a hill and ordered his followers to bring three sheep and three pigs. They would have brought three heifers, but the large animals were too frightened and unmanageable, what with all the noise and action below. They had to be content with a ewe, a half-dozen sparrows, a small loaf of bread, and a jug of ale. The offering was shabby, but Gutun could hardly have returned to the village amid the battle to find something better.

Now, he made perfect plans. At the zenith of winter, the sky cleared, allowing the full moon to have a luminous effect, a portentous sign. His men tied two sheep and a cow in a sheltered grove where they could graze contentedly until he needed them. He led a procession up the hill at midnight, petitioners carrying fresh gifts. The bigger, the better.

He dressed in colorful robes, layering them so that he appeared bulkier and more imposing than his slight build allowed. Though he had no human offering, once he regained control of the clan, he knew exactly whom he'd like to offer to the gods.

For tonight, he was content with the blood of animals and the largest fire to ever rage on their fair island.

As the animals were led forth and the ceremonial flame grew, the chant rose louder. The devotees writhed in frantic ecstasy.

Gutun transferred a flame to an offering bowl, then lifted his arms. “Thank you for saving us from the mighty Romans. In blood, we return to the old ways and worship you with proper offerings.” He wrung the neck of a wriggling sparrow, dropped its body in the offering bowl, and threw the corpse with a wild yell—“Ayee!”—into the massive flames.

The excited congregation screamed in jubilation.

Gutun accepted a cup of wine and drank deeply. He gestured for others to bring forth ale. “Partake, all!”

More birds and the sheep were slaughtered and thrown in the flames. Finally, a cow was led forth. Gutun reached for his bloody knife, while the chanting grew wilder and more demanding.

~~~

Rueben dreamed that he was at home in a circle of men, dancing and praising God as they would during festival time. As the chanting grew louder and weirder, so his dream became more menacing. Before he knew it, he was taken captive by a cavorting monster that grunted and pawed at the earth, urging him to despair with his threats and admonitions.

A woman shrieked.

Rueben sat bolt upright, his heart beating wildly. Blinking at the dancing flames, Rueben, hidden in the shadow of the oak, stared with amazement at the silhouette of wild dancers in the distance.

They circled around the fire which seemed to undulate to the chaos of their clamorous noise.

He clambered to his feet and shook his head, running his fingers through his hair, trying to comprehend the
~~~

scene. Step by step, he drew closer until about a stone's throw away.

A cow's anxious moo grabbed his attention. Two men dragged the reluctant heifer toward the fire, so intent on their duty they didn't even notice him.

Dressed in his flowing robes, Gutun stood ready with a large knife, glinting in the firelight.

Rueben leapt forward. Though he had often seen the sacrifice of a goat or a sheep in Jewish ceremonies, driving fury propelled him forward. No animal would be slaughtered for a false god before his eyes. He rushed from the shadows and tackled Gutun, wresting the knife from his hand.

Unprepared, Gutun dropped the knife, scurried to his feet, and raised his hands in surrender.

Seething, Rueben swung his gaze over the assembly and spat his words. "You serve an evil demon and offend the one true God. You must not do this!"

Recovering, Gutun caught his breath, dusted the dirt from his robe, and straightened his shoulders. Sliding a sneering glance from Rueben to the watching throng, he opened his hands and lifted his gaze to the night sky. "Blessed be the gods for rewarding our devotion with a great gift! A servant of Rome!"

Rueben glanced at the glassy-eyed assembly and realized his mistake. These were not Seanan's loyal clan members who lived and toiled in humble service. These souls had been captivated by Gutun's mysterious, demonic power.

Fear spread through Rueben, prickling his skin. There was only one answer to a devilish prayer. He lifted his face to the starry sky with his arms outspread and called, "Oh, God, I worship only You. If You wish, show Your power and majesty—"

A drop splashed on Rueben's face. And then another and another. He blinked as raindrops turned into a downpour.

Yelps of surprise, murmurs of fear, and loud calls for deliverance filled the air as drenching rain poured forth from a star-studded sky.

The drowned fire smoked in swirls of gray desolation, and the crowd dispersed, scampering away in confusion.

Shoving past the complacent cow, Gutun pounded down the hill, his robes dragging across the wet ground.

Exultant, Ruben threw back his head and savored the rain. He hated to disappoint Georgios, but now he knew where he must go.

The next day, Rueben returned to the village and packed his bags, preparing for his journey to Jerusalem. His only concern was whether Georgios would join him on the greatest adventure of his life.

Destiny called.

~~~

Georgios enjoyed watching Seanan tease Liam, encourage Earan, and listen respectfully to Ian's latest suggestion, all the while catching his wife's eye and winking playfully at her.

He could not take Seanan away from his family again.

As Seanan crossed the village, Georgios caught up with him. "Seanan, wait a moment. I want to talk about our next expedition."

Frowning, Seanan stopped at the edge of the village and crossed his arms. "What might that be?"

"Perhaps Olcan should lead it."

Seanan glanced away, rubbing his chin, his frown deepening.
~~~

Like a swimmer plunging into the cold sea, Georgios spoke faster. "I must take Father home. A ship leaves in three days. It can take us south, where we can trade in the village. Then we'll take the next ship heading for Rome, and I'll find a doctor to look after my father. Then Marcus will finally be free to go home. You'll be glad to be rid of *him*, certainly."

Seanan nodded, hesitating. He shrugged. "There is still a great deal for me to attend to here. I suppose Olcan could manage the next voyage." He peered at Georgios. "Will you be able to leave Alexios in Rome?"

Georgios met Seanan's searching gaze. "I must return to Patmos. Father has no part in that."

Seanan clasped Georgios' shoulder. "You're a man now. You decide." He turned and strode away.

Georgios closed his eyes, a sinking sensation drowning all newfound joy.

When he opened his eyes, Marcus stood in the doorway across the compound, staring at him.

Concern tightened Georgios' throat. He jogged over. "Is my father all right?"

"He is resting comfortably." Marcos rubbed one side of his face, his gaze scanning the hills. "It's time we left. He can't recover in this primitive place, and he wouldn't want to die here."

"I've made arrangements. We'll leave in three days."

Wide-eyed amazement spread over Marcus' face. Relief like euphoria altered his entire demeanor, making him stand straighter, a new spark in his eyes. "I know of the best doctors in Rome. They'll attend to his care as soon as I arrange it."

Georgios studied Marcus, his aversion twisting from hate to mere curiosity. "Why do you care so much,

Marcus? After all, he's not your father. Don't you have a father of your own?"

Marcus opened and closed his mouth, clearly stunned. He swallowed. "Y-yes, I have a father. I had a father, I should say. He died when I was young—but not with honor. Alexios knew my situation, so he adopted me, in a manner of speaking. When the opportunity came, he chose me for his second in command. I'll always remain as faithful to him as he has been to me."

Georgios' stomach tightened. Weary acceptance swept over him. Marcus' position of honor should have been his position. He should have been his father's most trusted friend and advisor. Instead, he opposed not only his father but the whole Roman Empire. Desolation crept into his heart. "When we reach Rome, will you stay with my father or return to your own home?"

Marcus cleared his throat. "I have many duties. You will care for your father." His stoic tone betrayed him.

Georgios nodded. "You belong to the Roman army, but you could still look in on my—Alexios—often, and help in his recovery, surely?"

Marcus' eyebrows rose, a hopeful gleam in his eyes. "Certainly. I could make arrangements to assist with his care. We are fellow soldiers, after all."

Georgios sighed. "That's the truth. I'll leave him in your care in Rome while I return to my grandparents. It's been over two years since I last saw them. They won't even know me."

A genuine smile crossed Marcus' face. "Don't worry; your father will be well cared for as long as I am alive." Marcus returned to his bedside vigil.

A shout turned Georgios' attention.

Seanan called across the compound, "Ian, Earan, come here! I have something fine to show you." The grin playing on his lips and the twinkle in his eyes suggested mischief, a teasing game.

Stung as if bitten by an adder, Georgios bit his lip against jealousy. His family had never been so close nor so fond of each other.

A silent figure caught his eye.

Rueben strolled forward, his hands clasped behind his back, his head bowed.

In deep thought or heart-wrenching grief? Certainly, they'd be friends forever.

God knows—I need one.

CHAPTER TWENTY-EIGHT

A GREAT DEAL WE DON'T KNOW

—GAELIC LANDS—

Gutun was not one to forget an insult. To be outmaneuvered by a foreign youth who looked inferior, acted superior, and called upon a foreign God tortured his mind like a barbed hook embedded in his flesh.

Though a ship had been made ready and Rueben, Marcus, Georgios, and Alexios would soon leave, Gutun could not allow Rueben to go unscathed or it might appear as if a Jew had outmaneuvered a Druid.

Meandering along the lakeside, the sky heavy with rain, Gutun observed Seanan and his sons preparing for a grand feast. The fire pit had been freshly scraped, new wood placed over it, and two oxen slaughtered. As the clan priest, prayers beseeching the gods for safe travels would be expected.

He smiled. He knew where the drinks were made and how ceremonies were performed, and he understood better than anyone the traditional songs, prayers, and invocations that must be utilized. He also knew when drinking cups were exchanged. To add a bit of fun, he would make Rueben's death appear as an act of treachery by a friend. Delight, like honey, always tasted sweet. He'd destroy two enemies with one drink.

~~~

Olcan straightened and rubbed the small of his back after moving a boulder from the spot Isadora insisted would be the only proper place for her desired bench.
~~~

Their eyes met.

Sitting on a simple chair that Olcan had brought for her comfort, Isadora blushed prettily. “Thank you, Olcan. You’re so much stronger than Rueben, and I would’ve hated to hurt the little man after all the kindness he has shown me.”

Olcan stared at the late afternoon mist as it descended from the hillsides. “I wish you wouldn’t call him that. He’s not a little man. It’s just that most of us are large. Rueben has a stout heart.”

Contrite, Isadora dropped her gaze. “I suppose you’re right. I’m a harsh judge. My husband corrected me often for being so.” She lifted her head and stared at him pointedly. “Perhaps you could teach me to be gentler?”

Heat flooding his body, Olcan rubbed dirt off his hands. “I’ll be leaving with Rueben and Georgios on the next ship bound for Rome.” He swallowed a bitter taste. “I’ll be gone some time…”

Spluttering, her eyes wide with shock, Isadora jumped from her chair and clasped his arm. “But you can’t leave. I need you! I can’t take care of Agnes and the little ones by myself. I don’t care for anyone here as well as you, except Brighid, and she’s going to be married—” Isadora pressed a trembling hand to her mouth, tears glimmering in silent appeal.

A storm of emotion filled Olcan. *Could it be possible?*

Gutun strode across the village, his gaze straying in their direction.

Irritated, Olcan clasped Isadora’s arm and led her to the lake.

Greenish water lapped against yellow grass stems. Multitudes of birds, startled at their approach, flew to the safety of bare treetops. The air, muted and grey, hung like a vaporous mist.

They strolled along the edge of the lake in silence. Isadora dropped her gaze.

After assuring himself that they were alone, Olcan stopped and gazed at the imposing woman before him. "It's time you knew the truth, Isadora." He cleared his throat. "I knew your husband, Leander. He was an excellent trader and a surprisingly good Roman. He spoke of you with such love that, through him, I learned the meaning of devotion. When word reached Seanan that he'd been charged with treason, we both knew it was a lie.

"We knew that Leander was blamed for another man's crime, but we were helpless to change his fate. Seanan told me then that if ever an opportunity came for us to make right the wrong, we should do it. When I saw you being led like a sheep to the slaughter, heading for the sale house, I prayed to the gods that you would one day come home with me and know freedom once again. I couldn't speak my feelings, for it seemed ungenerous to expect you to care for me after you had tragically lost your husband, so I told Seanan that I'd take Georgios and Rueben on the trip to Rome. But now…"

Crumpling like a broken doll, Isadora sat slumped on the boulder. "I ought to be ashamed. I didn't deserve my Leander's love, and you took such a chance in rescuing me. I never deserved your kindness, then or now." Isadora met Olcan's gaze. "Though I still love Leander's memory, I care for you, too. I know a man's word is his honor, but perhaps you could explain to Seanan, and he might find another to—?"

The same reckless passion that compelled Olcan to rescue Isadora gripped his heart.

"I have two good children. Timo will be strong and robust, and—"

Olcan laughed. "Zoe has already won my heart. Timo

is a good lad. Though I'm not sure about Agnes—such a sad girl."

Isadora sighed. "The girl plagues me. She watches Rueben's every move and sighs whenever he passes. I fear her heart will break when he leaves, but it's for the best. He is not the right man for her."

Olcan scratched his chin. "Rueben's heart is consumed with his search for a majestic God. I would dismiss his faith as a child's story, but Seanan respects Rueben, and even Gutun was amazed by his miracle—rain falling from a clear sky."

The white mist thickened around them. An owl hooted in the distance and day succumbed to evening.

Olcan perched on the boulder, sitting shoulder to shoulder with Isadora. "There's a great deal about God that we don't know."

Isadora rubbed her hands together. "Leander was educated by the Greeks and had a Roman's heart, yet he believed in the One God. I never knew what to believe, except in him."

Coming from the mist, Agnes led Timo and Zoe around the lake, shimmering figures breaking through a misty curtain.

Isadora clasped Olcan's hand, a smile wavering on her lips. "I wish she could be as happy as I am."

Olcan wrapped his arm around her soft, yielding shoulders. "We have men enough to spare in this clan. She'll love another. Rueben must follow his own path."

Agnes drew closer, smiling shyly.

Timo broke away, grabbed a stone, and quickly threw it into the lake.

Zoe crouched on the riverbank and swished her fingers in the murky water.

Grinning and lighthearted, Olcan stood. He gestured to

Agnes. "Sit and keep your sister company. I must speak to Seanan."

With an amused twinkle in her eye, Agnes took Olcan's place on the boulder.

Holding her gaze, Olcan pressed Isadora's shoulder. Then he took his leave with a polite nod and started toward the village. His mind felt at ease for the first time in ages.

CHAPTER TWENTY-NINE

WHAT JUST HAPPENED?

—GAELIC LANDS—

Seanan shifted his stance, crossing his arms over his chest as he watched his clansmen prepare for the coming feast.

The whole village bustled with happy anticipation. Smoke rose over firepits, mingling with the misty air.

The savory aroma of roasting meat tantalized his nose, though anxiety intruded on Seanan's pleasure.

Upon hearing Olcan's news, he wanted to throttle the man, but he had seen the first symptoms of awakening love so long ago, he could hardly be surprised. Still, no other man could be so well trusted on so important a matter.

He strode to a dead tree, leaned against it, and tried to cheer himself. Now Isadora would truly become a clan member and could settle down and make herself useful. Goban, one of his best smiths, had claimed Brighid for his wife. She'd be as busy as a bee making a home and taking care of the babes that would come along. Seanan kicked an acorn nut and reflected broodily. Brighid had better have a *large* family, or Goban would be the one to pay the price. A harassed smithy was a clan's nightmare.

No… Seanan exhaled a long breath. Marriage was a blessing, and here he was going to have two new families formed within a month of each other. Georgios' departure feast would mark the beginning of Brighid's wedding feast, and then a month later, they would celebrate Olcan's wedding with Isadora. Seanan nodded in approval, stroking his chin.

The white mist had turned into a gray fog. But who in

the world would he find to take Olcan's place?

Ian marched toward him, talking as he approached. "Father, all the trade goods are ready. Do you still want the three heifers and two goats to go? They'll slow the journey down a bit." Ian jerked his thumb at the packs neatly piled in the storage hut, then waited, his face a picture of wisdom and patience.

Lightning could not have brightened the world anymore for Seanan at that moment. He grinned. "You're right. Leave the heifers and goats. I appreciate your help." He clasped his son's shoulder and led him around the village. "It's too bad that Olcan can't return with Georgios and Rueben."

Ian nodded and then called to a man standing near, "Tell Liam to take the heifer and goats up to the meadow." With a grin, he faced his father. "I'll be happy to take his place. My things are ready. This will be a good opportunity to learn Roman customs."

Seanan blinked, surprised to have his idea accepted before he even offered it. "I thought you hated traveling...always so attached to home."

"When mother needed me, that was true, but now she has you. Besides, Georgios could use my help."

"Ah!" Seanan stroked his chin. "Though I am the clan leader, I'm barely one step ahead of my son. You're always kind enough to let me feel like I'm in charge."

With stoic composure, Ian deadpanned his answer. "You are a giant among men."

Seanan laughed, thumping Ian on the back. "I'll miss you with all my heart, but I can think of no other man I'd rather entrust on this mission." He glanced around and then returned his gaze to his son. "After Rome, take Georgios to Patmos. You'll learn a great deal and might even turn a profit." He shrugged. "Rueben might be right, and you'll find a new god for us to worship."

Seanan rubbed his temple, a headache building between his eyes. "Wait, no, don't. I can hardly keep up with the ones we have. I'm swamped with Gutun's devotions. Just be thankful he won't be going with you."

With a grimace, Ian turned his attention to the bustling village. "The feast is ready. I won't be with my family again for a long time, and I mean to make the most of tonight."

~~~

Georgios enjoyed the food and festivities, though he was a bit uncomfortable as the guest of honor.

A few stars twinkled through the misty veil. The air cooled with a breeze blowing in from the north.

The hogs turned to perfection, and boards laden with fish, eggs, honey, and breads put everyone in a convivial mood.

Even Alexios and Marcos were allowed to join in. The pleasure of seeing the last of the Roman warriors leave in dejection made the entire clan generous.

Offering a magnificent speech, Seanan stood tall and proud, while the crowd reclined comfortably in a circle. He recounted his adventures with Georgios: a skinny, sickly boy. But under Seanan's training and skillful direction, he drew the man from the child.

Men laughed, women chuckled, and everyone grinned at Georgios, but he was too aware of their generosity to be easily offended. He was more inclined to smile than frown and to accept all forms of raillery as well meant.

Rueben sat next to Alexios and Marcus, his expression as unreadable as theirs.

As the night grew old and cold, the mead and ale were
~~~

consumed in larger quantities and laughter turned exuberant.

When the clan became the most raucous, Gutun stepped out of the shadows. He wore his ceremonial robe and a stern expression.

Hushed silence fell, as if the father of a naughty brood of children had come upon them in the middle of their mischief. Laughter died and gazes dropped.

Georgios watched, perplexed. He couldn't imagine what Gutun had planned, but from the expressions of fear and dismay around the circle, no one expected anything fun.

~~~

Gutun lifted his arms to initiate the drama. "Sons of old, I bring you good tidings! I have read the signs of the times. We shall know good fortune for generations to come. Rome will never enter our lands again. We will enjoy prosperity while Rome will fall to destruction."

Groggy minds tried to follow Gutun's words. Several nodding heads attested to the lateness of the hour and the strength of the ale. Seanan covered a yawn.

Gutun would not have his moment dimmed. He raised his cup in offering. "There are many gods to thank for our success. We must pay them proper homage. The strangers in our midst do not know our traditions, so they must stand and offer a toast for their salvation." He handed his cup to Seanan. "As clan leader, you set the example and drink to the health of our gods. Then pass the cup to the travelers."

~~~

Seanan struggled to his feet. He had been having a

good time, but the scent of morning was in the air, and birds stirred in their nests. It was time to finish this celebration so that he could attend to the duties of the day. Unsteady, he had to step closer to Gutun to grasp the cup. He drank a good measure and then tried to decide who should have it next.

Gutun bumped Seanan's arm, knocking the cup aside. He snatched it, poured in another full measure and with a wide grin handed it back to Seanan, nudging him toward Rueben.

Irritated, Seanan drew back. He hated it when Gutun touched him. Such long, dirty fingers made him feel as if death were trying to grab him. Instinctively, he did the opposite of what Gutun wanted. Alexios certainly looked like he needed a drink.

With furrowed brow and confused eyes, Alexios shook his head in refusal.

Quick to save Alexios any discomfort, Marcus accepted on his behalf. He took the cup and drank deeply.

Gutun's cheeks flushed, and he seethed with spittle forming on his lips. He clawed at the cup.

Seanan slapped Gutun's hand away. "Stop, you idiot! This was your idea. Remember?" He looked around and met Rueben's stern expression. Clearly, he rebelled at the thought of drinking to a foreign god. Only Georgios and Ian were left.

Gutun's fingers darted as he spluttered, "Give it to me! It's not your place to offer to the gods!"

Weariness mixed with rage boiled Seanan's blood. "Oh? Why don't you enjoy good fortune yourself! Here, take a drink!" He smashed the cup into Gutun's face.

Gutun jerked backward.

Georgios stood and reached for the cup. "Stop. I'll drink. Then we can end—"

Ian called out. “Wait! Something is wrong with the Roman.”

Marcus clutched the air as spasms rippled over his body.

Ian jerked forward, knocking Seanan aside.

The mead splashed on Gutun’s face. “Aye!” He leapt to his feet, frantically wiping his lips.

All eyes snapped to Marcus as he fell limp, his eyes wide and terror-stricken. The frantic struggle, sudden and horrible, ended abruptly.

Alexios screamed, “No!” as he grabbed Marcus’ tunic and shook him as if to wake the man from slumber.

Georgios knelt at his father’s side, pried his fingers free, and closed Marcus’ eyes.

As one body, all eyes turned to Gutun.

Gutun jumped to his feet and pointed accusingly from Marcus to Alexios and finally to Rueben. His high-pitched scream sent early birds screeching from their nests into the dawn. “The gods have judged! They are guilty of heinous crimes. Kill them, now!”

A raucous din of voices rose as clansmen argued in favor or against the clan priest.

Seanan thrust his arms into the air, demanding silence. His voice matched his mood, furious and quite sober. He glared at Gutun. “I was going to offer that cup to my son! Georgios, who fought against our enemy, was about to drink from that cup! Of course, you wanted me to give it to Rueben first!” Rage blinded Seanan. “You wanted me to poison your rival? You devil!” Seanan swung at Gutun, but his encounters with the resplendent jug of ale ruined his aim.

Gutun ducked.

The fearful crowd sobered quickly, offering no response.

Tainair grabbed Gutun's shoulder. "You've escaped the punishment due a traitor once too often. We can't trust you to live any longer."

Ronan stepped up and gripped Gutun's other shoulder.

Together, the two men forced Gutun onto his knees.

Seanan slipped his knife from his belt.

Stunned, Gutun stared wild-eyed, his gaze darting around the crowd. "The gods will demand your blood if you harm a hair—"

Georgios clutched Ronan's arm. "Wait! I was an outsider and yet you welcomed me. My father was your enemy, and yet you allowed him to live. You have done no wrong in offering forgiveness. Let me take Gutun into exile. Then you will be free of him without blood on your hands."

Seanan glared at Georgios as he spoke, his words flying in a spluttering spray. "I don't *mind* killing him, Georgios! It will be my pleasure!" He stared hard at Gutun. "I will rid the world of his treachery!"

His arms flapping helplessly, Georgios shook his head. "But—"

Rueben gripped Gutun's shoulder, as if claiming him. "He meant to kill me, so he's mine."

Seanan tried to regain control of the situation. "He must die!"

Rueben stared Seanan in the eye. "In the end, he may prefer death." In silent understanding, Georgios and Rueben asked for rope, bound Gutun hand and foot, and led him away.

Seanan faced his eldest son. "What just happened?"

With red-rimmed eyes and a face drained of all color, Ian offered a weak smile. "Many think that the gods will seek vengeance if we kill their priest. This way, if he lives or dies, it'll be the providence of the gods."

Seanan pursed his lips in a petulant pout. “It won’t break my heart if he falls overboard during the journey. He’d survive. He’s the sort that always does.”

Chapter Thirty

We Need to Know

-OldEarth-

Noman loved proper ceremony. Irritation surged through him at the anti-climactic ending to Gutun's plans. Surprised by the stomach-churning reaction in his human form, Noman wandered through the village dressed as a simple merchant. With a sack of ornate knives that he had designed himself, simple and utilitarian, nothing to arouse suspicions or envy, he strolled about, eyeing the human specimens. Dirty, slump-shouldered, a defeated lot.

A piercing gaze caught his eye. A horned god-man carved into the trunk of a tree set his nerves quivering. CERNUOUS. Noman ran his fingers along the letters. He had seen something like this before. *Where?*

Ah, yes, Armand worshiped a snake-man figure—the same demonic power emanated from the figure that the Parthian schemer stoked with incense.

"You like it?"

Nearly tripping over his robes, Noman whirled around, his heart pounding.

A little girl with long, wind-blown hair stood with her hands behind her back. A dark wrap draped from her shoulders, covering a simple tunic. Her eyes shone against the drab colors. Her bare feet, calloused and dirty, stood wide apart, ready to run at a moment's notice.

Aghast at being directly addressed, Noman deformed his figure by tiny degrees, emanating a distinctly unpleasant odor. "Yes, of course. Beauty ought to be appreciated." He grinned, revealing black and broken teeth—a sight to frighten away any child.

Except this one, apparently.

Undeterred, the girl squinted through red-rimmed eyes. "It's one of Gutun's favorites. He enjoys his gods, he does."

Noman glanced around.

No one appeared to care that the child conversed with an ugly stranger.

Noman stepped closer and wrapped a hazy shroud around them. He grinned disarmingly. "What do the gods really have to offer, do you think?"

Tilting her head, her eyes rolling to the sky, the child took a moment to think.

Startled and nearly impressed, Noman stared at the other carvings on the ancient tree—figures carrying swords, staves, hammers, and lightning bolts. He rubbed his chin. Humans made the most of their primitive tools.

"They give us power." She grinned. "My da says the whole world conspires against him, and he'd do about anything to even the odds."

Noman's gaze swiveled back to the child. A shimmer ran down his arms. He nodded, banishing the murky charm.

"Hey, Aife! Come, girl. Give your mother a hand!"

Noman watched the small body scamper away, kicking up dirt as she pelted to the center of the village, where a ragged woman waited, one arm clutching a sack, a jug of water at her feet.

He surveyed the village, trying to see who had the unearthly power to alert his senses to such a degree.

The Luxonian was near—the one with his son. Crestonians annoyed him, while Ingots were a distinct bore, but Luxonians? *You sent a spy, Abbas?* He pursed his lips and considered the child's words. Power was key. Humans would do anything for control over their lives.

All he had to do was offer something worthwhile. Georgios and his friends would sink lower than beasts.

And the Luxonian could report the facts faithfully.

Clapping his hands free of dirt, Noman rounded the tree and blinked away.

–Helm–

Abbas sank onto the glossy hardwood bench amid the fragrant, tall-stemmed flowers and breathed deeply. “Only Bhuacs can create such beauty. It’s one of your many gifts.”

In her matronly elfin-style appearance, Song knelt in the vegetable section, snipping off ripe heads and pulling luscious roots. She placed each piece into a wide basket, her gaze flickering from plant to plant. “Fruitfulness and healing are our vocations. Some beings are warriors. Others guides, messengers, truth-tellers…” She glanced back and met Abbas’ gaze. “Some mere destroyers.”

Abbas stood, and paced along the narrow path. “I can’t do this without you.”

Song stood, arching her back. “Do what? Refuse your own?”

Abbas stopped, frustration sizzling through his dignified body. “Noman wants to prove that The Event was a mistake. He’s insecure about his place in the universe.”

“Your place, you mean.”

“All our places!” As his form shimmered, threatening disintegration, Abbas snatched a tall, red flower. The stem snapped, and the flower drooped, broken and unlovely. Disgusted, he tossed it aside.

Her jaws clenched as her gaze followed the destroyed plant. Song glared at him. “Noman is yours. Not mine!”

He threw his head back and laughed, bile rising. "He belongs to all of us! Given the right circumstances, we all betray our better selves."

"He is faithless. The Bhuaci are faithful."

"You're right…but incomplete. Can't you see? The danger he threatens us with is not simply the degeneration of the human race—that we could withstand—but the loss of what The Event represents. Hope. That we can rise. We can grow beyond our worst weakness and limitations."

Gripping her basket in hand, Song stepped from the garden and onto the path. Her long white dress flowed like a shimmering stream at midday. "No. We can't."

His heart spasming, Abbas pressed his hand to his chest. He needed a less alarming body.

With a deep breath, Song reached into the basket and pulled out a flower like the one Abbas had tossed away, perfectly preserved, its roots still attached. "I picked this earlier. I didn't know why. Just a silly inclination, or so I thought." She peered into his eyes. "There is more to this universe than we understand. No one is delivered from evil without help."

Breathing once again, Abbas fought tears welling in his eyes. "You will help me, then?" He held out his hand.

Song clasped it.

–OldEarth–

Ark paced along the shore, his tentacles perched on his hips, making him look like an irate school master fed up with his students' antics. "Surely, you're done! How long can it take?"

Zuri's head popped above the waves; he spluttered. "You're the water-creature! You should be doing this."

His eyes widening in horror, Ark smacked the air. "I

am a scientist, not a mechanic!"

"Scientist-smientist! I've done all I can with this thing." Zuri heaved himself out of the water and onto shore. He flopped onto the wet sand. "Bhuaci are glorious beings with the most perfect sense of beauty—but they don't know a blessed thing about shipbuilding."

"I thought they bought it from a Uanyi trader?"

Zuri rolled his eyes, resting his case.

"We need Teal. He's good at fixing things. Or maybe Cerulean can take a look. Children love to prove their worth."

Climbing to his feet, Zuri wrung water from his shoulder-length hair. "I already sent word—"

Teal and Cerulean appeared on the shore, grinning. Cerulean laughed. "He was waiting for you to say something. Here we are! Ready to save you."

Bubbles frothed as Ark glanced at Zuri, whose brows lowered noticeably.

Teal patted Cerulean on the shoulder. "That's not exactly what I meant."

In a flash, Cerulean disappeared.

Ark copied Zuri's astonished expression. They turned to the waves. "Did he—?"

Teal shrugged. "You're right. Children like to prove themselves." He scratched his chin. "Never ceases to amaze me." He looked at Ark. "You might want to give your pod a chance to prove himself."

Straightening to his full height, wishing his eyes were embedded with lasers, Ark decided this was an apt time to reveal the facts. "Just so you know what's really important, I have discovered a foreign signature on this planet. Someone—a certain Mysterious someone—has been gallivanting about the place. Probably wants to take over Earth and use it as a resort."

Zuri slapped his forehead. “For a moment, I thought you were serious.”

Teal shook his head. “Let’s get off the shore. We’re too exposed.” He headed inland to a grove of windswept trees.

Zuri pointed at the ocean. “Uh, what about—”

“He’ll let me know when he’s ready.” Teal shrugged. “Children like to manage their own affairs. Trust me. I learned the hard way.” He tromped forward.

Ark mumbled as he took up the rear. “I was serious, Ingot. There is a Mysterious being wandering around our planet, doing God-knows-what.” He stumbled over his thick boots.

Zuri stopped, grabbed one of Ark’s tentacles, and tugged him like a boat in tow. “I’m more interested in The Event—or The Events, really. Why does everyone act like there was just one?”

Huffing with the labor of land-travel, Ark hunched his shoulders. “The birth didn’t matter so much. Everyone gets born. And the miracles were interesting. At least, the ones I read about in the reports. But the dying and rising—I must admit—spooked me. Couldn’t sleep properly for five cycles.”

Teal glanced back. “We’re here to protect our own and that means keeping an eye on humanity. If someone is interested in them—we need to know why.”

“So, the restrictions have been lifted?” Ark arched his brows.

Teal stomped ahead. “Obviously. I suspect that we aren’t the only ones worried.”

Zuri shrugged off the concern. “If a Mystery being is here, then they can figure The Event out for themselves.”

Ark snorted. “Unless they can’t. Which means they need our help. That’s why they let us come.” He stopped and pointed to his feet. “Oh, they’re aching!”

Zuri sighed and glared meaningfully at Teal. The two gripped Ark around the middle and scooted him to the sheltering trees.

CHAPTER THIRTY-ONE

LET GOD DECIDE

—THE MEDITERRANEAN SEA—

Rueben did his duty on board the merchant ship in taciturn silence. He was not in a humor to engage in pleasantries or offer commentaries on the events of the day. Confusion pressed on his mind like a heavy burden. Only Alexios or Gutun could awaken his sympathy. Occasionally, he'd stop to speak to them, though they rarely answered direct questions.

The journey south across the blue-green sea toward the mainland took less time than anyone expected, as the winds were favorable to flying over the gushing crests. The sun shone bright and hot, and the days remained beautiful.

Attending to his duties like a seasoned sea traveler, which now included looking after his father and checking on Gutun, Georgios' good mood remained intact. He managed the pleasantries of harmless conversation with the crew as if he had been born to it.

Alexios and Gutun were little trouble, thanks to the mercies of others. For the most part, the crew ignored them.

By the time they reached shore and started on their overland journey, all the men were familiar with each other and their part in the shared labor. They knew each other's qualities so intimately that they marched swiftly to the nearest city and engaged in prosperous trade.

All through spring and into the summer, they continued on, traveling by ship and on foot and trading along the way.

Only Alexios did not prosper. He lost weight and winced in pain spasmodically. He rarely spoke, remaining stoic, as the men around him hurried about their appointed tasks.

In deepening depression, Rueben remembered Marcus' tormented death, and his spirits fell even further. Was there any purpose to human suffering or did one simply travel about in self-made importance, only to be struck down without rhyme or reason?

As a bright sun sank toward the horizon, Rueben once again found himself on board a small merchant ship.

Georgios edged his way near, stopping a few feet away. He clasped and unclasped his hands like a petulant child.

Irritated but uncertain as to why Georgios' presence annoyed him, Rueben draped a coil of rope on a peg and leaned against the railing. He masked his discomfort with a forced grin. "Something wrong?"

Georgios stepped closer, unusually hesitant. "W-we hardly talk anymore. You're so quiet. What's happened to you?"

Tight with suppressed anger, Rueben shrugged. "I have little to say. Only Alexios understands my misery."

Flushing a dark red under his sunburnt skin, Georgios lifted his chin. "What's this? I've done everything possible to take good care of him, while still supporting you and everyone aboard ship. What more could I have done?"

Rueben turned and faced the sea. Dark clouds loomed on the horizon. "You never talk to Alexios."

Clutching the rail beside his friend, Georgios faced the turbulent scene. His shoulders slumped. "You, a Jew, feel sorry for a Roman soldier! Has the world gone mad?" He stared until, with a sigh, he turned his back on the mounting waves. "We live in different worlds now. I can never train under him, and he can't return home with me."

Every clear thought drained away in weariness. Rueben exhaled a long breath. "Just tell him that you love him."

Tense with pent-up emotion, Georgios pounded across the deck. "What have I been doing all these weeks? Have I not proven that a hundred times over?" Suddenly, Georgios narrowed his eyes and lowered his voice. "Why do you spend time with him, Rueben? What do you say to the man who serves the army that destroyed your temple and was the ruin of your people?"

As if a candle had blown out, the sky darkened. Feverous waves crested higher.

Dismissing Georgios' fury, Rueben shrugged. "I wanted to know what kind of man could serve the Roman army—yet bear a son like you."

"What…did you learn?"

Lost in a reverie, Rueben leaned over the railing and gazed at the wild waves crashing against the ship, ridiculous swirls in an oversized pond. "Alexios reminds me of my father: strong, determined, sure of himself." He turned his back on the waves, swallowed hard, and met Georgios' intense gaze. "He isn't a monster. He's weak and suffering, confused by life. I find that I can't hate him. I tried to hate Gutun to fill the emptiness, but even that doesn't work. In a fit of madness, I spoke with the stupid man and discovered that he's not worth my hate." Rueben closed his eyes. "Lord, I feel so empty inside."

His eyes wide with surprise, Georgios chuckled. "What a pair we make!"

A torrential spray of seawater splashed over the deck and drenched them both. Black clouds circled overhead.

Rueben shoved Georgios toward the doorway. "It's getting dangerous. Head below. It is not safe to stay on top in one of these."

Georgios glanced around wildly. "My father! We must

get Gutun and my father to safety."

Rueben nodded. "Gutun went below earlier. We'll manage Alexios together."

The clouds broke and rain poured down in sheets, spraying across the deck. As the ship pitched, the crew swore, working frantically and pleading with every god they knew to save them.

Rueben and Georgios found Alexios shivering in a corner and hoisted him below.

The hold, dark and dank, stank of sweat, spoiled food, and wood rot.

Gutun crouched against a back wall.

Finding a dry place, Rueben and Georgios maneuvered Alexios against the wall and made him comfortable, draping a blanket around his shoulders.

Georgios turned to the doorway.

Gutun crawled next to Alexios, huddling at his side.

Alexios' eyes, wide and desperate, watched his son climb the steps.

In a flash of sympathetic understanding, Rueben called out, "Georgios, wait! Keep your father company. If we need help, I'll come get you."

Confusion flooding his face, Georgios frowned at Rueben. Then his eyes darted to his father. He retreated down the steps and stopped in front of Rueben, his gaze fierce. "Swear by all you hold dear that you'll call me if there is the slightest need."

For the first time in weeks, a spark of hope kindled inside Rueben. If reconciliation could heal the wounds deep inside, then life was not mad happenstance. He placed his hands over his heart. "I swear." Then he ran up the steps.

~~~
~~~

Georgios crouched next to his father as the storm raged overhead. Despite his anxiety, sleep burdened his eyelids, forcing them to close. A tug on his arm jerked him to wakefulness.

Alexios leaned forward, peering at him.

Like returning to a nightmare, Georgios remembered the storm and his father's illness. "Yes, Father?"

Alexios rubbed his legs and nodded. His hoarse voice barely rose above the pounding storm. "I need...to explain."

Georgios frowned. He couldn't decipher his father's meaning, and he had no energy to try. He only wanted the storm to end and to get above deck into the warm sunshine. "Keep your strength, Father."

With his trembling hand, Alexios gripped Georgios' sleeve, his eyes brimming with desperation. "Now."

Fear filled Georgios, but he could not refuse. He nodded.

"My father was orphaned young. When he married my mother, he accepted her God—the God of Israel." Alexios swallowed convulsively, gagging.

Georgios glanced around for the water barrel.

Gutun pulled a wineskin from a deep recess of his robe. His hand shaking, he held it out to Alexios.

Shocked at this kindness, Georgios froze.

Gutun shook the wineskin, grunting like an animal that has lost the power of speech yet refuses to be ignored.

Georgios plucked the wineskin from the Druid's hand and tipped it to Alexios' mouth.

Alexios took several sips and wiped his mouth with a dirty fist.

Though he was thirsty, the sour wine repelled Georgios. He handed it back.

Gutun snatched it and gulped down a long draught.

Alexios crossed his skinny arms over his knees, staring at the ground. "My father fought alongside the Jews. Just a boy, I was sent to Greece, raised by a scholar who cared nothing for me."

Georgios watched his father's face crumple.

Struggling with his emotions, Alexios shook himself. "I learned of the destruction in hushed whispers. The temple destroyed. Innocents murdered. I wondered why God allowed such an affliction to admonish His own people."

Tears welled in Georgios' eyes.

"When I was grown, I traveled far and wide. I found my father still alive, a shrunken man with poor vision who could neither read nor write."

Astonished, Georgios lifted his head and stared. "Your father survived?"

"My father but not my mother or sister. I could find no other relatives. I had neither family nor a home."

"But your father?"

"Humiliated by his poverty and ignorance, I left him and joined the Roman army."

Georgios squeezed his eyes shut and asked, "How could you abandon him?" His voice sounded high and strained, like a little boy's whine.

"We lost everything. There was no hope. I wanted success, not failure. I met your mother and started a new life."

Georgios blinked back tears. "You were never really a Jew then? Unlike your father, you never joined the family."

Exhausted by his efforts, Alexios closed his eyes and leaned against the wall, drained like an empty wineskin.

Georgios propped his head on his hands as Rueben's stories—Noah, Abraham, Isaac, Jacob, and Joseph—

crowded his thoughts. Moses should have died with the male infants of his generation but was spared for a purpose designed by God. Samuel advised kings. David, a shepherd boy, became a king. Solomon had been the wisest of all. The Maccabees, valiant brothers, held off defeat with noble courage. Georgios squirmed. How could his father have forsaken such a lineage?

The ship lurched.

Men yelled.

Gutun whimpered.

Alexios remained wrapped in his blanket, huddling like a child.

Contrary to his expectations, pride surged like fresh water through Georgios. Everyone met defeat eventually, but only those who never gave in outlasted failure and became worthy of renown.

Georgios eyed his father and then grasped his limp hand. “You lost hope, but I’m not ashamed of my heritage.”

Gutun shivered, his eyes wide with confusion.

Rising to his knees, Georgios stared at Gutun. “Make yourself useful. Take care of my father while I go above to see if I can help.”

Gutun scooted closer to Alexios.

Georgios looked from Gutun to his father. “The journey isn’t over. Don’t give up.” He mounted the steps and entered the maelstrom.

Heavy rain clogged the air. Waves crashed over the ship’s sides. The sea’s tempestuous roar collided with the crew’s shouts.

As the sea tossed the ship about, Georgios had to grip the wall and then clutch the railing to stay on his feet. He searched the deck.

Rueben and two others hauled thick ropes, wrestling with a sail overhead, attempting to turn it.

Struggling to keep his balance, rain pelting his face, Georgios pulled himself along until he grasped Rueben's shoulder.

Rueben threw Georgios a glance. Soaked from head to toe and squinting against the splattering rain, he maneuvered the sail into position.

"Where are we?" Georgios shouted, repeating the question twice before Rueben shook his head.

"Somewhere between heaven and hell!" A timber fell from above and toppled over the side. "It's not safe! Get below!"

"Gutun is near despair."

Rueben rubbed water from his eyes and grabbed a dangling rope as another lurch sent the ship listing. "He's not the only one. We're worn out, but the storm won't give way."

The crew clung to their supports while the ship groaned, lurching in her agony. "Lost at sea. It's a common fate."

Georgios shook his fist in the air. "I'll not give up! We still have much to accomplish!"

"Men die every day, Georgios."

Glaring at the black clouds, Georgios whispered, "Let God decide." He hugged the nearest post and stared into the storm, seeing something. His heart leapt as he pointed. "Mountains in the distance."

Rueben clutched the railing, fear and hope battling for supremacy in his eyes.

The rain slowed, and the wind calmed. Breaking through a curtain of fog, land appeared before their eyes, beautiful as a sunrise. The crew sailed at a brisk pace toward their salvation.

Suddenly the captain shouted, “Rocks! Turnabout!”

Georgios worked as hard as any, perspiring under the newfound sun. A lurching movement caught his eye.

Alexios, with Gutun’s aide, staggered upon the deck. Both ashen and stooped, they shuffled forward with their hands out for balance.

After tossing his rope to another man, Georgios sprang to his father’s side. “What’re you doing? It is not safe yet.”

Alexios lifted his wavering hand. “Stop fighting the wind. Soften her flight, but do not restrain her too much. Allow the ship to turn towards shore with a gentle curve. She’ll nest there.” He pointed emphatically. “You’ll see. I’ve been here before.”

Rueben hurried to the captain.

Georgios gripped his father’s arm, and Gutun hurried into the shadows. “You’ve done a noble—”

With a wave, Alexios cut his son’s comment short. “I did what I was trained to do.”

Georgios rubbed his aching head. “But I thought—”

“I had given up?” Alexios smiled weakly. “Not yet.”

After heaving over the side, Gutun leaned upon the railing, his face pale and his arms shaking.

Georgios reached out to guide him to the floor.

Gutun slapped his hand. “Don’t touch me! I’ve spent myself beseeching the gods for our salvation.”

“Georgios!” Rueben called from where he stood beside the Captain.

As he darted forward, Georgios mumbled over his shoulder. “You think too well of yourself and of your gods, Druid.”

Like a spent rag, Gutun slid to the ground.

With a somber expression, Alexios faced east.

As Georgios came to rest at Rueben's side, he gazed across the calm ship and out to sea. Relief settled his heart and gladness filled his soul.

CHAPTER THIRTY-TWO

THE FORTUNE OF CHANCE

—CARTHAGE—

Lysander did not intend to spend his life being a miserable servant to a miserable master. Endowed with a conscience that spoke loud and clear, he found that when a recent business deal turned cruel, he could not agree to the transaction. He was paid back with treachery. All his hopes were dashed by his ill-timed goodwill, and he was slandered near and far.

But when he put his mind to it, Lysander could manage sly tricks as well as any man. As long as he appeased his conscience with noble deeds, he was satisfied. But this impossible mission from Myron made him uneasy. He traveled halfway around the known world and found nothing to satisfy his conscience or his employer.

Georgios had disappeared off the face of the Earth.

Lysander returned to the island of Patmos intending to face the disappointment of Myron, but his employer no longer lived there. Myron had left his estate in the care of an old servant, with the cryptic message that he had gone "to discover the truth." Absurd! And from a man normally in command of himself, too.

Flummoxed, Lysander wandered aimlessly until a worthy transaction took him to Carthage, where he got drunk and decided to spend his life talking politics and philosophy, while believing in nothing and caring for no one.

In a happy state of haziness, he sat in a public house, expecting the usual afternoon crowd. When a miserable group of castaways came through the doors, he grinned.

He loved a good tale, and this looked like an assembly that could fill his empty hours with details of a bold and disappointing adventure—his favorite kind of story.

A long-haired, muscled young man led the group and spoke in low tones to the innkeeper, who took a long appraising look at the things held out for inspection and then beckoned the wayfarer to a back room. The other refugees glanced about for a place to make themselves comfortable.

The leader and a second young fellow followed the innkeeper, directing the others to wait.

A third young man clasped the arm of an older, clearly ill man and led him to a corner piled high with cushions. They promptly sat down.

The shabbiest fellow among the set sidled into the room and found a place not too close to make anyone uncomfortable but not so distant that he couldn't see and hear everything that was said.

Lysander watched the disheveled crew with mocking interest. After they settled, he lifted his carafe of wine in salute. "Join me in a salutation to the gods, for it has been a warm day, and we could use a cooling breeze!"

The shabby fellow wasted no time. He ambled to Lysander's table and bowed. "We are poor, shipwrecked men who have barely made it to shore—no one else has offered us such kindness. I'm Gutun, a Druid priest, and I'd be happy to read your fortune. My gods are as powerful as any upon the earth."

Lysander motioned for one of the serving boys to bring more cups, and the boy retreated into an inner chamber. Lysander beckoned the others to come nearer. "Come! Don't be afraid. I mean no harm. I have the means to be generous today. Let me offer you food and drink, and you can regale me with your adventures, for I like nothing better than a good story." Lysander bellowed out an order and an answering yell boomed from the inner room.

A weary smile spread over Gutun's face.

One of the young men led the frail man closer. "I am Georgios, and this is my father, Alexios of Rome."

Lysander motioned for them to sit on the bench across from him.

The serving boy returned with mugs, thick bread, and a bowl piled with fruit.

"Anything else, sir?"

Lysander waved him off. "More of everything! These men have suffered and need material comfort."

The boy bowed and retreated again.

Gutun helped himself to the bread and wine.

On closer inspection of the old man, Lysander frowned at Georgios while pointing at Alexios. "The old man is ill? Do you need a doctor?"

Georgios poured his father a cup of wine and placed it before him.

Alexios ignored it, staring vacantly across the room.

Returning his attention to his host, Georgios met his gaze. "That's why we came here. Our ship was caught in a storm, and we landed off the coast several leagues away. We salvaged what we could, and our men are making repairs, but we fear it's in vain, for the ship may never recover. We were told that there's a doctor in the village, so we came to ask for his services."

"Yes, there is a doctor here. I will send for him." He called the boy and gave him new orders. With an exaggerated bow, Lysander introduced himself. "My name is Lysander—of many lands."

Georgios bowed. "Thank you for your kindness. I will replay you as soon as I can."

Lysander smiled. "You're from Rome, eh? So is half

the world. Though my grandmother was Persian and my grandfather Greek, I carry in my veins Roman, barbarian, and even a smattering of Jewish lineage long past."

Tearing off a piece of bread, Georgios glanced at his father. "You do not class the Jews with the barbarians, then?"

Lysander scoffed and poured out a generous cup of wine and placed it before Georgios. "Would I do such an ignorant thing? I'm proud of my Jewish blood. As a matter of fact, I wish I had more of it." His eyes slid to where the two young men had gone with the innkeeper. "Your companion is a Jew, if I don't miss my guess."

"Rueben is, but Ian is from the Celtic lands." He motioned toward Gutun. "And you have already met Gutun."

Giddy with the magnificent assembly, Lysander grinned. *Such a collection! Most interesting*! "Ah, yes, the Druid." He met Gutun's interested gaze. "I travel a good deal, and I make it my business to know something about everything!"

Gutun sipped his wine and broke off a large chunk of the bread.

The serving boy returned, offering fresh wine and bread to the other men sitting at nearby tables.

Lysander motioned for them all to partake. "Please, eat and take your ease. You're among friends here." Suspicion tickled his imagination. He waited until Georgios ate a few bites and sipped his wine before beginning again. "So, tell me about your journey, then. Where are you from and where were you going when you were driven off course?"

Alexios took a draught of wine and chewed his bread thoughtfully. Color suffused his cheeks, and his eyes gained more focus.

An older serving boy distributed hard cheeses and ripe figs.

Gutun snatched the offerings eagerly.

Lysander waved to Georgios, who offered cheese to his father.

Alexios accepted it with trembling hands.

"Thank you, Lysander." Georgios held his cup and leaned against the wall. "In gratitude, I'll tell you of our recent adventures."

Pleased that his evening entertainment was so fortuitously arranged, Lysander leaned against the wall and listened with delight, imagining every detail.

Chills ran down Lysander's spine as he listened to Georgios' recounting of his personal adventure, his leaving Patmos in search of his father, his joining with Rueben, his service with Seanan, the battle with the Romans on the Celtic lands, and his reunion with his father. Lysander suspected that many unpleasant details had been left out, but the story proved remarkable, nonetheless. The coincidence that here sat the very man he had been searching far and wide for left him breathless.

As if wearied by his storytelling effort, Georgios refreshed himself with more bread and wine.

A question burned on Lysander's lips; his head spun with the fortune of chance.

Ian and Rueben strode into the room laughing.

Georgios stood and took a step forward.

Lifting his hand, Ian stalled him. "We've made arrangements to stay here a few days. A doctor will come this evening to see your father. The innkeeper knows of another ship that'll leave for Rome in a week or so. We'll make arrangements with them then. In the meantime, you might as well get comfortable. Rueben and I will scout out the town."

After climbing to his feet, Lysander bowed in his most gracious manner. "You must be exhausted. Refresh yourselves first and join our company."

Ian grinned as he rubbed his belly. "The innkeeper doesn't have an empty room back there. Once we came to an agreement, he was very generous. We'll be back soon." Ian started toward the doorway.

Rueben hung back, gripping Georgios' shoulder, his gaze flicking to Alexios. "How is he?"

"The food does him good. We'll wait to see what the doctor says. Perhaps he'll have medicine to ease his pain." He sighed. "Go and have a good time." He nodded to Lysander. "Our host has been very kind."

After Ian and Rueben sauntered out with most of the other men in tow, Georgios returned to his seat and faced Lysander. He frowned. "Are you all right? You look rather pale."

Lysander inhaled a deep breath and leaned closer. "Answer one question. Do you have a grandfather named Myron?"

Georgios and Alexios glanced at each other and then at Lysander, astonishment in their eyes.

Lysander grinned. "Now, I've got a good story for you."

CHAPTER THIRTY-THREE

VICTORY RISING

—PARTHIAN TOWN—

Armand, named after the Parthian Empire when it was young and beautiful, never appreciated irony. His spine twisted as he grew, deforming his appearance, though his mind developed beyond the normal scope of men. Expressing an affinity to the gods, many believed he was favored with unique insights. His father sent him to the best scholars, and despite his unfortunate appearance, he made important friends and his future shone bright.

Until one day when a legion of Romans, full of strong wine and bitter from a recent embarrassment, marched through his village of Dara and unleashed their fury on the inhabitants. When the military line swept away after a daylong rampage, only sobbing voices and hazy smoke rose from the ruins.

Armand returned to his desolated home to discover that his future now lay sprawled across a bloody village.

As the remnant pulled itself together, so did Armand. He moved to another town, lived with a surviving uncle, and planned revenge. He found in his nephew Pacorus a handsome man so personable that few could resist his charm. With his nephew's beauty and his own connections, a new plan took shape. He called for a meeting.

On a bright morning, with a swaggering step and dressed in a flowing green and gold tunic with white trousers, Pacorus entered the banquet hall. "You called for me, Uncle?"

Resting his aching back on a pile of colorful pillows

and dressed in a belted white tunic over baggy trousers, Armand watched the young man through hooded eyes. He beckoned his nephew to his quiet corner.

With a graceful halt, Pacorus bowed low, a smile playing on his lips. "Most wise Uncle, I'm honored to be in your presence. How may I be of assistance?"

"I have an opportunity for you."

Pacorus' eyes gleamed.

"You're to travel to Jerusalem. It's nearly Passover, and you'll meet many people there. I'll give you money and letters of introduction. You'll attach yourself to one of the distinguished families and become their trusted friend and invaluable aide. When they return to Rome, you'll offer further assistance and become acquainted with their friends and anyone related to the king's household. Once you've been accepted, I'll give you further instructions."

Pacorus nodded, his mouth a firm line but his eyes shining. "I'll set out at once."

"Through the cultivation of powerful friends and the knowledge of their gods, I hold the keys to the Empire. All you have to do is become someone everyone wants to know."

Clasping Pacorus' arm, Armand labored to his feet. He gripped the young man's arm. "In the morning, I will introduce you to your guides. As the center of a religious maelstrom, Jerusalem is the perfect place to become indispensable to a lonely widow or an anxious elder. Take your time. Make sure that the family you choose plans to return to Rome. I'll meet you there. Together we will right a terrible wrong."

The two men ambled across the room, through the main doorway and into an open garden, alive with fresh flowers.

The sun sank behind distant mountains, while across the burnt-orange sky, birds sailed to lofty nests.

Armand inhaled the sweet scent of victory rising to the gods.

CHAPTER THIRTY-FOUR

TO HIS IMMENSE SURPRISE

—CARTHAGE—

Georgios choked on his wine.

Lysander laughed.

Ian, Rueben, Alexios, and Gutun stared at Lysander, their eyes wide and their mouths gaping.

Gutun lifted a trembling hand. "Arranged by the gods, so it is."

Ian grinned as he nudged Georgios in the arm. "You have luck beyond the lot of most men!"

Rueben shook his head. "In such a miracle, there is intent and purpose. Your grandparents need you. You must return home with all possible speed."

"But I-I..." Georgios stammered, turning to Alexios. "My father must return—"

"I've nothing to return to." His voice low, Alexios dropped his gaze to the floor. "I'm injured beyond repair. Rome will merely replace me and forget me, as is their custom."

Stunned, Georgios rose and paced across the room. "But what will you do? Where—" Georgios' face grew hot.

Alexios met Georgios' gaze. "I'll go with you."

Georgios sighed; a heavy weight pressed on his heart. "Rueben is right; my grandparents have waited long enough. We have good doctors on Patmos—"

"I'll join you then." Ian raised his glass. "Let's drink to our voyage!"

Rueben, Georgios, Alexios, and Ian lifted their cups in salutation.

Lysander fluttered his hand impatiently. "Wait, you are naming the wrong place. Myron isn't in Patmos. He went to Jerusalem to find some preacher or teacher called Jesus, who I hear is dead, but that doesn't seem to matter to anyone. Myron and Roxanna left months ago."

Dizzy with the constant turn of events, Georgios gripped the wall. "What? Have they given up on me?"

Lysander chuckled. "No, they'd been told by some wise man that you'd find your own way home."

Rueben jumped to his feet, a light in his eyes that had not been seen for months. "Let's go to Jerusalem, Georgios! It has been so long, and I've heard such things—"

"I'll go to Patmos first and see if my grandparents returned. At least then, my father will get the care he needs." He met the disappointed eyes of his friend. "But we'll go to Jerusalem after that. Even I'd like to learn about this God you seek."

Ian smiled and raised his drink again. "To Patmos and then on to Jerusalem!"

Reseating themselves, the young men began discussing their plans.

One bitter voice broke through the happy chatter. "And what about me?"

Rueben recovered first. "You'll come with us, Gutun. We'll see the wonders of the world together."

Like a forgotten child offered a place in the family, Gutun's eyes widened. "You won't leave me?"

Ian snarled, "You could stay."

"I have nothing to trade, no useful—"

Georgios took pity on the old man. "Come with us, Gutun, and perhaps my grandfather will welcome you."

Disgusted, Ian shook his head. He turned his attention, tapping Lysander on the shoulder. "How about you? You want to be reunited with your benefactor? Surely, Myron owes you!"

Lysander stretched out expansively. "I wouldn't mind traveling a bit and being paid, but I am afraid my position has been taken."

Georgios took another sip of wine and broke off a large piece of bread. "You found me. How could your position have been taken?"

"In his last message, Myron mentioned that he had acquired the perfect guide, some jewel of a man."

Georgios frowned. "I'll see that you're paid for your services. Come with us, Lysander. You can do no good here."

Lysander grinned. "I might learn a thing or two from this jewel from Jerusalem. Some men have all the luck." His grin widened. "With you all along, I might become one of them."

With a long, relieved sigh, Georgios patted his father's arm. To his immense surprise, Alexios patted him back.

CHAPTER THIRTY-FIVE

PRIDE AND JOY

—GAELIC LANDS—

Seanan exalted in his good fortune. The Romans were gone, Gutun was exiled, and best of all, his wife appeared to like him. Happiness settled in his heart.

Sitting on a tree stump, he stretched his legs and yawned.

As birds chirped their goodnight songs, a shout rang out, followed by high-pitched laughter, ending in evening quiet. Fading flowers swayed in a late summer breeze.

Ian and Georgios had been gone for months. He imagined them traveling in Rome, trading and possibly getting into trouble. Seanan frowned. Why had he let them go into the vicious world without him? He sighed. The die had been cast, and there was little he could do to change it now. He could only hope that Georgios would get to Patmos safely and Ian would grow homesick and return soon.

Fiona strolled forward, a smile hovering on her lips. She wrapped her arm around his neck and kissed him on the cheek.

Seanan nearly fell backward. He peered at her. Though she had become a cheerful companion, he couldn't deny a suspicious anxiety that raised the hair on his arms every time she drew near. When would the next transformation take place, and what it would mean for him?

Fiona perched on the trunk, nudging him over a bit. "Beautiful night." She inhaled a long breath as if to make her point clear.

Seanan nodded. "Like last night and the night before that—"

Fiona pinched his arm. "You know what I mean. I feel like Xana Mega, the queen of the fairies."

Seanan tilted his head, considering his wife. "I am no king, to be sure. I don't remember any stories of the Sidhe ever being attacked by Romans. Gaels maybe, but not Romans."

An anxious scowl marred Fiona's perfectly oval face. "But you're happy, aren't you?"

"Why?"

"Why?" Fiona's disbelieving echo matched her confused expression.

"You worried?" Seanan faced her, narrowing his eyes. "You're planning something, aren't you?"

A quick shake of her head denied the possibility. "Not at all. I simply like to imagine that we'll live here forever in perfect happiness. That's all."

"That's all!" Seanan snorted. "Happiness is never perfect. Do you remember when we were first married? You were terrified of me! You seemed to think I was a mad man."

"I still think that."

Seanan grinned. "We learned to help each other and when the children came along, we were happy, even if not perfectly."

"And then—"

"Our baby died, and you blamed me because Gutun lied."

Tears filled Fiona's eyes. "Do we have to discuss *that*?"

"I left home an injured man." He stared at the distant hills. "But I found solace in helping Rueben and Georgios. They would've been caught and sold, but with me, they were safe. I took good care of them."

Fiona wiggled one finger in humble protest. “Except for that incident with the Romans.”

Seanan shrugged. “We won, didn’t we? Rueben and Georgios grew into strong, valiant men under my care.”

Fiona’s shoulders hunched, and her smile dissolved. “So, you remember my mistakes and your goodness but nothing else?”

“I have a vivid memory of coming home to that strangling hug of yours.”

Not a trace of a smile lightened her expression.

Seanan tried again. “I also remember that I had a home to come back to because my wife and my sons remembered their duty. I remember that you lost a child and yet you never lost your love for your other children.” Seanan wrapped his arm around her and drew her close. “I remember a great deal.”

“But do you see what is before your eyes now?”

Seanan sighed, his chest tightening. “More than you think.” He looked around and frowned. “Where is Brighid?”

“At home. She’s tired, rather old to be having her first.” With a back-to-business expression, Fiona slipped out from under her husband’s arm and rose.

Disappointment filled Seanan. “Is that all you wanted to talk about? How beautiful the night is and how I should remember things?”

Tears filled Fiona’s eyes.

Shoving all resentment aside, Seanan stood and clasped his wife by the shoulders. “Don’t worry so. I won’t leave again. I wouldn’t have left in the first place if—”

Fiona covered her face. “Won’t you ever forget that?”

Seanan pulled her close, resting his head on hers. “I’ll let it go. It has done me no good anyway.” As a pulsing desire rose, Seanan stepped back. He battled his inclination and glanced around. “Let’s find Olcan. I’ve been wondering how he’s surviving—”

Fiona smacked his arm.

“I mean, how much he’s enjoying his married life.”

“Isadora loves him, so he’s doing quite well.”

His good mood bouncing back to full measure, Seanan grinned. “She’s just following your example.”

Fiona clasped his hand as they headed for home.

Olcan, with Earan at his side, intercepted them. An angry scowl marred his usually placid face. “Men from the north say that raiders are attacking villages along the coast. They haven’t come this far inland before, but they might now. We should be prepared.”

Seanan dropped Fiona’s hand. “How far away?”

Earan spoke up. “I’m not sure, but they’re aggressive. They have a mind to acquire new lands, it seems.”

Seanan gripped his son’s shoulder. “If we could defeat the Romans, we’ll defeat this threat as well.”

Evening shades of pinks and purples with streaks of gray clouds textured the sky.

A new sense of purpose filled Seanan. He was needed at home, and he’d never leave again.

CHAPTER THIRTY-SIX

FATHER AND SON

—ISLAND OF KOS—

Georgios suppressed a sigh as a throbbing ache rose from his middle. The distant Greek mountains, barren and rocky, reminded him of home. The stunted cypress and gnarled olive trees spoke volumes, bringing childhood memories fresh to mind. The Gallic lands he had left behind, lush and green and brimming with vegetation, made the contrast more startling. But this was familiar, the land of his birth.

A bittersweet joy filled him. He was so close to his anticipated return home, just a little further would have landed him on the Patmos shore, but fortune had led them to Kos first. With a raging fever, his father was sinking fast.

Hippocrates was from here, so physicians were held in high esteem. Engaging the services of a good one was easier than elsewhere, as they were all considered the best the world had to offer. At least, that was what everyone told him.

They soon found an inn and a kind attendant who promised to get his own physician to see to Alexios.

Georgios settled Alexios in a white-walled room with two large windows facing east, a neat abode with lush cushions and beautiful murals. Georgios knew it had been due to Ian's skill and Rueben's arguments that they had been able to secure such a high-quality arrangement.

The innkeeper, a garrulous old fellow, loved to recount stories about everyone who had ever stayed in the place.

The fact that Alexios was an ailing Roman warrior returning home with a long-lost son made a good tale to tell. Georgios suspected that before the night was out, he had already invented heartbreaking scenes between the beloved son and his stern father as the final leave-taking was forced upon them. The old man's dramatic skill was enough to make every woman for leagues around sob into her pillow.

Pushing all other thoughts away, Georgios tried to get his father to eat and drink.

With a wave, Alexios brushed his efforts off. "I'm not hungry." He took a sip of wine and leaned back on the pillows. "Please, just leave me in peace. There's nothing left to do but let me die."

With bowed head, Rueben stood in the back of the room in respectful silence.

Swallowing back a desire to coerce his father into trying once again, Georgios turned away.

A stout, dark-skinned man appeared in the doorway.

Irritated at his father's refusal to eat, Georgios scowled. "If you've come about the room—"

Rueben jogged forward, intercepting his friend. "Are you the physician our innkeeper sent for?"

The smile that broke across the wide face beamed with kindness and intelligence.

Relieved at the physician's arrival, Georgios led the stranger into the room. "Your patient, Alexios, is over here. I'm his son, Georgios."

The man's kindly face focused on Georgios. "The son is no less important than the father. My name is Kleitos, and I will do all I can to help you both."

Confused, Georgios glanced at Rueben, who stood watching the exchange with avid interest.

Kleitos crossed the room and took Alexios' hand. He spoke low, introducing himself and asking a series of questions.

Alexios mumbled his answers, though after a few moments, he attempted to sit up and clear his throat to speak more distinctly.

Kleitos held Alexios' wrist, listened to his heartbeat and the grumbling of his swollen stomach, checked his eyes, had him turn his head, and performed various other diagnostic procedures.

When Alexios' eyes drooped with exhaustion, Kleitos told him to rest, reassuring him that he would return soon.

Alexios lay down on the bed and closed his eyes.

With his hands clasped behind his back and his face grave, Kleitos strolled to where Georgios and Rueben had retreated, on the far side of the room. He motioned for them to follow him to an outer courtyard.

Questions darting through his head, Georgios stopped beside a bench beneath a large tree and faced the doctor.

Kleitos lifted his hand. "You are very anxious about your father, but I'll not lie. I have seen this sickness before. It is nearly impossible to cure at the best of times, but he is already in the last stages—"

Fury flooded Georgios; his face flushed. "In one visit, you can make such a despairing prognosis?"

Rueben pressed Georgios' shoulder. "We've all seen the signs. He's not telling us anything we didn't know. The surprising thing is that Alexios has lasted this long."

Kleitos nodded. "Yes, I was going to say that. Your father is alive for a reason."

Clenching his hands into tight fists, Georgios lost control and shouted, "What then? If you know so much, tell us why he has survived!"

Kleitos gestured towards a bench near a large, spreading tree.

They all sat and Kleitos faced them. "Remember what I said: the son is no less important than the father?" He glanced at Rueben. "May I be so bold as to inquire who you are?"

Laughing at mad absurdities, Georgios waved him aside. "He's a friend, Rueben. What you mean—"

"You are a Jew, are you not?" Kleitos rested his back against the bench as if he had all the time in the world.

Rueben leaned in, nudging Georgios. "Yes, I am. Does that bother you?"

Kleitos grinned. "Not in the least. I am also from that noble race. From a brilliant Jewish doctor, I learned to heal the sick."

Rueben's eyes narrowed. "But—"

Kleitos' smile softened. "Let me tell you a little story." He crossed his legs and relaxed his arm over the back of the bench. "I have always been a faithful Jew looking for the coming of the Messiah. I have seen the misery of our people. Sometimes I am able to heal, but at other times, I am forced to watch my patients die despite my best efforts.

"Some years ago, I heard about a man, Jesus of Nazareth, called the Son of the Living God. I wanted to see Him but then discovered He had died. I was disappointed, for the stories were most amazing. But a dead savior was of no use to me. Yet, one day, as I knelt weeping in prayer, I felt a presence and heard a voice say, "I am the God of the living. He who believes in Me shall never die." I was like a man struck deaf and dumb. I couldn't eat or sleep for days. In time, I realized that I must not just treat the body but also the spirit. My mission is to bring spiritual hope as much as physical healing."

His mouth dropping open, Rueben stared at the doctor.

"You know about the Nazarene? Tell me everything you know! I'll never betray my people, but I so long for hope."

Kleitos patted Rueben's shoulder. "God will help us both."

Squeezed between anger and despair, Georgios stood and stared at the two men. "My father is sick. He needs medicine, not philosophy."

Kleitos got up too, shaking his head. "You must see for yourself. Your father cannot be healed from this ailment. It has progressed too far. But I insist that he has been kept alive for a reason. Tell me—where were you going when you stopped here?"

Grinding his teeth, Georgios seethed. "Home to Patmos."

Kleitos smiled. "Finish your journey. With God's help, you will find your answers, and your father will die in peace." Straightening his shoulders, Kleitos wandered inside the inn. "I will give your father medicine to ease the pain. It'll give him strength for his last journey."

Desperately wanting to strike someone, Georgios clenched his hands.

Rueben stared at the empty doorway.

Hurrying inside, Georgios saw his sleeping father. "A useless waste of time! I hope Ian did not pay that man."

"You remember why I hated you when we first met?"

Caught off guard, Georgios jerked back. "I was a Roman, and you were a Jew."

Rueben shook his head. "No. It was because I had decided I knew you before I really did. I thought I knew the worth of every Roman in the whole world."

Georgios scowled, ready to let his fists loose once again.

Rueben shrugged. "You think that your worth depends upon your heritage—being a good Roman, Greek, or Jew.

Don't you ever wonder what God thinks of you?"

Georgios slammed his fist into his hand as he watched Rueben stomp out of the room.

The next day, after Ian announced that they needed to catch the tide, Georgios arranged everything in bitter silence. If there was a God, He should have taken his father when Georgios had been ready to let him go, not now when they had finally found each other's friendship.

As they boarded the merchant ship, Rueben handed Georgios a note. "It's from Kleitos. I'll look after your father."

Georgios had boarded the ship that would take him home, and he read the note that made his journey meaningful.

Dear Georgios,

You are not alone in sorrow.

Perhaps this will take you from faith in a father to faith in the Son.

I am in every heartbeat, every breath,
every hope, and every Death.
In grief you are born, but in forgiveness, you overcome.
Life
Begins with God's love for His Son."

~Your Servant,

Kleitos

CHAPTER THIRTY-SEVEN

TOWARD THE EASTERN SKY

—PATMOS—

Georgios let the large man's arm press heavily on his shoulder and said nothing.

Lysander had advice to offer. "Listen to me, boy. I've seen much of the world, and I know how hard it is to come home again. The world changes and so do you. Don't expect it to be as you remembered. Your grandparents may not be the people you thought they were. Surely, you are not the boy you were when you left. Myron told me to look for a child, but I am bringing home a man."

With a sigh, Georgios let Lysander's arm fall to the side. "Thank you for your counsel. I'm more aware than anyone that I am not the person I was."

Lysander studied Georgios and seemed satisfied.

After they arrived on shore, Georgios took Rueben aside and said softly, "Take Ian, Gutun, Lysander, and the others down the coast. You'll find an inn run by a man named Zoticus. He's a distant but friendly relation, so if you tell him that Georgios, grandson of Myron, sent you, he'll take good care of you."

Ian sauntered up, took an appraising glance around, and smiled at Georgios and Rueben. "You don't need the whole tribe appearing at your grandparents' door, I imagine. I'll take care of matters while you settle in with your family." With a grin, he tilted his head to where Lysander assisted Alexios to a waiting litter, while Gutun hovered in the background. "You think Gutun and Lysander can behave themselves?"

Georgios shot a quick look at Rueben. "They'll behave

as well as the rest of us, I suppose."

Rueben chuckled dismissively. "How much trouble can anyone get into on this little island?"

Alexios climbed into the litter, while Lysander beckoned two hired assistants to make ready to carry it up the steep road.

Georgios stepped toward his father, then stopped and faced his friends. "I'll send for you soon. I'm not planning on staying long. I promised to go to Jerusalem, and that's a promise I plan to keep."

Ian patted Georgios' shoulder. "No worries. Just take care of your father. I love little islands. I am sure I'll find all sorts of opportunities..."

Rueben snorted. "Don't you ever think of anything other than commerce?"

Ian laughed. "Of course. I think about food and-"

Rueben grimaced.

Nodding his farewell, Georgios jogged after his father.

Ian tugged Rueben's sleeve. "Let's see what this island has to offer."

Rueben called after Georgios, "Don't get too comfortable! Call for me soon."

Georgios grinned. "If you could manage Seanan, you'll have no trouble with this one."

Trudging away, Rueben muttered, "Oh, I did marvelously well with Seanan! Led all over the world, set to fight in a battle that wasn't mine, and now—"

Ian yanked Rueben along.

Georgios could just make out Ian's laughing banter as they strolled away. He followed the hired attendants carrying his father's litter up the steep roadside.

The day heated up, but after a morning of uneventful progress, they finally halted at his grandparents' home.

Everything was eerily still and quiet.

Fear shivered through Georgios. *Have I come for nothing?* A sound caught his ear.

An old man shuffled among various plants in a small garden beside the house, a small spade clutched in his hand.

Georgios trotted forward. "Grandfather? Is that you?"

Stoop shouldered and with a haggard face, Myron stared at Georgios. A scar ran across his face and his left hand hung limply at his side.

Shock sped over Georgios to see his stern, most noble grandfather old and damaged.

When recognition entered his eyes, Myron smiled, though it trembled on his lips, afraid to reveal itself. "Georgios?" He shuffled closer and then hobbled as fast as his legs would carry him. "Your grandmother would be so happy."

Georgios blinked in surprise. *Would be?* Fearing that the old man might fall, he strode forward and intercepted him.

Myron clasped Georgios in a feeble embrace. "I knew you'd come, though I didn't know when. I was hoping we'd meet before—but never mind. You've come; that's all that matters. And you're so grown up! A man now, I see. God brought you home just in time." He peered intently into Georgios' eyes. "Trouble is brewing."

His stomach clenching amid his confusion, Georgios glanced at an approaching servant. "Come, help your master. He's been out in the sun too long."

With assisting hands, the two led Myron through the narrow doorway and into his home.

Once inside, Georgios stopped in his tracks. "Oh, I almost forgot. I've brought someone with me."

Myron shuffled to a bench covered with pillows against a large picture window. "Bring him in. We live simply now, but I am sure you'll not mind."

Georgios stepped forward and spoke low. "Will you accept my father? Will you offer him hospitality?"

Straightening, Myron shifted his gaze to the entryway.

An attendant assisted Alexios out of the litter.

Myron sighed. "Yes, I'll accept your father. My judgment has become better informed."

Unbidden tears welled in Georgios' eyes.

He soon settled Alexios on a soft bed in a quiet room and then strolled through the house, reacquainting himself with his old home. Memories flooded him at every turn. Everything from the furniture to well-crafted artwork proclaimed his grandmother's touch, but he could find no sign of her.

Once back in the main room, he plunked down at his grandfather's side and pressed the old man's cold hands. "Where is she, Grandfather?"

"I'll tell you everything—in time. It's a hard tale to tell."

With a sigh, Georgios paid the attendants who had cared for his father and returned to Myron. "Father is resting comfortably. Thank you for allowing him to stay. I understand why you never loved him."

Myron waved off the comment and gazed out the window, lost in thought.

His heart heavy and head dizzy with weary confusion, Georgios longed for Rueben and Ian's lighthearted chatter. Even Lysander's paternal assistance would be welcome. "Grandfather, I have a lot to tell you."

Myron's mouth twitched. "I have much to explain as well."

Shifting with doubt, Georgios plunged ahead. "I want to hear your story and to tell you mine, but I left some friends near the shore, and I'd like—"

His face shining in sudden excitement, Myron met Georgios' gaze. "Why didn't you say so? You could've brought them. I wouldn't have minded. I'd be grateful for the company. It's been lonely since Roxanna—" Myron's face crumpled. He waved Georgios along. "Go get them."

"Are you certain? They're not your sort of people."

Gathering his composure, Myron clapped his hands and let out a cackled laugh. "I hope not! I realize now that I would've done better to travel less and associate with people—even not my sort—more."

Shaking his head at his grandfather's altered personality, Georgios felt comforting warmth spread through him. "In that case, I'll send word. It won't take them long to get here. They're good, strong men." He rubbed his chin. "Except for the Druid. He's—"

Myron blinked like an innocent child alive to a new wonder. "A Druid priest? I imagined that you'd met with many people, but a Druid never entered into my dreams...or my nightmares, for that matter."

Clapping his hands, Georgios got up and approached one of the servants. He spoke over his shoulder. "Gutun is a mystery. Rueben is the only one who really talks to him. You can judge for yourself." Georgios gave directions to the servant.

With a formal bow, the servant hustled away.

Georgios seated himself at Myron's side and leaned against the warm wall while the night settled over the day. In quiet, remembering tones, he told his story.

Myron listened without interruption, though he nodded often, reflecting on matters Georgios could only guess at.

The sky faded from a blush pink to dark purple, finally to black night. The stars twinkled in silent glory. A cool breeze descended, and sharp night air invaded the room.

Georgios' stomach rumbled. "Are you hungry, Grandfather?"

Myron shrugged. "I eat when I feel like it, but I am sure they have prepared something for you." Myron stood, rubbing his back. Pain contorted his face. With a shiver, he stiffened and clapped his hands.

A young, unfamiliar servant arrived in the doorway.

His curiosity aroused, Georgios stood at his grandfather's side. "Where are all the servants I knew?"

Myron gestured to the young man. "Set his evening meal in his room. I'll retire for the night." He turned and clasped Georgios' hands. "When I came back, I discovered many of our servants gone, along with many of our things. But that is no matter now. They wanted to serve a man of wealth, not one in poverty. Your old nurse is still here but in fragile health, so she stays with her family. I still see to the needs of those under my care." A grin twisted his lips. "The servant is served by the master in the end, eh?" Myron patted Georgios' back. "How you've grown!" His eyes lit up. "You must take after your father. There were giants among them, I heard. I'll see to him tonight. It'll give me something to do during the long, quiet hours."

Georgios frowned. "I can't ask that of you. Besides, he might be—"

Myron's wan smile trembled. "He'll be surprised, but sickness and injury make brothers of us all."

Exhaustion overtaking him, Georgios nodded through an enormous yawn. "If you're sure, then thank you. Wake me if he seems troubled. I want to be there when…the time comes."

Myron shuffled away.

Georgios wandered to his old room.

A plate of bread, a dish with spices and oils, a bowl of

figs, grapes, nuts, and a hunk of cheese had been set on an end table. A carafe of wine stood to the side. He poured himself a cup, drank, and ate in silence. Drowsiness enveloped him. He stretched out on his pallet and looked toward the eastern sky.

Tomorrow would be another eventful day. Thank God he wouldn't meet it alone.

CHAPTER THIRTY-EIGHT

A COMMAND

—PATMOS—

Ian arrived first, his heart pounding from the exertion of the climb and the news ready to spring from his lips.

Georgios stood in the doorway, his face a mask and his eyes weary.

Ian stopped before his friend, his words bursting forth like a flooded river. "Trajan is about to attack Darcia! He's taken his men north of the Danube, and the Parthians plan to raid the eastern shore. He'll be forced to fight two wars if he's not careful."

Georgios held his ground, his stoic expression unwavering.

An old man hobbled forward, nodding in wise agreement. "Trajan will have to hold tight to his power if he's to accomplish anything. Rome wasn't built in a day, but it could fall faster—" He shook his head and beckoned Ian inside with a smile. "Come in. I'm getting ahead of myself."

With a worn grin, Georgios stepped aside and whispered, "My grandfather, Myron, if you didn't guess."

Sighing, Ian put the world's troubles aside and focused on the situation at hand. His father's advice when he'd attempted to fashion his first sword sprang to mind. *Keep the long-range goal in sight, son, but take short steps.*

Myron called to the assembly, beckoning with his hand. "Come in and rest. You must be tired after your long journey." He wagged his finger as he hastened them along. "You must be, Ian, son of the Celtic leader, Seanan. My grandson told me much so about you. Glad to meet you."

When they entered the main room, he bowed low. "Georgios reports that you have a merchant's wit, an eagle's eye, and the hands of an artist. A rare combination, indeed!" The old man's eyebrows rose with emphasis.

Pride and embarrassment fought for dominance, forcing a half-laughed snort to the surface. Discomforted, Ian studied the elegant room. Quality furnishings adorned the neat space: a carved end table, matching chairs, two benches, one stool, a low couch, ornate vases and urns perched on a high shelf, and a large tucked into a wall niche. Ian's shoulders relaxed. His heart settled peacefully amid the room filled with beauty and light. Rustling and chatter turned his attention.

Rueben strolled forward, chatting with Lysander, while Gutun tagged at their heels.

Myron clapped his hands, his eyes widening as they focused on the newcomers. "Ah, you must be Rueben, Lysander, and the Druid priest." He hobbled forward, his hands beseeching. "Please come in! Sit down. Make yourselves comfortable. My servants will bring refreshments."

A sickly wheeze from behind caught everyone's attention.

Georgios led a weak, trembling Alexios toward the couch.

Alexios heaved each labored breath but managed to settle in a semi-reclined position and force a smile.

Dread filled Ian. *If Seanan were to ever suffer so…* He shook the image away and strolled to Georgios. He directed him aside and leaned in. "How is everything—really?"

Rubbing his red-rimmed eyes, Georgios yawned through his words. "I hardly know. Nothing but surprises. Grandfather spent the night with father, chattering away like boys till early morning."

Ian tilted his head, confused. "That's good, isn't it? They're getting along…"

"It's beyond my understanding."

Gutun hovered near the entrance, scowling. He grunted in obvious dissatisfaction.

Across the room, Rueben gestured for Gutun to come in and sit down.

Gutun slid onto a stood before the window, folded his hands, and peered at the sky, appearing aloof to worldly matters.

With a snort at the Druid's pretense, Ian turned his attention to Lysander. He nudged Georgios with a meaningful nod.

Chuckling, Georgios strolled across the room and interrupted his grandfather's conversation with Rueben. He took Myron's arm and led him to Lysander. "Your long-lost servant, Lysander, Grandfather. He has returned after accomplishing his mission—difficult as it was."

Frowning, Lysander lifted his hand. "Georgios, don't. Everyone knows I didn't find you; you found me. I deserve no—"

Myron's eyes widened. "Honest man! I certainly set you on an impossible task. I must pay you for your service."

"Your humble—" Lysander bowed.

Myron snorted. "Humility has nothing to do with it. My grandson is home again. I'd thank the whole world if I could." His eyes twinkled. "I may have another mission for you, but I'm getting ahead of myself again. Here, sit and be comfortable. We have much to discuss. But eat first."

Ian perched on a stool. His stomach grumbled in anticipation as he accepted a dish of bread, cheese, dates, and figs. Enjoying himself as servants offered various refreshments and cups of wine, he watched Myron circle the room, chatting with each of his guests. Gutun arrested his attention the longest. Ian scratched his head and then returned to the task of filling his stomach.

As the sun touched the horizon, Myron called for everyone's attention. "It's time for me to tell my tale. I wish my wife were here, for she was better with words." A shadow crossed his face, but he brushed it away.

Ian and Lysander drew close. Georgios sat with his father on the couch. Gutun turned just enough to see Myron but still faced the window. Ian leaned his back against the cool wall and settled himself for a good story.

Myron spread his hands wide. "As you all know, I sent Lysander off to find Georgios. Soon after, Roxanna traveled to the other side of the island to visit the home of an old man, a prophet named John, who I'd never heard of. After a couple of strange letters from her, I became concerned, so I went to investigate the matter for myself. To my surprise, Roxanna had become a new woman, more patient and understanding than ever before. It turned out that John had died years before. He had been an apostle of a man named Jesus who claimed to be the Christ, the Son of God. Roxanna introduced me to her friends, who told amazing stories about John and Jesus. I listened, watched, and even had an experience in John's cave that defied all..." Myron's gaze turned inward.

Intrigued, Ian listened quietly, but Lysander cleared his throat in impatience.

Myron recollected himself. "I learned that Jesus had been crucified in Jerusalem and then rose from the dead. Many believed this, so we traveled to Jerusalem to learn more." He blinked back tears. "After traveling in His footsteps, hearing about the miracles He performed and stories of His life, I, too, came to believe. Jesus Christ is the Son of God."

His skin prickling, shock spread over Ian. He glanced around.

Georgios frowned.

Lysander shook his head, derision in his eyes.

Rueben's face glowed in joy.

Gutun's eyes narrowed.

Myron fluttered a hand in quick dismissal. "Don't be alarmed. I'm not asking you to believe. Jesus does not force anyone to come to Him."

Georgios straightened, his face tight and strained. "What happened to—"

Myron nodded. "Yes, I'm getting to that." He exhaled a long breath, a man readying himself for a sprint to the finish. "We saw where Jesus had lived, preached, performed miracles, and we met many interesting people. We even met some old friends. But after a time, we grew concerned because we had not heard from Lysander. With all our moving about, I feared that we had lost track of Georgios forever."

Lysander shrugged. "When I didn't hear from you..."

Myron nodded. "Eventually, we met a learned man named Polycarp who had known John. He showed us John's writings, such extraordinary words. If you read them, you'd—"

Georgios scowled, his gaze sweeping the assembly. "If you'd just tell us what happened—"

Myron sucked in a breath and blinked, a glimmer of tears in his eyes.

Irritation snagged Ian's mind. What's wrong with Georgios?

Myron lifted his hands in surrender. "I met an old acquaintance, and he had in his company a man named

Pacorus, a knowledgeable man hoping to be of service as a guide. Later that evening, we met Polycarp again; he warned us against Pacorus and insisted that we return home immediately. He'd had a premonition that our grandson would return home soon. The next day, I went to make arrangements, leaving Roxanna alone at the inn." Myron twisted his hands, his voice shaky as tears slipped down his cheeks unchecked. "If only I had taken her with me!

"While I was gone, Pacorus came to see Roxanna, and they quarreled—about what exactly, I don't know—but I found her unconscious. Later that night, she died in my arms. Polycarp believed that Pacorus was a Parthian spy in the service of a man named Armand. As Trajan had been adopted and made the ruler of Rome, so Armand hopes to rule through his chosen one, putting Rome under the power of the Parthians. But—" Myron stretched his crooked arm and pointed to his scarred face. "I learned all of this at a cost. On a lonely street, I was attacked and beaten nearly to death."

Georgios jumped to his feet. "Grandmother was murdered, and you were attacked?"

Lysander's face turned dark; his jaws clenched.

A hot flush worked over Ian, his stomach sickening with the cruel images. "What did you do?"

Myron shook his head. "There was nothing to do. The Roman authorities cared nothing for a Greek family attacked by unknown assailants. Polycarp grieved with me, but he insisted that I must return home. Grieved beyond words, I buried my beloved Roxanna in a tomb with other followers of Christ to await her resurrection. My only hope is that this life is a prelude to a world yet to come." He shuddered through a deep breath. "It must be—or nothing makes any sense." Myron dried his eyes with his sleeve and then gestured toward the food left on the table. "Eat and drink. My story has been long, and you need refreshment."

No one moved toward the food except Gutun, who snatched a cluster of grapes.

Georgios plunked down on his chair, his face haggard.

Rueben's voice broke the silence. "You said earlier that we have some part to play. What did you mean?"

Georgios glanced up. "Yes, last night, you told me that my coming was an answer to a prayer."

Myron nodded. "Rome is not the greatest country on the Earth because she earned the right but because God has allowed it so. Rome has a part to play in the future that we cannot yet see. But dark forces covet power and the ruin of us all. I cannot let Roxanna's death have the final say. Georgios, you must find Pacorus and stop him before he traitorously turns Rome over to the Parthians."

Georgios stood and stared out the window into the dark night. Then he turned and faced his grandfather. "I will avenge my grandmother's death, but I care nothing for Rome. It makes no difference who rules. All kings are the same."

Gutun, to all of their amazement, shuffled closer. "You do not know dark powers, Georgios. The battles that you see are nothing compared to the ones that you do not see. Pacorus is not acting alone."

Georgios shook his head. "You'd side with Rome, then? You who hate the gods of other nations?"

Gutun shrugged. "I side with no one."

Georgios stared at Rueben. "What do you think?"

Rueben smiled. "We did plan to go to Jerusalem—"

Lysander waved his hand. "First, we need to find out where Pacorus went—"

Rueben lifted his hand. “If we go to Jerusalem, we’ll find—”

Excitement filling him, Ian leaned toward Georgios. “I’d like to see the city myself.”

His face flushed, Gutun’s shrill voice rose high. “You’d leave me on this barren rock?”

Myron pressed Gutun’s shoulder. “I could use your help—”

A man’s voice called out strong and clear.

“Go, Georgios!”

A shiver ran down Ian’s spine. The voice sounded like Alexios’. Everyone looked around wildly.

Georgios leaned over; his attention fixed on his father.

Alexios lay unnaturally stiff, his gaze staring, unseeing.

A lump formed in Ian’s throat and lodged there. Tears filled his eyes. He could hear Alexios’ voice in his head. There was no doubt; it was a command. Georgios must go.

~~~

Georgios stood under a bright blue sky, leaning on a gnarled tree, as ocean waves crested and fell. It had been three years since that fateful day when he and Alexios had planned his future so near this same spot.

Myron shuffled close. “Am I disturbing you?”

Georgios shrugged. “I am trying to decide what to do. I know what you want, what Rueben, Ian, and Lysander want, but I don’t know what I want.”

With a hesitant smile, Myron opened his hands in a silent invitation. “The night Alexios and I talked, he told me a story.”

Sighing, Georgios waited for the inevitable.

Myron settled on a flat boulder and clasped his hands on his lap. “Before the count of time, clans roamed the
~~~

land of Ur. The leader of one tribe, a man named Aram, had many adventures and suffered terrible misfortunes, but when he died, he left a powerful legacy. Throughout the ages, his name has strengthened the fainthearted and emboldened the fearful. Alexios told me that in the lonely hours of night, the stories of Aram gave him fresh courage. Remembered for his faithfulness to his family, his people, and God, Aram knew the One when most were lost in a sea of doubt or wrapped in treachery. Before we parted, Alexios told me that his greatest wish was that you would become a man like Aram." Myron stood and pressed Georgios' shoulder. "Whatever you do—do it heroically." With that, Myron hobbled away.

Laughter rose in the background.

Rueben and Ian strolled along the shore, chatting, as Lysander jogged forward, gesturing toward the port where a ship awaited their departure. Lysander's voice rose against the wind. "It's time! Let's go."

Georgios shoved away from the tree and faced the rising sun. It was time. He had to go.

CHAPTER THIRTY-NINE

CHOOSE WISELY

—ROME—

Armand knew the truth: greedy people were always unreliable. Yet what he learned concerning Pacorus disturbed him. Apparently, the man couldn't control his mouth, his moods, or his temper. Relaxing on a soft couch in the most luxurious room he could find in the bustling port city of Ostia, Armand steepled his fingers under his chin. A gentle breeze wafted over him. What he needed was an innocent; someone longing to do good in the world.

Armand smiled. Such a man could move easily in favored circles. An honest face, upright character, and purity of heart disarmed rich and poor alike.

Annoyance crawled over his joy. He'd have to deal with Pacorus soon, but he must find a replacement first.

He stirred from his statue-like posture, stood, and stared out the window over distant fields. The best gardens had well-worked soil. Just off the coast of the awakening village, fishermen sailed in port with the night's catch while merchants loaded their wares on tables, chattering with neighbors as they toiled.

He'd take a stroll and consider his options. Surely, he could find someone out of work, a noble-hearted fool wandering through town. With a chuckle, Armand imagined the boy he needed. Not another Pacorus. This time he'd choose more wisely. He'd treat his protégé like a son and plant him right in the heart of Rome.

Chapter Forty

Who on Earth?

–Rome–

Noman's heart fluttered. Someone heard my prayers. He scowled. He didn't mean that. Just a happy coincidence. Nevertheless, Armand's desire for a man like Georgios played right into his plans. In Noman's longing to prove humanity's worthlessness, he'd placed too much hope in Gutun. And that had proven a dismal failure. He was pathetic rather than a prime example. *Couldn't use him to prove much of anything. Except weakness. How obvious.*

He yawned as he looked out the window of his Roman villa. All he had to do was give Armand a little help and remind Gutun of his purpose as a useful slave. *He can do that much at least!*

He turned from natural beauty and faced the ornate door leading to Trajan's palace.

~~~

Teal had had enough. He'd spent far too much time attempting to track down the Mysterious being. *Clearly, there's more to this situation than meets the eye, but—*

Standing in the middle of the dusty road with a staff in hand, Cerulean cleared his throat, waiting impatiently.

Dressed in shepherd's garb in accordance with the setting, Teal remembered his present duty. He nudged Cerulean ahead while glancing fitfully at the six sheep wandering every which way. "Keep them together, son, or we'll have some explaining to do."

"Why couldn't Zuri help? He's good with animals."
~~~

Teal snorted. “He’s good with Bhuaci animals. Don’t forget; he only tells selected stories. If Kelesta hadn’t prepared him, he would’ve had a heart attack on their first nature trip.”

“Ark, then. He could help.”

Teal frowned, baffled.

Cerulean grinned. “Just joking. Like when I said the ship sank.” He laughed at the memory. “They looked like the sun had just exploded!”

Smacking an errant sheep back into the fold, Teal harrumphed. “I still don’t know how you got it to work.” He waved off an explanation. “I don’t want to know. I just want to find the king and see what’s going on inside the palace.”

“He’ll let us in?”

“No. Even if he did, he wouldn’t tell us anything. It’s the servants and slaves who know everything. We’re going to get invited to the palace kitchen. Then we’ll learn something.”

“Why will—”

A guard shouted, waving his spear, “You! Take them to the sheep gate! You’re not supposed to go through here.”

Teal nudged Cerulean toward the proper gate. “Let’s go. I noticed a young man, Georgios, who interests me. He has a certain look, as if I’ve met him before.”

“Is he here?”

“He will be. I have Ark and Zuri keeping an eye on him.”

“How? As birds?”

“No, bugs.”

One of the sheep darted ahead, rushing mindlessly into the throng.

Teal swore under his breath. *Lord Almighty, what a thankless task—being a shepherd!*

CHAPTER FORTY-ONE

IN SERVICE OF THE GODS

—ROME—

Armand knelt on the stone floor, rocking in rhythm with his words, more a hum than a chant. Armand knelt on the stone floor, rocking in rhythm with his words, which were more of a hum than a chant. He pressed one hand to his chest and stroked a serpentine figure with the other. The figure stood near a fire burning in the center of a circle drawn in red chalk upon the floor.

A snake with a man's head appeared ready to devour a small offering directly in front of it—a clay figure of a young man standing indifferent to the snake.

The snake was not indifferent to the boy. Its enormous mouth appeared ready to devour the figure in one swift, undulating gulp.

His rhythmic chant died as his hand went from the snake to the boy. Tragic perhaps, but sacrifices had to be made. A picture of his son rose in his mind. An inquisitive child who discovered a poison Armand was perfecting and suffered an early death as a result.

The boy's mother had not understood.

Armand rubbed his thin lips with his well-manicured fingers.

When he had learned that someone else was searching for Pacorus, he discovered everything he could of the young man and ascertained that he was from a rich merchant's family on the island of Patmos. He sent a servant to further investigate his background and learned all he needed to know from a stranded Druid priest. Such irony tickled his sensibilities.

With his bare toe, Armand shifted the clay boy closer to the snake. The snake would not kill him; it would only bite him, making him more powerful. Then the boy could become a real man, and wasn't that the wish of every boy?

Armand lifted the snake and peered into its black eyes. "I serve you truly, but a son must be restored to me."

The figure stared through blank eyes.

Armand tapped the serpentine figure, sliding it closer to the boy but slightly turned away. He smoothed down his white tunic and straightened his shoulders. It was time to meet Georgios.

—PATMOS—

Gutun strode to a spot distant from Myron's home and knelt on the hard ground under the night sky. He folded his hands, murmuring in a language few Romans, Greeks, or Jews would care to understand.

His gods were angry; he had been away too long. Most likely, they hadn't received a proper sacrifice since he'd left.

One day, a messenger had offered a flicker of hope. The man wanted to know about someone named Georgios. In return for all he knew, Gutun had been given enough money to ensure his freedom. Confident that he served his gods first, the coins offered practical support.

That night, Gutun thanked his gods for the day's good fortune. A tug jerked his body, and he glanced up. Finding nothing but empty air, a chill ran down his spine, and an image filled his mind—a serpent with a man's head. His body stiffened. By serving the servant of another god, had he been called into its service too?

Gutun rose to his knees, huffing laboriously as he struggled to his feet. He could not serve two gods.

Countless stars filled the night sky above Gutun. Perhaps the gods are like the stars, the same in essence but called by different names? Not likely. They were much too different.

Gutun wiped a hand across his sweaty forehead and trembled. In a battle between the gods, he was doomed. What could a poor mortal do?

An inspiration ignited his imagination. *I'll offer Georgios. When they release their wrath on him, I'll make my escape.* He exhaled a long, relieved breath.

CHAPTER FORTY-TWO

THE HEART FOR REVENGE

—ROME—

Georgios ran his work-roughened fingers through his hair. At almost seventeen, he had grown tall and strong. His short tunic and shoulder-length hair matched his shipmates' style, but in Rome, pedestrians stared, and their whispered commentaries did not flatter. Being mistaken for a barbarian made Georgios laugh out loud.

With Rueben, Lysander, and Ian's help, he had followed Pacorus' trail, but every time they drew near, they found him protected from both strangers and their questions. As a trusted member of the imperial household, Pacorus even found favor with the emperor.

Weary of traveling and frustrated by their lack of success, Ian announced that he would board a ship heading home the next day. Though he had adopted the Roman style, short hair and no hint of a beard, he looked more Roman than Georgios ever had. Still, he complained endlessly about the frenetic pace of city life.

Seemingly at peace in every situation, Rueben set no plans and merely followed wherever Georgios led, demanding nothing but absorbing everything.

Lysander enjoyed himself and made the most of every inn and meal. With his charming nature, he turned simple events into friendly gatherings.

The memory of his father's face flitted through Georgios' mind at odd moments. That and the image of his grandmother haunted his steps. But he could do nothing to change the past. He had trouble enough managing the present.

As Georgios reclined at an outdoor table, enjoying a cup of strong wine, he studied the complacent Romans around him. What did it matter if Rome were overthrown? Who were the Parthians but members of another empire? Could they be any worse than Rome? Commerce ran the world, and that would never change.

Georgios studied the various ships rocking on gentle waves in port. He could return to the Celtic lands with Ian, but a silent command held him in Rome. He sighed.

Lysander arranged a sendoff party for Ian with food and enough libations to feed a small army. He had been drinking freely since early afternoon and was warmed up for an enchanting evening. Laughing, he leaned toward Ian. "You must bring home a Roman bride. That would please Seanan beyond measure!"

Ian flushed and whapped Lysander on the back a little harder than necessary. "That would please my father but annoy my mother. She has undoubtedly picked out a nice girl for me."

With a wicked gleam in his eye, Lysander grinned. "You don't need a nice girl; you need a strong woman."

Georgios glanced at Rueben, and they rolled their eyes in mutual commiseration.

His gaze sweeping over the throng that milled through the inn, Lysander suddenly stood and stared intently into the distance.

Ian tugged his arm. "You've had enough. You don't need another—"

Mumbling, Lysander pulled away and ran off.

A headache pounding behind his eyes, Georgios rubbed his temple as he glanced from Ian to Rueben. "What's gotten into him? He's been acting strange all day."

Ian shrugged. "He's always strange."

Rueben shook his head. "Lysander is a mystery. No use

trying—"

His voice booming, Lysander returned chatting and leading two women toward their table.

The younger woman, small and plump and about Georgios' age, wore her brown hair wrapped on her head in Roman fashion, wore no make-up, and wearing a plain and unornamented dress. She met his gaze a moment before glancing away.

The older woman had a square jaw. Stouter and plainer, she marched behind the younger woman, her gaze studying every face she met.

Georgios stood and bowed, darting a glare at Lysander.

With a hint of a grin, Lysander lifted his hand. "These are two noble ladies, mother and daughter. I know them well. Well, I know them a little. I actually know their servant—he's over there. See?" Lysander pointed to a fat man clasping a large cup of wine, chattering and laughing in unrestrained fits.

Lysander held Georgios' gaze. "An interesting man, and these ladies have quite a story—one I'm sure you will find fascinating." Lysander bowed graciously. "This is Georgios, the son of a loyal Roman soldier named Alexios." Lysander pointed in turn. "And here is our honest friend Rueben, and there, the quiet one with the serious expression, is our excellent trader, Ian, son of Seanan." Lysander lowered his voice to a conspiratorial whisper. "He's a barbarian, but don't be afraid. He doesn't bite, unless in fun!"

Lysander's laughter slammed the inside of Georgios' head. He winced.

Glancing around at the unwonted glares from nearby patrons, Ian shook his head.

Struggling to keep his irritation in check, Georgios turned his attention to the girl.

She blushed and her gaze dropped, downcast and dispirited.

Pity shoved anger aside, and Georgios beckoned them forward. “Come and rest until your servant is ready—”

The older woman snorted. “Don’t pretend to be concerned about us. Our servant is merely in need of refreshment. He’s been guiding us around the city. We’re looking for someone—”

“Mother!” The girl’s blush deepened. “We don’t know these men or who else may hear you!” She looked apologetically at Georgios. “We aren’t usually so forward; it’s just that—”

“As I was saying—” Her mother straightened and pressed her daughter’s shoulder. “My name is Volga and this is my daughter Mithra, and we are looking for my son. He left home over a year ago. We know that he’s in danger, so we’re trying to warn him.”

Lysander’s smile nearly engulfed his entire face.

Ian frowned and glanced at Rueben.

Rueben searched the two women’s faces.

Confused, Georgios massaged his temple, his headache throbbing. “We can sympathize. We’ve been trying to find someone too. It’s exhausting work. Perhaps you need more help. Rome is hardly the place for two women—”

Volga spat, “No one that can help us. My son was deceived by a conniver who imagines himself—”

“Mother!” Mithra hissed.

Volga nodded. “You’re right.” She craned her neck, peering across the room.

Her servant had disengaged himself from a throng bantering in animated conversation.

“He’s ready now. It’s time we left.” She gripped her daughter’s hand and attempted a gracious bow.

Lysander returned the formal salutation while Rueben

and Georgios merely nodded.

The two women headed for the door.

Ian patted his lean stomach. "I'm going to get something to eat."

Lysander laughed. "You're always hungry!"

Rueben wagged his finger. "That's because he's always working–something you know little about."

Georgios' gaze followed the women until they were lost to his view, then he plucked Lysander's sleeve. "Why did you do that?"

Lysander propped his head on his hand and leaned on the table, a relaxed storyteller launching into his newest tale. "I met that idiot servant a few days ago, and he tried to tell me some ridiculous story about how his master had been kidnapped—" He slowed his speech to an irritating degree. "But, after some investigating, I discovered that no one had been captured. Rather, the woman's son had run away from home and has been missing for some time. Normally that would not interest me, but it turns out that they are Parthian and had left their native lands a few months ago. And *that* did interest me."

A spark ignited inside Georgios. "Are you sure?"

Lysander took a hearty swig of his drink and then slammed it on the table. "The son's name was interesting as well."

Ian returned with a chunk of cheese and a loaf of bread. He brandished the bread like a weapon, the amusement in his eyes belying his serious tone. "Tell the rest quickly!"

Lysander considered each man in turn. "It might interest you…to know…that his name is…Pacorus!" A satisfied smile spread across Lysander's face. "He was sent here to accomplish a certain *business*, but someone figured out that the fool couldn't be trusted, so a replacement has been found. Volga wants to find her son before the replacement does, or there might not be a son to bring home."

Rueben whistled low.

Ian tried to swallow an inordinately large piece of cheese.

Dizziness engulfed Georgios.

Lysander slapped his thigh. "I knew you'd be amazed! I hear everything important in town and, of course, it helps to get people properly drunk!"

Irritated, Georgios tried to clear his head. "Why didn't you tell me earlier?"

After taking another swig of wine, Lysander waved his hand. "Don't get in a tangle! I didn't expect to meet up with the mother and daughter so soon. They'll be of invaluable assistance to us."

Rueben frowned. "What under heaven can we possibly say to them? 'Hello, turns out we're looking for your son too, but we'd like to visit vengeance upon him for murder and treachery?'"

Lysander clasped his hands primly. "I wouldn't put it precisely like *that*."

Georgios shook his head. "No, they can't know the truth. But with their help, we may find Pacorus soon."

Shrugging, Ian spoke between chews. "Why bother? Once the replacement kills him, what's left for us to do?"

Lysander scowled. "You're taking a ship out in the morning, so your opinion doesn't count."

His stomach tightening at the thought of the girl searching for her brother, a man that killed a harmless old woman, Georgios stood. "I want to speak to that servant." He glanced from Lysander to Rueben, and finally stopped on Ian. "Get some rest, Ian. You've a big day tomorrow, and we'll see you off early."

Lysander stood and stretched lazily. "Ian and Rueben

can take care of themselves. I plan to make a long night of it."

Rueben patted Lysander's arm. "You were never young. You've always been a troublesome old man."

"True!" Lysander meandered to the door.

With a sinking sensation working its way down to his toes, Georgios watched Lysander leave. He faced his two friends. "I want to look around." Before the two could protest, he raced out the door.

Dark and quiet as night set in, the streets lay bare of merchants and shoppers. Georgios strolled along, the fresh air reviving his spirits and clearing his confused mind. As he headed north, he saw a familiar figure standing near a low wall.

Lysander hadn't appeared this serious and alert all night.

Georgios stopped before him. "You find the servant?"

Lysander gestured with his chin. "He's sitting by an inn wall over there. He's not as incompetent as I thought. There's more to this situation than meets the eye, Georgios." He looked around warily. "We must be careful."

Georgios padded toward the silent figure. Once within range, he crouched low and whispered, "You're searching for a man by the name of Pacorus?"

A silent nod.

Georgios leaned in. "We'd like to find him too. Could you help us?" He pressed coins into the man's hand.

The clipped nod repeated itself.

Georgios waited.

The man drew from a deep pocket a tiny papyrus scroll. He handed it to Georgios.

Taking the note, Georgios straightened. "Thank you."

The man neither moved nor made any acknowledgment.

Georgios returned to Lysander.

Lysander took the note, unrolled it, and read it in the bright moonlight. "It says that the holder of this note has vital information for one known as Pacorus. It's signed Volga." Lysander scowled. "This won't help us."

"But once he responds to the note, we'll have him. We'll just have to keep an eye on Volga."

Lysander shook his head. "This note doesn't make sense. Why give the note to us? Unless he has already given it to others, and he's keeping an eye on everyone to see if there's any response. Impossible to be sure."

"Pacorus will surely recognize the name and do something."

Lysander faced Georgios and gripped his arm, a father having to give bad news. "Pacorus will meet his end soon enough. Why bother any longer? Besides, what are you going to do if you find him?"

Georgios sighed and leaned against the wall, his headache throbbing in full force. "You're right. I don't have the heart for cold-blooded revenge."

His eyes full of understanding, Lysander nodded. "Who would want a mercenary's life? Long days full of nothing you ever want to talk about."

Georgios pressed his hands together, deciding at last. "I'll let Pacorus know that his mother is looking for him and leave it at that."

Lysander snorted. "You'll face the man who killed your grandmother and say, 'After a long and arduous search, I've come to inform you that your mother is looking for you?'"

Georgios seethed. "You'd leave the mother and sister roaming the city—" He glanced aside. The place where the servant once sat was now vacant. A knot tightened in his stomach.

His eyes growing wide, Lysander sucked in a breath and smacked Georgios' shoulder. "Let's go!" He took off running.

Confused and irritated, Georgios scowled and stood his ground. He crumpled the note and then tilted his head as a strange sound caught his ear, the rhythmic pounding of many feet.

He could think of only one source for such a perfect step—the march of Roman soldiers.

He pressed against the wall to let the battery of soldiers pass.

To Georgios' surprise, rather than moving on, they stopped and surrounded him.

CHAPTER FORTY-THREE

TOO OLD TO CRY

—ROME—

"*Georgios*, son of Alexios, you have been summoned to appear before Armand, a faithful servant of the Emperor."

Since the Roman warrior was doing a fair imitation of a mountain come to life and was assisted by several well-armed men, Georgios decided to comply, though his mind raced with questions.

As they marched along the dim alleyways, he glanced warily at the men who marched in perfect formation, indifferent to every assaulting smell. Georgios tried to study the man nearest him, but his face remained composed and his gaze averted. Georgios could read nothing. When he searched the expression of the leader, he realized with sick foreboding that this man simply acted on orders and probably knew little about the matter. And what was worse, this man didn't care about the outcome.

The sun crested the horizon as they reached a whitewashed mansion, the home of a very rich Roman.

Georgios blanched.

Surely Armand was not brazen enough to make an example of him in a public spectacle?

The Roman soldiers stepped to the side as an immaculately dressed servant hustled forward from an open doorway.

Their duty complete, the soldiers marched away.

As Georgios followed the servant inside, enticing scents tickled his nose. He glanced at the rooms they passed; high ceilings, bright artwork, and glorious statues caught his eye.

Halting before a large door, the servant tapped Georgios' chest.

Disgusted by the thin, manicured hands, Georgios sneered and slapped them away.

The servant's hooked nose rose higher. "Listen and obey!"

Georgios pursed his lips. If the man were not so effeminate, he would have enjoyed pushing the overdressed fool to the side, but hard-earned wisdom deflected the temptation. He nodded.

The servant pushed wide the wooden, ornamented doors, and exotic scents engulfed them.

Nudged forward by the servant, Georgios braced himself and took a deep breath.

A sharp-featured, middle-aged man sat on a couch covered with embroidered cushions. He sat straight; his hands folded as if in prayer.

Georgios took a step forward and stopped cold when the stranger looked at him.

A subtle, sensual smile slithered over the stranger's pale face. Wearing a long red robe over a white tunic, he beckoned with manicured hands. "Come, sit down and be comfortable, Georgios. You've had a long night, and I know you'd like to see your friends off on their voyage this morning."

His skin prickled. To regain his composure, Georgios shifted his gaze away from the stranger and glanced out the window at the pink hues signaling the start of a new day. He cleared his throat. "How do you know—?"

"It's my business to know, yet there is one thing I still long to learn, and only you can tell me."

Irritation replaced nervousness as a blush heated Georgios' cheeks. "I'm a free man, and I have every right to know why I have been summoned here."

The man laughed, a gentle chuckle cascading like water over a rocky brook. "What words you use. Rights? Who gave you rights, Georgios? Your long-dead Greek mother or your recently deceased Roman father? Can the dead give the living rights?"

The man stood and stretched. "We'll take a stroll. I have beautiful orchards that I'm sure you'll enjoy."

"Just tell me who you are and why you've brought me here." Georgios crossed his arms, planting his feet firmly on the highly polished floor.

The smile on the stranger's face widened. "What a bold young man you are!"

Georgios continued to stare, stuffing his irritation down.

"You allow no leisure, Georgios—that is something we need to remedy. My name is Armand, and I'm from Parthia. I'm here to uncover a nefarious plot. One of my men intercepted your message and, realizing that you and I search for the same man, he gave me your name. We can work together, since it is in our best interest to put our mutual enemy in a place where he can never hurt anyone again."

Glancing at the ceiling, Georgios tried to untangle truth from lie. If only he had Lysander's ready tongue, Ian's wit, or Rueben's wisdom. Depression surrounded him like a cloud.

"I hate deception and the confusion it causes. That's the root of my disagreement with Pacorus."

Georgios' legs felt weak.

A knowing smile wavered on Armand's lips. "Pacorus was once a friend. He became entangled with dangerous men and decided that he was wiser than me. He nearly destroyed one of my most cherished dreams. I was almost forced into exile, and after living in such circumstances..."

Armand gestured to indicate his surroundings. “Surely you can imagine what a sacrifice that would be.”

Georgios held his tongue.

In a fatherly gesture, Armand clasped Georgios’ arm and strolled into a garden.

Ancient olive trees, an expansive grape arbor, and rows of flower beds created a colorful feast for the eyes.

“Why have I been brought here?”

Ignoring the question, Armand pointed out the natural treasures and fine pieces of art.

Fears of a Roman cohort or being attacked from behind kept Georgios from reacting on an impulse.

When they finally returned to the main room, Armand gestured toward the door. “I’ve bored you enough for one morning. Run off now and see to your friends. I gave strict orders that their ship was not to leave until you arrived. After you have said goodbye, come back, and have dinner with me. Once your friends leave, you’ll be without any dependable support, so avail yourself of all I have to offer. I’m a generous man. I once had a son who would be about your age now... But enough. Go, see to your friends and return quickly.”

His garments billowing like a blooming flower, Armand strode off into an adjoining room.

Alone, Georgios mulled over Armand’s mistake. He had said *friends*, when only Ian was leaving. He shook his head and pounded down the hall, past the staring servants, and into the morning air.

He followed the path to the inn he had stayed in the day before. The city had awakened from sleepy murmurs to hectic action. After passing the inn, he headed to the ship, fear spurring his steps. Ian might have sailed already. Georgios began to run. Sweat broke out on his forehead.

With a sigh of relief, he soon saw both the ship and his

friends. He waved a greeting. Imagining what Lysander would say when he told him the tale of his adventure, amusement replaced his earlier fears. Racing the last steps, Georgios pounded Ian on the back with a laugh. "I am so glad I made it on time. You won't believe what happened! But never mind, you'd better get on board. The captain must be nearly frantic. The tide is almost gone."

Ian, Rueben, and Lysander stared at Georgios as if they were seeing a vision. Not a flicker of a smile or the slightest greeting.

Georgios glanced from one frigid face to another. Apprehension tumbled over his momentary joy. "What's the matter? Sorry I'm late, but something strange happened." He scowled at Lysander. "Thanks for leaving me at the mercy of—"

Ian and Rueben started to speak, but Lysander raised his hand and his voice. "There's not enough time to explain." He glanced nervously over his shoulder. "See—here comes the captain and his men. I'm sure his orders are as strict as ours. Go on, Ian and Rueben. I'll tell Georgios as much as I can, but we'd better not wait, or we'll all be—"

With a petulant frown, Ian folded his arms. "I'm not leaving—"

Rueben tugged Ian toward the ship. "Lysander is right. We'll find a way to come back and—"

Snapping an order, the captain gestured toward the ship. "Hurry up, or I'll get the whips out, and you'll be wearing your skins in strips, you hear?"

Horror clenched Georgios' stomach. He glared at the captain and the approaching men, his fists at his sides. "What does he mean—"

Lysander swung around and gave Georgios a swift hug, forcing a small parchment into his belt. When he loosened his grip, he looked Georgios in the eye and stated in an undertone, "Trust no one. We'll be back." Lysander followed Ian and Rueben up the plank and onto the ship.

Stupefied, Georgios watched the merchant ship pull away from shore. He searched for his friends on deck, but they were nowhere in sight.

When the ship was no more than a dot on the horizon, Georgios turned away. With the last of the coins in his pocket, he bought a meal from a street merchant. He found a grassy spot near the water's edge and chewed his bread meditatively. He could not make sense of anything. Armand had known that they were *all* leaving. But how could he know? He might be rich, but he couldn't send his friends off at a moment's notice. *Could he? And even if it were possible, why would he want to?*

Georgios wiped his hands clean, adjusted his tunic, and remembered Lysander's note. He pulled it out, looked around at the children playing nearby, ran his fingers through his hair, and read the few lines.

Accused of murder, we've been sent into exile. If we protest, we'll be killed on the spot. Someone wants us out of the way. Trust no one! We'll be back.

Heart pounding and confusion making his head spin, Georgios crumpled the note and glanced around.

No one seemed to notice him. Even the children were gone. Alone and uncertain, Georgios wrapped his arms around his drawn-up legs and rested his head on his knees. He stared at the empty expanse where his friends had gone. He was too old to cry, so he closed his eyes and wished he could.

CHAPTER FORTY-FOUR

A SILENT PROMISE

—GAELIC LANDS—

Gutun knew that his services had been invaluable to someone, but to whom? He rubbed his chin and watched the purple horizon melt into the night sky. Someone had wanted to know everything about Georgios. He had complied and was well paid for his efforts.

A disturbing noise broke his concentration.

Myron hobbled about his house, humming off-key.

Gutun frowned. He had no reason to tell Myron about these developments. Besides, the old fool had become difficult of late, always wanting to share stories of his risen God. Now that Gutun had a heavy bag of coins, he could find his way off this barren island and return to his native land. He suppressed a chuckle. The shock on Seanan's face when he reappeared in the village well-dressed and with golden bands on his arms would be worth all he had suffered.

Myron called, "Gutun, come in and eat now."

Gutun swore under his breath.

Myron shuffled forward. "You've been out here so long. Is everything alright?"

"Certainly. But I wish to get a message out. I've had a forewarning." He pursed his lips and dropped his gaze to the ground. "I won't be much longer in this world, and I'd like to amend matters before I pass to the other side. You understand, don't you?"

Myron pressed Gutun's shoulder. "Of course. What can I do to help?"

"A servant left a message for me a few days ago, a

young boy with a limp. Would you send this boy to me?"

Myron nodded. "I know him, a worthy child. I'll have him come tomorrow."

Gutun bowed his head, gratitude incarnate.

Myron patted Gutun's shoulder as he led him back to the house. "Come eat now, and I'll tell you a story. You'll find it fascinating."

Reluctantly, Gutun followed, but he turned once with a silent promise to the sea.

CHAPTER FORTY-FIVE

THAT'S YOUR JOB

—GAELIC LANDS—

Seanan sat at his sister's kitchen table and smiled through his grief.

Brighid was one of the strongest women he had ever known. When she was angry, it was for a good reason, and when she had a whim, no one cared to know the reason. Brighid had an uncanny knack for being right about things, and though this unnerved him, he also found it helpful, for she was never one to break under pressure, and her advice was as solid as a hardwood tree.

Now that her twins had proven deaf, her confidence wavered like candlelight in a strong wind, and Seanan suffered with her.

Her first child, Etan, a fat and fair-haired little boy, would grunt and scream lustily, but he couldn't speak a coherent word. The second child, Cian, a dark-haired and black-eyed girl, remained forever silent.

Goban strode in from the high country, swinging a bulging leather bag. He had been in the hills and brought fresh milk. He saw the children tugging and pushing and heard his son squealing like a furious hog. A dark scowl crossed Goban's face. Flushing deep red, he shouted, "Go outside to make your racket!"

They ignored his command, merely grappling with less enthusiasm due to exhaustion rather than obedience.

Her face pale, Brighid stared at her husband and placed her hands on her hips. "You know perfectly well they can't hear you. Why not command the trees to jump into the sea instead?"

Seanan stepped over to Goban and clasped his shoulder. "It's a trial, to be sure, with the young ones struggling so. But you mustn't ask more than they can give. Being deaf as they are, they cannot be held accountable."

Swinging his glare to Seanan, Goban flung the strap of his bag over a hook and stomped to the open doorways, huffing.

Seanan faced his sister. "They're intelligent, surely, but you must work with what they have, not grieve for what they don't."

With a wan smile, Brighid shook her head and pointed to a pot of stew hanging over the fire. "Eat with us, brother."

Seanan waved the offer away and glanced at Goban's back silhouetted against the sky. "The children will learn, but first, you must teach them."

Brigid ladled the stew into a wooden bowl, strolled to the doorway, and tapped her husband's arm. With a sad smile, she handed it to him.

An apology in his eyes, Goban met his wife's gaze and then returned to the center of the room. He perched on a stool by the fire and blew on the steam rising from his bowl. He glanced at Seanan. "I've tried to help, but it's a hopeless task."

A moment later, Fiona stepped into the doorway, catching her breath as if she'd run clear across the compound. "Good morning," she said, her eyebrows rising and her gaze darting from her husband to her sister-in-law.

With a smile for Fiona, Seanan picked up little Cian and swung her into his arms. "Brighid cannot manage everything. The difference between disaster and destruction is that you don't let a disaster have the last word." He kissed the child and landed her back on her wobbly feet.

The little girl beamed with pleasure, all altercations forgotten.

Fiona motioned to Brighid, and they stepped into the evening air striped with slanting shadows.

Seanan clapped Goban on the shoulder. "Keeping your wife happy in good times is easy. Helping her to remember her strength in bad times is a much bigger challenge. But that's your job; don't forget it."

Seanan nodded goodbye, passed the two women deep in conversation, and headed toward the hills, wondering if he would ever heed his own advice.

CHAPTER FORTY-SIX

AN INVITATION

—AT SEA—

Rueben wondered where he was going. He sat on the deck of the strange ship, his arms wrapped around his knees, sailing against his will to the edge of the Roman Empire.

In Jerusalem, he had felt vibrant and full of purpose, fed off the teachings, miracles, and—most of all—the stories of Jesus' death and resurrection. He longed to learn about God, the God of Abraham, Isaac, Jacob, and his ancestors going back to time immemorial. He had hoped to join one of the Christian sects in Jerusalem, but when Georgios decided to follow Pacorus to Rome, he decided that he must remain by his friend's side.

But now, separated from Georgios, what use was he? Rueben rested his head on his knees and closed his eyes, hoping to silence the questions rattling his mind.

Shuffling footsteps nearby caught his attention, and he opened his eyes, though he remained motionless. Men gathered nearby, though a barrel and a stack of rope kept him hidden.

The group formed a tight knot, and a deep voice spoke, "All quiet?"

A higher, nervous voice spoke. "Yes, sir. Not a word from anybody. It's been an uneventful voyage so far. I thank the—"

The image of the slight, pale-faced man with a high voice, Epicharis, who was forever giving orders, rose in Rueben's mind.

"Oh, shut up!" A voice rumbled like distant thunder.

Rueben recognized the captain's stern tone. He had

wondered why the captain kept Epicharis on board but then learned that he was the son of the captain's brother, who owned the ship. With a sigh, Rueben closed his eyes again and slowed his breathing, not wanting to give himself away.

The captain growled, "We have to get this over with. I don't want trouble."

A new, low voice responded, "What could go wrong? We outnumber them twenty to one. Besides, they won't be arguing once we give them their cups. They'll cooperate, I assure you."

Rueben thought he knew who spoke: one of the thickset crewmen who never said much, although his eyes glared messages that Rueben didn't want to receive.

"A brute and nothing more," was Ian's unflattering assessment of the seaman the first time they laid eyes on him.

Every muscle in Rueben's body tensed.

Apparently in no mood to be pacified, the captain said, "I know you, Britain, you think that every murder is the same—a quick thrust and overboard—but I have a hunch these men are different. If you had received the orders I did, with the kind of warning that went with them—a strange curse that nearly took my scalp off—you'd be wary yourself."

"Stars above! What in Luna's sky is that?" Epicharis shouted.

Rueben jerked his gaze upward, where a series of eerie colors washed across the sky.

The captain gasped but then resumed control. "It's as I was saying. We can't wait. We must act soon!"

Epicharis wailed. "But what if their gods are more powerful than ours? Look at that sky!"

"Shut up!" Britain was clearly irritated. "So, what if the

sky turns colors? It means nothing. We see colors during the day, don't we? What difference does it make if we see them during the night?"

A smack and a grunt met Rueben's ears.

The captain growled his next words. "There is light to see by in the day; colors are natural then, but not now, idiot! Regardless, I don't care about colors, day or night or gods or sorcery. I only care about the man who gave me my orders. He promised more than enough money to make every effort worth my while if I do my duty. He also threatened the destruction of every member of my family if I fail. Now that I take note of!"

Epicharis spoke up again. "Why not tonight? There's enough darkness to cover our deeds."

The captain hissed, "Not with that rainbow showing over the sky! If anyone wakes up, they'll take it as an ill omen, and we'll have trouble. You know how the men are. I'll not have tongues wagging. Rumors ruin a man. Tomorrow night is soon enough. But be ready. Make sure their drinks are good and strong and be prepared as soon as darkness falls to drop them overboard. Bind them tight and make sure there is not one splash! I want no questions!"

Epicharis stuttered, "N-no questions, certainly. Who wants to know anything? We just obey—"

"Shut up!" both the captain and Britain hissed together.

It would have been amusing under other circumstances, but a freezing shudder worked over Rueben's body. He waited until the gathering broke apart before stirring.

Suddenly, Britain circled around the barrel and kicked Rueben in the shins, whispering low. "Don't get up till the sun's above the horizon, or you're a dead man. I'll only season your drink—you'll be able to swim."

He sauntered away, stretching expansively.

Frozen, Rueben clenched his jaw. A friend or foe? Before he could take another breath, Britain sauntered back, thwacking his stick against the railing.

Tying a knot, Britain bent in close. "The ropes'll be threadbare." The man sauntered away, whistling.

Rueben's muscles slumped in exhaustion. A few minutes ago, he had wondered where he was going. Now he wondered why someone wanted to murder him. *Oh, God, help. I am as lost as a man can be.*

After a long, restless night, a cooling breeze rushed across the deck, and the light of a new day warmed Rueben's face. He did not dare move until large and clumsy feet tripped over him. A hand grasped his shoulders and shook him. "There you are! I've been looking for you. Get up, man. It's a new day!"

Rueben lifted his head and stared into the smiling face of Lysander, who wagged his finger and chuckled to the man beside him. "I told you he'd still be sleeping."

Ian stood beside Lysander with a wry look lighting his face.

An ironic laugh wormed its way through Rueben, but he held himself in check. Though no one was eyeing them, he imagined that ears were cocked to hear every word. He swallowed and rose. "I am as hungry as a lion. Let's get something to eat."

Ian unceremoniously dumped food on top of the barrel. "The captain was in a generous mood this morning and said we should eat now since we're nearing land. He's afraid we'll tell tales and ruin his reputation. He's even planning some kind of festivity tonight, and we're invited. Honestly, I'd thought that he was all bluster and fat with not an ounce of heart."

Rueben squeezed Lysander's arm and lowered his voice. "We're about to be murdered!"

Ian shoved a piece of fruit into Lysander's mouth before the man could reply. His eyes serious, Ian snorted. "I had the most amazing dream. It seemed to me that there were spirits roaming. Do you have the power of revelation, Rueben? You come from a long line of dream readers."

Rueben took a small bite of bread and chewed, feigning thoughtfulness. "Yes, I think I understand, for I had a similar one. But in my dream, I saw demons—"

A large hand gripped Rueben's shoulder from behind. Britain's voice boomed. "You believe in dreams? My captain would take your heads off if he heard you talking nonsense. Stop chattering and eat while you still can."

Sweat beaded on Lysander's forehead. "We want nothing more than to please the captain! After all, his generosity is well known."

Britain snorted as he turned away. "Dreams turn to nightmares if you're not careful."

Lysander clapped Ian and Rueben's shoulders. "We must stick together at all times. No wandering off."

Rueben bit off another piece of bread, but his stomach churned faster than he could chew.

The three men worked together all day. At sunset, the captain formally invited them to his cabin for refreshments. "I was unkind, hurrying you away from Rome as I did, but orders are orders. Now that we are far from spying eyes, I wish to make up for my harshness. I hope you understand."

Acting pleased, Rueben returned the compliments and assured him that they would be happy to accept his invitation once they made themselves presentable.

Pleased, the captain swaggered away.

Lysander leaned over the railing and studied the rushing waters. "We could jump now and save time."

Ian scanned the watery horizon. "I won't die here. My

father needs me."

"Above all, do not drink or eat anything." Rueben's eyebrows arched in silent command.

Lysander groaned. "What are we to say? We've all come down with cramps?" With a resigned air, he went back to work.

After a long day, the sun finally touched the sea, and the crew settled in for the night.

The three friends leaned against the railing and enjoyed the cool evening breeze. They silently watched Britain lumber by, humming an off-key tune.

Gesturing for the others to wait, Rueben jogged forward. He dropped his voice low. "About the food and drin—"

Britain smacked Rueben across the face, swore, and shoved him away. "Don't go telling the captain tales, either. I know your sort. If the captain is nice for a moment, you think you can work a deal with the rest of us. Get that out of your head before I throw you overboard!"

Hanging his head low and rubbing the red mark on his cheek, Rueben refused to answer Ian or Lysander's inquiries. He strode straight to the captain's door and knocked loudly.

CHAPTER FORTY-SEVEN

LOST INNOCENCE

—ROME—

Mithra's mother was in trouble; that much was obvious. Though an intelligent woman, she often acted impulsively. In their culture, it was in a woman's best interest to ask a man's opinion about every matter and take his advice as soon as possible.

Volga managed skillfully, but unspoken fears kept mother and daughter from discussing anything important.

Mithra wondered how she could ever understand her mother's reasoning if they never discussed her plans.

A hard rain fell, and a chilly breeze scoured the walls and roof of the shabby inn.

Mithra tugged a long, black cloak tightly around her shoulders and stared at the stained, mudbrick walls. Freezing in this dingy room would never do.

She knew all too well that Pacorus was not her mother's son. He used to visit their house as a guest rather than as a member of the family. Tilting her head, Mithra wondered if Pacorus was the son of her father—a mysterious someone who must never be dishonored. She shook her head. How could Pacorus be in danger? *He's a man, after all!*

The sky darkened, the room dimmed, and rain hammered the roof.

Volga hurried through the doorway and slammed and barred the door. Wet strands of hair plastered her face. Her eyes were wide and fearful. "Hurry, get your things—we must leave quickly. They're coming, and they must think this room has been vacant some time."

Mithra instantly obeyed, grabbing every article of clothing within reach and stuffing them into a small bag. She threw scraps of food into the fire and glanced at her mother. "What happened? Please, you must tell me!"

Volga continued her mad rush around the room, swirling dirt, smudging candles, even breaking a pot on the floor and scattering the fragments. "The less you know, the better."

Mithra grabbed her mother's arm. "We're in danger?"

"Do you think I'd wander all over this horrible kingdom for the pleasure of it? If I don't stop Pacorus, we'll be blamed and you—"

"Why would we be in danger from anything Pacorus does? He's a vain child with ridiculous ambitions. Why does he matter? Does he hate me or something?"

Volga groaned. "Oh, there is no time to discuss this! They may be here any minute."

"Who will be here?"

"The men that he's sent to find us! I can't explain now, but you must trust me. I love you more than life itself. You are the hope of our people; you're not stained with madness—"

Shuffling footsteps drew near.

Mother and daughter froze, but the sounds padded on.

A flash of lightning and thunder rumbled overhead.

Volga snatched two bags, tossed the straps over her shoulder, and ordered her daughter to take the rest.

After spying through the doorway and down the street, the two inched forwards.

The rain settled to a soft pattering as they rushed into the alleyway and skittered along as fast as they dared without slipping.

Mithra hissed, "Where's our servant?"

"Dead—serves him right!"

Aghast, Mithra followed in silence, gripping her bags tight against her chest.

When they turned a corner, a group of idle soldiers stood chatting before the gate.

A cold sweat broke over Mithra, and her body trembled.

Volga marched purposely toward them. "You there, direct me to The Shipyard Inn."

A tall, slim soldier replied, pointing. "By the docks. See the edge of the sign?" He grinned, his gaze roaming over Mithra. "Need help finding your way?"

His peers scoffed and leered.

With a nod of dismissal, Volga swept her daughter forward.

Mithra jogged at her mother's side, her arms aching as she held the bags bundled under her cloak. She glanced at the inn's sign, recognizing it as the one they had entered earlier. "Why here? We don't know anyone—"

Volga ran her fingers through her daughter's wet, disheveled hair. Her eyes softened. "Someone here can help us, for as God exists, I believe he was sent for this purpose—to save you so that you may fulfill your destiny."

"Have you lost your mind? Who—?"

"The handsome, young man named Georgios. He followed us the other day. He knows something, and he'll help us once he understands."

"But *I* don't understand!"

"As it must be for now." Volga patted her daughter's cheek and then pulled open the door. "Don't fret; it makes wrinkles, and that will never do. There will come a day when you will cherish your lost innocence and wish you had it back."

Mithra watched her mother stride into the dark interior.

Biting her lip, she followed along. Couldn’t she both keep her innocence and not be so ignorant?

CHAPTER FORTY-EIGHT

TO RIGHT THE WRONG

—ROME—

Georgios crept from under the dock where he had found shelter from the worst of the storm and wandered along the shore. Soon it would be time to return to Armand's home and discover what the man wanted to tell him.

He pictured Mithra's face, and he wondered if she had returned to The Shipyard Inn. Without thought, he raced ahead and almost ran into a woman just leaving the inn. With a quick apology, he plowed ahead, but a hand grabbed his arm.

"Are you Georgios, the one looking for Pacorus?"

Georgios nearly lost his footing as he backed up. Recognizing Mithra instantly, a flush warmed his cheeks.

Coming out of the inn, Volga spoke before Georgios recovered his breath. "May we speak privately?"

Georgios glanced around. He could not imagine any place without spying eyes, but then perhaps the safest place would be in a crowd. "How about the butcher's shop? No one would notice two women shopping with a servant following behind."

Volga flashed a smile, grabbed her daughter's hand, and sped toward the market. Volga motioned for Georgios to carry her bags. She sauntered to a meat stall, surveying the dangling fowl and various meat slices arranged on tables. With a quick wave of dismissal, she entered the evening throng.

Georgios sidled up to her, his head bent and his gaze downcast.

Volga whispered, "Have you learned anything about Pacorus?"

Impatience gripped Georgios. "Did you give your servant a note telling Pacorus that his mother was looking for him?"

Her face draining of color, Volga stopped and faced Georgios. "No, I did not. Did you receive such a note?"

Georgios motioned for her to walk ahead again. "Tell me the truth, for lives hang in the balance. Is Pacorus really your son?"

Volga glanced over her shoulder. "No."

Georgios spied a bench under a large shade tree. "Let's rest a moment."

Once the women were seated, Georgios stood like a waiting servant. He kept his voice low. "Lysander and I followed you because we were worried that you were in danger. I was given a note but soon found myself surrounded by soldiers. I was marched to the house of a man named Armand. Apparently, he has some service he wants me to perform. He invited me to dinner tonight."

"Will you go?"

Georgios bit his lip. "My friends have been exiled, so I'm alone." He quickly restated his position. "I want the truth."

"Are you sure? It might lead to disappointment."

Matrons sauntered past with their heads held high. Dawdling boys lounged on a distant pile of feed sacks, staring vacantly at each passerby. A servant managed baskets and bags, shuffling along and murmuring under his breath.

Georgios cleared his throat. "I've had to endure many unwelcome truths. I'll not shy away now."

Volga snorted. "Good for you. Now, tell me why you want to see Pacorus?"

Georgios' gaze swept from Volga to Mithra. "He murdered my grandmother."

Mithra gasped.

Volga shrugged. "I'm not surprised. He's become a dangerous man, but why would he want to kill an old woman?"

Georgios dug his sandaled toe into the dirt. "I don't think he intended to. He may have feared that she'd heard rumors of his misdeeds. They quarreled, she fell, hit her head, and died. My grandfather was devastated, and I vowed to right the wrong."

"Will vengeance bring your grandmother back to life?"

Mithra jumped to her feet. "He has the right to seek justice, Mother!"

Volga nodded. "Pacorus may have been the one to knock your grandmother to the ground, but there was another, a more dangerous man, who gave Pacorus his mission. He's the one at fault. Pacorus would never have become so desperate but for him."

Both Georgios and Mithra stared and spoke at the same moment. "Who?"

Glancing about, Volga shook her head. "We're not safe here." Her brow furrowed. "Tell me, what does your friend Armand look like?"

Rubbing his chin, Georgios pictured the man in his mind. "He was—"

Marching footsteps echoed through the marketplace. A trumpet blast announced the procession of a person of importance.

Not wanting to be caught off-guard again, Georgios stepped into the watching crowd.

The procession marched by, carrying a covered litter.

Georgios turned to speak to Volga, but she was nowhere in sight. His stomach clenched. Now he would have to meet with Armand as ignorant as he had been that morning.

He watched the last of the marching soldiers disappear around a narrow lane as the sun dropped behind the hills and sent faint pink fingers into the sky.

Weariness enveloped him. The marketplace was closing, and the last pedestrians hustled to their homes. He'd have to find something to eat. It would never do to arrive at Armand's table hungry.

CHAPTER FORTY-NINE

AN ADVENTURE FOR BOTH OF US

—GAELIC LANDS—

Seanan jerked awake, stiff with fear, his heart hammering violently in his chest. He peered around the cold, dark room, sensing shadowy evil. He patted the thick coverings until he felt his wife's soft form resting peacefully.

Seanan pursed his lips. "Go ahead, rest easy while the rest of us are being *murdered* in our beds!"

Fiona shifted her head onto her other arm but quickly drifted back into deep slumber.

Seanan snorted. "He's your son, too. The least you could do is lose a little sleep over him. *I am*!"

Fiona sighed, stretched, and slept on.

Seanan scooted back in bed and leaned against the wall, propping his head on his clasped hands. He squinted into the black pit that surrounded him. Only the sharp edges of a few objects shone in the faint moonlight.

He shivered. Was he being watched? His mind returned to his nightmare, and he sucked in a deep breath. Ian was being chased by attacking warriors. The look on Ian's face…his eyes had grown wide with determination but also traced with grief. He could not outrun his enemy.

Desperately wanting to put his own body between Ian and the approaching dread, Seanan's muscles tightened, but a roaring river held him back, keeping them separated and helpless. One of the enemies threw a well-aimed spear, piercing Ian in the middle of the back.

Instinctively, Seanan jumped and found himself in the middle of the river. He tried to reach his son but sank, grabbing warm, flowing water that could not hold him up.

He was going to die.

Then he woke up.

Seanan straightened. *No use trying to fall back asleep.* Why was he having this dream? Malevolent forces desired the utter destruction of men, but surely there were other spirits not without kindness.

He rubbed his jaw, glanced at his wife's slumbering form, and exhaled. Did belief inform his dreams, or did dreams inform his beliefs?

Clearly, Gutun's gods were of no use to him. Rueben had described his God and how He had chosen a people for Himself to protect and love. A wave of jealousy passed over Seanan.

How comforting to belong to a tribe assured of the benevolent care of God, who claimed them for His own. But then again, the Jews didn't have an easy time of it.

Seanan drummed his fingers on his legs. *I can't become a Jew; too many rules.* He considered the Savior Rueben had blathered about. He had heard rumors of a new religious sect while traveling, but he had paid little attention. A God-man didn't seem very useful. *Now, if a man could become a god—that'd be something.*

Seanan sighed. It was hopeless. He wasn't a religious man; he paid homage to whomever his wife told him he should, and he pretended to listen to the priests whenever he attended a ceremony. But deep inside, he felt nothing. He just wasn't a believer, except in the evil that men could do. That was real enough.

If his dream meant anything, it warned of coming danger. Seanan slapped the bed and accidentally hit his wife's leg.

With a yelp, Fiona sat up. "Why'd you hit me?"

Seanan blinked in surprise. "You're sleeping the day away!"

Fiona squinted at the darkness.

Not one bird sang, but an owl hooted in the distance.

She leaned on the pillows and clasped her fingers on her stomach. "You have a headache? A stomachache? You certainly ate your fill last night. I wouldn't be surprised if you were sick—"

"I'm not sick, woman."

"Have you done something?"

"What does that mean?"

"If I feel bad, I wake up in the middle of the night and—"

Seanan waved his hand dismissively.

"Tell me then. I can't guess what is on your mind."

Seanan snorted. "Isn't that a turnabout? Usually, I'm the one wondering what's going on in *your* mind. If anything."

Fiona swatted her husband's arm.

Seanan smiled at her impotent fury. "If you *really* want to know, I'll tell you, but I don't want you getting upset."

Fiona exhaled a long, exasperated breath.

"I've been plagued with bad dreams lately."

"That I forgot to make dinner or something?"

Ignoring her humor and kicking off his blankets, Seanan rose from the bed and paced the room. "For three nights in a row, I've watched Ian being brutally murdered. Each time I was helpless to save him."

Fiona gasped. "Oh, not Ian, not my beloved Ian."

Knowing that he'd said too much, Seanan tried to undo the damage. "In the dream, *I nearly drowned.*"

Fiona continued to groan, "Oh, my son!"

Seanan winced. What had possessed him to tell her?

Fiona rose and gripped his hand. "We can't allow this to happen, Seanan. This is a warning. That means that whatever is threatening Ian has not hurt him yet. We still have time."

"But in the dream, I'm powerless to help."

With a savage grunt, Fiona shook his hand. "What's making you powerless?"

Seanan shrugged. "A huge lake or a river or something, I can't cross it. Every time I try, I nearly drown."

Tugging her husband along, Fiona strode to the doorway.

Fingers of sunlight brightened the sky. Birds burst into morning song and the villagers began to stir. Smoke rose from chimneys.

She stared ahead, a frown traversing her forehead.

Seanan snatched the blanket and wrapped it around her shoulders. "It's only a dream, and you know how I am. I ate too much, and I had a nightmare."

"No. Each night I dream about a boat setting off on a voyage, and I'm very afraid, but I know I must go." She swallowed and stroked her husband's chin. "Ever since you picked up those boys, you've wanted to go back."

In stillness, Seanan tried to make his face unreadable. "You don't know that."

"Yes, I do. It's time. Do what you're meant to do and find Ian. Bring him home."

Seanan's heart leapt. He longed to tromp over wildlands sail out to sea, travel wondrous distances, meet new people, and face challenges. Most of all, he wanted to find Ian and bring him home. Seanan gazed at his wife and stroked her face, his hand trembling. "I'm glad you're my wife."

Fiona hugged him. "I'm glad you're my husband." She pulled away. "You'd better make arrangements. This will be an adventure for the both of us."

Relief flowed through Seanan. He turned with a new

spring in his step, then stopped. What did she mean, an adventure for the both of them? He shook his head. Wives stayed at home. Fiona was a reasonable woman. He frowned.

Fiona hummed as she busied herself for the day.

Seanan smiled. After all, Ian was her son, too.

Chapter Fifty

No Explanation

-OldEarth-

Noman wasn't going to make the same mistake twice. This time, no banquet and little in the way of personal comfort awaited Abbas.

The circus crowd jostled and shouted as the last of the formal procession marched into the arena.

Perched on the edge of his stone seat, Noman planted his feet on the hard ground, one hand sheltering his eyes from the blinding sun. Whatever news Abbas had, he could bloody well share it amid a fight to the death. The perfect setting for the sort of drivel Abbas considered as momentous.

Horns blasted. Cheers and jeers sprang from the assembly.

Trajan stood, ready to signal the opening of the day's first contest. Grinning like a fox, he knew better than anyone how to control the masses—bread and circuses.

Brilliant concept.

Warmth spread through Noman. He snatched his wine sack from the ground, took a long draught, and then cheered with the men around him as the gates opened and an assembly of well-armed gladiators charged forward.

A hand pressed his shoulder.

Jerking aside, Noman glanced over his shoulder. A middle-aged, perfectly-attired Roman met his gaze. *Abbas*?

"You chose a public setting for our private chat, I see."

A palpable sneer crossed Noman's face. "Nowhere better to hide than in plain sight."

The crowd screamed at the first sight of blood. A gladiator, down on one knee, struggled to rise.

Abbas winced and shook his head, his gaze bouncing through the throng.

Men of all sizes and shapes leaned forward, their wide eyes shining and mouths gaping.

"Could we perhaps—"

As his mood snapped, heat flushed Noman's face. "What are you afraid of? That my point is made abundantly clear without even the slightest effort on my part?" He waved his arms, indicating the heart-pounding, blood-thirsty mob.

Abbas wrapped his toga tighter. "Your point?"

"Beasts! Not a soul worth dying for in the whole lot. The Event failed dismally and completely."

Abbas stared into Noman's eyes. "My wife gave birth to a son yesterday."

Despite the burning rays of the sun and hot bodies packed in close proximity, a searing chill spread over Noman. "Is that supposed to mean something?"

Abbas gripped Noman's arm. "I never acknowledged your primary place—it wasn't fair, I realize that now. But they chose me, and I prayed for an heir, someone better than both of us to inherit the role. You must understand, I—"

Noman leapt to his feet, joining the crowd as the gladiator fell full length, blood pouring from multiple wounds. He shouted, "Can't you even die like a man?" In one swift jerk, he yanked Abbas forward, almost knocking him into the frenzied crowd. "I choose my own worth!"

Wiping the spittle from his cheek, Abbas scowled. "You'd have no worth if it did not come from above."

Emaciated slaves dressed in short, flimsy tunics, dragged the bloody body from the arena. Gates on the opposite end opened wide. Wild boars and wolves raced onto the scene.

The crowd screamed in frenzied delight.

Power surged through Noman, dark and terrible, filling him with unheard of potential. "Not from above but from below!"

Pity in his eyes, Abbas blinked out of sight.

Triumphantly, Noman raised his arms and joined in the crowd's screams.

~~~

Teal read the message transmitted before his eyes twice, then he gasped, panting for air. He blinked the emergency signal away, his gaze raking the narrow alley.

Cerulean paced sedately at his side.

"We have to go. Now!"

Cerulean met his gaze, a frown building. "Why?"

"Your mother is ill—the baby came too early and—" A sob choked his throat. He grabbed Cerulean's hand. "We have to tell Ark and Zuri first."

"They're on the ship, observing Georgios and the others."

Teal pulled Cerulean into a dark corner. "That's where we'll meet them."

The two shadows shimmered, and a dog barked at empty air.

~~~

Zuri stood on deck and tapped on the console, deleted words, started again, deleted a whole line, and started again…

My Love,

Though I have missed you beyond comprehension, I have managed to publish regular reports to the Ingilium, keeping my superiors happy and my conscience clear.

Teal, as professionally astute as usual, keeps us at our respective tasks, and his son, Cerulean, is wiser than any child ought to be. I wonder what will become of him. He seems to have a natural affinity for humans.

Ark remains as ridiculously obsessed with all things scientific, to the grief of his son, Tarragon. He recently informed the pod that he could not accept the role as father, and he should find a mentor in his place. Can you imagine? I fought the urge to yank off Ark's breathing helm and give him a taste of pain, but his wide-eyed ignorance, damning himself to future misery, made me nearly cry.

As usual, humanity struggles along in its state of corrupted innocence.

We haven't discovered the Mystery player's identity. He's too smart for that, but we do know that he has influence in high places. Apparently, he has made good on promises to allow certain humans unnatural luck, all the while placating their consciences with deceptive accomplishments. Trajan has gained popularity through mob entertainment. He has also risked the loss of his kingdom on more than one occasion. Someone has been encouraging risky choices.

We've been following a boy named Georgios, a descendant of Aram and Ishtar. He, too, is offered alluring choices at the cost of his soul.

I have followed, as much as possible, the course of The Event, and I am as amazed as ever. No explanation accounts for it. The reports are remarkably unified. Life beyond death; hope after despair. Song would be pleased.

You're ever in my—

A bright flash scattered Zuri's attention.

Teal and Cerulean stood before him, their eyes much too wide.

"What's wrong?"

Teal glanced around the room. "Where's Ark?"

Rising from a chair against the back wall, Ark waved like a pod called upon in class. "Here. You returned rather early. I haven't finished—"

"Sienna is ill. We must return to Lux immediately."

Ark bounded forward, his tentacles fluttering. "Go, then, Hurry. We'll manage. See to your wife!"

Zuri swallowed a rising lump. "The baby?"

Teal shook his head, tears in his eyes. He gripped his son's shoulder.

Crushing pain squeezed Zuri's heart. "We'll be here—or there—wherever you need us."

With a nod, Teal sucked in a steadying breath and glanced at his son. They blinked away.

Ark shook his head. "Why stop here? They should've just gone directly."

"He knows I understand."

Ark harrumphed. "I understand too!"

"If only." Zuri hit the send button.

CHAPTER FIFTY-ONE

THE MEANING OF WORDS

—ROME—

Georgios strode to Armand's home. Though he made two wrong turns in the confusing labyrinth of narrow streets and tiny merchant shops, he finally found himself at the right location.

A well-dressed servant motioned Georgios inside and led him to the back garden.

Armand rested on a carved bench near a gnarled, old tree. A fountain mounted on stone lions sent a spray of water into the air. Burning incense further enhanced the rich, exotic atmosphere.

The servant bowed his way backward, leaving Georgios standing alone.

Armand patted the seat beside him with his bejeweled hand. "Come, sit and tell me about your exciting day."

The skin on Georgios' arms prickled. "I've been sitting all day, so I'd rather stand."

Armand smiled, his gaze reflecting both mirth and a sneer.

Heat rose in Georgios' cheeks.

"I know where you've been, Georgios, and I hardly think that crying like a lost child on the shore until you fell asleep, running to the inn to meet with two manipulative women, and then hurrying through a miserly supper qualifies as sitting all day. Do you?"

Desperation clutched Georgios' mind as he detached himself from frantic terror. He pictured Connan in his mind and formed an exaggerated pout, feigning anger. "You're following me? Did you send my friends away? I should report you to the Roman authorities!" Georgios' heart pounded. He was acting a part but only a little.

Armand sat up straighter and sighed, clearly disappointed. "An interesting act but not you at all. You have no interest in Roman authorities."

Georgios leaned against the tree; his fury spent but his need for answers unquenched. "The questions remain."

Armand flicked a fly off his arm. "So, they do. I know all about your short, misdirected life, Georgios. Your Greek grandfather and Roman father. Your mother undoubtedly once told you that good men act with honor. But do you even know what the word means? You can't possibly understand the real world with what little traveling you've done." Armand rose, staring into Georgios' eyes. "But you could grow into a man of consequence. So much depends upon your willingness to learn the honest meaning of words."

All but frozen in place, Georgios scrambled for a coherent thought.

Armand motioned toward his luxurious home and started forward. He stepped through an arched doorway. "Though you may not be hungry, I am, and the food is ready. I assure you; it's not poisoned. You may eat your fill and stroll back to your inn and sleep comfortably through the night."

Georgios called after him, "But you haven't told me—why am I here?"

Armand continued to walk away, his voice like a child's plaintive call, "Because I need you. Without your help, my life might as well be over."

Staring at the strange man as he stepped into his luxurious house, Georgios shivered.

CHAPTER FIFTY-TWO

AN EVENING GLOW

—GAELIC LANDS—

Earan brushed spindly branches aside and thrashed his way through a tangled wood. The stupid cow had wandered in this direction, but he had no idea where she was now. Her calf had been sold yesterday, and she was acting moody and unpredictable. Chasing an unhappy cow through the woods did not please him, but he allowed himself the pleasure of thinking about a particular young woman, the most exasperating and unmanageable girl he had ever known. Still…the thought of her long, thick hair gleaming in the sunlight and her sparkling eyes brought a smile to his lips.

He stepped from the woods into a wide, lush pasture.

A noisy grunt caught his attention.

When he looked over, he saw not the oval face of his beloved with her teasing eyes but rather a massive black bull with sharp horns and eyes that sparked in fury.

Apparently, the cow also had a relationship she wanted to continue.

Earan glanced around, keeping an eye out for sudden movement on the bull's part. He slapped his thigh in irritation.

The bull didn't appear particularly pleased by the meeting either. The massive animal pawed the ground, its snort growing louder and more aggressive.

Earan shuffled backwards, ready to return to the enclosing woods while the bull rocked, preparing to launch itself forward. Heart racing and palms sweating, Earan searched his memory. Which god should a man turn to when faced with a charging bull?

A piercing whistle from the opposite side of the field rang out.

Undeterred, the bull kept his head low and bellowed.

The whistle rang out louder, higher, and more insistent.

The bull paused and turned its head, the whites of its eyes glaring.

Liam's voice called, "Earan, where are you? I found the cow, and I am bringing her home."

Recognizing his little brother's voice, Earan rushed to the edge of the woods, an area populated with saplings.

Irritated, the bull glanced aside and glared a warning.

Could he shimmy up one of these trees to its lowest branches? Knowing his heavy weight and the pliability of young wood, Earan dismissed the possibility. He wanted to shout a warning, but he didn't want to anger the bull any further.

Clearly unaware of the unfolding drama, Liam strolled into the clearing.

To Earan's amazement, his brother smiled and stopped to stroke the cow he was leading. "Oh, there you are. I'd been wondering. Are you looking for—?"

His heart leaping to his throat, Earan forced out a few strangled words. "Stop, Liam! The bull!"

Grinning at Earan, Liam led the cow forward.

Earan's heart stopped. "What're you doing? The bull is—"

"Oh, him?" Liam threw a lazy glance at the bull. "Feisty, isn't he?"

The cow and the bull met and shared a private moment.

Earan blinked, glancing from the bull to the cow, who was now eating grass in great mouthfuls. He swallowed. "You knew the bull was here?"

Liam patted the contented cow's side. "It's my job,

isn't it? She likes to wander afield." He jutted his jaw at the bull. "He's just nosy." He stroked the cow's head affectionately. "She should be milked. See how full she is?"

Earan took his brother's word for it. "And the bull?"

"He'll head to the other side of the hill like he always does. Father says it keeps us safer having a bull wander about. Few people trespass if they know he's around. Besides, he likes the cows. Can't blame him for that."

No, Earan admitted, he couldn't.

Liam tugged on the cow's rope as he spoke to his brother. "Come on. It's getting late, and father has news. He's going to sea again."

Earan followed, rolling his eyes. "That is why I was sent to get you and the cow. There's a feast tonight before he leaves."

"He's going so quickly?"

"He's worried about Ian."

"That sounds more like Mother. Then again, he's wanted to return to sea for some time now. I hope everything will stay calm while he's gone."

The sun faded behind the hills, and twilight set in.

Standing on the brow, Earan admired his village, peaceful and glorious in an evening glow. He sent one furtive glance back to the dark woods then patted Liam on the back. "Don't worry, little brother; I'm here to protect you."

CHAPTER FIFTY-THREE

GOD OF SEA

—AT SEA—

Rueben looked up when the door opened, nodded to the cabin boy, and passed into the captain's quarters.

Ian and Lysander followed close behind.

The captain bounded forward. "Thank you for coming. I know you must be wondering what could possibly have made me act—"

Lysander plastered a smile over his face and, with a sing-song tone under his breath, said, "Threats and bribes..."

Ian jabbed Lysander in the ribs, staring directly ahead.

A servant marched forward with a tray laden with drinks.

The captain took a tall cup from the sideboard, swished it dramatically, and swept toward them. "Here is to your health and long life!"

Lysander began a new song. "*Liar, liar*, you're quite-"

Ian choked.

The captain pounded him on the back.

Lysander stood back, staring as if in a trance.

The cups were passed around, each man accepting one.

Without hesitating, Rueben drank the contents in one gulp. He smiled blankly and plunked his cup on the sideboard. "Very good, Captain. Thank you."

The captain bowed low and motioned for the others to drink.

Lysander pouted. "My stomach has been weak of late—"

Rueben snatched Lysander's cup and drank its contents as fast as he had the first. Before Ian could stop him, he grabbed his cup and gulped it down just as swiftly. His mission accomplished, Rueben smiled, though his eyes watered and his throat stung. "Very good again, Captain."

Lysander glared at him, stricken.

Ian grabbed Rueben's arm.

"I can take my drink with the best of you. Let me be."

Lysander gestured weakly. "But you drank ours too. Was that wise of you?"

Rueben pursed his lips and waved his hands aimlessly. "It seemed like the right thing to do. When do we eat?"

His face flushing, the captain grumbled orders to his cabin boy.

The boy scurried to arrange the captain's table in short order.

"While he's making everything ready, let me tell you about my most exciting voyages!" The captain clapped his hands. "And let's have more drinks!"

Ian glared at Rueben.

Lysander leaned in. "Hold back your enthusiasm this time, would you?"

Dizziness enveloped Rueben, and his legs buckled.

Ian grabbed one arm, and Lysander caught the other. Bobbing his head apologetically, Ian motioned toward the door. "We'd best take him outside for some fresh air."

As they arrived on deck, an uproar met them.

A spectrum of colors rippled across the sky. Although this night's demonstration was not as startling as the night before, it evoked dire predictions among the men.

"The gods are angry!"

"The ocean will rise from the deep and drown us all!"

Britain slogged between the men, cursing and shoving. "Colors in the sky don't mean anything. We aren't thieves and murderers. It's only when the gods are displeased with terrible injustice that they send such warnings. Since we're innocent men, we've nothing to fear."

Epicharis pointed at Lysander, Ian, and Rueben. "What about them? They're exiled for a reason!"

Britain shouted above the tumult. "Perhaps you are right! Or perhaps they're unjustly accused, and the gods are angry because we've taken part in misdeeds."

Flushing deep red, the captain shouted above the cacophony of voices. "I've done nothing wrong! If there is guilt, it's on them."

A background voice clamored, "Throw 'em overboard!"

Lysander scratched his chin. "They change their minds so quickly."

Recovering in the fresh air, Rueben shook his head to clear his mind. He pulled free and stood tall. "As a son of Israel, I belong to the God of sea and sky. He has seen my people through many tribulations, and He will see me through this voyage. Drop us off at the nearest landing, and we'll gladly leave you in peace."

A general murmur met this proposal.

Britain shouted, "We'll be in port day after tomorrow. We'll leave them there and have no more trouble about it."

Refusing to face his crew's wide-eyed stares, the captain turned and stalked into his cabin.

Lysander slumped in relief.

Ian slapped Rueben on the back. "Quick thinking."

Rueben slid against the railing and plunked down on the hard deck. He rested his head on his arms. "I wasn't thinking."

Lysander laughed. "Someone must be looking out for you." He took a deep breath and slid down next to Rueben. "I'll rest too." He glanced up at Ian. "You keep watch and wake me early." He chuckled. "I can't wait to see what tomorrow brings!"

Sighing, Ian faced the sea and leaned on the railing.

Rueben closed his eyes. The gentle waves rocked him like a child in his mother's arms. For the first time in days, he rested easy.

CHAPTER FIFTY-FOUR

HOW WOULD SHE FARE?

—GAELIC LANDS—

Fiona stood at the table in the dimly lit room, warm loaves of bread laid out before her, and brushed her hair away from her face.

A breeze blew from the hills and swept over the valley. The sun still hovered over the horizon, while clouds descended from the highlands, spreading white mist and softening its pink rays.

She packed food bags with care and considered the shrouded green hills, a lump rising in her throat.

This was her home, and only her love for her son could draw her out. Those she left behind would carry on as they always had, in perfect rhythm with the seasons. *But how will I fare?*

Ancient legends told of forebearers who had traveled from distant lands. Through uncounted seasons, newcomers settled in this valley and built homes and livelihoods. Would she, Fiona, wife of Seanan, mother of Ian, Earan, and Liam, still belong after she had traveled the world? Worse yet, would she have to brave the ire of her entire clan to make a voyage she dreaded?

Fiona straightened, stretching her neck to loosen the tight muscles. Her instincts told her that there was nothing so vastly different in the great world that was not already in her small corner, but she would have to prove that to Seanan and her sons, perhaps to herself as well.

A cheerful hum drifted closer.

Seanan strode into the room, smiling cheerfully.

"It's good to hear you so happy," she said.

Seanan's grin disappeared. "I'm not happy to leave, but the sooner I depart, the sooner I return—with our son, I might add."

Fiona wrapped the leather thong around the necks of the food bags, her hands trembling. She braved a smile and stepped a little nearer. "That makes sense. I'm happy that you're going."

Seanan's eyebrows arched.

"I'm not happy that you're leaving. I'm just happy that you will find Ian. I've been so afraid that I may never see my son again." Fiona's voice broke.

Seanan wrapped his arms around her and stroked her hair, resting his chin on her head.

Fiona nestled contentedly in his arms.

Seanan lifted his head and took a step back, staring at her with a strange look in his eye. "Come with me, Fiona. Brighid made the trip, and it didn't do her any harm. The boys are old enough to manage on their own and, who knows, we may have good luck and find him quickly." Seanan's words tumbled to a stop.

Tears overflowing, Fiona hugged Seanan with all her might. His offer gave proof of the rightness of her desire. She was meant to go and search for her son. Hope swelled in her heart as she gazed up at her husband.

Fear and doubt raced with hope and joy across Seanan's face. He gripped her tightly, anxiety springing to his eyes.

"You'll not regret this, Seanan. I'll do whatever I can to help. You know how well I cook."

With a gulp, Seanan nodded.

Content with her decisions, Fiona led her husband to the doorway and gazed out at the others.

Liam and Earan strode into view, smiling at the crowd gathered by the hogs roasting on spits. Women with toddlers tugging at their dresses set bowls and platters on a table in the center of the village. Men sharpened knives and joked with each other. A father teased his son, pretending to jab him with a knife. The son parried the blow, both of them laughing.

Fiona stood in the doorway, holding her husband's hand. Though she could not see where her future would lead her, she trusted that the home she loved would be here when she returned.

CHAPTER FIFTY-FIVE

A SHADOW DREW NEAR

—PATMOS—

Gutun shifted uneasily as fading light softened white walls, and the sea glowed like burnished gold. He savored the beauty unfolding before his eyes like a canvas in an artist's shop.

As darkness swallowed the day, a peculiar sensation crept down his spine—a nauseating loss of self-control. He had once called the spirit world to do his bidding; now, he was being called to do their bidding.

A shadow drew nearer.

Disgusted by the unwelcome presence, his skin prickled. He backed toward a steep cliff. If he leaned back too far or was pushed— A shiver ran through him. Gathering his courage, he spat his words, "Who are you? What business do have you here?"

The shadow hovered and in the next instant enveloped him.

A voice spoke…or was it an impression? "You serve two masters."

Gutun wanted to laugh. He served *no* masters.

"You forget your duty."

Gutun attempted to clear his throat, but a spasm incapacitated him. He had no reason to remain loyal to gods that had not protected him.

A furious hiss spat in his ear, "You serve another!"

Gutun shook his head in wild denial. *There's no one to serve on this barren rock.*

A new thought slapped him. "You do not serve us!"

His body grew cold. His unknown benefactor had paid

him handsomely, providing a good opportunity. "How could I serve you from here? No one helped me!"

Jerked upward so that he stood on his toes, Gutun blinked in terror. "I'm loyal to you!"

An insect-like being crawled inside his mind. He retched. Gritting his teeth, he tried to maintain a bit of dignity. Horror loosened his mind. He began to giggle.

Blazing pain licked his skin from the tips of his toes to the frizzled ends of his hair.

He dropped to the ground and groveled. "I serve you. Whatever you want!"

A combination of wrenching and throbbing pain replaced the searing fire. Relief settled in, and Gutun wrapped his arms around his middle and swayed on his knees like a child lost in the dark.

In the moonlight, a distant ship rocked on gentle waves.

Gutun stared ahead. Slowly, he climbed to his feet and faced the shore.

CHAPTER FIFTY-SIX

HIDDEN FAITH

—CARTHAGE—

Rueben held Britain's arm longer than necessary at their leave-taking. They looked into each other's eyes. Britain's hidden faith had surprised Rueben, but they both knew how to keep a secret. The understanding in their eyes spoke for them.

Tapping his foot impatiently, Ian watched but said nothing.

Lysander pushed the line along. "Hurry, would you? This plank is about to fall to pieces, and I can hear the captain calling, probably inviting us to breakfast!"

With a parting glance, Rueben jogged off the ship and joined his friends on shore. "What now?"

Ian nodded toward another ship. "I need to find out where they're going. I'll be right back."

Without further discussion, Lysander led Rueben to a food stand. "I'm starving. You must be, too, despite your rambunctious night. Come, and let's get something to eat."

After ordering a simple meal and starting with weak wine and bread, Rueben's stomach unclenched and his mind cleared.

Ian jogged forward. "I found a ship that'll take me home."

Lysander swallowed and cleared his throat. "Did you forget about Georgios?"

Rueben jabbed Lysander's arm. "Seanan is waiting." He faced Ian. "Go home to your family. We'll head back to Rome, find Georgios, and free him from whatever—"

Lysander pounded his fist on the table. "Mess he got

himself into! Won't he be surprised to see us? I can't wait to see his face."

Rueben studiously ignored his friend. "This humble meal will have to suffice for your farewell party, Ian." Standing, Rueben placed one hand on Ian's shoulder and the other on his head. "May God, the Father of all Men, go with you, and may you find your family safe and in good health."

Lysander chuckled. "And may the good God find you a beautiful wife!"

Ian embraced Rueben, patting him heartily on the back. "We will meet again." Then, with his well-packed bag slung over his shoulder, he trotted toward the ship. He turned and called out, "Tell Georgios I'll be waiting for his visit!"

Lysander beamed and called after him, "He won't be coming alone!"

Ian marched away.

Smiling dreamily, Leander took a long swig of wine.

A nameless grief tugged at Rueben. *If only I could go home...*

CHAPTER FIFTY-SEVEN

A PERFECT MATCH

—ROME—

Alexandra knew that she was beautiful. Endowed with long, thick, black hair, piercing eyes, arched brows, a chiseled face, and a body only a talented artist could dream up, confidence exuded from every pore of her body.

The only child of a powerful senator, a leading citizen of Rome with many important connections throughout the city and devoted to his gods, she had found temple dedications an effective means of making herself admired.

Whoever controlled the city's temples controlled the minds and hearts of its citizens. As a devoted worshipper of Jupiter, she was expected to dress with the greatest care, wear the finest jewelry, and eat the best foods. Simpletons envied her, as if she really did sup with the gods, but she knew the emptiness of her role. No god ever spoke to her. No one answered her yearning prayers for a worthy man to fill her empty arms.

As with any evening party, she strode into the main room with her robes flowing like colorful, billowing clouds.

Only one man did not look up.

Annoyed, she sidestepped her appreciative audience and flowed over. She stopped, allowing him time to properly appreciate the vision before his eyes. She inclined her head.

He lifted his eyes. His penetrating gaze pierced her. Suddenly vulnerable, she covered her unaccustomed nervousness with a laugh. "Do I know you?"

He patted the cushion at his side.

She sat, wondering at her sudden shiver.

Though not handsome in the traditional Roman or Greek style, his eyes held her. Spellbound, she shook herself and unloosed her most sensual, melodious voice. "I've never seen you here before. Are you a senator or a member of the imperial household?"

Armand smiled and clasped his hands. "I'm a friend of a friend."

Her brow wrinkled. She was attracted, but she could see no reason for her sudden interest other than his eyes. "I am the daughter of—"

"I know all about you. In fact, you are the answer to a prayer."

Alexandra relaxed. Back in familiar territory, her smile widened. "I'm merely the daughter of a Roman senator, not so very special."

Armand chuckled.

A shiver ran over her arms.

"Brilliant—your voice, beauty, modesty—a picture of glorious innocence." His eyes roamed over her. He leaned. "But I know the truth. You are a daughter of the gods. You've never been innocent, have you?"

A flush heated Alexandra's cheeks. "I am not a child you can flatter. I am as pure as the day I was born. I serve my people by serving the gods. My father has sponsored three temples—"

Armand waved his hand in dismissal. "Your father is of no use to me. I need a woman who knows her own mind. I may have misjudged you."

Alexandra blinked, indignation rising. "No ordinary man can understand me!"

Armand smiled, a game to be played to the finish. "Too true. And I know just the man for you. As innocent as you but extraordinary just the same. A perfect match. One the gods will approve—have no fear."

Her heart leapt. Alexandra clutched her hand to her chest. Perhaps she had been wrong about the gods. They had been listening all along.

CHAPTER FIFTY-EIGHT

LITTLE CHOICE

—ROME—

Mithra faced her mother. Standing in a corner of a cloth merchant's stall, sheltered from the pounding rain, they talked in urgent whispers. "What happened to our servant, Mother?"

"Don't ask." Volga's eyes drooped in exhaustion. "We've done all we could; we must accept our fate. Pacorus is gone. We've only one hope left, a tremulous one at best."

Mithra wanted to scream. "What would that be?"

"Pray that our enemy's enemy is not our enemy and that we can escape without detection."

"Oh, Mother, you always speak in riddles!" Mithra rubbed her eyes and tried not to let her frustration dissolve into tears. "Won't you explain anything? It's all because of me, isn't it?"

Volga thrust her bag behind her and reached for her daughter. "Don't be ridiculous. It's not about you. People like you don't cause wars. You're a good child, a mother's perfect wish, but some people will try to use us to achieve their own ends." Volga paced across the small space. "It's not your doing, but it does involve you. Our lives depend on the will of others, for good or evil." Volga clasped her daughter's hands. She glanced around.

The stall remained empty.

"You're the eldest daughter of the king, the only legitimate daughter of me, his first wife. I have counseled peace and patience, but others bend the king's ear to their schemes involving war to achieve wealth and power. The king used to heed my words, and we decided that you shall marry a neighboring prince to strengthen our kingdom. But that alliance depends upon peace with Rome, a peace that will not be kept if Armand has his way.

"We kept you ignorant of the truth until the time was ripe for you to take your position as first daughter. Armand plots to overthrow the Roman Empire, but he would not stop there. He desires your father's throne as well. Besides, any attempt to overthrow Rome would be an act of war. Your father sent assassins to take care of Pacorus and Armand, but they failed."

Volga smiled wanly. "I decided that we could do what no one else could: *we* could search for Pacorus and have him killed so the danger would end. But in my obsession with Pacorus, I underestimated Armand. I hoped that when his servant was overthrown, Armand would forget his schemes, but he has already chosen another to take Pacorus' place."

"What happened to our servant?"

Volga's voice trembled. "He was killed. I do not believe he meant to betray us, but I'm afraid he was left little choice."

"Who killed him, then? The emperor or Armand?

"Armand, of course."

"Why did he give Georgios a note in your name?"

Volga shrugged. "He probably thought he could draw Pacorus into Georgios' hands and solve all our problems."

"But Pacorus wouldn't come to you. Surely, he knew that."

"The fool thought he knew everything, but in fact, he knew little. He was supposed to draw Pacorus out and have him killed, but I discovered too late that he tried to win the emperor's favor by betraying our secret to a friend and got himself killed in the process." Volga sighed. "I had hoped that perhaps our young friend, Georgios, might be of some use, but now I fear that Armand has got his claws into him as well." Volga sighed and rubbed her hands across her eyes. "I've made so many mistakes. I've been the cause of more confusion and death." She looked at her daughter. "I must bring you safely home and face the just wrath of your father."

Stricken, Mithra gasped. "None of this is our fault! Besides, we can't leave Georgios to face Armand by himself!"

"We had only a fool's hope. As long as I see you safely back home, I don't care what happens to me. I just want to get away from Rome as soon as possible."

"But if the emperor ever learns the truth—"

"Rome will demand justice—your father and all his household will be marked for slaughter."

"We'd be killed though none of this is our fault?"

Volga snorted. "Many innocents have died in the name of justice. We would not be the first nor the last. Besides, if you look at it from the emperor's perspective, he'd be right. One of our own is trying to destroy Rome."

Mithra's eyes glazed with unshed tears. Daughter of the *king*. Divinely created for a precious role. "I won't run from Armand, abandon Georgios, or leave our people to a treasonous fate. I'll find Armand and stop him, even if it costs my life."

Volga wiped her tears away with the back of her hand and sniffed. "Your courage gives me strength. Come, we must do what great men tremble to think about."

~~~

Armand sat in his chamber, resting on a pile of overstuffed pillows. Perfumed air caressed his face. He
~~~

had arranged a meeting tomorrow night with Pacorus. Georgios would finally confront the man who killed his grandmother. The outcome was inevitable and would solve numerous problems.

If threats meant anything, Volga and Mithra were on their way home.

Georgios was coming to understand his new role as a favored friend, practically a son to a powerful man.

Armand rubbed his chin. Under his care, Alexandra had cultivated a friendship with Georgios and fallen in love with the boy who looked and acted like a benevolent Greek god.

Armand chuckled.

They owed all their happiness to him.

Now, it was a simple matter of introducing these two worthies into the Emperor's most intimate household. Through the arms of others, he would finally bring his plans to fruition.

Armand's gentle laughter wafted into the spice-scented night.

~~~

Georgios tried not to stare at Alexandra, who sat across from him as the living embodiment of serene beauty.

Armand paced in and out of the room, arranging a religious service.

As he observed Armand's ornate robes billow behind him, memories of Gutun soured his stomach. He darted a glance at Alexandra.

She observed Armand closely even as she met Georgios' gaze repeatedly.

Finally satisfied, Armand swept into the room with an ornate figure cupped in his hands. He centered it in a ring
~~~

of flaming candles surrounded by a black oval. He clapped his hands, and servants deftly set incense burners around the oval.

The room filled with pungent odors and undulating smoke.

Armand sat cross-legged and beckoned the two nearer. He gestured to indicate their places.

As he crossed his legs, Georgios resented the heavy incense wafting in his face. Sweat broke over his forehead. Why had he let himself be talked into this? He wished that Rueben were here. If not Rueben, then Ian with his blunt assessments would be of some help. At this point, even Lysander would be useful—he would say something so ridiculous that it would break the spell that wound around him like a treacherous snake.

Armand murmured a slow chant. "Rest easy, Roxanna, your murderer will meet his just end, no fear."

Alexandra closed her eyes.

Georgios tried to control rising panic. He took a deep breath of the perfumed air, and his body soon relaxed, soothed, entering a dream-like state.

A deep voice broke the stillness.

Georgios glanced up to see a young man standing only a few steps away, his arms folded across his chest and a sarcastic smile curling his lips.

Seeming to move in slow motion, Armand rose, approached the newcomer, and whispered in his ear.

The newcomer's sneer grew uglier as he stared at Georgios.

Suddenly, Georgios knew the identity of the man before him. This was his grandmother's murderer. With gut-wrenching clarity, he imagined his grandmother—innocent and harmless—on the day she died. Fury swelled. He rose, his heart pounding, his breath rapid. He stepped forward, caring about nothing other than his building rage. His tongue felt oddly thick, but he choked out, "You deserve to die for what you did!"

Something cold and hard was slapped into his hand.

His fingers curled around the knife. He took a step forward.

Pacorus shrugged. "I merely relieved the world of a miserable wretch."

Armand shouted, "He wants to kill you!"

Pacorus swung at Georgios' head.

His fury taking him, Georgios blocked Pacorus with his left and plunged with his right.

Pacorus jerked but stayed upright, as if held in place by strings.

Georgios released his grip.

Pacorus fell to his knees with a surprised grunt.

Armand stepped back from the body, accusation in his eyes.

Weak and confused, Georgios tried to make sense of the blood spreading across the floor and the knife slipping from his fingers, then clattering down.

On her feet, Alexandra was screaming loud enough to alert the entire household.

Armand slapped her and yelled at Georgios, "You've killed a favored member of the Imperial household. Do exactly as I say, or your death will not be so quick and merciful."

Alexandra's eyes widened in horror. "But he didn't mean—"

"Some might question your association with a murderer."

Alexandra gripped Georgios' arm, a woman taking possession of her man. "What must I do?"

"Pretend that this never happened. When questioned

about it, look innocent. I will explain to Trajan that Pacorus met with an unfortunate accident and that you two are being offered as replacements for his loss. He'll be pleased with the exchange." Armand gestured to the figure. "See your new god. After I instruct you in the proper protocol, you will erect a temple in his honor and collect all dutiful homage. In service, you'll find protection."

Georgios stared at Pacorus' dead body. It happened so quickly. Dizziness enveloped him.

Once Armand snapped his fingers, servants came to Georgios' aid.

Alexandra looked from Georgios to Armand, to the dead man. She nodded and then prostrated herself before the figure.

After being led into a quiet room, Georgios stumbled onto a bed, his ears ringing and his mind numb.

CHAPTER FIFTY-NINE

AN INTERESTING VISIT

—ROME—

Rueben knew how to fight, but he also knew he was too small to intimidate anyone. Lucky for him, Lysander's growl and irritated squint masked a soft heart, though few were willing to test him. Instead, Lysander put all his fatherly qualities into guiding Rueben safely back to Rome. Once there, Lysander insisted that they deserved a reward, so he spent their first night eating, drinking, and retelling stories at a bustling inn. Rueben crawled onto his side of the bed and fell asleep, letting Lysander talk and drink himself into a stupor.

During the night, Rueben dreamed of fish flying overhead. He awoke in a sweat, thrashing his blanket aside.

In the morning light, Lysander stood over him, grinning. "I didn't kick you hard, just sort of toed you. Think I was a thief?"

Groggy and faintly disturbed, Rueben rose and flung on his cloak. "A strange dream is all."

Lifting his hands as if to ward off the sign of death, Lysander groaned. "Don't describe your dreams. I had enough of those on board the ship."

Rueben brushed Lysander aside as he headed for the door. "We ought to find that girl we met and talk to her servant."

Lysander's smile widened. "I'm one step ahead of you." His grin turned into a grimace. "Turns out, their servant was murdered." Lysander rubbed his chin. "Nasty way to go, I mean, why torture him?"

Rueben's eyes widened. "Tortured to death?"

"Well, a man doesn't do such a thing to himself! He must've known more than we realized. Anyway, I did find the girl and her mother."

"Where?"

"Hold on. I was up early, and you know my motto—"

"Spare me!"

Lysander pouted with exaggerated forbearance. "Well, my lord, they're not far. I thought that we could go—"

Rueben ran out the door, his cloak billowing behind.

They approached the inn and knocked. No one answered. Lysander tried the handle. It was locked. Flummoxed, he stopped a passing boy. "Where's the owner?"

The boy pointed to another shop up the road.

His shoulders squared, Lysander nodded and paced ahead.

Anxiety rising, Rueben covered the distance at a sprint. Stepping breathlessly inside, he approached the weaver. "Have you seen the mother and daughter from the inn down—"

"Excuse me." After nudging the hanging baskets out of his way, Lysander stopped before the weaver. He threw one arm around the man's shoulder and met Rueben's inquiring gaze. "This here is a good friend of mine, an innkeeper and quality weaver. He's survived the world's troubles by knowing how to keep his eyes open and his mouth shut. A lesson I wish you'd learn!"

The weaver shuffled toward an unfinished basket leaning against the back wall. "Don't flatter me—I've learned a few tricks, is all."

Rueben leaned forward and dropped his voice. "Do you know the mother and daughter staying at the inn?"

"Many people came through, two women among them,

but they left before the Romans came and shut the place down."

An ache throbbed through Rueben's head. "Roman soldiers shut down the inn?"

"For the time being."

"You didn't protest?"

The weaver shrugged. "I have two businesses for a reason. When the Romans' shut one, I open the other."

His eyes shining like a cat's, Lysander grinned.

The weaver plunked down on the hard ground, grabbed a handful of thick grass, and wrapped the ends together. "Tell me about your adventures. I love exciting stories, especially when I'm not in them."

Lysander rubbed his hands together then pointed to the door. "We'd love to, but right now, we have a mission to accomplish—I know just what to do."

A headache threatening, Rueben pressed his forehead.

Lysander grinned at the weaver. "When we meet again, I hope you'll have finished that basket."

"You wouldn't know this basket from a thousand others. But I hope you find your friends."

Lysander nudged Rueben into the sunshine.

Faltering from the pain in his head, Rueben shaded his eyes and grimaced.

"This won't do. You're not feeling well." Lysander waved in the direction of a food stall. "Here, get yourself comfortable. Eat and rest. I'll be back."

Rueben grabbed his cloak. "Wait, I can be of some use. You might need me to translate…or something."

"I can do all the translating that needs to be done. Don't move until I get back. It may take a while, but promise me that you won't leave."

"I'm not a child."

Lysander patted him on the back. "I know. I just don't

want to lose another friend."

With a sinking feeling, Rueben dropped heavily on a stout bench and watched Lysander fade into the crowd.

~~~

Lysander folded his arms over his chest in the middle of the marketplace. "I've been looking for you all over Rome."

Mithra met Lysander's gaze and jumped up.

Lysander grabbed her arm. "No, you don't! I found you and I mean to keep you, at least, until I get answers. Where's your mother?"

Mithra's gaze darted to the butcher's shop.

Lysander smiled. He sauntered into the shop, found Volga, and steered the two ladies to an unoccupied spot under the canopy of a large palm tree. He motioned toward a low stone wall.

"Glad you weren't drowned at sea. We've been under the impression that your lives had been made forfeit."

Lysander winced. "Thank you, Volga. We had a little trouble, but we managed to stay alive." After taking in the nearby scene, Lysander dropped his voice. "Our real concern is the fate of our friend Georgios. You know where he is?"

Mithra opened her mouth, but her mother waved her off. "We know where he is, though he may no longer be your friend."

The bright sun stung Lysander's eyes as sweat trickled down his back. He glared at the woman, not liking her accusation.

Volga nodded. "First, you should know why we are here."

Mithra hissed, "Is that wise, Mother?"
~~~

With an appraising glance at Lysander, Volga shrugged. "We've barely escaped. We must trust someone." She faced Lysander. "I am the King's first wife, and Pacorus, acting on direction from Armand, is about to upset the delicate balance of power in our two countries, using your friend to seize control of Rome and lay blame on my family."

Convinced that his heart had stopped beating, Lysander froze every muscle as he listened. "But what happened to Georgios? Where is he?"

Volga snorted. "Can't you guess? Your old friend Georgios is now the new Pacorus. Armand has a new obsession and seems to have forgotten all about us."

Lysander stared, stunned. "Georgios, the new Pacorus? He hates Pacorus."

Volga sighed. "Rumor is that he killed Pacorus and took his place. The emperor is quite pleased with him, I hear. Armand is using Georgios and a senator's daughter to acquaint the world with a powerful new god. Not really a new god, if anyone knew their history. Such provincials! Put madness into verse, and they will fall on their knees and worship!" Volga snorted. "Idiots!"

Lysander spent the failing afternoon questioning Mithra and Volga about the plot to overthrow Rome. Had Georgios not been in the middle, he would have dismissed the notion as a woman's ridiculous story.

The sun dipped under the horizon.

After standing and stretching, Lysander gestured for the ladies to follow. "We need to find Rueben. Let's go."

The three strolled towards the vendor's booth where Lysander had left Rueben, but no familiar face met his gaze.

Lysander fumed. "I told him to wait here!"

A boy jogged close. “You’re looking for a man named Rueben?”

Lysander looked the boy in the eye. “Yes, what do you know about it?”

“He told me to watch for you. He’s gone to the shore, but he’ll be back by nightfall.”

“The sun just set!”

“Lysander!” Loping forward, his face too pale for Lysander’s comfort, Rueben huffed. He stopped short before Mithra and her mother. “You found them!”

In no mood for pleasantries, Lysander bellowed. “Where have you been? I told you to stay put!”

Rueben nodded to Mithra. “I was afraid you were in trouble. After what happened to us—”

Lysander exploded, waving his arms. “Stop talking to them and start talking to me! Why did you go to the shore?”

“It’s a long story, but I wanted to see a family off safely. They were being persecuted, so I gave them money for—”

Fury heated Lysander’s face. “You decided that someone else needed our money more than we do?”

Rueben clasped his hands, calmness incarnate. “Yes. They’ll be welcome in Carthage. A thriving colony lives there. It was a miracle, really. The ship was ready, I had the money on hand, and they were willing to go.” His grin fading, Rueben faced Mithra. “If you can tell us where to find Georgios, my day will be complete.”

Lysander cleared his throat. “We know where Georgios is; we just don’t know who Georgios is.”

Rueben tugged his fingers through his hair.

At a loss for how to explain, Lysander nodded to Volga. “You tell him.”

Mithra stepped forward. “Yes, it might be better

coming from me." The four wandered to the stone wall, while Mithra retold her story.

Leaning against the stones, Rueben clasped his hands, a picture of confidence. "I know Georgios. He'll see through Armand's lies." Talking through a yawn, he started forward. "We'll find Georgios in the morning." He smiled at the women. "Meet again tomorrow?"

Mithra furrowed her brows but nodded.

Volga sighed in resigned acceptance. "We leave for home the day after tomorrow. We pray that Georgios is spared."

Lysander chuckled. "Don't worry. Rueben is right. What difference will one more night make? He's not going anywhere." Lysander bowed low. "Goodnight."

The two women walked along the shoreline.

Lysander clapped Rueben on the shoulder. "I'm exhausted."

Snorting, Rueben stumbled.

After they found a room for the night, Lysander stretched out on a thin pallet and yawned mightily.

With a sigh, Rueben sat in the corner, leaning against the wall.

"Aren't you going to sleep?"

"Not yet. Go ahead. We'll talk in the morning."

As he closed his eyes, Lysander wanted to say, "Don't go anywhere." But sleep took him before he could get the words out.

~~~

Rueben crept out of the quiet room. He was not sure where Armand lived, but he could find out. There were always men milling about who had answers for those willing to pay. It would be a matter of finding the right
~~~

person, but with some luck and the grace of God, he would find Georgios tonight.

A few hours later, Rueben met Armand on the threshold of his home and knew that he had met his match. A knot tightened in the pit of his stomach. “Sorry to have disturbed you so late, but I was told that you might know my friend Georgios. I have an urgent message for him.”

Armand looked pleased, though Rueben could think of no reason a man would welcome an interruption in the middle of the night. “You’ve not bothered me. I enjoy interesting visits on quiet nights.” Stepping aside, Armand ushered Rueben into an ornate room.

Exotic wall hangings and miniature serpentine statues added to Rueben’s unease. An odd scent emanated from one corner.

Attempting a calm demeanor, Rueben strolled to the window and breathed in the clean night air. After squaring his shoulders, he faced Armand. “I’d be grateful if I could speak to Georgios.”

Though he smiled, Armand hesitated.

Movement caught Rueben’s attention.

A woman slipped into the room.

Armand’s eyes narrowed, his hands tightening.

The woman sashayed forward. “I’m Alexandra. I can show you where Georgios is sleeping.”

Rueben met Alexandra in the middle of the room, clearly against Armand’s wish. Rueben didn’t care. *I won’t leave Georgios behind again.*

Chapter Sixty

Enough Trouble

-Mystery Planet-

Noman poured burgundy wine into a silver goblet, paced across the Persian carpet, plunked down on a plush couch, and stared at the sober family portraits hanging discreetly across the stone walls.

Abbas certainly knows how to decorate. Or at least, his wife does.

Footsteps echoed down the hall.

Noman glanced up.

Abbas, appearing younger and stronger than ever, nodded as he stepped into the room. "You made yourself comfortable. Good."

Noman sipped his wine and stretched before the comforting fire.

Bypassing the decanters, Abbas strolled to the arched window. "You'll meet everyone at dinner—they're arriving now."

Noman grinned. "I do enjoy the exquisite flavors of a well-appointed table. Trajan's offering included the indecent, as did many of his friends, but that only heightened my delight."

Abbas stared at the flames. "This meal is simple enough: meat, bread, honey, fruit, some spiced wines." His gaze shot to Noman. "But no one will care about the food."

"Speak for yourself. I've developed a cultivated palate. Nothing but the best. If you can't provide, I'll—"

"That's not why you came."

Rising, heat sizzled through Noman and his form

blurred. “I’m here to make my case before the assembly. You may provide a meal, but make no mistake, I will provide a feast!”

~~~

Abbas listened to the prattle around him as the assembly, arrayed in their accustomed forms as representatives from Lux, Helm, Ingilium, Sectine, Earth, Crestar, and farther reaches of the universe ate in calm demeanor, catching each other up on personal news and recent events in their respective placements.

At the foot of the table, Noman chattered, a happy child telling all who would listen about his adventures among barbarian humanity.

Subtly, Abbas tried to catch his attention.

Ignoring everything but his set purpose, Noman rose and saluted the assembly. “Welcome, all, to our humble gathering!” He winked at Abbas. “My friend sets a simple table, but I’m sure his excessive humility can be amended.” Noman snapped his fingers.

A colorful variety of exotic desserts, from tall glasses of foaming red liquid to delectable sparkling cakes topped with creamed icing, appeared on the table. A heady scent of spicy sweetness filled the air.

The assembly gasped—then clapped in hearty approval.

Abbas rubbed his forehead. *Pompous idiot.*

Noman lifted his goblet, topaz and sapphire gems glinting off flickering candlelight. “To Humanity. Our own beasts! Intelligent and crafty, but animals, nonetheless. They rise in one generation and tumble in the next.”

One member, appearing as a prime Cresta scientist,
~~~

languidly smoothed down the green cilia on top of his head as he smiled through golden eyes. “Don’t they all? Lessons hard-earned are soon forgotten.” He glanced at a tiny Bhuaci female who glared straight ahead. “But then, we’ve heard promising things about this race. That they’d been favored…”

Noman spluttered and waved his goblet, slopping the amber liquid across the table and onto his neighbor, an annoyed Ingot. “Favored? By whom—God?”

Abbas chewed his lip. Noman had taken more than his usual fill this evening, and it showed. “We don’t name—”

“God! God! God!” Noman slapped his cup on the table and swung away. He charged beside the long table and halted at the head. He stared into Abbas’ eyes. “It was nothing! A trick. A test, perhaps. Humanity has proven itself unworthy of our attention, much less His!”

The heavily armored Ingot tapped his foot, his jaw clenched.

The Bhuac cleared her throat and gazed around the room. “That’s not for us to decide.”

Spittle flew as Noman raged. “An idiot could decide!” He thrust his hand into the air, ticking reasoned points on his fingers in quick succession. “Alexios, the grand Roman soldier, a sick failure. Myron, moldering in his grave, left his life’s work to slaves. Seanan wanders about, a befuddled child unable to protect his own. Armand, like Trajan, at least knows what he wants—power! And who can blame him? Humans exist in chaos; why not grasp a moment’s pleasure?” He slapped his hands together. “It all ends the same.”

Abbas shoved his chair back and rose to his full height. “Those are only some examples of humanity. There are others.”

Throwing his head back, Noman chortled. "Who can you be thinking of? Witless Georgios? Pathetic Rueben?" Noman thrust his arms into the air and raged. "Let us extinguish vain hope and dedicate the planet to a worthy reason for existence."

Cursing the inevitability of the answer, Abbas choked out his words. "Such as?"

Deadly serious, Noman's fiery eyes burned deep into Abbas. "Me."

–Lux–

Teal plunked down on the offered chair and dropped his head onto his hands.

Sterling paced before him, his hands clasped behind his back and head down, a low murmuring hum emanating from his chest. "I can't say I understand since that would be patently ridiculous. Not married, have no children; I don't even do well with plants. But I can feel grief. Just because I am rising through the ranks, so to speak, hardly means I've lost touch with basic emotions."

Numb beyond even wretched anger, Teal lifted his head and stared out the open window.

The sky bustled with luminous activity. Delivery systems ferried goods to every available home, business, care center, and government facility. Though Sterling's apartment wasn't at the highest level, it still commanded a glorious view of the surrounding cityscape and even a margin of the Wildland Preserves. Memories of his last camping trip with Sienna sent searing pain through his chest. He heaved as his stomach roiled.

Jerking back, Sterling glanced around, an anxious frown building between his eyes. "Perhaps you should return to Luxonian form before you do something…disgusting.”

Teal wiped his mouth with the back of his hand, his nausea abating. He stared at a clay vase, one he had brought from Earth and gifted to Sterling. “I made a full report to the Supreme Council. I’m ready to go back as soon as Sienna recovers—”

Sterling’s large, surprisingly warm, hand dropped onto his shoulder. “Your son and your wife need you, Teal. I’ll go. Though I hate the food, the climate, and humans in general, still, I wouldn’t mind catching the Mystery Race in the act.”

His throat closing somewhere between a choke and a snort, Teal glanced up, his vision blurry.

Sterling dropped his gaze, his dark eyes brooding, belying his light-hearted tone.

“You’ll keep me informed?”

Sterling laughed and slapped Teal’s back. “By the Divide, I’ll send you a daily report. That way, you can tell me everything I’m doing wrong.”

Teal sighed and let his gaze fall back to the floor. “It’s hard to do anything right these days. Right just isn’t enough.”

—GAELIC LANDS—

Zuri tiptoed after Ark into the quiet village during the dark of night, searching the perimeter for any movement. He sniffed the acrid scent of offal, a waste pit, and rotten fish. *Blast it, how do they survive here?*

The hushed village slept in secure routine. Only an occasional hooting owl and a distant wolf’s howl broke the stillness.

As clouds skidded across the sky, the moon’s glow illuminated the landscape.

Ark halted near a smoldering fire in the center of the village and whispered, "He was here recently."

Zuri frowned and attempted to match Ark's low tone low. "How can you tell?"

Ark waved a tentacle. "I can smell him."

A quick roll of his eyes relieved Zuri of the need to sputter his disbelief.

"I'm serious! You have sensors that detect movement in distant galaxies, while I have"—Ark waved his tentacles in the air—"very sensitive skin. I feel that a non-human was here recently."

Exhaling a long cleansing breath, Zuri fought to regain control of his shattered concentration. "Could've been a chicken or—"

A child's cry pierced the night.

Zuri stiffened.

Ark thrust his tentacles over his ear holes and scooted as fast as his booted feet would allow to the far edge of the village.

Zuri raced along behind.

They met beside a boulder, panting with the exertion.

Once his irate heart had steadied, Zuri scowled. "Sensitive skin! Your waddling into the center of the village almost got us caught."

Ark shrugged. "I wanted to get closer. They amaze me."

With a sigh, Zuri let his gaze roam the bucolic setting. "They are beautiful. Their natural simplicity, commitment to honest labor, family traditions…it's enchanting."

Ark blinked. "I meant that they moved so far from water. What was the point? I mean, they could've had a perfect existence if they'd just stayed near water."

Like a patient tutor with a slow student, Zuri shook his head. "Humans like to do things the hard way. Haven't you figured that out yet?" He stomped forward. "Let's go."

Ark yanked his friend's arm and held him. "Where?"

"We'll follow your skin—then maybe we'll have something to report to Teal before Sterling gets here. By the Divide, if I didn't have enough trouble."

Ark huffed as he waddled along, bubbles rising from his breathing helm. "Sterling is all right."

"Does your skin tell you that?"

"No. My heart does."

His chest tightening, a empty cradle flashed before Zuri's eyes. "By God, next time I look, you'll be human."

CHAPTER SIXTY-ONE

SENSIBLE

—GAELIC LANDS—

Brighid glared at her husband, a wail hovering on her lips. By the blood of their ancestors, could she never teach her children to mind, even for a moment?

Cian and Etan remained as incorrigible and defiant as ever. They were not simply deaf and dumb to words; they were deaf and dumb to reason. Every attempt at teaching them manners had failed.

Appearing undisturbed, Goban arrived for his mid-day meal, smiled, and grabbed Cian around the waist. While she wiggled, grunted, and kicked, he laughed. Then he put her down and did the same with her brother. He ended the matter with a friendly pat, something he might offer an unruly pet.

Brighid lamented cruel fate. "Don't you care that your children act like beasts?"

Goban wiped the tears from his wife's face and shrugged. "I accept them for what they are. You must do the same."

"I can't." She dropped her head on her husband's shoulder.

Wrapping his arm around her, Goban held her close and sighed.

Fresh tears sprang to her eyes as her children tumbled across the room like unrestrained puppies.

~~~

Liam shoved daub into the crack of his house, then
~~~

pressed it smooth with the palm of his hand. Too preoccupied to hum, as was his usual practice, he kept his eyes and ears alert for any sign of village unrest. Since his mother and father had left, everything appeared calm, but uneasiness strained his peace of mind.

Irritation surged at the memory of Earan smiling at a silly girl named Maggie. It was natural for a handsome man to fall in love with a beautiful woman, but if Earan felt he was next in line to rule, he might be looking for a wife. And Maggie was an unsteady boat even in the calmest sea. Liam shook his head.

Laughter rang out.

Liam had a fine view of the entire village from the top of his ladder. He glanced around.

Finishing with an extended chuckle, Earan leaned toward Maggie as they stood together in the middle of the village.

Maggie giggled and nudged Earan with her shoulder in mock severity.

Liam's gut twisted.

The sun sank behind the hills, and the light dimmed. Storm clouds approached from the west.

Satisfied with his work but concerned about the weather, Liam called out, "Earan!" He pointed to the dark clouds building the sky.

Earan frowned and waved his brother's concern away.

Frustrated, Liam climbed down the ladder, wiped his hands on a rag, and strode across the bare, hard-packed earth. "Earan, we need to get the cows in."

His face flushed, Earan dragged his gaze from Maggie and flung it at Liam. "You can take care of them. I'll come in a bit."

Liam knew his brother's temper. If Earan became clan leader, it would not do to make him resentful and angry now.

Wishing that Maggie would leave, Liam tromped to the corral and set to work opening the gates and filling the water trough.

Agnes shuffled by, her feet bare and a ragged shawl wrapped around her slumped shoulders.

Liam called out, "What's the matter? Has the sky fallen?"

Raising her eyes, Agnes blinked at Liam as if coming out of a trance. She glanced at Earan and Maggie. "It's sad. She doesn't even care about him. She just wants to become the next clan leader's wife. If Ian were here, you'd see a change soon enough. She wouldn't have a thing to do with a younger brother then, would she?"

Liam stared at the pair and sighed. He returned his gaze to the woman before him. Agnes suffered not solely because Earan was deceived but because Earan never noticed Agnes. No one noticed Agnes. She carried her isolation about her like a second skin.

Liam's heart skipped a beat. Living in the shadow of older siblings was never easy. He forced a smile. "It's not as bad as—"

A drop of rain splattered on his arm. Alarm bells rang in his mind. He met Agnes' gaze and pressed her arm. "Tell my brother I've gone after the cows. I don't want them slipping down the hill. If I hurry, I should be able to get them back safely."

The rain fell faster and heavier.

Drops crowned Agnes' head and streamed down her face. "But the bull. What with the lightning and thunder crashing about, he might—"

In perfect imitation of his older brother, Liam waved

her concern away and puffed out his chest. “We’re old friends. He won’t bother me.” He glanced at his brother. The rain poured harder. He lifted his voice above the raging storm. “Tell Earan to hurry!”

Agnes’ pensive face lengthened as her eyes widened in fear.

Searing pain clutched Liam’s heart. A strange girl who cared when few else did.

A distant moo was answered by an angry bovine snort.

Without further ado, Liam sped up the slippery slope, hoping that the cows would be more sensible than humans.

CHAPTER SIXTY-TWO

SOMETHING HAS CHANGED

—GAELIC LANDS—

Gutun despised mud but he hated flies even more. He scowled at the dark sky and muttered an oath that should have shriveled every green thing in sight.

He cast a sidelong glance at his companion—a middle-aged man with a grizzled face who seemed to care little for the impending storm or the flies.

Gutun had found him living in his little hut on the other side of the island. Why the seaman had landed there, Gutun could not say. The merchant who had dropped him off was more interested in getting his goods to market than to seeing Gutun safely settled.

Once Gutun paid him at the beginning of the voyage—the only deal the man would accept—Gutun was as good as on his own. He had told the captain that he would like to be let off on *his* side of the island, but the fellow had merely stared, then spat a little too close for comfort. Without ceremony, he had dumped Gutun's few belongings on shore and spat again before waddling to the noisome port town. Gutun had picked up his belongings and asked nearby vendors for assistance. No one appeared interested in helping.

In desperation, he plunked down at a small hovel that sold the worst gruel he had ever tasted.

In response to his inquiry, the serving woman pointed to a shack near the water's edge. "He knows this land better than anyone, and though he usually stays home, he'll ramble about at times, but you better ask soon. He goes to bed with the birds."

Gutun was not sure if she meant that the man went to bed early or that he literally slept with the hens, for his shack looked like a fowl's delight.

He trundled over and called out, "Man for hire?"

A grumble answered, "We want no man for hire!"

Gutun sneered and tried again. "I'm looking for a guide to take me home. I have only a few things, but I wish to get there as soon as possible."

A grizzled head poked out of the shack. "Where'dya live?"

Gutun jogged a few steps forward and tripped on his soiled robe. "I live with the people of...Seanan was the leader…his sons, Ian and Earan, are worthy metalsmiths and..."

"I know the place. There've been goings on there I hear, but it's not my business. I'll take ya, if ya make it worth my while."

Gutun held out a Roman coin.

The old man snorted. "That's how you reward a man's service? Can I eat or drink a piece of metal?"

Gutun smiled. "If it's meat and drink you are looking for, then come, and I'll give you a supply to last a year."

"And how would I carry such abundance home, I wonder?" The old man's grin exposed yellow, broken teeth. "Just give me my due, some meat and cheese to last from moon to moon, and I'll be happy enough. A couple days' travel to be fed a month. That'll do, aye, that'll do."

And from that moment forth, Gutun could not get another word out of his companion. They traveled in silence except for the whine of mosquitoes, the buzzing of flies, and his incessant slaps on every part of his body.

So glad to be nearing home, Gutun imagined the food he would heap in the man's arms as a reward. But as the leagues fell away, the day wore on, and another day followed, Gutun's enthusiasm dwindled. By the time they reached the village, a steady downpour had soaked through the layers of his ragged clothes, and Gutun's nerves had strained tighter than the straps on his mud-spattered sandals.

He squinted at the dim, deserted village. Exhaustion directed his weary feet to the doorstep of his own home.

His determined guide followed close on his heels.

Gutun stepped inside and found to his amazement that it wasn't his anymore. All his personal items were gone, replaced by the tokens of another man and the marks of a woman's touch!

Gutun smothered his fury and tried to imagine anyone with the audacity to attempt such a thing. He turned swiftly around and bumped into his guide. "Still here? You've done your job; you can go!"

The old man straightened, narrowing his eyes at Gutun. "Oh, that would not be a nice game to play, my friend." He looked around at the fine things in the roundhouse and smiled. "I see by ya surprise that something has changed since you were here last, but that does not surprise me. If you please, I'll take my rest while you get my provisions. I'll be happy to leave ya in peace, but I'll not take a step away from this place until ya do as we bargained."

The old man stepped to the immaculately made-up bed and stretched his wet, dirty body upon it. "Yes, I'll be happy to rest a bit. Go about your business. I'll wait."

Amazed by the length as well as the meaning of the speech, Gutun realized that he was not going to extricate the old man easily. Fuming with impatience to get answers, he stomped out of the house and into a drenching rain.

A flash of lightning and a clap of thunder reflected his current mood.

CHAPTER SIXTY-THREE

SEPARATE PATHS

—AT SEA—

Seanan's hands shook as he carried Fiona's bruised and bleeding body over the foreign shore. She stirred in his arms, murmuring Ian's name.

Despite the vicious storm in the wee hours of the night, most of the crew had survived, though three men had been washed overboard. Once the sea unleashed her fury, it appeared determined to see them sink. But luck, skill, or an unknown force had saved them. Now they needed to retrieve the last survivors from the sinking vessel before the waves grew strong enough to wash the broken ship out to sea.

Pushing himself beyond pain and exhaustion, Seanan swam from ship to shore several times, rescuing injured crew members and salvageable materials.

By evening, the weary, battered men staggered along the shore and watched the last of their ship disappear under the rolling waves.

Fiona and two other women tended the injured men and organized the pitiful foodstuffs.

Seanan limped to his wife's side and sank to his knees.

She offered him a near-empty flask of wine.

Stretching out on the grass, he exhaled a long, ragged breath. "You think we made a mistake?"

Tears filled Fiona's eyes. "I've always believed that dreams were directed by spirits who knew more than mortals. But now—" She glanced up as a man trudged by carrying a heavy cask on his shoulder. "Perhaps it was just a dream and nothing more."

Seanan rubbed his temple. "Now you tell me."

Fiona's face crumpled, tears spilling down her cheeks.

Seanan clasped her hand with a remorseful chuckle. "It's not as if I was full of wisdom myself. I was determined to go, with or without you." He rubbed his chapped lips. "I regret that you're in this mess." He sat up and surveyed the open shore and high rocky cliffs to his left and right. Had the ship broken on the rocks either north or south of here, they would have found themselves shipwrecked with no shore within reach. "It could've been worse."

He considered his wife, who sat rigid and silent. "Listen now. We'd only been traveling a few days when the storm hit. We're alive and safe and not far from home. We'll soon get another ship." He shrugged. "The question is—do we continue forward or...?"

Fiona stared mutely ahead.

Seanan understood. This adventure had been conceived in fear and ended in terror. He wrapped his arm around his wife's shaking shoulders. "I know what I'll do."

She swallowed, blinking warily.

Seanan chuckled. "I'll take you home, and then I—"

A seaman jogged forward. "Men on the cliff called down. There's a village close by. We can get provisions and make arrangements for another ship."

Eager to get moving, Seanan snatched at a bundle within reach.

With a look of concentration, Fiona stood, smoothed her torn dress, and brushed dirt from the folds.

Tucking a second bundle under his arm, Seanan straightened and laughed. "You look like a cat dragged from the sea!"

Fiona smiled grimly. "You're looking bedraggled yourself. But for a man, that isn't unusual." She swept wet strands of hair from her face. "So, what are we going to do?"

"What we should've done in the beginning. You're going home, and I'll travel alone." He dearly wanted to caress her pale face. "Sometimes, we must take separate paths."

Fiona stared ahead, agony in her eyes.

Seanan recognized the truth of his words, but grief gnawed at him, nonetheless.

~~~

Ian watched the navigator fall to his knees with gasping breaths and clutch another seaman who brutally pried his clinging fingers from his arm.

Of the seven men who had fallen ill, only two remained alive. The navigator had panicked and ordered men overboard, dead and sick alike, but no one obeyed his orders.

Now the navigator had fallen ill.

Ian watched with fascination and disgust, though as a passenger, he had no authority to intervene.

The navigator reached for the seaman a second time, but the seaman backed away, his movements sharp and cold. Mercy was a rare commodity. Everyone was frightened.

Pity tugging at him, Ian stepped forward, but no words came.

The navigator, now prostrate before the crew, mumbled in breathless haste a devout prayer.

Rueben had often bowed in the same manner, murmuring prayers Ian never could understand. Ian had no wish to meddle in the unseen world. He never liked to imagine that any priest, Gutun especially, had a
~~~

relationship with the rulers of the natural world. But when Rueben spoke with conviction about his God, Ian understood that Rueben knew God in a manner Gutun did not.

A burly seaman dragged the navigator to the prow of the ship.

"Please, don't. I'm still alive! I have a family—"

"Shut up! It's as much as you deserve. You were ready enough to throw others overboard. Now it's your turn."

Ian heard his own voice as if someone else spoke. "Are we beasts that throw living men to the sea?"

A crewman on the perimeter of the watching circle shouted, "The Romans do so all the time!"

"Are we all Romans, then?"

Another crewman responded, "Good as or better."

Ian nodded. "A wager then. If God spares him, will you?"

The men glanced at each other doubtfully. Ian could read their thoughts: the gods were hard to comprehend. Sometimes you could please them with mercy, but more often, they liked nothing better than strict justice.

The navigator fell on his face in an exhausted stupor. They hardly needed to choose, for he was dying fast.

Pity nudged a memory. When he had first boarded the ship, the navigator had boomed out, "Good to have you aboard, boy." As he looked down on the man slipping into death's fierce grip, Ian made a decision. He wanted to see this man live beyond his mistake. His heart stretched out to something beyond his understanding.

The navigator's contorted face stilled.

Grief washed over Ian. Before anyone could protest, he bent down and kissed the man's forehead. Then he stared at the disgusted crowd. "He is beyond us now."

A quavering voice rose. "He's not dead."

The navigator stirred.

One of the men stepped nearer. “He was never dead. He fainted from fright!”

Relief swept over the throng. A crewman shouted, “Stop gawking, fools! Have you never seen a man faint before?”

The navigator combed his fingers through his hair and rose, fresh spirit in his eyes. “Get back to work before the ship flounders. I’m not ill, so get moving.”

Dumbfounded, Ian stood apart and watched as the crew returned to their former duties. He searched the deck for the two sick men and realized that the miracle had not extended to them. They were dead and soon flung into the sea.

Grim-faced, the crew hustled to direct the ship on to the next port.

Still stunned, Ian leaned over the railing and watched the rushing waves bubble and foam against the ship’s sides. *How could God do so mighty a thing and yet—?* Heaving a sigh, he returned to his duty repairing the anchor rope.

When they reached their appointed port, Ian stepped onto land and gratitude relaxed every muscle in his body.

From deck, above the tumult of bustling crewmen, the navigator called out, “Ian, remember me the next time you pray to your God!”

Ian nodded. He wanted to say something, but he couldn’t find the words. He turned toward his next destination, praying that it would lead him home.

CHAPTER SIXTY-FOUR

OUT OF LOVE

—ROME—

Rueben heard Armand's invitation to come in and have something to eat, but he wasn't hungry, only tired. A strong scent nearly overpowered him. Then his eyes faltered, the stucco walls and textured ceiling appearing out of focus. His legs trembled, and he lurched unsteadily for the door.

Armand's servant gripped Rueben's arm.

Instinctively, Rueben attempted to pull free, but he could hardly lift his arms, much less jerk them out of a strong grip. As he fell, he noticed that everyone else in the room wore a veil. His mind seized on this incongruent detail, but all mental activity was arrested in the grip of drowsiness.

~~~

Georgios awoke to a bright new day. He lumbered from bed, rubbing his aching back. A pounding headache brought his hand to his temple.

A basin and water jug sat on a table near the window.

He lurched toward them. After splashing the tepid liquid over his face and rubbing it vigorously with a towel, he staggered to the doorway.

Voices murmured down the long hallway. He forced himself to stand upright, not wanting his host to see him in this weakened condition. *What a fool I've been!*

Armand had played the host too well.

All Georgios' attempts at self-discipline had been cast
~~~

to the wind in time. Nothing seemed to please Armand more than to see Georgios surpass his limits. Like everyone else, he enjoyed the feasts and Alexandra's company.

Armand never cared what they talked about, so long as they enjoyed themselves, though he never answered any of Georgios' questions.

Late at night, Georgios would wander the coast in hopes of discovering his friends' return. He had asked the seamen if they had seen anything of them, but invariably, no one knew anything useful.

Georgios rubbed his eyes and ignored the persistent nausea boiling in his stomach. His friends would never come back.

Distant voices rose in a heated argument.

Georgios eased forward.

Alexandra's voice grew shrill. "I told you that someone would come looking for him. He's—"

Armand's sibilant hiss interrupted her. "Nobody! He—"

Georgios lost his grip on the doorframe and fell into the hallway.

Armand and Alexandra halted, their exchanged glares as angry as their voices.

Alexandra blurted in a hurried tone, "Georgios, we were coming to get you. We've met your friend—"

Armand stepped in front of her. "He met with an unfortunate accident."

Alexandra gasped, gathered up her robe, and marched away.

His head still foggy, Georgios tried to comprehend the situation. "What do you mean? Who—?"

Armand lifted his hand, stalling Georgios.

Alexandra screamed from a distant room. "Georgios!

Come quickly!"

Swallowing back bile, Georgios raced down the hall, glancing in each room. He halted in the doorway of a tiny room next to the servants' quarters. Coiled ropes, a ladder, and planks of wood lay stacked against the walls.

The body of a young man lay stretched upon the floor.

Armand stopped beside Georgios.

Alexandra, kneeling beside Rueben, glared up at Armand.

How did Rueben manage to get here? Remembering his own preoccupation with assorted pleasures, guilt tore through Georgios.

Alexandra beckoned. "He's not dead yet, but I'm afraid he won't live much longer." She brushed Rueben's hair out of his eyes. "He came seeking you, Georgios, but he was ill, and we didn't know what to do."

His mouth falling open, Georgios stared at the coils of rope hanging from wooden pegs and the planks of wood with dirt clinging to their edges, and then at the rush ceiling. He turned to Armand. "You laid my friend in here?" Georgios shoved Alexandra aside and cradled Rueben's head in his arms. "Rueben, I knew you'd come back. It's me, Georgios. Wake up. I have so much to tell you!"

Rueben's head flopped to the side.

Georgios shot an accusing glance at Armand. "This man is as dear to me as a brother! Why have you laid him like a dog on the floor? Where are the others?" In rising fury, Georgios eased Rueben down then stood and faced Armand. "Tell me the truth!"

A knowing smile crept across Armand's face. "Ask Alexandra. She was with him."

Her faced flushed and eyes flashing, Alexandra climbed to her feet. "Would you make Georgios believe that I had something to do with this—this treachery?"

Ignoring Alexandra, Armand clasped Georgios' arm. "He was sick when he arrived, so naturally, I could not have him in the main house, though I did leave him in Alexandra's care. We both know how jealous she is..."

Alexandra slapped Armand's face and turned to Georgios. "It's not what you think! I could tell—"

Armand gripped Alexandra's arm, his fury flashing.

A servant yelled from the hall, and a deep voice shouted.

Armand turned to face this new challenge.

Georgios heard the commotion but was too intent on Rueben to care. He knelt and pressed his ear to Rueben's chest. To his infinite joy, he heard not dead silence but a beating heart. He chaffed Rueben's hands, calling his name. "Rueben? Wake up, Rueben."

Though intent upon his ministrations, Georgios froze at the sound of synchronized marching feet. Torn between fears, he chose to stay on his knees.

The marching halted, and a voice demanded, "Armand, come forth!"

Armand paled.

Alexandra stared in fascination.

The same deep voice commanded. "Forward!" The Roman soldiers marched down the hallway. Two soldiers detached themselves and moved towards them, sour expressions proclaiming their mood.

A demented smile curled around Alexandra's lips. "Friends come to visit, Armand. Will you honor us with introductions?"

The larger of the two men stopped before Armand.

Armand recovered his senses and swung his arms in welcome. "This is no place to meet. My servants must have lost their senses to lead you this way. Come, we'll go out to the orchard!" Armand whisked around and started toward the garden.

"Stop, Armand!" The commander brooked no disobedience. "I've been told enough to kill you where you stand, but someone from the Imperial household would like to speak with you." His eyes narrowed. "Some would risk their lives to keep a friendship and halt the advance of war."

Armand's gaze slid past the Roman officer to a gathering just inside the doorway.

Georgios stood and looked over Armand's shoulder.

Lysander, Mithra, and Volga huddled close together. He should have known.

Alexandra turned to Armand, a furrow digging into her brow.

Mithra stepped forward and scowled. "You are the man who caused us so much grief? Not at all what I imagined."

Armand bowed mockingly. "You're hardly the princess I had hoped for."

"You came to topple a throne, but you have been toppled instead. Did you think my father would let you set the stage for war without his consent?" Mithra shook her head. "The only one you deceived was *yourself*."

Armand laughed. "Who are you to bring such charges against me? I see you brought your mother. She thinks lies can bend the ear of emperors." Armand waved toward the door. "Away with you! You may tell those who sent you; I am not pleased. I will certainly take action—"

The commanding officer stepped forward and gestured to his men. "Take him."

The soldiers advanced.

"I am a friend of important senators, and the emperor himself considers my advice—"

Two soldiers grasped Armand's arms, bound them

behind his back, and despite his protests, forced him through the doorway.

Silently, Mithra and her mother stepped aside.

Lysander strode closer. "Noisy fellow." He glanced around. "Nice place, but where is Georgios? And whatever happened to Rueben? I was sure we'd find him here."

Tears sprang to Georgios' eyes. Rueben's emaciated body lay in stark contrast to his own bloated flesh. His conscience condemned him as he remembered the sumptuous feasts, his drinking, the silly flirting, and the luxurious hours he had spent stretched out on a soft bed.

Stirring, Rueben struggled to rise.

Relief and joy flooded Georgios as he helped Rueben to a sitting position. "You all right? Armand made it sound like you were dead. For a moment, I thought you were."

Rueben shuddered. "Not dead yet…though, apparently, I've been through the fires of Hades."

With his gaze glued on Rueben, Georgios relaxed. "You're among the living again. I'm sorry that you had to get caught up in this mess. I should never have come here." Georgios sat back and slapped his hands on his face. "I've been a fool. If only you'd been here, I would've made wiser choices."

"We learn from our mistakes." Rueben sighed and glanced around. "Where's Armand?"

"He's been…called away."

Lysander chuckled. "That's one way to put it."

Georgios stood. "Lysander!"

"You can thank Mithra and Volga. They took their lives in their hands, went to the Emperor, and told him everything." He exhaled a long breath. "Good thing Trajan was in a mood to listen." He frowned and wagged his finger admonishingly. "You have any idea what you've put us through?"

Georgios' face flushed. He offered Rueben his hand. "Can you stand?"

"I think so, though I feel like I've had enough wine to make ten men drunk for a week." He swayed, putting his hand to his head.

Lysander smiled. "You have a way of taking chances—and living through them. Armand could've killed you on the spot."

Rueben nodded ruefully.

Lysander and Georgios helped Rueben to the front door.

Georgios stopped as his gaze fell on Alexandra, waiting in the shadows.

She ushered him forward with her eyes.

Mithra and Volga stood waiting. Volga bowed. "We're glad you're both safe. I was worried when we couldn't find you, Rueben, but Mithra guessed the truth."

Rueben nodded. "God bless your kindness. Armand would certainly have killed me."

Alexandra strolled forward dressed for traveling in a long cloak and hood. When she spoke, her voice barely rose above a whisper. "Not if I could've helped it." She stopped in front of Georgios and met his gaze. "He was doing more than molding you. He was destroying you."

His stomach churned and his heart twisted; Georgios could hear his own voice pleading, "I thought you wanted me to be different."

Dropping her gaze, Alexandra stepped away. "I wanted many things different but never you."

As Georgios led Rueben into the fresh air and the bright light of a new day, his gaze followed the beautiful woman until she disappeared around a corner, even as he felt his friends watching his back.

~~~

Armand trod forward, his head high. He fumbled twice on the uneven pavement but righted himself quickly. His thoughts ran rampant as the Roman soldiers marched him through filthy, Roman alleyways.

He could see Georgios' face in his mind. That Volga and her daughter had dared to go before the emperor and report their suspicions should not have amazed him. That Alexandra and Rueben tried to rescue Georgios shouldn't amaze him either. They acted out of love for the man.

To have Georgios for myself is all the revenge I need.
~~~

CHAPTER SIXTY-FIVE

HOME AGAIN

—AT SEA—

Ian watched the throng of forlorn humanity hustle up the incline that led to a small fishing village and wondered if they needed his help. They certainly looked bedraggled. He munched a handful of dates and, though he was thirsty, he was satisfied for the moment to lean against a boulder and observe with little real interest.

Obviously, they'd met misfortune and needed to find another conveyance to their hoped-for destinations. Offers arrived from competing ships' captains.

Dropping the last date into his mouth, Ian merged into the crowd.

A distinctive voice rose above the noise and confusion.

Ian stopped and cocked his head. He scanned the crowd of weary travelers, but they hustled by so quickly, he could hardly discern faces.

A deep-throated laugh lifted the hair on his arms. *Father*? Ian twirled around, his gaze raking through the crowd. There he was! Ian jumped forward, fumbled, then stood frozen by the astonishing sight of his mother and father. *What's happened*? Ian took off and weaved through the crowd.

His mother's shoulders slumped as she clung to her husband.

Meandering along at an easy pace, his father spouted humor at a fellow traveler. The two men burst into laughter.

Wiping a dirty lock of hair from her eyes, his mother blinked in the strong light. She looked out, her gaze sweeping over the crowd. Her gaze passed right over Ian, then back. She halted, catching Seanan off balance. Then her eyes opened wide and her jaw dropped, a woman ready to scream. "Seanan, look!"

Carrying on his conversation with the strange man, Seanan waved his wife's interruption away.

Though unwilling to lose sight of his parents, Ian had to stop in his tracks as one traveler and then another blocked his way.

Fiona shrieked, "It can't be!" She jabbed Seanan in the ribs.

Irritation digging a furrow in his brow, Seanan snapped, "I told you; we'll get aboard soon! Don't be—"

His heart pounding wildly, Ian jostled through the last of the crowd and called, "Father!" At last, he stopped before Seanan, his face hot and flushed, his heart bursting with anticipation, and his mind swirling in confusion.

Seanan turned and stared, uncomprehending. "Yes?"

Panic flooded Ian's whole body. *He doesn't recognize me*? "It's me, Ian! Your son!"

Seanan blinked, then a grin spread over his face. "By the great sky above! Do you think I don't know my own son?" He glanced from Fiona to Ian, his chest out. "My son!" He threw his arms around Ian, pulling him into a fierce hug.

Fiona squeezed in.

Relief like a cool breeze swept over Ian.

Once onboard another ship and seated in a quiet corner, Ian related his adventures and listened, in turn, as Seanan and Fiona described their terrifying search for him.

When Ian explained that he left Lysander and Rueben to look for Georgios, Seanan chewed his lip. "It doesn't seem right, leaving those two to manage that task."

Fiona scowled. “You’d rather that Ian were still out there?”

Seanan glared at her, then shrugged. “I wish they would’ve stayed together. It was a real trick to separate them like that. Some men like to play with other men’s lives.”

Ian leaned against the railing. “I’m sure they’ve found him, and all is well. Lysander has experience, Rueben has wits, and Georgios has amazing luck. I’m so glad to be going home. Finally, peace, quiet, and a chance to work at the forge. Has Goban been busy without me?”

Seanan sighed. “Not so you’d notice. Nothing changes much.”

Fiona grinned, a sparkle in her eye. “A dream come true! Not a nightmare, for once. We’ll never leave home again.”

Ignoring his father’s odd expression, Ian agreed and closed his eyes.

CHAPTER SIXTY-SIX

AS A LEADER SHOULD

—GAELIC LANDS—

Liam let the rain pelt his head and drip down his body as he tugged at the lead rope with every ounce of his strength. In a struggle between himself and a cow, Liam was determined to win. And he was winning—until he saw the bull waiting with flaring nostrils at the bottom of the hill.

He had pulled the cow far enough down the slippery slope that backing up, turning around, or going in any other direction was no longer an option. Yet, standing on the high end of an incline in a driving rain, holding a rope tied to a cantankerous cow with a bull in the way hardly seemed the best option.

The bull bellowed to the cow. The cow returned the call with a pathetic groan of her own and twisted her head around—

Suddenly, the cow slid down a bit, then a bit more, unable to find secure footing in the mud, jerking the rope from Liam's wet hands, throwing him off balance.

Arms flailing at his sides…he did not…want to…fall!

The two of them slid, scraped, and tumbled down the slippery slope. Would the bull be stupid enough to stand his ground as they plummeted toward him?

The answer came hard and fast as the cow—and then he—collided with the less-than-brilliant bovine that hadn't moved one bit out of the way.

Though the rain beat down mercilessly, Liam didn't care. He attempted to rise, but his aching body protested, and his head swam in confusion.

Snorting, the bull admonished the cow. She took it in

stride and swished her tail.

Liam lay prone upon the ground, a hammer pounding his head.

In bovine bliss, the cow and bull sauntered off.

Liam closed his eyes as images of fitful cows, red-eyed bulls, and slippery hills danced in his head.

~~~

Earan trudged through the pelting rain, heading for home. The love of his life had told him to go away, and Earan knew better than to argue when she was in such a mood.

He was grateful that they had been heading to her parents' dwelling when her mood struck, for he would not have appreciated it if she had told him to get out of his own home—as she had on other occasions.

Ever since he had taken over Gutun's dwelling, he had allowed her to alter his new house to her heart's content. It had kept her satisfied, and that was how he liked her best. Earan chuckled at the thought of Gutun's rage if he ever were to see the womanly touches made to his home. No need to worry about that. Gutun was gone for good.

As he approached the place, he noticed something strange. Light undulated from its depth. Earan stopped, puzzled. Had someone made up the fire? Not Maggie, for he had left her at her parents' door. He strode forward and rushed through the doorway.

To his amazement, he saw not a warrior or a thief but merely Agnes and some old man sitting on *his* fur rug chattering amiably in front of *his* cheery fire.

Jumping to her feet, Agnes reached out. "Oh, Earan, I'm so glad—"
~~~

Earan wiped the wet from his face and stared at the old man.

The stranger rose. "Don't be angry; we're not intruders. I was invited here by the owner himself, and this young woman came seeking you. We'd settled down just a moment ago. Gutun should be back with my provisions soon; then I'll be on my way."

Earan's heart all but stopped. "Gutun?"

The old man tottered to the doorway. "Has the rain stopped? At home on the shore, I know when the slightest wind blows—"

Confusion like the roaring of the sea rattled Earan's senses.

Agnes tugged his sleeve. "We must look for Liam. He went after the cows and hasn't returned yet. Have you seen him?"

Too disturbed to respond to her plea, Earan glared at the old man. "Did you say *Gutun* has returned?"

Agnes tapped his arm impatiently. "Earan, didn't you hear? Liam had to go out in the storm, and the bull—"

Earan ignored Agnes. "We sent Gutun away! He can't come back."

The old man plopped down on the rug before the fire. "I know nothing of that. I'm just the guide who brought your priest home, and he promised me enough meat for a month. He should be here soon."

Stomping feet and muffled grunts turned Earan's attention.

Gutun shuffled into the room with his arms over-full of items wrapped against the weather. His filthy face, torn clothes, and hunched shoulders matched his sour expression.

Agnes hurried over and caught items slipping out of his grasp.

The guide rose with a wide grin. “See, I told you.” He snatched the packages from Gutun.

With a grimace, Agnes untied her shawl, slung it into a bag shape, then packed in each item, wrapping them securely. She handed the cargo to the old man.

Gutun settled himself by the fire and pulled off his ragged outer garments.

Earan watched, cold horror spreading over him.

Agnes led the guide to the door. “Be safe on your journey!” She faced Earan. “I’m really worried about Liam—”

Blinded by fury, Earan grabbed Gutun by his ragged collar and jerked him to his feet. “Get up, dirty dog, and go back outside where you belong! This is no longer your house. I live here now. You are an exiled enemy.”

After jerking away and slapping at Earan like a madman, Gutun then stumbled to a pallet and flopped down. “You’re the leader and priest, too, I suppose? You own the sky and the earth? Stupid fool—you’re nothing!”

A strange gleam in Gutun’s eyes sent a shiver through Earan. Much of what Gutun had said was true. Earan turned away. He stepped into the cool night air, and struggled to calm himself, huffing deep breaths.

Agnes came up beside him.

Earan let his eyes rove over her.

Not beautiful or exciting, Agnes did nothing to catch his attention.

“Earan, your brother…”

Wearied by her unrelenting obsession, Earan snapped his words. “What about Liam? The boy knows how to bring in the cows!”

Hanging her head, Agnes shrunk, looking every bit the image of a chastened child. “Won’t you look for him?”

The image of Liam’s innocent face rose, and Earan

sighed. “Which way did he go?”

She pointed to the dark hills undoubtedly slick with rain.

Earan glanced aside. The girl did have nice eyes. He snatched his cudgel by the door and headed toward the hills, calling for his men.

Three of his friends jogged from their homes and joined him.

Whistling, Earan composed his nerves and set his mind to the tasks ahead. He’d find his brother, throw Gutun into the sea, and then make peace with the woman he loved.

CHAPTER SIXTY-SEVEN

PEACE

—PATMOS—

*Myro*n walked outside and stared at the place where Gutun should have been. He nodded in understanding. His fingers gripped the letter he had been writing to Georgios. He had sent his grandson off on a useless mission. Rome rose by a power beyond him, and it would fall by a power beyond any he could name.

Myron slapped the letter against his knee as he seated himself on the bench Gutun usually occupied. The priest was a danger to himself and others, but there was little Myron could do now. Gutun had to follow his own destiny.

Myron heaved a sigh and gazed at the unfinished letter. Perhaps he would see his grandson again…but unlikely. He could hear Alexios' voice in his head. *We must leave some tasks for others.*

Myron blinked. *Is my job done? Have I failed or succeeded?* Not knowing the answers, he rose and returned to his room. He finished the letter, and then, still clutching the last connection to Georgios, he lay on his bed.

As darkness spread over the land, the parchment slipped from his hand and fell softly to the floor.

~~~

Diane, Myron's oldest and most faithful servant, found him the next morning, cold and lifeless.

She lifted the letter from the floor but could not read it.
~~~

According to custom, everything would stay the same until Myron's grandson returned and decided their fate. She would see to matters. Georgios must be informed, and the letter would stay in her custody until his return.

In the meantime, her master's body must be made ready for burial. She considered Myron's serene expression. Though tears cascaded down her cheeks, at least his heart rested in peace.

—ROME—

Georgios understood that death had a mind of its own and claimed whomever it wanted, but his heart rebelled. He let the letter fall onto his lap as he sat before a window at a seaside inn.

Rueben patted Georgios on the shoulder and murmured, "He's at peace now."

Lysander snatched the letter and began to peruse its contents. After a brief reading, he looked from Georgios to Rueben, and back to Georgios. "What are you going to do?"

"What I should have done all along. This whole adventure has been a misadventure. I should never have left him." Grief overwhelming him, Georgios ran out the door toward the roaring seashore.

Rueben followed behind. He yelled out, "Why? Could you have kept Myron young and alive? Besides, it was his idea!"

Georgios swung around, arms flailing. "What did I accomplish? I nearly became as bad as Armand, his tool no less."

Lysander strolled forward, a forced smile on his lips but a grim look in his eyes.

Rueben raised his hands. "Mithra and her mother cared

about you, Georgios, and that forced them to do what they had feared to do from the first. And Armand would've trained his attention on killing them, if he hadn't been distracted by—" Rueben glanced aside. "In the end, they're headed home, Rome is at peace, Armand is in a dungeon, and we're free. I think we've done well for ourselves."

The wind played with Lysander's hair and knee-length robe. "And don't forget that Ian did well while under our care, and he's undoubtedly home, helping Seanan become leader and prophet. Not bad for a few honest men."

Georgios dropped down on the sandy shore. "I can never boast again. I played the fool. If it hadn't been for Alexandra, Rueben would have died."

"All right, you were an idiot! We've accepted it; why can't you?" Lysander's grin widened.

Rueben chuckled.

Lysander stepped up to Georgios and patted his shoulder. "When do we head to Patmos? I can't wait for a good meal."

Georgios glanced at Rueben. "You still want to go with me?"

His eyes teasing, Rueben smiled. "Like old times." Serious again, Rueben shrugged with nonchalance. "I heard a rumor about a cave on that island of yours. One of Christ's friends lived there."

Lysander shook his head. "Just when we get a chance to rest, you want to look for some mysterious fanatic. Can't you enjoy life a little?"

Rueben closed his eyes and exhaled long and slow.

Lysander laughed. "Come, Georgios. We have plans to make, and we're running out of money. You don't know how glad I am that you're coming into your inheritance. I feared that I might have to find work, and I wasn't looking forward to that prospect."

Exhilaration and grief warred inside Georgios as he traipsed across the sandy shore. He would miss his grandfather, but the idea of returning to Patmos as the master of all Myron's land and property nearly took his breath away. Despite his sorrow, Georgios paced between his friends, half-listening to Lysander babble on about his plans for a grand feast and wondering what Rueben might find a mysterious cave on the other side of the island.

CHAPTER SIXTY-EIGHT

BREAK FREE

—ROME—

Marcus Ulpius Trajanus was surprised by the request, but since it came from a powerful and influential senator, he listened rather than killed the traitor who had been brought before him.

Trajanus was no fool; he had a healthy respect for the gods and even more for his peoples' faith in the gods. If challenged, Trajanus liked to show that he was not intimidated. By all accounts, he loved war; thus, he was good at it. At the moment, however, he had other interests to occupy his mind.

Armand was a Parthian, and though the warning had been brought to his attention by a Parthian loyalist—a family member of the imperial household—he still felt the unspoken threat. He had ascended the throne through adoption, and the idea of having a traitor set up as his inheritor hit too close to home.

Luckily for Armand, Trajanus had other battles to win at present. Dacia was a problem, and that situation would brook no delay. Without further consideration, Trajanus accepted the senator's request and allowed the traitor to live for a year and a day upon the mercy of his god.

Since the emperor had an abiding fascination for all gods, he was interested in discovering how long Armand's god would succor him in a dungeon with no food, no water, and no hope of assistance.

To his surprise, a report arrived the next day.

The jailer in charge was perturbed to the extreme to discover no sign of Armand's presence—except for the bodies of two sprawled guards who had died, apparently, without a hand laid upon them.

Upon hearing the news, Trajanus decided, quite logically, that this had not been the act of a man but of a supernatural power. The best he could do was to pretend it never happened.

All record of Armand's imprisonment was erased from every public document and private record. Every man who participated in the matter was given strict orders never to mention the event upon pain of death.

Trajan tried to forget, but this display of mysterious power made him realize that perhaps he had not given the gods their proper due. Therefore, he promised to arrange the grandest festival in history. Not only would the people cheer his generosity, but the gods would be pleased. He would win favor on high, always the best plan for an emperor who hoped to enjoy a long and prosperous reign.

~~~

Armand, on the other hand, made no promises.

Alexandra had sent word through a well-bribed guard that he was going to be reprieved for a year and a day, and all he had to do was pray to his god. She had sent him the proper incense and scrolls for his prayer ritual.

The guards saw no reason to keep them from him. Their shortsightedness sealed their fate. Armand burned the incense at the grated door near the guards, while burning the parchment before his face, creating a smokescreen.

By the time Alexandra's men arrived at his cell door, Armand's guards were sleeping. It was a small matter to leave enough of the incense burning between their slumbering bodies to finish the job, leaving only a lingering scent and a scattering of white ashes.
~~~

Once freed, Armand burned for vengeance and the right to reclaim his own. He would travel to Patmos, find Georgios, and together they would change the course of history.

~~~

Alexandra made the necessary arrangements for Armand to slip aboard the departing ship the night of his escape. She also made sure that no awkward questions would be asked when he appeared on deck the next morning.

Though she had not received one word of thanks for her efforts, she knew that Armand owed his life to her. A pain twisted in her gut when she remembered Georgios.

Armand may plan to reclaim Georgios, but Georgios held the secret to her heart. In the coming battle of wills, she would stand by Georgios' side. Proving once and for all whose will was strongest, she'd finally break free.
~~~

CHAPTER SIXTY-NINE

STRONG AND PURE

—ROME—

Mithra stood on deck as the ship sailed from the Roman shore. She saw Georgios' face in her mind, budding friends, never to be more.

Before she boarded, Georgios had taken her aside and placed a silver pendant in her hand, an image of the sun with mysterious inscriptions carved around the center. Georgios had clasped her small hand and pressed the gift into it, saying, "I'm glad we met. We are one in spirit, and I think, maybe, we were brought together for a special purpose."

A distant voice called Mithra's name. Her mother beckoned her to the eastern side, facing their new home. They would be well guarded, even honored, when they made their entrance into the capital of their kingdom. Mithra would not meet her people as a daughter to an unknown father. Word of their success had reached the king, and he was pleased. She had been claimed.

Mithra could imagine the city gates opening before her and the blaring of trumpets as the procession gathered speed. She was now a valued woman. More importantly, Georgios would forever remember her as a worthy woman, a woman who had risked much on his behalf.

Heart aching, she blinked away tears. Though her love would no longer be free, she would remember a time when it was. Few women had the luxury of marrying the man they loved, but she had glimpsed the possibility, and it offered hope.

~~~

Georgios watched the procession take Mithra and her mother out of view.

Rueben and Lysander strode down the shore to arrange their own voyage.

As the mighty ocean surrounded the sailing ship, Georgios tried to ignore the ache rising in his chest. Mithra had a glorious life ahead, and though both their futures were uncertain, he was glad that they had met. Strong and pure, her heart was not confused; she would always choose duty over personal ambition. He admired her and only wished he could've loved her.
~~~

Chapter Seventy

Strength of Will

–Mystery Planet–

Noman leaned back on his golden chair centered within the assembly and basked in satisfaction. A job well done. He stared at the glaring stage, empty now except for residual blood splattered on the floor. All had gone so well. The meal. His fabulous dessert array. The after-dinner entertainment…

He had snagged a few captives, who exemplified humanity's most dramatic entertainment. His choices weren't any worse—or better for that matter—than Trajan's games: blood sports involving men, women, and children. He'd vaporized them as soon as the show ended and whisked a spicy scent throughout the room to absorb the lingering odors.

After making his point abundantly clear, he rose from his throne and faced the silent throng.

Their mouths open, eyes unnaturally wide, and limbs shaking, several lost their formal shape. Noman chuckled. They didn't know whether to be amused, fascinated, disgusted, or furious.

As one body, they glared at him in profound silence.

Why?

A shiver ran over his body. "I sense your displeasure, but you must understand, I didn't demonstrate anything that humanity hasn't revealed to me."

Like a chameleon who fits his surroundings most perfectly, Abbas, now with white hair and an air of ancient authority, rose and stepped to the center of the theater.

Irritation flashed through Noman. "It's not your turn!"

He flung his arms high. "I arranged this whole thing. I have shown you the truth! Don't put me on trial now."

Confusion rippled across Abbas' face. "No one has suggested that this is a trial."

Cold stiffened Noman's body. "You're always putting me on trial, Abbas. Admit it. I'm never good enough. You and all the rest"—he encompassed the whole assembly in a sweeping gesture— "of you think I'm mad. Or a silly child who can't keep track of the truth."

The Crestonian representative stood and strode onto the stage, stopping beside Abbas. He then morphed into an elongated, thick-haired creature with slanting eyes, thick grasping fingers on muscled arms, and a robust waist over massive legs. "I spent twenty cycles on Haj. The cruelest beings I've ever encountered. Yet, even they had exceptions. A few always rise above and prove their worth." He morphed back into Crestonian form, glaring at Noman. "You made the point you wanted to make. Truth had little to do with it."

The Bhuac representative, her form now settled back in place, paced up to Noman and lifted her chin defiantly. "Through your display of the worst of humanity, you have revealed yourself."

One by one, each of the representatives rose and aligned themself with Abbas.

Frost gave way to furious heat, and rage blinded Noman to the figures arrayed before him on stage. He knew he would combust soon, but before he left— "Damn you all beyond the divide. Disregard the evidence at your own peril. Humanity will destroy itself. They have no strength of will. They are slaves, nothing more."

Noman burst into flames.

~~~
~~~

Abbas sighed as he stared at the wavering, heat-laden air.

The Cresta sniggered. "Always was overly dramatic."

Thrusting his hands on his hips, definitely put out, the Ingot tapped his foot. "Where's he gone to now?"

The Bhuac clipped her words. "He wants everything his own way. He'll probably obliterate humanity."

Abbas squeezed his eyes shut.

–Lux–

Teal sat on the edge of a white canopied bed and held Sienna's limp hand. Time stopped. "I cannot lose you."

Too weak to move, Sienna's half-lidded eyes stared without expression. A whimper rose from her throat.

Teal leaned in, his human body wracked with more pain than he could process.

Her voice, barely a whisper, rose shakily. "Not lose. Find."

"Think of Cerulean." It was a cruel move, but he had to try. "He won't understand."

A tear slipped down Sienna's face.

Teal's heart clutched so tightly he could hardly breathe. His words, a strangled scream, sounded far away to his ears. "We need you!"

With desperate effort, Sienna turned her head and met Teal's gaze. She swallowed and opened her mouth, but no words came.

Teal caressed her cheek. "I love you. Forever."

Her softened expression spoke of acceptance. "Ever." She closed her eyes. Her human form shimmered, and a vaporous mist rose from the bed, luminous and glorious in colorful array.

His own form breaking into light rays, Teal tried to join his wife, but her essence dissolved into the air, spread to the window, and joined the sunlight.

As he spread out to follow, a slight figure caught his attention.

In his human-child form, Cerulean stood in the doorway sobbing.

-OldEarth-

Zuri stomped over the barren ground and glared at Sterling. "What are you doing here?"

Elongating his form to tower over the Ingot, Sterling scowled down. "I told you I was coming. Teal is…indisposed."

Ark hustled across the short green grass, his tentacles hovering, a mother ready to end the latest squabble. "Now, please, you two. This is no time to unleash our inner beasts."

Sterling tilted his head, eyeing Ark with fresh interest. "What an odd expression. Where did you learn such profane language?"

Smug, Ark laughed and tugged Zuri's arm. "Come on. Teal will come along in a bit. He just needs to help Sienna get—"

A cloud hid the sun, and darkness settled over the landscape.

Zuri glanced up, perplexed. "There wasn't a cloud in the sky a moment ago."

With a groan, Ark stumbled. "Uh, oh."

Sterling lifted his hand. "Don't imagine things."

Waddling forward, all six tentacles pressed to his hips, Ark's eyes narrowed. "What happened?"

Alarm spread through Zuri. "Something happened?" A

blast of fear washed over him, shattering his composure. "Sienna!"

His shoulders slumped, Sterling's figure shrank as he plodded up the emerald hill, crushing the grass underfoot. "I'm not supposed to say anything. He wanted to tell you himself."

Ark hunched forward as he struggled up the incline. "Poor Teal. It'll break his heart—so to speak." He glanced at Zuri. "And Cerulean? How is he taking it?"

Sterling shrugged. "I didn't stay to find out." He climbed a large boulder and faced the valley below. "I had to come here and discover what the Mystery Race is going to do next."

Zuri jumped up and stood next to him. "One of the children here told her mother about a stranger who came—a man named Noman—that had special power."

Ark stood at the base of the boulder and lifted a tentacle beseechingly. "That's where I heard the term inner demon. The child reported that the stranger wanted her to release her demons." He flapped his tentacle with renewed vigor.

Annoyed, Zuri grabbed Ark's tentacle and yanked, eliciting a howl of pain from the Cresta.

"Oh, by all that shines bright, get up here, Ark." He grabbed the Cresta by the front of his bio-suit and pulled him forward.

With a yelp, Ark grabbed Zuri for balance and found a place on the boulder. Wincing, he smoothed his stretched tentacles,

Zuri glanced around. "He has visited Seanan's village several times and seems to be keeping an eye on Georgios. I wouldn't be surprised if he helped Armand now and again."

Ark chuckled. "Probably what haunts Gutun. I always thought the Mystery Race was above such intrigue, but

I've begun to wonder if they don't have pompous fools like the rest of us."

Sterling cut his gaze to Ark. "A very intelligent, powerful fool."

Ark shrugged.

With a sigh, Zuri flopped down on the ground and let his legs dangle over the edge of the boulder. "I feel bad for Teal."

Sterling pulled a handful of figs from a satchel that hung at his side. He offered them with an open hand. "Not Sienna?"

Ark accepted one fig and squinted at it.

Zuri took one fig and bit into it. "Sienna can come and go as she pleases. She isn't bound now."

Ark sniffed the fig and then dropped it into his breathing helm. "But Teal and Cerulean lost her, so she must suffer as they do."

Zuri shook his head. "Not if they believe that she still lives."

Sterling peered at the bright sky. "Loving without bounds is one thing. Loving without suffering is impossible." He pointed to the descending sun. "Come on. Noman has come back. We'd better hurry."

Leaping off the cliff and then assisting Ark down, Zuri raced after Sterling. He shouted, "What are you afraid of? He's just watching humanity like we are. He hasn't done anything bad."

Sterling looked over his shoulder and winced. "Anyone who wants to release inner demons isn't up to any good."

His heart aching, Zuri plunged ahead.

CHAPTER SEVENTY-ONE

WAS IT A DUTY?

—GAELIC LANDS—

Liam awoke to rumbling in his ears, a sound like a creek in spring thaw. Fiery pain seared every limb of his body. Had he fallen in his brother's shop? He forced his eyes open.

Brighid stared down at him, anxious lines crowding her eyes.

After patting the soft blankets on his own bed, Liam reorientated himself. His dry mouth made speech difficult. "Drink?"

Brighid's worried expression broke, and the worry lines smoothed. "You're back among the living! Poor lad, you shall have whatever you want. Imagine going up on that treacherous mountain to bring down cows on such a night! What were you thinking? Is a cow worth more than your life?"

Liam licked his lips. He was afraid his aunt might forget his request. "Drink?"

Brighid rose to her full height. Her head disappeared from his view and only her voice thundered over him, hammering his head with multiple blows. "What? You think I don't know my duty, poor child? That fall must have done more than damaged your leg; it must've addled your wits. Am I not the best caretaker in the village? Of course, I will get you a drink! Why, I have a flagon here of the best mead with the finest herbs mixed in to soothe those hurts you're feeling. Don't tell me you don't feel them—I can see with my own eyes what damage you've done to yourself! Why, of all the things—going up a slippery mountain in the midst of the worst storm of the age! If I had only known, I'd have—"

"Oh, by the god Dagdg, get the boy a drink!"

Relief surged through Liam and a bit of a grin teased his lips at the command of his older brother.

Earan tread across the room, toward Liam, and stared into his eyes. "You feeling all right?" Turning, he took the offered flagon from Brighid and tipped it on Liam's puckered mouth. Most of the liquid dribbled down his chin and neck, chilling his hot body.

With a spluttered, "Ank 'oo," Liam wiped his lips with the back of his hand.

Brighid chuckled as she patted Earan's shoulder. "Seeing that you're in good hands, I'll go on then. I have a husband and children who need me as well." She leaned in and met Liam's gaze. "'Tis a pity that you got laid up, for it is said that there's a ship not far offshore unloading wares and passengers, and I would've sent you to see who's arrived. But 'tis no matter; Gutun says he'll see to such things now that he's back. Old fool! No better off than you, sick with fever and all. But he raves that he has mighty friends. I wish he'd stayed away. What were they thinking, letting him return?"

Liam's eyes widened, and he looked pointedly at Earan but said nothing until Brighid bustled out the door.

"Gutun?"

Earan nodded, his mouth a grim line and his eyebrows knotted in anger. "Went all the way to Patmos, stayed with Georgios' grandfather, received money from some mysterious source, and to our misfortune, found his way back here. He still believes he is our high priest." Earan shook his head. "He's no more than a raving lunatic."

Closing his eyes as exhaustion reclaimed his body and mind, a sudden thought demanded his attention and his eyes popped open. “But that was your home!”

Earan waved the concern away. “I didn’t give it back. I told him he could sleep on the floor the first night, but after that, he’d have to find a new abode. I wish we’d killed him when we had the chance.”

Pain sizzled through Liam. He winced.

“What? You think we should spare him? He’s a menace.”

Liam sipped from the jug. The thick brew tantalized his tongue. “It’d be best to let the gods deal with him.”

Earan frowned. “Those who hate Gutun wish to see him dead, while those who believe in him are afraid of offending the gods. But the gods themselves? You think they care?”

Morning light slanted across the room, and birdsong twittered through the air.

Liam blinked and licked his dry lips. “Gutun tries everyone’s patience, even powers he doesn’t understand.”

“You’re too wise for your years and too brave for your own good.”

“It wasn’t wise to go after the cows in a storm.”

Earan blushed. “Not alone, anyway.” He sat on the edge of the bed. “But we have more important things to speak of. Brighid was right; there are ships off our shore, and materials are being unloaded. With troubles in the north, we can take nothing for granted. I’ll go and take a look.”

“When?”

“Early tomorrow. I’ll take Olcan and Goban and leave Tainair and Ronan here.” His gaze fell back to his brother. “I’m counting on you to keep your eyes and ears open.”

Liam’s brow furrowed. “But—”

Earan’s countenance darkened. “Tainair has grown too fond of his mead. I can’t trust him as I once did. And

Ronan, though a good man, is no leader. I need someone who can see a problem before it starts and take action."

Liam shrugged. "From my bed?"

"I'll send Agnes. She has something worth more than strength of arms—persistence. She wouldn't leave me be until I went up the mountain to find you. To my shame, I had to be reminded of my duty by a girl."

Liam looked into his brother's eyes. "Was it a duty?"

Earan cleared his throat as he stood and studied his little brother once more. "I'll send word if I find anything serious to report. Keep your ears and eyes open. Tell Agnes if something should be done, and she shall set things right as only a persistent woman can."

Liam nodded and watched his brother head toward the doorway. "Oh! The cow and the bull? Whatever happened to them?"

Earan turned. "Well, your little cow, despite her difficult night, gave enough milk to be made into several rounds of cheese. The bull, on the other hand" —Earan strode out of sight— "is attending tonight's feast in all his glory."

Though he chuckled, Liam frowned at the thought of strange men landing on their shore. And worse yet, Earan had taken the mead with him.

CHAPTER SEVENTY-TWO

MY GREATEST WEALTH

—PATMOS—

Georgios led Rueben and Lysander up the mountain pass to his home, where the sun glared off the white walls and the sea crashed against the rocks below. Weary but filled with expectation, they entered the atrium.

Servants met them with wash water, towels, and goblets of wine. The elderly servant, Diane, delivered Myron's last letter into Georgios' hands with a deep bow and backed away.

He strode to a far corner and opened the scroll, his hands shaking.

With a happy "Ah-ha!" Lysander strode to a round table set with a golden bowl filled with dates, figs, grapes, and pomegranates, and a platter of dainty sweet cakes. He pointed at Rueben, who stood staring out the window. "If you'd relax, you'd be so much happier. Here!" He tossed a pomegranate across the room.

Rueben caught it handily and shook his head. "I'll be happy when I know what Myron wrote in his letter."

Lysander shrugged. "What do old men write about before they die? Enduring love, their greatest loss, and their vain wishes. Same as the rest of us."

Horror galloped over shock as Georgios read and reread the letter. He lifted his gaze, staring first at Rueben then at Lysander. "Nothing. He's given everything to those Christ-followers! His house is to be sold with all his possessions, and the money is to be given to a poor community. He left me—only my name and my memories."

Choking and swallowing a huge lump, Lysander pounded across the room. "You must be joking, or Myron must've been mad! What about his name? Everything he built? He's just going to scatter it to the wind?"

Still facing the open window, Rueben spoke low. "He didn't scatter anything. He gave his wealth to the poor."

Lysander turned on Rueben. "Who are the poor to him? What did the poor ever do for him that he should give everything to them? This is outrageous! I hope you plan to ignore this, Georgios. Let me see that letter! It must have been written in a fit of insanity. Perhaps one of those Christ-followers talked him into this absurdity, using whatever tricks they're good at and then...and then... They killed him!" Lysander's eyes bulged with imagined horror.

Both Georgios and Rueben stared, taken aback.

Lysander lunged for the letter.

Quicker, Rueben intercepted it.

Georgios reached for it back.

Rueben held it aloft. "Wait! Before Lysander lets his imagination go any further, let me read it out loud so that we all understand. Perhaps then Lysander won't be so ready to undo a dying man's wish."

My Dearest Georgios,

Know that I think of you every day. I have much I wish to tell you. I once heard a story about a rich man who built up great storehouses and planned to take his ease, but then his life was required by the Master, and he lost everything. The only treasure he could carry to the other side was inside himself.

I have given all my worldly goods to a community that serves the Christ. The house and furniture will be sold and the money given to the poor.

I am not leaving you without a fortune. Do you still remember the story of your ancestor Aram? A man remembered and revered even still. Like him, you have the noble blood in you, though you may not realize it. You already have your treasure—within yourself.

I hope to see you one last time, but if this is denied me, remember what I have said and know that I have not left you without a heritage, for in my love, I pass my greatest wealth to you.

Your grandfather,

~Myron

Tears welled in Rueben's eyes as he leaned against the wall. "You are a blessed man, Georgios. What I would give to have such a letter as this!"

Georgios' eyes narrowed. "Then take it then! It's yours! What value is it to me?"

Rueben's expression darkened.

Lysander stepped between them. "This is bad news, but there's no need to get mad at Rueben. I understand how you feel. It's a hard loss. But there's nothing you can do now unless you want to break his word."

Rueben's face flushed. "Don't you see? He's made the greatest sacrifice he could in offering your inheritance. He is entrusting you into God's hands, and he knows that God is never outdone in generosity."

Georgios spat his words. "Does God make deals then? Does He take a man's livelihood and offer him protection in return?"

Rueben stepped to the doorway. "Any man who just lost his fortune would be upset, but I never thought you were like other men. You have so much. You've traveled and have friends near and far, you have encountered evil and lived to tell of it, yet still, you are not happy because you think that wealth would have made you a richer man." Rueben crossed the threshold.

Blind fury filling him, Georgios shouted, "Where are you going?"

"To see where John lived, where Myron found his joy."

Rueben's footsteps pounded away.

Georgios looked at Lysander. "You want to go, too?"

Lysander shrugged. "I wouldn't mind having a look. How often does a man see a place of miracles?"

Georgios snorted. "Miracles?"

"Your grandparents found their lost love there."

Sick at heart, Georgios slammed the table with his fist. "Rueben will soon be disappointed."

"We might find a good storyteller to liven the place up a bit, but then, it is just the other side of the island."

Trapped between disappointment, fury, and concern, Georgios hesitated. Suddenly, he jogged forward. "Hurry up! I don't want to lose him as the night descends."

Lysander's eyes widened in alarm. "What? *Go now*?"

"He's going!"

Lysander followed, glancing back at the well-laid table. "We don't need to be impetuous. We haven't even had anything to eat!"

Striding across the courtyard, Georgios glanced around for any sign of Rueben. "He might need me. I promised I would protect him." *I already lost one fortune today. I won't lose another.* With that thought giving speed to his steps, Georgios began to run.

CHAPTER SEVENTY-THREE

OFFERINGS

—GAELIC LANDS—

Gutun ran his fingers across his twitching lips. He mumbled loud enough that those nearest him flinched but dared not intervene. They no doubt knew when a man was conversing with the gods, and no one would want to be blamed for breaking a trance.

Gutun stretched to his full height. "Be merciful, oh lords of the underworld, Dagdg, Rannach Crom Dobh, Aine, Anu, and Macha, masters and mistresses of the land beyond. Hear me, your faithful servant."

Searing pain sizzled through his body. "I serve only you!" Gutun fell to his knees, clutching his abdomen. "Do not take out your anger on me. I am innocent!" Gutun fell on his face, beseeching.

Several men in the surrounding circle stepped back. An old man with a toothless grin chortled, "The gods are 'ard on their servants. If you please 'em, all goes well. If you make 'em angry, it'd be better to die in an instant than endure their torments. I always say, keep 'em happy, and you'll live longer."

Nods of somber agreement made their way around the circle of watching men.

A robust man crossed his arms. "Appears that he meddled with some foreign god, and there's a heavy price to be paid. Never allow strange gods about, or you'll have trouble." He spat off to the side and hitched up his shoulder strap. He nudged the old man. "I have to go to the high field. Tell me what happens later, da." He started forward, then paused. "We ought to get his house back for him. Earan overstepped his bounds when he moved in. Gutun hadn't been officially declared dead by all the laws that were proper and just. Soon as I come back, I'll gather the men, and we'll see Earan and settle things. We don't want blame falling on us."

Genial assents followed.

Satisfied the meeting had ended, the crowd wandered off to their daily duties.

Gutun stirred in the dust. He huffed to his feet and straightened his back, rubbing the sore places, then he shuffled toward his old home. "Won't Earan be surprised?" He stopped in the doorway and fingered the crude sign in the doorpost: *Tu'atha De Danaan*—Paradise of Peace and Plenty. He smiled and hobbled inside.

~~~

Agnes swept the path to her sister's house, watching Gutun out of the corner of her eye.

Dark clouds mounted across the sky.

"Another storm brewing." With a shake of her head, she ambled inside.

~~~

Earan crouched in the frozen grass and observed the line of men trailing from shore. His men ranged on either side of him, all watching with the same silent intensity.

A couple of strange-styled long boats bobbed at sea in the distance. Not the best example of merchant ships he'd ever seen. He smiled in relief. Nothing more than a bedraggled band of travelers. An image of his brother flashed through his mind. *Could Ian be—?*

Considering it best to play it safe, Earan used his staff

and gestured for his men to fan out and approach from different angles. He straightened and strode forward at an even pace, a benign expression on his face. If Ian was among them, Earan wanted his elder brother assured that he was in perfect control of the situation.

He glanced around and frowned. No one he knew. Or wanted to know by the look of them. Dressed only in rough tunics, their bare arms and legs spoke of a primitive lifestyle. Their ragged hair hung in their faces while shoddy short capes were thrown off their shoulders. A new thought chased away his disappointment. Perhaps these newcomers brought news.

About two dozen in all, they had stopped and stood facing him, still and silent.

A prickle moved down Earan's spine. He forced a smile. He knew full well what the laws of hospitality demanded, so he marched forward prepared to offer shelter and food.

While Earan kept an even pace, one of his men, Branm, outpaced him. Branm's curiosity had clearly gotten the better of him. Irritated with this breach of protocol Earan scowled at Branm. Branm didn't see the look, though; he stopped before a man with flaming red hair and started asking questions.

Close enough to see what was happening but not close enough to correct Branm, Earan clenched his jaw and imagined the punishment he'd mete out to the idiot once they got home.

As Earan strode closer, one of the strangers circled around the group. Branm chatted on, not noticing him. The stranger obviously didn't notice Earan because, in the next instant, he raised a cudgel and struck Branm across the skull.

Branm fell without a sound.

Earan jerked to a stop, freezing up. What just happened? He glanced aside. His line of men stood stupefied.

The cold threat of challenge in the stranger's eyes demanded a response.

Earan swallowed a lump rising in his throat as icy realization washed over him. His hand went to his knife tucked in his belt. Every bit as fierce as the Romans, these invaders would steal everything they could get their hands on, including slaves. They would die for the glory of the kill or the glory of death itself.

Since running was neither an option nor honorable, Earan marched forward, ignoring the frantic gestures of his men. Two steps later, likely realizing that Earan meant to face the enemy with or without them, Olcan and Goban swept to his side, and his eight other men took up the rear.

Earan halted before the red-headed leader. "You struck down one of my men without cause! I demand an explanation before I take you in for judgment."

The barbarian stood waiting, his fingers tapping his thigh. The tattoos on his upper body undulated with each movement. Grinning, he gestured for one of his men to translate.

A thickset man stepped forward, muttered in a strange speech, and stepped back.

The barbarian leaned forward, a knowing smirk on his face. "I Othos! Obey or die."

Earan's gut contorted. Clutching a knife in one hand, he raised his staff with the other, but one of Othos' men moved faster.

The barbarian threw one of Earan's men to the ground, gripping him by the hair and forcing him to his knees before Othos.

Othos whipped out a blade and placed it against the young man's throat.

As Olcan—on Earan's right—hurried forward, Goban shouted, "No!"

With a surge of adrenaline coursing through his veins, Earan threw his body at Othos, grabbing him around his substantial waist and knocking him to the ground.

The two sets of warriors clashed like waves against a rocky shore.

In a matter of moments, four of Earan's men lay in pools of blood. His own head spinning in dizziness, Earan tried to rise from his knees.

A horn blew. For a moment, hope surged, but the look of satisfaction on Othos' face obliterated the spark.

Othos stood panting, his red hair aflame with the falling light. He shouted enthusiastically as a throng of warriors swarmed down the hill, torches alight with flames of red and blue and their eyes blazing.

Calling for retreat, Earan jerked away, sprinting blindly ahead. Blood and sweat obscured his vision, but he pelted through the bracken and raced forward. How many of his men survived, he could not guess. His only prayer, to reach his people, so that they could face their doom together.

~~~

Agnes washed Liam's wounds, unburdening her mind of recent concerns. "Did you know? More and more men side with Gutun now. I think it's because of the sacrifice he's planned for tomorrow night. And the feast that follows. Red meat, strong mead, bread and honey—not to mention the two hogs and what's left of the milk and cheese. It's just the thing to lift everyone's spirits, don't
~~~

you think? I wish you'd thought of the idea first."

While bandaging Liam's leg with care, commotion outside caught her attention. Shrill yells, calls for help, men shouting for their weapons, and mothers screaming for their children sent shivers down her spine.

Agnes ran to the door, her worst fears realized. Men clutched spears, swords, and cudgels, while terror filled the air.

Retreating inside, she grabbed Liam's arm. "Hurry! Invaders are never merciful to injured men. You must hide!"

Carefully balancing himself, Liam gestured for his cloak. Draping it over his body, he hobbled out the door toward Ian's forge as fast as he could manage. Slipping behind the ironworks, he fumbled at the latch on the hidden door.

Following close, Agnes slapped the latch back and grasped the edge. The two pulled with all their might, opening it enough so that one body could slide inside.

Liam blinked at the dark opening and then back at Agnes. He reached for her, but she sprang nimbly away.

"No! You're the last of Seanan's line. He cannot come home to find you killed. It would take the heart out of him. Besides, this way, you can raise a rebellion. You must be safe!"

Without answering, Liam tried to shove her through the doorway.

The screams and yells intensified.

Sick with dread, Agnes glanced at Liam's crippled leg. Without another word, she yanked the crutch away, shoved him backward, tucked his feet inside, and forced the door closed. She piled wood against it while Liam shouted from inside.

"Shush or they'll hear you, and we'll both be killed!"

A heavy, bulky figure with a nasty snarl and furious eyes lumbered into the room.

Agnes shrieked but never once looked back as she was dragged out the door.

~~~

Othos surveyed the beaten clan with disgust. On the one hand, he would take healthy slaves, ample stores, and a few warriors. On the other hand...*ugh!* He spat to the side. *Not one altar to worship the gods?*

The defeated clan lowered their heads in humiliation.

Looking over at the main prize, the one who had escaped from their attack on shore, Othos grinned. *Loyal warrior or offering to the gods?*

Othos stood over the man and lifted his battered face. He waved his arm, encompassing the entire village. "So where be gods?"

The man's body slumped in exhaustion. Barely able to hold himself up, he glanced aside.

Othos followed the gaze and smiled. He waved for his men to follow him, then grabbed the beaten man by his hair and dragged him along.

At the engraved doorpost, Othos stopped and called. "Come out!"

A bedraggled figure cowered at the door, his gaze shifting from Othos to the prisoner kneeling in the muck. His eyes widened and a ghost of a smile shimmered over his lips. "Earan, you meet a fitting end, I see."

Othos pounded his chest. "Where be gods?"

The figure crossed his arms over his chest and bowed low. "I am Gutun, a humble servant. I serve the gods
~~~

there"—he pointed to a distant hill—"offering whatever pleases them best."

With a frown, Othos glared at one of his men, who then scrambled forward and muttered in his ear. Othos lifted his gaze and grinned. He shoved Earan ahead and forced him to his knees. "Gift to gods!"

Gutun gave a crooked smile and clasped his hands together, clearly delighted. He bowed and motioned toward the hill.

Othos nodded and then surveyed the assembly of beaten men huddled in the center of the village. He muttered and gestured to his translator, who blurted, "Other gifts?"

Tainair and Ronan stood, bruised and bloody, tied together like hogs for slaughter.

Gutun pointed and bobbed his head.

Othos waved to Gutun, directing him to take his gifts up the hill.

The translator clapped his hands. "Gods be happy!"

Grinning, Gutun offered a bow of obeisance and took the lead toward the hill, his garments trailing in the mud.

Othos sighed. Though this had not been a rich conquest, the sacrifices would please the gods. And, as far as Othos was concerned, the pleasure of the gods made him rich beyond measure.

~~~

Agnes, held fast in the brawny grip of a barbarian in the center of the village, tried to control her trembling body. She glanced at her home, where Isadora lay sprawled on the floor, senseless to the upheaval. Brighid had administered a strong draught to the terrified woman at the onset of the battle and sent Timo into the woods with the
~~~

other women and children. When Goban had urged her to flee, Brighid had insisted that Olcan and Goban leave with her so they could organize a resistance.

Agnes looked to the hills. She watched Gutun lead three bloodied and beaten me: Earan and his uncles, Tainair and Ronan. Tears were only consolation now.

CHAPTER SEVENTY-FOUR

YOUR WILL BE DONE

—PATMOS—

Rueben sat on the rock ledge inside the cave and listened, his chin cupped in his hands. The speakers took turns, a large family of itinerant carpenters. *Clearly not rich, but they must've made a good living.* Rueben had never met anyone who had seen as many holy sites. The plainspoken grandfather had been present at the feeding of the 5000 and had been converted on the spot. Like Rueben, they had come to venerate the place where Jesus' holy disciple had lived.

Rueben appreciated their willingness to share their experiences, though he had been disappointed to find that John's dwelling looked so much like any other cave. Not a hint of supernatural qualities about the place.

As the night deepened and the gathering broke up for a night's rest, Rueben strolled outside and stared at the stars, pondering the glory of God. The ancient refrain, "The Lord swore…a priest forever, after the order of Melchizedek," repeated over and over in his mind. Bread and wine, the transformation of food that nourished the body into food that nourished the spirit, struck Rueben as too wonderful to comprehend. God's majestic invitation beckoning through time and space, life support for developing humanity.

Alone the next day under a bright blue sky, Rueben wandered where John must have walked, perhaps where he'd had his vision, "I saw a new heaven and a new earth..."

Images of his father's crucifixion mixed with Christ's

offering upon the cross. *Your will be done, Lord.* He stared at the roaring sea and shuddered. *The sooner, the better.*

~~~

Armand disembarked the ship, ate a leisurely meal, and then wrote a note in his careful script. He handed it to a boy to be delivered in person to "Georgios of Patmos." As the sun sparkled upon the bright water and a gentle wind blew in his face, Armand basked in near-forgotten pleasure. With Georgios at his side, he would be master of his destiny once again. Slinging a bag over his shoulder and taking a staff in hand, he started the long trapse to the Apostle's Cave.

Once at the top of the hill, the sound of heavy breathing as someone labored up the incline caught Armand's attention. Using his foot, he shoved his bag out of sight and leaned back on a warm boulder. His right hand rested on a favorite weapon tucked inside the pocket of his tunic.

Rueben shuffled forward, his gaze down and his eyes thoughtful. When he reached the pinnacle, he straightened and turned to the gorgeous panoramic view of the sky kissing sea. Joy suffused the young man's features.

Surprised, Armand grinned. *Lovesick fool.* "Hello, Rueben. I was expecting Georgios."

Consternation replaced serenity. "You have powerful friends."

With a shrug, Armand pursed his lips. "How strange to find you alone. Dreaming of love, perhaps?"

Rueben returned to the path. "You're a sick man, and I don't have the cure you need."

Lilting laughter halted Rueben's steps.

Shock stiffened Armand. *Where did she come from?*

Alexandra stepped forward, shaking her finger at
~~~

Rueben. "You can't walk away. Don't you know why he's here?" Her grin twisted. "He wants Georgios. The question is—what does Georgios want?"

Rueben glanced at Armand, his eyes wide, horror flooding his features. His gaze flickered to the woman. "And you?"

"Good of you to ask. I almost feel human now. Armand has done so little for the human in me. He prefers gods, beasts, and young men."

Annoyance flittered through Armand. He should've realized that she'd follow him—to find Georgios, no doubt. The woman's obsession knew no limits.

Alexandra broke into his thoughts. "So, Rueben, what did Georgios inherit? He won't need his old friends anymore, will he?" She attempted to stroke Rueben's arm, but he jerked away.

"There is no fortune, if that's what you are looking for. Not the kind you are supposing. Myron saved Georgios from the bitter fate of discovering wealth's empty promises."

Alexandra's face paled. "What is wealth but the happiness to decide your own destiny?"

Rueben stared meaningfully at Armand, his face flushing. "No point in throwing pearls before swine."

Suddenly, the decision was easy. Armand pulled the warm blade from inside his tunic and advanced.

His hands lifting in self-defense, Rueben backed up.

Alexandra's mouth fell open as she stood motionless, a spectator at a game.

Armand pointed his knife at Rueben as he approached. "Don't think you are so different. We just call our gods by different names."

Stopping on the crest of the cliff, Rueben stared into Armand's eyes. "Do you have a son?"

A distant voice called, "Rueben! Where are you?"

Georgios! Armand darted forward, grabbed Rueben's arm, and twisted it behind his back. He pressed the blade against his throat.

Struggling, Rueben shouted, "Stay back, Georgios!"

Coming into view from up the incline, Georgios raced forward. He stared at Rueben held tight in Armand's grasp and jerked to a halt.

Right behind him, Lysander jogged forward. He took in the scene and slowed to a stop.

One arm clutching Rueben, Armand dragged him over the hard-packed earth to where he'd stashed his bag. Using his foot, he retrieved the bag and positioned it amidst the group. Carefully, he yanked the bag upside down.

A large, venomous snake slithered out.

His eyes expressionless, Armand followed the movement of the slithering snake. "We've been waiting for you, Georgios."

Rueben struggled, trying to free his arm, but Armand tightened his grip and pressed the knife harder against his throat.

Fear in her eyes, Alexandra clenched her hands and tottered on her feet, ready to run forward or back.

Lysander crouched, an athlete preparing to tackle his opponent.

Memories whirled through Armand's mind. Flashes of childhood, his mother, his father, his destroyed village, Roman soldiers wreaking havoc, and the face of his dead son. His gut twisted in the grip of hot pinchers. "I was wronged! Everyone misunderstands. I told you the truth. I have your best interest at heart. Your friends—not so." He pricked Rueben's neck with the knife but kept his gaze focused on Georgios. "Rueben plans to make you a servant of his god, but I'd protect you like a good father."

He snatched the snake by its tail, dangling it near Rueben's throat.

Like a deer leaping through high bracken, Alexandra jumped forward and slapped the serpent.

Furious, the snake twirled and bit her on the wrist.

Shocked, Armand dropped the snake. "You *idiot*! I wasn't going to *hurt* him."

Alexandra clutched her arm and fell to her knees, her breath rapid, her eyes terrified.

Both hands free, Rueben slapped the knife from Armand's hand and jerked away. He ran to Alexandra's side as she sunk to the ground.

She grimaced, anguish suffusing every feature.

Georgios crouched at her side. "Alexandra!"

Her body spasmed, and she cried out in pain.

Numbness invaded Armand. He watched the woman struggle for gasping breaths, her wrenching cries straining for air, and then the final frantic jerks, until her body slumped, still, inert, lifeless.

Cradling her head in his arms, Rueben bent low and kissed her forehead. "Peace, Alexandra."

Rising, Georgios turned on Armand, his face flushed red with fury. "You call yourself a father? You're a beast!"

Disturbed by the sudden turn of events, Armand's body grew weak and his legs trembled. The knife slipped from his hand.

Lysander gripped Armand's arms and yanked them behind his back. "How you escaped the King's dungeon is more than I can guess, and the only person who knew the truth now lies dead."

Rueben stared at Armand. "You're known by your fruit." His gaze roamed to Alexandra's body.

Flashes of his wife's hate-filled eyes wavered before Armand. "It was the snake, not me! It's everywhere—"

Glancing wildly about, Lysander jumped back and loosened his grip. "Where?"

Armand wrenched free, snatched the knife from the ground, and flew at Rueben, stabbing with renewed strength.

Georgios flung himself on Armand and tried to pull him off, while Lysander attempted to pry the knife from his fingers.

Filled with renewed strength, Armand sliced Lysander's wrist and nicked Georgios' arm. He squirmed away, ran around the boulder, and crouched low. As if separated from his own body, coherent thought ceased. Sweat blurred his vision as he peered around the rock.

In a pool of blood, Rueben lay sprawled on the ground.

His face wracked with grief, Georgios clutched Rueben's tunic, attempting to stop the spurting flow.

Jaw clenched and eyes narrowed, Lysander pounded toward Armand.

Armand chuckled and heard the sound as if from a far distance. He climbed wearily to his feet and faced Lysander. "You're foolish to oppose me. Don't you see? I have powers you know nothing of." He stepped forward. "Only Georgios could've—"

Pain surprised Armand. A sharp bite, deep into his thigh. His legs buckled, and he fell to the ground.

Georgios rose to his feet, his mouth gaping.

Lysander reached out in warning. "Stop! There's another snake. He glanced around. "Dozens in these parts, I'd say."

Panting and helpless, Rueben turned his head and squinted through the strong light at Armand. "Your son? What happened?"

"I killed him." Nearly blind, Armand glanced wildly around. He could not die. Not by a snake bite.

"Georgios…I would've—"

Darkness rose. No sun or sky. Only a face. A boy with trusting, innocent eyes.

~~~

Georgios clutched Rueben's arm.

Rueben shuddered each labored breath.

His vision blurring, Georgios tore the hem of his tunic and pressed it against Rueben's seeping wounds. "No, you shall not die! You must live."

Rueben sucked in air, blood gurgling in his throat. "Not much longer—Georgios—I can't stay—"

Burning tears trickled down Georgios' face. "I need you."

Rueben choked. "If I could—" His gaze wandered to the other two lifeless bodies. "Rest in peace."

Lysander crouched at Rueben's side but stared at Armand. "May his soul burn in hell."

Rueben squinted at the bright sky, a smile ghosting. "He didn't make me hate him."

Georgios made a sweeping gaze of their surroundings. Nothing but rock and sky and two dead bodies. He and Lysander couldn't save Rueben by themselves. How far to town? Certainly, a physician could be found. "We need help!"

"I'll go." Lysander sprinted away.

A lump swelled in Georgios' throat, choking him as he tried once again to hold death at bay.
~~~

CHAPTER SEVENTY-FIVE

OH, GOD, SAVE MY SON

—GAELIC LANDS—

Seanan halted, huffing deeply, on the top of a steep hill where verdant green warred with lengthening shadows. While thankful for his blessings—they could've shipwrecked in some uninhabited lands or sailed for months and never found their son—he longed to reach home, to sit and recuperate.

Looking back, he appraised the ragged trail of men, and at the very end, his wife. "Come along, will you? It's getting late, and I'm hungry!"

Grunts of agreement echoed down the line.

Fiona clutched Ian's arm as they trudged up the hillside, hunch-shouldered and exhausted. She was not built for this extended hardship, physically or emotionally.

Seanan attempted to tease her into good cheer. "When we get home, we'll have a feast in celebration! Even Ian will get his fill of fat and red meat!"

Ian smiled.

Flinching, Fiona glared at her husband. "We've been traveling forever. I've lost count of time. Before any mighty feast, I'm going to crawl into bed and sleep for three days. After that, we'll see."

Seanan adjusted the bag over his shoulder. "We'll see, will we? Well, *you'll* see! First"—he raised one finger—"Ian will go to the high country and bring down the fattest young bullock we have and a couple of hogs. Second"—up went the second finger—"while the men are getting those ready, Ian will lay wood for the greatest fire ever seen by man. Then third"—the third finger moved into position—"the women will bring out tasty provisions and serve all the wine and mead that we have and..."

Fiona raised her hand, interrupting him. "Seanan?" She stared toward the western horizon, her eyes narrowed and puzzlement passing over her features.

A fire flickered on one of the distant hills.

Ian jumped forward. "The sacrificial fire, the one Gutun always lit when making an offering to the gods!"

Seanan blinked uncertainly. Surely, Earan hadn't taken to offering sacrifices, and Gutun was long gone. He'd heard no reports of Romans near and, besides, they offered their sacrifices in temples, not under an open sky. Seanan scratched his chin. "Well, if the fire is ready, we'll just need to bring the feast, though it'll be mighty inconvenient to drag the food up *that* hill!"

Both Ian and Fiona glared at Seanan.

Seanan wanted to pull his hair out by the roots. "Oh, all right, I'll go look. Wait here." He started forward, but then he stopped and glanced over his shoulder. "Ian, aren't you coming? You should know how to deal with idiots like this."

Ian jogged forward, doubtful. "You think an idiot did this?"

Seanan snorted. "Anyone who follows Gutun's example must be an idiot. Look what happened to him!" He sighed. "I just don't like seeing a fire on *that* particular hill. It brings back bad memories!" The image of past sacrifices rose in his mind. Seanan yelled for three other men to accompany him. "The rest of you go to the grove of woods. When I'm ready, I'll come get you."

Fiona wrung her hands. "Fate is set against us. Seanan, I'm afraid."

"Stop worrying. We'll get home and have our feast. It just might take a little longer."

Fiona stood her ground, her eyes straining in the dim light. "I hope so."

When Seanan and Ian reached the hill, a veil of smoke enveloped them. Ian coughed and wiped his teary eyes. "What are they doing, using green wood?"

Seanan choked and winced, his eyes stinging from the smoke. "Wait till I get my hands on the idiot who did this!" He climbed the hill, and the other four men followed, covering their faces with their sleeves.

At the top, they stood staring at the immense fire and the encircling, tense crowd. None of the typical chanting or dancing frenzy accompanied this ritual. Seanan groaned. "The most depressing sacrifice I've ever witnessed."

A goat bleated in the distance, followed by the plaintive moo of a cow.

His eyes adjusting, Seanan stared at the strange crowd—not men from his clan. These were thickset men with unkempt hair, ragged tunics, and short fur capes flung back from their shoulders. Black irregular lines ran up and down their arms. *Tattoos?* They hardly appeared human. Shock waves exploded in his mind. He peered more closely.

Several of his men huddled together—tied up! A Druid priest with attendants began chanting in low, dolorous voices, focused solely on their ceremony, oblivious to their surroundings.

Seanan glanced at the stone altar. Sweat trickled down his spine. Tainair and Ronan stood tied together like hogs on festival day. Other tied men, as well as a few women—was that Brighid?— stood hunched and dejected. *It would be just like her to be sacrificed twice!*

Fury fought fear inside his mind. Were these human beings or devils from the underworld that some barbarous fool had called forth? Perhaps Gutun had left some evil spirits behind to haunt the clan when they were least expecting them. Where was Earan or Liam? His eyes scanned the crowd again. *At least they weren't captured! But where—by God—were they?*

A hand pressed Seanan's shoulder. His heart jumped to his throat.

Ian beckoned him.

"What? Don't you see we have a problem on our hands? Devils arisen from the depths are about to sacrifice half our clan!"

Ian pressed his finger to his lips, pointing to two other men standing near the edge of the woods.

"It's me Olcan." Olcan pointed to the man beside him. "Goban and I escaped before the invaders took control." He clutched Seanan's arm. "It's a miracle you've come back now. We were caught unaware, and several of our best men have been killed or captured. They're about to sacrifice human victims to the gods for their good fortune. Tainair and Ronan are among the victims...and Brighid." His eyes flickered toward Goban in misery. "We must do something fast!"

His heart pounding, Seanan choked out his words. "Where's Earan? These invaders fell from the sky—did they—that you were so taken by surprise?"

Goban hissed, "Not now! We must plan our attack."

Seanan rubbed his temples, forcing his fury down. "I wish Gutun were here! For once in his wretched life, he would've been useful!"

Goban stared, deadpan. "You want Gutun? He's over there dressed in the long ceremonial robes. See, that's him. He convinced these barbarians that he has the ear of the gods, so they are allowing him to lead the rituals. He has Earan—and he wants revenge, badly."

Haunted by the spectacle, Seanan winced. “He has Earan?” He craned his neck. *Oh, God!*

Gutun chanted louder and faster, working himself into the frenzy necessary to accomplish the dreadful deed.

Trembling, Seanan glanced into the starry sky. *Rueben, if only I had your faith! Oh, Lord, save my son!*

Taking out his knife, Seanan rushed forward. “No-o-o!”

First, one barbarian turned toward him, eyes and teeth glimmering in the firelight, then three more. Before Seanan could plan his next move, they surrounded him. Someone cracked him on the back of the head with a shock of pain that knocked him to his knees. Another pinned his arms behind his back. His knife knocked from his hand, he knelt on the hard ground, stunned and immobilized and all alone.

Two figures strode forward. One, a garishly painted figure, wore fine ceremonial robes, while the other, a robust figure painted even more garishly, wore only primitive attire.

Seanan snorted.

“I wondered when you’d return.” Gutun grinned, his broken teeth gleaming. “Thought you destroyed me, but I do not serve alone—”

The other figure stepped forward. “Who?”

Gutun swept a humble bow. “Seanan—the leader.”

With nothing to lose, Seanan’s courage returned full force. “You think he”—Seanan pointed with his chin—“will keep you alive, Gutun? He’ll kill you as soon as it’s convenient. He might even make a sacrifice of you!”

“Bind him and prepare the fire. He’ll die first!” Gutun reached for the knife.

Othos gripped Gutun’s hand. “No! I kill.”

Gutun bowed low, adjusting his robe with a neat flourish.

An angry snort bellowed from the woods, like a cow being slaughtered.

Gutun hissed over his shoulder to his attendants. "We'll offer the cows later!"

Murmurs and confused denials followed.

"I didn't."

"Wasn't me."

Agonized bellowing broke the stillness.

Chills chased confusion down Seanan's spine.

Othos laughed and pointed to the sky. "The gods play!"

A nervous chuckle reverberated through the watching crowd, eyes glancing every which way.

Gripping the knife with both hands, Othos closed in and raised his arms.

Another bellow, not a disturbed cow but an angry bull.

Intakes of breaths all around.

A snorting, furious bull broke from the tree line. Like a vision from hell, a man painted red rode the creature. He swung a spiked mace, toppling everyone in his path.

Yells and screams rose higher than the flames swirling in the gusting wind.

The bull and rider charged, heading for Othos.

Knife at the ready, Othos lifted his hands to confront the charging mass of muscle and fury. He lunged.

The rider swung his spear, knocking Othos to the ground.

The deranged animal turned and vented his fury with stomping hooves on the prostrate man.

Terrified screams rose to new heights as three more bulls raced onto the chaotic scene.

Men fled in all directions.

Stupefied, Gutun stood with his arms at his sides. As

the rider eyed him, a strangled gurgle bubbled up. Gutun scooted away as fast as his draperies would allow.

The stench of panic and blood filled the air.

After struggling to his feet, Seanan fought his way through the chaos, searching desperately for his sons and sister.

The bulls ran riot, gouging and killing at random.

By the light of the flickering fire, Seanan called above the tumult, "Earan!"

A weak reply caught his ear, and he turned toward it.

Through the hazy smoke, he saw him. Earan knelt before a figure who stared down at him, a knife poised above his head.

Desperate to save him, Seanan raced forward. At the same moment, he glimpsed movement out of the corner of his eye. Then it was too late. A bull in full charge knocked him into the muck.

Seanan struggled to rise, but a powerful hand gripped his tunic, and a hard blow knocked all sense from his body.

CHAPTER SEVENTY-SIX

A LONGING HEART

—PATMOS—

Georgios packed everything he wanted to take—childhood mementos mostly.

Sunrays shone through the window, slanting across the floor.

Rueben sat on his pallet and watched through weary eyes. "Seanan will be glad to see you, even without all the gifts."

Georgios scowled. "What gifts? These are mine, and I intend to keep them. No one will care about these...but me."

"I can't see well. Tell me, what you are taking to your new home?"

Georgios shrugged. "Don't call it my new home just yet. I don't know that Seanan will accept me, or if I am doing the right—"

"You have to go somewhere—wandering is no life. Seanan cared for you, and I think, in the end, you cared for him. You need to start over."

With a headshake, Georgios pressed his few belongings into the wooden crate. He lugged it to where Rueben lay on his pallet. "All right, since you're so curious, I'll show you, but don't make any comments you can't defend. These are important. I must take them along."

Rueben nodded through a wan smile.

Georgios lifted a small, ceramic figure. "A gift from my father, a figure of Jupiter." Georgios swallowed a lump in his throat.

Rueben reached inside the box. "And this?" He held up

a small scroll bound by a thin ribbon.

Georgios laughed. “My first attempt at poetry.”

“What does it say?”

Georgios blushed. “Nothing but gibberish. I can’t think why I’ve kept it.”

Rueben stared at him, his brows rising.

Georgios shrugged and held the papyrus to the light.

“I am the son you never see.
The son who peers over ocean waves—waiting.
The son who loves through endless days.
The son you never see.”

Georgios grimaced. “Told you; it’s no good.”

“A longing heart is nothing to be ashamed of.”

“Hardly matters now. We were friends in the end. That’s enough. I shouldn’t cling to old memories.”

Rueben lifted his palm. “May I keep it, then?”

“Why? You knew your own father, didn’t you?”

“Yes, I knew my father, and we were friends, but I have another Father I long to see. Can’t have too many fathers.”

“Riddles again.” Georgios handed him the scroll.

Rueben tapped Georgios’ hand with the tip. “When are we leaving?”

“If Lysander has everything set, we’ll sail tomorrow.” He looked Rueben over carefully. “I hope this journey won’t be too much for you. You’re sure you don’t want me to take you back to Jerusalem? You’d be better cared for, and you must have family who want to see you.”

“I want to see you settled first.”

A stab of fear pricked Georgios. “Seanan never liked my father. Perhaps I won’t be so welcome.”

“You’ll be welcome, have no fear. Go on now and take your treasures with you. We need to take you home.”

Rueben fell back on his pillows, a spasm of pain rippling across his face.

Georgios pretended not to notice, though his heart clutched into a hard knot. Home. He had to find one soon, for both their sakes.

CHAPTER SEVENTY-SEVEN

THE FORTUNE OF MY DAY

—GAELIC LANDS—

Seanan awoke. The sun had risen on a new day, but what world was he in, Earth or the Otherworld?

A misty haze swirled, hanging like a tattered rag over the scene that opened before his stinging eyes. Groans filled his ears and searing pain clutched his head. He was so nauseated, he couldn't stand.

He attempted to sit up, but pain convulsed his body and he fell back, dropping his head on his outstretched arm. He resigned himself, for the moment, to simply lay there awakening to his surroundings.

In the next moment, he noticed something cold against his hand. Fingers? Cold fingers very close to his own, almost as if he had been grasping someone's hand, or someone had been grasping his, when he'd fallen. Gritting his teeth against the pain, he craned his neck.

An outstretched arm lay near enough to touch him, bloody and filthy, but he could not make out the figure.

His eyes burned. A sob rose in his throat. A hideous sight met his eyes. Mangled bodies in the distance, some gruesome not only in death but in their tattooed decorations. Memories overwhelmed his mind. He stifled a groan.

Shuffling, whimpering, a gasp, and quickened steps.

Fiona sobbed, "Seanan, are you alive then?"

Seanan merely blinked in a silent salute.

Fiona crooned, "Oh, you're alive, brave man! The gods couldn't have allowed us to endure so much, only to be separated now. Such a battle! We thought there'd never be an end to it. After an age, the enemy was driven off." Fiona's voice trembled. "They burned everything and took slaves. We were helpless to stop them!"

Seanan waved a heavy hand. He tried once more to sit up. "The boys?"

Fiona pressed a hand to his chest. "Don't move until I can get help." She glanced around. "Ian is fine—he's helping—and Liam is—though he must've hit his head, so full of mad stories. Said that he rode a bull!" She peered at distant figures. "Ian, come! I found your father!"

Sprinting forward, Ian kicked up dirt in his wake. He knelt at his father's side, blood and anxiety spread over his face. "Father, are you hurt? Can you rise?"

Seanan grinned weakly. "If you help, I can stand. This is hardly a restful spot."

Fiona backed out of the way, glancing to each side as if to avoid stepping on anything…anyone. But then she stopped in her tracks, her hand shooting up to stifle a scream. "No," she groaned, covering her face with her hands.

As Seanan gained his footing, he stared at the white arm and lifeless fingers that had reached out to him. Grief rose like a torrent.

Brighid lay in death's cold grasp.

Seanan swayed.

Tightening his grip on his father's arm, Ian steadied him and looked around. "Liam! Come help!"

Limping through the bloody battlefield, Liam wiped muck and sweat from his face. He stared from his dead aunt to his father. With a heavy sigh, he took his father's other arm.

Seanan's head dropped onto his chest as he was half-carried across the slaughter. Though death had not taken him wholly, it had taken far too much.

~~~

Seanan awakened five days later to a fresh morning, questions still swirling through his mind. He sat up in bed and faced his two sons, who had assisted Fiona in caring for him during his slow recovery. "Where is Earan? Is he hiding? I probably said some things I shouldn't have, but it was a devil of a situation, and I was justly angry."

Liam glanced at Ian.

Ian clasped his hands in his lap and leaned forward. "Earan is no longer the man you knew."

"What does that mean? I'll see him now! I don't care if you have to tie him up and carry him in here by force!"

"He can't walk." Ian frowned. "He just sits and stares with no mind to converse with, not with you—or anyone."

Seanan looked from one son to another and then bellowed, "Fiona!"

Fiona hustled through the doorway, her eyes inquiring but her lips shut tight.

"Why didn't you tell me Earan was hurt?"

"You've been sick yourself. I've done my best, running and doing—" She choked back a sob.

Ian gently caressed her shoulder.

Liam scowled at his father.

With a sigh, Seanan gathered his strength. "Bring him to me."

Ian bowed. "As you wish."

Liam followed his brother, his crutch digging a furrow across the dirt floor.

Flushed, Fiona stared at her husband. "Earan is not the only one changed for ill."

His thoughts jumping, old horrors mixing with new fears and furious with his helplessness, Seanan seethed.
~~~

Four men carried Earan on a pallet and placed him on the ground in front of his father.

Kneeling, Seanan peered into Earan's eyes.

Though his pink skin and clean face suggested health, Earan's lack of expression, stiff lips, and placid body represented only the shell, not the man.

"How! How did this happen?"

Tears slipped down Liam's face. "I knew the charging bulls would break up the gruesome ritual." He choked down a sob. "I saved Earan from the knife, but the damn bull—"

Seanan dropped his head onto his arms, his fury spent, his guilt rising. "I should never have left. Oh, God. Is this how you save my family?"

~~~

Georgios felt the wind on his face and smiled. The rise and fall of the waves as they neared shore heightened his giddy joy.

The green island practically glowed in the twilight. He glanced at Rueben, and his smile faded.

Rueben offered an impish grin, reigniting Georgios' joy.

Lysander slapped the railing, his voice tight. "What are you two grinning at?" He grimaced. "You can't wait to see Seanan's expression when you saunter into his village?"

Rueben shook his head, a picture of gravity.

Georgios frowned. "But this was your idea."

Rueben lifted a limp hand. "Lysander just means that Seanan will be surprised. And he won't be the only one."

Lysander worked his jaw, ready to retort.

Georgios pointed to shore. "Make ready." He clasped Rueben's arm. "Will you be able—"
~~~

Rueben waved him off. “Well enough. Don’t worry about me. It’s you and Lysander who have to do all the talking.”

~~~

Georgios stood by and watched Lysander struggle to get his bearings as he plodded along the shoreline.

Resting on a log, Rueben called to a boy playing outside a thatched hut. “Are there any guides about?”

With a nod, the child ran off.

Amused by Lysander’s dogged efforts and Rueben’s quick thinking, Georgios glanced from Rueben to Lysander. “Come along, and we’ll get you set right.”

The boy quickly returned, leading a grinning old man.

Georgios jogged forward. “Can you lead us to Seanan’s village?”

“Ay. I was there not so long ago that I’d forget. Seems to be a place that attracts notice. But I’ll say no more. You best eat and rest up first. It’s no easy jaunt and, besides, you might find a surprise when you get there. There’s little to spare in that village now.”

Alarm rippled through Georgios. “Why? What’s happened?”

The old man shrugged. “I’ve heard that they were attacked, many killed, and the whole place set to blaze. Not much left, I expect, but if you still want to go, I’ll take you. You best get me some food now and pay me with something that I can use, for I don’t expect much hospitality from them.”

Lysander pursed his lips and rubbed his hands together. “Tell me what you want, old man, and I will get it! We leave as soon as possible.”
~~~

Rueben stalled them. "Who did you take there? A Druid?"

"You're clever! No, I'll not say. I don't want his kind of trouble. Besides, he may not even be alive anymore. Many dead, you understand."

The four moved toward the shops that crookedly lined the shore, and they ate in brooding silence.

Finally, Lysander stretched and considered the long shadows. "If we don't go now, we'll never make it there before nightfall."

The old man cackled. "By nightfall of the second day, maybe!"

Georgios groaned as the old man called for more bread.

~~~

Gutun knelt on the hard ground before Seanan's stern figure.

Standing in the middle of the village with most of his clansmen circled around, Seanan glared at Gutun. "You're a murderer, a coward, a betrayer, a liar, and a deceiver, a villain without repentance and not worthy of redemption!"

Ian stood by his father, staring down at the humbled figure, his brother Liam standing at his right hand.

Earan's blank-eyed face stared at nothing from the corner he occupied as he leaned against the wall of his father's house.

Seanan's cold voice listed Gutun's crimes. "You caused the death of my good sister, Brighid, her husband, Goban, one of the best smithies the village ever had, my brother Tainair, and other worthy men. Grieving widows, mothers, and sisters share sorrow that will never go away, even after years of rain have washed the blood off the field."
~~~

Madness reigned in Gutun's mind. It was not his fault. The invaders had been sent from the gods; he'd had no choice but to obey. He whimpered.

Seanan unsheathed his knife.

Gutun bowed his head. Death was welcome. If he couldn't trust the gods, life held no meaning.

~~~

Seanan stared at Gutun and knew that if he hesitated, even for a moment, he might lose this one chance to kill his enemy.

A familiar voice rang out. "Seanan!"

Thwarting his rage, a burst of joy ran riot over his soul. Georgios? The knife slipped from his grasp.

Four men strode in his direction. With Ian and Liam flanking him, Seanan stepped forward to intercept them.

The watching crowd turned as one.

Bits of charred remains stood in silent testimony to recent horrors.

As the distance closed, Seanan marched faster, but as they came within easy distance, he halted.

Georgios stood beside Rueben, Lysander just behind, and an old man leaning on a staff to the side.

Ian shouted in gladness.

Tears coursing down his cheeks, Seanan lifted his arms in welcome, beckoning to his friend with longing in his heart.

Georgios matched him step for step.

The entire clan turned from Gutun's imminent death and cheered as the two men embraced.

Seanan sighed as he clutched his friend. "You've changed the fortune of my day forever, my friend."
~~~

CHAPTER SEVENTY-EIGHT

MARK A NEW BEGINNING

—GAELIC LANDS—

Agnes rubbed her sore foot, then tried to slip her sandal back on, but it was useless. The leather, little more than a tattered remnant, would never hold together, no matter how elaborately she tied it. She perched on a rotten log by the edge of the stream on the outskirts of the village and sighed.

A lump rose in her throat. She should not complain. Many suffered worse. Earan was alive, yet he seemed dead. Maggie had dropped all interest in Earan as soon as she learned of his condition. Though she hunched her shoulders and put on a sad face, it was amazing how perky the girl became whenever Ian walked by. Agnes snorted.

A feminine figure strolled down the well-traveled path from the village, swinging an empty bucket and smiling up at the treetops. Recognizing her—Maggie—Agnes turned her attention back to the soothing sounds of water gurgling over rocks in the stream.

A moment later, soft footfalls came up behind Agnes, and Maggie spoke. "Hello, Agnes. What takes you to the river so early?"

Noticing a twig next to her on the log, Agnes picked it up and forced herself to speak in a civil tone. "Just gathering sticks."

Maggie swung the bucket and laughed. "My scatterbrained sister forgot the water, and Mother says she has a headache, so she asked me."

Agnes frowned, anger flushing her cheeks.

With a scowl, Maggie puffed air and squeezed the

bucket's handle so hard her fingers turned white. "You shouldn't judge me for being glad that Ian has returned." She shot a cold glance at Agnes. "I've seen your stares."

Agnes stiffened. "I judge your actions."

With a carefree chuckle, Maggie swung her bucket high. "Why can't I have a good man for my own? Besides, who would be a better wife for Ian?"

"What about Earan?" *Did you ever really care about him?*

"That's not my fault!" She glanced over her shoulder in the direction of the village, where a crowd now gathered. "Old Gutun will be getting what he deserves. Though in truth, I don't think it's fair."

Agnes huffed. "How's that?"

"He is a Druid, after all." She stepped closer to the stream. "He's supposed to do the will of the gods. Is it his fault that they brought our enemy?"

"You think the gods arranged for our destruction?"

With a thrust, Maggie dunked her bucket deep into the current. "They do as they please, don't they? My father always says that the gods look out for themselves, and men have to do the same."

Agnes ached to slap the woman.

Once Maggie had the dripping bucket in her grasp, she expertly balanced it on her hip. She gestured to the crowd with her chin. "Why aren't you over there with the rest?"

"I hate to watch an *animal* being sacrificed, much less a man."

Maggie shrugged. "Men or gods—all the same to us, isn't it?"

Annoyed by Maggie's prattle, Agnes watched the crowd as it started to break away. "Must be over now."

"Hope they drag the body away quickly."

Agnes nodded, though her attention stayed focused on

the villagers who seemed in a strange mood. Shouts and laughter? Has everyone gone mad? Tired of the conversation and curious about the villagers, Agnes left the stream and headed back. Drawing close enough to understand what she saw, she stopped in her tracks.

Gutun lay sprawled on the ground, heaving spasmodically. Seanan stood, his arm around Georgios, grinning like a happy child, while Rueben leaned on a strange man's arm.

Her heart beating like a drum, she pressed her hands to her hot cheeks, struggling against tears.

Fiona hustled forward with Brighid's orphaned children trailing behind, their eyes wide but their mouths pressed shut.

Tears overflowed as Agnes watched the confused children. Poor Fiona, exhausted by travel, shipwreck, invasion, battle, her husband's injury, and her sons' near deaths. *On top of all that, she's taken in those poor, crippled children.*

Agnes stared at the scene and marveled, whispering her words, not caring who heard. "Will wonders never cease?"

~~~

Rueben glanced around at the assembled clansmen in the center of the village and listened to Seanan and Georgios chatter away, catching each other up on recent events. He stood quietly by and smiled—until his eyes strayed to the ragged body lying on the ground. *Gutun?*

Alexandra's face floated before his eyes, but there was no use wondering why she who had loved, died, and Gutun, so proficient in hate, still lived. Could it be that evil conquered not so much because it was strong but because
~~~

men were gullible—they believed they could make hate work for them?

Rueben knelt at Gutun's side as he lay sprawled in the dirt and pressed his shoulder. "The crowd has gone."

Not understanding, Gutun stared blankly ahead, mumbling.

Rueben tried to rouse him. "Gutun, you're safe. You can stand now."

Rising on his haunches, Gutun's murmuring grew into wailing cries of madness. He glared at Rueben through vacant, bloodshot eyes. "I had no choice." He squeezed Rueben's arm. "Father dedicated me to the gods as a boy. Remember? A sunny day, like this one." Gutun waved a shaky finger at the cloudy sky. "Took me to the river—threw me in. Said if I survived, it'd be a sign from the gods I was favored. Mother screamed, but the gods saved me." His eyes narrowed. "Seanan drank too deep of his father's cup! When the Romans brought their deceiving gods, I could've saved the clan but was banished instead!" He wrung his hands. "The invaders brought their gods—same as ours—I recognized them." He hissed into Rueben's ear, "They are mine, and I am theirs." Gutun collapsed in a convulsive fit.

Rueben rubbed his aching head. How odd the man who'd caused such destruction could move his heart to pity.

Georgios turned, scanned the area, then frowned. Leaving Seanan mid-sentence, he strode forward. "What are you doing?" He froze at the sight of Gutun sprawled on the ground with Rueben crouched at his side. "How can he be here?"

Seanan trotted forward. "You arrived at an inopportune moment. I was on the verge of setting him free from his torment." He glanced at the ceremonial knife held by one of his men.

Pounding his feet like a child, Georgios stomped to Seanan. "How'd he get here?"

Offering only a shrug for an answer, Seanan accepted the long, sharp knife from his man, and, with a grim expression, he took aim. He glanced at Rueben apprehensively. "You don't need to hold him. Just step away—"

With a violent shudder, his breath coming in sporadic bursts and his strength draining away, Rueben dropped to his knees. He clasped his hands in prayer.

Georgios grabbed him and tried to pull him to his feet. "No, Rueben! Spare your strength. He's not worth your prayers—or your life."

Rueben refused to budge. "Do not discount the mercy of God, Georgios."

"Mercy?" Georgios seethed. "Remember Armand? Some men do not change."

"You changed, Georgios." Rueben closed his eyes, his body falling limp. "Just let me rest somewhere. I'll go when God calls me, not a moment before."

Georgios knelt at his side and gripped his shoulders. "You're not going anywhere."

Seanan frowned at Gutun, who lay sprawled upon the ground, and he gestured impotently with his knife.

Agnes stepped forward. "I have a room attached to my house. We can lay Gutun there, away from watching eyes."

Olcan sighed. "Let her have him. He's so mad; he'll die soon enough."

Seanan glanced around. "Aye, let it be then. Olcan, carry him over to the empty room, but no one else shall attend to him except for that girl there." Seanan pointed.

"She asked for him, so she can attend to him, and when he dies, she can see to his burial as well!"

Fiona clasped the orphans' hands and led them away, but Seanan shouted after her, "I've waited long enough for my feast. I will not have it delayed any longer now that we have our son home again!" He smiled at Georgios and Rueben. "Sons, I should say. We will forget these evil days and mark a new beginning." He leaned toward Ian. "Take Rueben home and see that he is given every comfort."

Rueben closed his eyes and let himself be carried.

CHAPTER SEVENTY-NINE

WE UNDERSTAND HIM BETTER

—GAELIC LANDS—

Georgios did not know what to make of his new life, but he didn't *need* to know. As it turned out, there was a great deal of work to be done, and he found his mind moving in tune with his body. In timelessness, he found consolation that soothed his aching spirit. His simple skills involved repairing and building houses using the native materials of sod and stone. When he wanted a change, he would sit quietly with Earan.

One misty morning, as he strolled through the reconstructed village with only three charred homes as stark reminders of the violence of recent events, he looked around, trying to decide where to start his day's work.

The sound of laughter caught his attention. He stopped. Seanan had gone off to the high country, and Fiona and the children were at the river, washing clothes. He frowned. Who was left behind and laughing? He knocked on the wood frame of Earan's dwelling.

"Come in, if you've a mind to. We're not going anywhere."

Agnes? Having taken over where Brighid had left off, she proved to be a healer of sorts—soothing babies and everyday aches and pains. She even calmed the two deaf orphans, who communicated with her when no one else could manage it.

Peeking inside Earan's hut, Georgios blinked in surprise. He found not only Earan with Agnes but Rueben too. With flushed faces and sparkling eyes, the threesome seemed to be making rather merry. Georgios waited on the threshold, strangely embarrassed. "What do we have here? Something secret, perhaps?"

Agnes rose with a washcloth and basin in her hand. She made a deft swipe to Earan's face, and she brushed hair from his eyes. "Come, you silly man, don't play with us. We're just enjoying a quiet moment together."

New light shone in Earan's eyes. The man was back in his body. A thrill tingled Georgios' spine.

Rueben glanced out the open doorway. "Seanan knows, but he can't accept that the mind is back while the body remains helpless."

Agnes knelt at Earan's side, clasped his hand, and stroked it. "Earan's strength was never in his arms or legs. He was always more than that, and now we understand him better."

Rueben patted the ground at his side. "Come, sit and tell us your latest work. Your industry is prodigious. Do you plan on rebuilding this entire village all by yourself?"

Georgios smiled and padded softly next to Rueben. "I've not done much. Seanan tells me what to do, good planner that he is, and Ian helps. Liam takes care of the animals. He even calls them by name—marvelous lad."

Agnes chuckled. "If you continue to say things like 'marvelous lad,' strangers will take you for one of our own!"

Earan gurgled, his eyes glittering with humor.

She blushed. "True, I'm no more a native than he, but I certainly feel like I've come home." Her eyes glanced off Rueben and landed on Georgios. "I'm of service here in ways I never could've been before. Isadora is content, her children are thriving, and I am useful." She dropped her gaze.

Rueben exchanged an understanding look with Earan.

An ache pressed on Georgios' chest. He peered at

Rueben. "What happened to Gutun? I never see him."

Rueben indicated Agnes with a tilt of his chin. "She is his caretaker. She sees to his needs while he lays weak and silent upon his pallet."

Georgios blinked. "Oh—"

A peaceful glow about her, Agnes folded a blanket and laid it at the foot of the bed. "He's no trouble. Olcan made him a room between our dwellings, and he lies still and silent most of the time, just blinking like an owl."

Rueben grinned. "He fits right in."

Georgios shook his head. *How can they be so happy?* He stared at Agnes, a beautiful woman, really. *How did I never notice before?*

Agnes smiled. "You wonder at us, Georgios?" Her voice was light. "We are alike, you see. Rueben and Earan are men who have faced the other side, and I once wished to leave this world. But strangely enough, we're all now content."

"I am glad." Georgios met Rueben's gaze. "When are you going to get up? I could use some help." He pointed at the doorway. "We need you out there."

Rueben stared soberly at Georgios. "I offer what little strength I have left to Earan."

Agnes snapped her words. "Don't talk like that. It's not for us to decide who sits and who stands, who walks and who must be still. That power comes from those who know better."

"I am at the mercy of the One who has the power." Contentment settling on his brow, Rueben closed his eyes. "I'm very tired, but before sunset, bring Seanan to me."

Sudden emphatic jerking movements turned Georgios' attention to Earan.

"Ot im—eee!"

Dread clawed inside Georgios. He glanced at Agnes,

who knelt by Earan, caressing his arm to soothe him. "Maybe we should let them rest."

With a nod, Agnes rose and followed him outside.

Walking past a group of children under a large shade tree, Ian caught Georgios' eye and walked in their direction. "Rueben feeling any better? I offered to take him to the warm springs, but he said no."

With a long sigh, Georgios shook his head. "He wants nothing special except to see Seanan before the end of the day."

"I'll bring him myself." Ian smiled wryly. "Don't worry, Georgios. Those are resilient men. They'll get better. Just wait and see."

Bewildered by Rueben and Earan but comforted by Agnes' presence, Georgios forced a smile. "I promised Fiona I would fix her back gate, and if she comes home and sees it not done—well, I best get it busy." He nodded goodbye.

Agnes fixed her eyes on him with an unreadable expression.

Georgios' throat went dry. Would there be no end to the confusion in his heart?

~~~

Seanan grumbled as he trudged down the hill.

Ian jogged at his side, silent but insistent.

"I don't know why you have to hurry me home. I've plenty—"

"This is more important." Ian stopped short, staring at a large crowd milling about outside Seanan's door.

Seanan forced an unconcerned grin. "What's this? Have I called a council but forgotten?" He pushed through the throng and peered at Liam standing by the door. "Why
~~~

is everyone gathered like crows at nightfall?"

Liam swallowed but no words came.

Fiona stepped over the threshold. "Seanan, finally! Rueben said—" She clasped her trembling hands, moved aside, and waved her husband inside.

Seanan scowled. He hated mysteries. With an annoyed sniff, he strode forward.

Fiona clutched his arm. "Don't be afraid."

Irritation and apprehension increasing, he stepped inside.

The evening light had faded, but a modest fire blazed in the hearth. The burning peat moss added a pungent odor.

Four men stood by the back wall, watching and waiting. Georgios knelt at Rueben's side, and another man stood hidden in the shadow behind them. Sucking in a deep breath, Seanan understood. Rueben's death had long been expected. He crouched next to Georgios, taking Rueben's hand. "I'm here. I came as soon as I could."

Rueben opened his eyes and smiled.

Seanan blinked. Rueben's expression spoke more to him than words ever could. *Rueben knows I didn't want to come, that I'd stayed away on purpose, afraid to face this day.* But Rueben's smile assured him. "Is there anything I can do for you?"

Rueben nodded.

The watching crowd held their breath.

Rueben pointed to the shadows and said, "Your son."

Confused, Seanan leaned closer to catch the meaning of the words. Ian and Liam had hung back and waited in the doorway. Which son?

Rueben looked up.

The man stepped from the shadows.

Seanan rose, an uneasy feeling rising into panic.

"Father."

Seanan knew the voice, the body, the eyes—his son.

Earan stood straight and tall, his mind back in his body and a light in his eye.

Seanan staggered. Only Rueben's voice held him up.

"Your son has been returned to you, Seanan."

Earan limped forward and embraced his father.

Joy smashed into grief and broke open Seanan's wounded heart. He lay his head on his son's shoulder and wept.

~~~

Georgios strolled under the full moon toward the center of the quiet village.

Seanan sat alone by a fire.

Wearily, Georgios plunked down on a stump. "Everyone in bed now?"

Seanan nodded. He shifted his weight and peered into the bright, starry sky. "Why?"

Too exhausted to think, Georgios shrugged off the impossible question. "It's been a long day. Why don't we get some rest?"

Seanan took a deep breath. "It has been a long life! And you didn't answer my question."

Georgios looked toward the flickering flames. "I don't have the answer, Seanan, but I suspect that answers are not what is expected of us." Georgios closed his eyes. "Rueben wanted me to come here. He knew you'd take me in and treat me like a son."

Seanan smiled. "I'm glad you've come back."

"We've been guided and directed, and sometimes we've been stupid. Well, at least, I've been stupid. But always there has been some kindness, some generosity,
~~~

some goodness to help me along."

Seanan sniffed and dragged his hands along his face, a weary man. "I would say you're right. But what about Brighid and Goban and their suffering children? Were they guided and protected? I think not."

Georgios sighed.

Seanan stood and stretched. "Rueben knows something, though I can't see what it is. My son has been given back to me, even when I had given up, and now you're home." He sighed and started shuffling home. "Rueben wants you tonight."

With a nod, Georgios struggled to his feet.

Rueben's weak smile met Georgios when he entered. "Come and sit with me at my end, my friend." He clasped Georgios' hand. "I'm not afraid to leave now."

His throat aching, Georgios struggled to keep his composure. "We've been such good friends, Rueben—can't we just…"

Rueben's voice, thin from strain, whispered his words, a man confiding life's secrets. "You must keep growing…becoming one with God. No matter how bad things became, I can now leave in peace."

A sob choked Georgios as he pressed Rueben's limp hand, holding on, peering into his friend's eyes.

Rueben's gaze traveled where few could follow.

Calm spread through Georgios. He looked down. Rueben's hand—dead to this world but alive in another—still embraced his own.

Chapter Eighty

And You?

-OldEarth-

Song grieved. She shuddered at the sight before her, yet she dared to exhale consummate loss and inhale a prayer of hope. If a young human could peer into the mystery of Providence, could not she, a being of vastly greater years and experience, trust in the glorious Unseen?

In her form as a native spider, she crawled around a boulder and made her way down the winding path. In a sheltered spot, she shape-shifted into a peasant girl. After plucking a wayside flower, she strolled down the hillside to the shore and waited. Her ship would not arrive until darkness enveloped the land.

Rueben's words, "*I can leave in peace*." replayed in her ears. Her entire planet had suffered from the loss of a sister planet, and now she and most of her people were exiled to the outer universe, searching for new hope among ancient worlds. Would she ever know peace?

Rocking on her haunches, Song twirled the fading flower in her fingers.

The eastern hemisphere lay in blackness as thick clouds covered the sliver of a moon. Before Song's eyes, the sea bubbled and foamed as a rounded, black shape emerged just offshore. Her ship rose dripping and glimmering in her sight. She stood.

A long mechanical arm arched toward her from the ship and stretched out flat before her feet, like a slave offering obeisance before its mistress.

Song stepped forward, her bare feet tingling at the sensation of warm water on hard metal. When the door of the ship opened, a shaft of light nearly blinded her, but she continued her ascent into the interior.

Within seconds, the door closed, the arm folded, and the ship sank into the depths of the sea, only to emerge leagues away in the center of an ocean no human had yet explored. Then it rose into the night sky and slipped away.

Song dropped onto a padded lounge chair and folded her legs under her.

A tall elven-looking male with green eyes and black, curly hair strode forward, holding a crystal cup in his hands. With a stiff bow, he passed it to Song, his grim gaze appearing to penetrate her human form. "Everything went well?"

After sipping the honey-colored liquid, Song motioned to the lush divan before her. "Please, no formalities, Romtov. I'm too exhausted to play Queen today."

Perching on the edge of the seat, Romtov clasped his hands in his lap. "I'd help...if I could."

Song swung her legs over the edge, righted herself, and hunched forward. She set the cup aside. "I no longer despair."

Romtov watched her intently and waited.

She stepped to the oblong observation window. Earth's western hemisphere glowed in the light of the sun's rays. "There is beauty in simplicity, yet it has taken the complexity of space travel, invasion, and encountering new worlds to remind me that hope lies—not in the conquering of evil—but in the admittance of grace."

A spark ignited in Romtov's eyes. "You've had a vision. I see it."

Song turned, a smile warming her face. "Yes, but it will take a long time to fruition." She tapped the window. "One day, this planet will become home to our people, home to many peoples. Humanity has no idea that we exist. But like a couple that knew nothing of each other while in the cradle—yet intertwined so close as to become one—so the human race will embrace the larger universe. We shall grow together. Beyond hate and despair lies hope for us all."

~~~

Abbas stared at the filthy little girl, and his heart clenched in pain. He tugged his long brown robe tight about his shoulders.

She stared at him through brown eyes crusted at the edges with grime and soot. She wiggled her little, reddened toes into the cold dirt. "Why do you want him?"

Without thought, Abbas told the small inquirer the truth. "I want to see if he is safe."

Her searching eyes roamed and then focused, a sly smile forming. "Why not ask him yourself?"

Noman, dressed as a traveling merchant, stepped from behind Abbas, clutched his shoulder, and grinned. "I'm well and hearty." His gaze cut to the child. "Run along; your mother needs you."

Unsatisfied with the lie, the girl waited. "You said you'd show me things."

Noman snapped his fingers and a flower appeared in his hand.

The girl started, her mouth falling open.

He flicked the flower in her direction and nudged her toward the center of the village. "Go."

Snatching the flower from the dirt, she twirled the fragile, out-of-season blossom in her fingers. With a screech of triumph, she skedaddled home, calling, "Mother! Mother!"

Dread filled Abbas. "The mother will ask questions.
~~~

The whole village will want to know where she got it."

"Not for long." A gigantic spark ignited inside Noman, and he disappeared.

Throwing back his head, Abbas stared at the gathering clouds and groaned. He frowned. The swirling mass was much too large and dark, too powerful for anything natural. "Oh, God!" He blinked away.

~~~

Abbas knew just where to look. Noman was nothing if not predictable.

Winds rose to enormous speeds, rushing through the village, up and down the hills and valleys, sending the ocean into a rage.

Noman stood on the pinnacle of the highest mountain in the land, a rod in his hand and a smile spread wide across his face. In cross form he stood, his arms flung out, legs firm, his tunic flapping. "I am the Alpha and the Omega!"

"You can't take them by storm, brother." Abbas stood before his mother's other son. The unwanted one.

Noman screamed above the savage wind, "I can take them any way I want!"

Never in all his eons among his kind had anyone ever dared to subvert the whole. Not like this. Many had challenged, even threatened, the ordered balance of the universe, but no one had openly defied the consensus.

"You cannot take these people or this planet. It has been decided. You are to remain hidden, powerless on the other side of the Divide, until we know what to do with you."

Surprise fluttered over Noman's face. He dropped his arms and the wind died. "I made my case perfectly clear. Humanity is worthless. Everyone can see that. I'm just
~~~

cleaning up so as to begin my great work." He spread his arms again and the wind roared. "You'll see!"

Alarm spread over Abbas, and his whole being trembled. In the matter of this choice, there could be only one victor. "Please! Remember the child—you gave her a flower."

Noman laughed as he lifted his arms higher, enjoying the stimulating game, his form glowing, trembling with obscene pleasure. "This feels so good!" He glanced at Abbas. "No one will suffer. It'll be over quickly." With a low voice, he chanted, "By my will…" His form grew to enormous size, the wind shrieking, lightning flashing, and dollops of rain pelting the ground.

Abbas, diminutive in comparison, stretched forth his hand and touched Noman's chest. "You are not here."

Horror filled Noman's eyes and his mouth formed a wordless O. Dissipating like vapor on a hot morning, Noman's body disappeared.

A crack of thunder tore the sky and broke upon the land.

On the mountaintop, Abbas bowed his head and sobbed, bearing the loss of his brother alone.

~~~

Abbas stood beside a bassinet and stared down at the wide-awake baby boy.

His beautiful wife strolled forward and wrapped her arms around him. "He's the image of your father. A kind servant of all. We'll be blessed if he—"

"Did you choose a name yet?"

The woman frowned. "You're still upset?" She lifted the child from his bed and held him out, facing Abbas. "You must move on. We must show him how to survive
~~~

in our growing, ever-changing universe."

Running his fingers gently along the child's face, Abbas eyed his wife, his question waiting.

"I'll call him Omega. It'll bring a better end to the tragedy if we teach our son to do what your brother never could."

"Noman was never recognized—not as he wanted. He never had an identity."

"He had one. He just never accepted it. He never grew up!"

"I inherited grace, he madness."

"It was his madness to insist that he was wiser than he was, that he knew better than everyone else." She clasped her husband's hand. "In humility, you found both power and hope."

"I am the second son. Younger and lesser. I should be nothing."

"Your elder proved unworthy."

Abbas stared into his son's bright blue eyes. "And you?"

CHAPTER EIGHTY-ONE

THE GIFT

—GAELIC LANDS—

Georgios met Agnes outside the hut and asked to see Gutun.

Startled, Agnes led him into Gutun's dwelling.

Gutun rocked upon his pallet, humming tunelessly.

Georgios grimaced. "I was hoping that he'd fix this one last problem."

Agnes' brow furrowed. "Who?"

Dispirited, Georgios shrugged. "I'd hoped that Rueben would take Gutun with him when he died." A hot flush spread over his face. "It was a stupid thought."

Agnes studied Georgios. "When did you last eat a good meal?"

She sounded so much like Brighid, he faltered. "I'm not sure, but I think—"

"Follow me." She led him to a quiet spot near a large shade tree. "Sit, and I'll bring a hot stew. I made some for the children earlier, and they are running about as if they've never been sick a day in their lives."

"Were they sick? I didn't hear about it."

"It's no wonder; you've had other things on your mind." Her eyes flicked toward something in the distance. She chewed her lip. "Here they come. They'll be harassing you before I get back. If they're a bother, just call me, and I'll take them away." She scurried inside her hut.

Pelting forward in delight, the two children ran right at him.

Georgios tried to brace himself, but it was all he could do to not fall backward as Cian barreled into him. When

Etan came right behind, the combined weight sent him sprawling, his back thudding against the hard ground and his feet unceremoniously pointing towards the sky. Fury fed by embarrassment filled him. "Stupid children, hasn't anyone ever taught—"

The children clutched their ears, confusion written on their faces.

He glared at them.

They dropped their hands.

"What's wrong with you—"

Up went their hands, plastered against their ears.

Incensed, Georgios raised his voice. "I wasn't yelling!"

A stone's throw away, Fiona shot a look in his direction. She wiped her hands on a rag and bustled back to his side, her eyes round as moons.

Defensive, Georgios tried to explain. "I didn't do anything but scold them. They're acting like I hit them."

"I could hear you from over there." Fiona pointed to a cluster of women who watched the proceedings with interest. "What happened?"

Etan slapped her ears and babbled.

Fiona lifted Etan into her arms. "What's wrong, child?"

The little girl tapped her ears, wiggling wildly and grinning.

Fiona swallowed. She hugged the child tightly and peered into her eyes. "Can you hear me, child?"

The little girl nodded, her eyes wide with wonder.

Cian stood staring up at them.

Georgios' throat dried up. "Can you hear me, Cian?"

Cian grunted and slapped his hands to his ears. Then he eased his hands off his ears and looked at a bird chirping in a nearby tree. His eyes glowed.

Agnes trotted forward, bearing a tray with a steaming bowl of stew.

Georgios accepted the proffered gift. “Thank you.”

Innocent of the recent exchange, Agnes turned to Fiona, her voice light and easy. “Soup?”

Cian grunted, while Etan tapped her ears.

Agnes stared, puzzled, and then looked to Georgios for an explanation.

Georgios glanced at Seanan’s home, where Rueben’s body still lay. “They can hear now. Don’t ask me how.”

Fiona rubbed her hands together. “Do you suppose the second sickness undid the damage of the first? How, by the gods—”

Georgios took a sip of the stew. “I don’t know.”

Agnes lifted Etan and gazed into her smiling eyes. “You hear me, love?”

The child nodded.

Taking a deep breath, Agnes glanced at Seanan’s home. “I wonder if—”

Fiona’s brow smoothed. “It doesn’t matter how it happened. It’ll make things easier.” She stopped a moment. “Georgios, don’t say anything to Seanan just yet.”

Georgios cleared his throat, amazement struggling with curiosity. “Why?”

Fiona grinned. “Let’s see how long it takes him to notice.”

CHAPTER EIGHTY-TWO

FATHER AND SONS

—GAELIC LANDS—

Lysander stood by the gravemound and heaved a long sigh. He stared at the rounded heap of stones that marked the burial place of the most amazing man he had ever known. "If ever I become someone, Rueben, it'll be because of you. You made me realize there is something to become in this world."

Georgios stood by silently, holding Agnes's hand.

—TEN YEARS LATER—

Lysander stood alone on the crest of the hill and looked upon the bustling village. He smiled, glad to be back. It had been five years since he had last visited.

Probably thought I died.

But, in fact, he was in the business of helping people. He had assisted two innocent men to escape unlawful deaths, found homes for sixteen orphaned children, given money to countless widows, and even arranged four marriages between beautiful but poor young women and promising, though perhaps not so handsome, young men.

Unmasking devious plots against honest men had become something of a personal sport, while his own impeachable decency rarely fell into question. He drank moderately, spent his income wisely, and managed to save a little in between his creative industry, which included giving good advice to the right people at the right time, trading, translating, and traveling with those too skittish to go to strange ports alone. Merchants loved him. He had a way of changing their fortunes for the better.

A brood of children and their pretty widowed mother stood behind him on the brow of the hill, peering with concerned expressions at the village below.

Once she's happily settled, her thoughts might turn to love again. If I'm near at hand, useful as well as handsome, well, we'll see...

One son, Benjamin, buried his intelligence under a heavy mound of grief. The boy's eyes brooded with a familiar expression that spoke wordlessly, like a prophet of old. Lysander's ears twitched whenever the boy spoke. No, there could never be another Rueben, but this boy's splendid nature stirred tired blood, and Lysander could not leave him or his kin behind to be destroyed by cruel fate or cold omission.

Lysander looked behind himself and whispered to the woman to wait a bit. "I'll be back." He motioned for the children to relax. "We're almost home now."

Lysander bounded down the hillside and headed straight for Earan. "By the gods above, you've not changed since I last saw you! What, you have special magic which keeps you young?"

His eyes sparkling in joy, Earan called out, "Lysander!" He glanced around and shouted, "Father! Come see what the gods have brought home!"

Seanan, with streaks of gray running through his hair, trotted forward, chuckling with pleasure as he clasped Lysander's hand. "I always said you'd return. I'm proven right once again!"

Lysander stroked his chin and raised his eyebrows. "Are those streaks of concern I see in your hair?"

Seanan laughed and pointed to his sons as they assembled at his side. "They do all the work. What do I have to worry about?"

A passel of children raced from a large hut, followed immediately by Georgios and Agnes.

Joy spreading through him, Lysander gripped hands, tousled hair, pounded backs, and laughed until he thought his sides would burst. He told his story in snatches and listened to everything with rapt attention.

As the sun descended, he found his courage, grabbed Seanan's arm, pointed up to the hilltop and told him about the family that awaited his decision.

Amazed, Seanan slapped Lysander on the back. "Bring them! Let's see what gifts you've brought!"

Lysander nodded to his old friend. "Georgios, come with me. I've brought them this far, but you must help me to bring them the rest of the way!"

Georgios readily agreed, and together they strolled to the hill.

"Fill me in on all the news. I heard everything and nothing."

"Ian married as did Earan, though Liam has stayed single. Some say it's because he loves his animals too much, while others believe it's because the animals loved him too much. Olcan and Isadora live simple lives, and my Agnes raises our children like lush grapes on the vine."

Warmth spread through Lysander. "It's good to be home."

~~~

Georgios and Lysander sat on logs before the communal fire, under stars sparkling in a clear sky.

Movement caught his attention.

A four-year-old boy with black eyes, dark curly hair, and fine, white skin approached with measured footsteps.

Georgios grinned. "Come, son, and meet your uncle."
~~~

Lysander's eyes beamed in the firelight as he held out his arms.

Instead of going to Lysander, the boy ran to his father and climbed onto his lap, where he nestled his head just under Georgios' chin.

Georgios adjusted the child's head, snuggling his son comfortably under his muscular arms. An old ache rose in his throat. "I am glad you've done so well for yourself, Lysander. I suspect that there are many who will remember you with kindness."

"I have much to be thankful for. God has been gracious, but I am exhausted! Bringing a new family home has been my biggest adventure. I best rest up for the feast Seanan has planned tomorrow." He grinned. "You remember how to build a house?" He stood, stretched, and meandered toward Earan's home, where lights flickered, highlighting two women's figures bent together in private conversation. "See you in the morning, my friend."

Georgios smiled as Lysander passed.

With the warm little boy resting comfortably on his lap, Georgios sat under the stars, visions of his life-journey passing before his eyes. After a bit, he sighed and stood up. He strolled home, cradling his child in his arms and whispering into his young son's hair, "Yes, Georgi, God is gracious."

Epilogue

You'll See

-OldEarth-

Teal stood on the hilltop, his arm around Cerulean's shoulders.

Countless stars filled the night sky as calmness settled over the land. The village below lay in repose; even the central fire had burned down to mere embers.

Cerulean spoke into the quiet night. "You think she sees us now?"

His throat tight, Teal had to steady himself before responding. "Certainly."

"Because you believe in The Events?"

"I didn't, at first. But the gifts of those who have, their resiliency in spite of so much evil, speaks as loud as The Events themselves."

"You mean Rueben and Georgios?"

Teal clenched his jaw to keep his composure as memories flooded his mind. "I mean all those who have trusted in something greater than themselves. Aram, Ishtar, their friends and family…through generations. They have held true."

"And the Mystery Race. How about the one called Noman? What happened to him?"

A new voice rose from the stillness. Ark waddled forward. "You don't want to know." He shrugged, moonlight glinting off his pale face. "Some things are not meant for us to know."

Zuri climbed the last paces up the hill and joined the company. "I can hardly believe my ears. Did a Cresta just say that there is a limit to his inquiries?" He tapped the datapad on his wrist. Your High Tribunal made it clear; they want you back soon, and I have to give a full report before I get home." He glanced at Teal. "You're heading back to Lux?"

Cerulean stiffened, alert, waiting.

Teal pressed his son's shoulder. "Yes, we're going. Cerulean has a lot to learn before he becomes a guardian. I'll get him enrolled in the academy as soon as possible." He peered down at his son. "Don't you think?"

His shoulders relaxing, Cerulean nodded.

Zuri chuckled. "He'll be at the top of his class before the first cycle is half over."

Ark waddled forward, one tentacle admonishing. "If you have any questions, just let me know. If I don't have the answer, I can find someone who does." He sighed. "In the meantime,"—he glanced at Zuri—"we should get on board. I must check on my progeny." He gulped, sending bubbles swishing to the top of his breathing helm. "He's only a pod, but if he's anything like his mother, I'll have my tentacles full for a long time to come."

Zuri waved down the hill. "The ship awaits. Song will meet us on board to discuss our future here. I wanted to surprise her with a detailed description of all The Events, but she seems to already know."

Teal stepped forward and gripped his shoulder. "Tell Kelesta. It might make her feel better."

Ark harumphed. "Once your duties are in hand, I expect everyone to come visit me, and then we'll plan a trip back here. Even if the Mystery Race is quiet, there are always new threats to humanity." He flipped his tentacles in all directions. "They're always getting into trouble!"

Teal chuckled. "Unlike us." He bowed, pressed Cerulean's shoulder, and the two blinked away.

Ark held out a tentacle beseechingly.

Zuri gripped it, and the two descended the hill together.

~~~

Abbas held a baby boy in his arms, floating above Earth. “Look, my son. Humanity is just starting out. No one knows what will become of them, but there’s a whole world of possibilities here, Omega. You’ll see.”
~~~

About the Author

A. K. Frailey, an author of a historical sci-fi and science fiction series, short story collections, inspirational non-fiction books, a children's book, and a poetry collection, has been writing for over ten years and has published 17 books.

Her novels expand from the OldEarth world to the Newearth universe-where deception rules but truth prevails. Her nonfiction work focuses on the intersection of motherhood, widowhood, practicing gratitude, and rediscovering joy.

As a teacher with a degree in Elementary Education, she has taught in Milwaukee, Chicago, L. A., and Wood River, and was a teacher trainer in the Philippines for Peace Corps. She earned a Masters of Fine Arts Degree in Creative Writing for Entertainment from Full Sail University.

Ann homeschooled all eight of her children. She manages her rural homestead with her kids and their numerous critters. In her spare time, she serves as an election judge, a literacy tutor, and secretary/treasurer of her small town's cemetery.